£25

Bird Inside

Bird Inside

Wendy Perriam

For Lorna,
What a pleasure it was
to meet your lovely
husband!
Wishing you every blessing
Wendy.

HarperCollins*Publishers*

HarperCollins*Publishers*
77–85 Fulham Palace Road
Hammersmith, London W6 8JB

Published by HarperCollins*Publishers* 1992
1 3 5 7 9 10 8 6 4 2

A catalogue record for this book
is available from the British Library

ISBN 0 246 13407 0

Set in Bembo

Printed in Great Britain by
HarperCollinsManufacturing Glasgow

For Keith New

il miglior fabbro

I

Jane jolted out of sleep. A bomb had just exploded right outside the house. She could feel the cottage shaking, as if its whole foundations had been snapped or shocked apart; the faintest shudder still throbbing through her body, through the thin and scratchy mattress laid out on the floor. She jerked up from the mattress, kicked aside the pile of tangled rugs.

'They've come,' she thought immediately. 'They've found me.'

She could hear their noise, the noise she heard in nightmares, but real now and all round her: a constant muted roaring, as if her small one-storey refuge had been wrenched up from its stretch of lonely shingle and resited in the centre of a motorway. She reached out for her torch, startled by a sudden louder booming – an articulated lorry overtaking in the fast lane, its huge reverberating bulk juddering through the room. The torch felt clumsy – cold beneath her hand. She probed her fingers up and round, to find the smooth bump of the switch. The beam flickered for a moment, died. She shook it, terrified. Everything was not just dark, but damp – torch, walls, bedding, mattress, uneven wooden floor. She was crawling on the floor now, fumbling in the blackness for the lamp. She only knew she'd found it when she knocked it over, felt paraffin ooze between her fingers like warm wet blood. She inched back to the mattress, wiped her hands clean on the rugs, found the matches where she'd left them, on her bedside orange-crate, used her sense of touch again to locate the rough side of the match-box. She struck one and then another – three, five, seven, eight – their tiny futile raspings refusing to flare into a flame. Damp, like all the rest.

She must get out, escape. She couldn't stand the darkness or that insistent threatening roar. It wasn't just the sea noise, which she was used to now, accepted – waves pounding on the shingle, encroaching

7

on the house – but something far more menacing, like war. She felt her way across the room, negotiating obstacles in a stumbling zigzag course between the wrecks of tatty furniture she had arranged around her mattress, to try to turn a bolt-hole into home. Now they simply slowed her, tripped her up. She groped out to the poky hall, unbolted the front door, was knocked half off her feet as the wind swooped belching in – a pouncing, frenzied, violent wind, which forced an entry like a mugger. A shower of whirling debris struck her on the legs – old plastic bags, dried seaweed, litter, scraps of shells – scuttling to the corners of the hall, a scrum of desperate victims seeking sanctuary. It took her all her force to close the door again, as the wind tugged the other way, lashing out at her now, clawing at her clothes, whipping strands of hair against her face.

She stood huddled in the outside porch, trying to fight the wind off with her hands. The roaring noise was louder, and what she'd taken as a bomb was just an empty oil drum which had been dashed against the house and was now lying like a spent exhausted missile. It *was* a war – a war of wind and weather – the most savage storm she'd ever seen, raging round the row of crumbling cottages; maybe even a hurricane, like the vicious one four years ago, which she'd watched safely on the television news. She'd felt secure and almost smug then, living in a sturdy home in a solid street in Shrepton, a rugged little grey-stone town between Newcastle and Hexham; the whole brave northern county more or less unscathed.

This time she was totally exposed, camping all alone in a dilapidated house, precariously positioned on the sea's edge; a house already old and sick, and now crying out in pain. Its fragile walls were creaking and complaining, its tattered roof-felts ripping in the wind, and the lopsided garden swing, which had been left, a rusty relic, behind the last cottage of the row, rattling like a mad thing on its chain, crashing against the metal struts with a hideous clanging noise, which seemed to echo and re-echo down the beach. She could barely glimpse the sea, only hear the waves thwacking with a fury on the strand, battering the wooden groynes somewhere far beyond her. The shingle seemed alive, grinding on itself, as stone slashed angry stone; old cans and lengths of driftwood spinning up like frisbees. The light was mean and grudging – just a slice of frightened moon caged in swollen clouds; clouds moving far too quickly, as if delirious and ill, the whole sky churned, inflamed.

She took a step out from the porch, terrified, yet needing still to check her eyes, make sure she wasn't trapped in some wild nightmare. Through the whirling salt and spray, she could just make out the shapes of towering breakers, surely too high and violent to be real; glimpse cascades of fluorescent white, foaming from the black hole of the sea. Her eyes were stinging, streaming, flecks of spume clinging to her clothes. She turned her back, half-fell against the door, wrestled with the wind again, to tug it from its grip, rammed the bolts home, stood against it, trembling. The old tracksuit which she slept in felt wet against her body, her bare feet numb with cold. She needed tea, tea to warm her, calm her. She blundered to the kitchen, stopped a moment, rigid, in the doorway, reached out both her hands. She had suddenly lost all sense of boundaries in the stumbling clotted darkness, lost the shape and feel of things, like someone just struck blind.

She shambled on, bumped into the dresser, clung on to it, arms around its solid jutting bulwark, face against its wood. The darkness seemed to thicken, blank her out. She was being switched off, disconnected, as the electric-light supply had been cut off in this cottage, months before she'd come there. She had found the row of houses dark and derelict, threatened by erosion, in danger from the sea – a perfect place for hiding, or so she'd thought naïvely. Now she was defeated, bullied by the elements as well as prey to cold and fear. She would have to go back home, face all the fuss and questions, a new round of lies, or rows. It had been hard enough to live here in a smugly gold October, with winter just a word still, a vague and distant threat. But tomorrow was the first day of November, and had come raging in so spitefully, it was just as if they'd planned it, laid it on deliberately, to break her spirit, force her home. She hadn't done too badly, had survived a month alone, living like a tramp, collecting scraps from litter-bins, or daring some large supermarket when she could find the strength and purpose to walk the three miles into town, but where at least it was impersonal and no one probed or pried.

She would go there now – to town – go there for the light, whole sweeps and streams of light: lamp-posts, headlamps, neon, bright arcs in shops and houses. And the houses would be homes, not shivering gouty shacks, but healthy and alive: rooms with beds and curtains, gardens with real flowers, instead of sand and stones. She edged back to the largest room, which she had made sleeping-room and eating-room, the one room she kept warm – or tried to, when the stove worked, or she could coax damp logs to burn. She had always been untidy, cursed her own stupidity as she tried to find her trainers, which she had kicked off somewhere late last night, socks flung somewhere else. But she'd been relying on the lamp –

that loyal and faithful lamp, which hadn't failed her in twenty-seven days. She had chosen it herself, lugged it back from town with a super-pack of matches, a dozen instant packet-soups with names like Golden Vegetable, which sounded rich and comforting, but actually tasted thin and salty-sour. She was learning how things lied – not just parents – everything: false promises, false names. She didn't have a name now, could hardly go on using theirs, had never liked it anyway – too fancy with plain Jane. 'Plain' was right, at least. She shook back her damp hair – straight and boring brown. Pretty girls were blonde, or had hair which held a curl, tendrilled in the rain instead of forming rats'-tails.

Everything seemed difficult: tying shoes, forcing fiddly toggles through their loops, as if the wind had struck at coats and clothes, not just roofs and windows. The windows were all rattling, so hard she feared they'd break; sudden cold and squally gusts blitzing through new gaps in roof and wall; a sheet of corrugated iron beating an SOS against the shed. She tried the back door, this time, steeled herself to battle down the path, bent double like a soldier advancing into fire. The wind scalpelled through her body, slashed away its contents – lungs, heart, liver, womb – all those vital organs which doctors claimed you had, but you never quite believed in, never saw to check. She felt so light without them, she was barely able to stand, the wind pummelling her hollow frame, determined to uproot her.

The moon had dared to show itself, cowering out from behind a cloud, a three-quarters moon, looking lumpy and misshapen, as if it had also been manhandled by the wind. She used its light to pick her way along the rutted track which led on to the coast road; fighting for her balance, struggling for each breath. It was madness to be out. She could trip and break a leg, or be killed by flying debris – wooden slats from smashed and scattered beach-huts, cruelly splintered window frames. Yet she had to find some help, defeat that terrifying sense of being the only person alive in all the world. Perhaps it was her punishment. She had left her home and parents, left her school and friends, her neighbours, county, safe and sheltered cul-de-sac, and only now had she really grasped the concept 'on her own'. She had always been called brave – independent, self-sufficient, spirited – all those words which were only empty syllables, disproved now by the fear she felt; fear so raw and choking it seemed to be closing in and round her like another sort of darkness.

She stopped a moment, blinded, crouched down face to knees, to rest her smarting eyes. Strange how calm she'd been the night she'd actually left – a careful concentration on just the practicalities: the clothes she'd need, the route she'd take, money, food and train-times. She must do the same thing now, blank her mind of everything save the next step on the path: how to strike a bargain with the wind – sidestep it and dodge it, using guile as much as force; accept its boom and roaring as just some loud, crude background music she had no way of turning off. Just one step at a time, one step at a . . .

At last, she reached the road, stopped in shock as she saw a boat flung upside-down across it. Could the gale have hurled it quite that far, turned tarmac into sea? She longed to set it right way up, comfort it, explain. But what could she explain? The 1987 storm had been called a fluke, a one-off horror unlikely to occur again. Yet only two years later, there had been a second almost-hurricane, killing forty-seven people, striking at the trees again, the whole landscape scarred for life. Surely twenty million trees lost was enough destruction for a hundred years, yet here were the survivors, fighting for their lives once more: Scots pines bent almost double, as if the branches sought to touch their roots, huge limbs scythed off, or hanging maimed and helpless. She, too, was being blown away like some puny trifling twig; would never make the town, not even make the next few yards, since she could no longer even stand up on her feet. She should have stayed in bed. Even the claustrophobic darkness of the cottage was better than this sense of being trapped; too frightened to go on, too fragile to go back.

Suddenly, the stretch of road in front of her was magically lit up, light gleaming on the puddles, flickering the trees. A car – behind her – slowing down and stopping. The driver might be dangerous, a rapist or a Ripper. She hardly cared. At least the hand was human, winding down the window – another person in the world, another blessed voice. She couldn't understand the voice. She knew a little German, had just done French at A-level, but this exotic guttural language was one she'd never heard. Signs were quite enough though – a friendly hand gesturing to the passenger-seat, a welcome opened door. She scrambled in, shouting out her thanks above the wind, then stunned to silence by the sudden warmth and calm; the roaring muted, the shock and sting against her face miraculously removed. She was in a small cocoon, a heater blowing warm air on her legs, powerful headlights slicing through the black. She stole a quick glance at the driver before daring to relax. He seemed old and pretty harmless, from what she could distinguish in the gloom – a bald and plumpish man, wearing a comfy tweedy jacket and an old home-knitted cardigan in some sludgy nothing-colour she couldn't quite make out – someone's favourite uncle, judging by his looks.

She could hug him, kiss him, just for turning up, rescuing her from terror and exhaustion.

He was talking to her still, but the words made no impression, bounced off her like water off an oilskin. She tried a little English, in the hope he'd understand, but he answered in his own tongue, with a few eager flash-on smiles. Stalemate. Though perhaps it was a blessing that they couldn't actually communicate. Questions were so dangerous, and she wasn't good at lies yet.

They were travelling little faster than her previous walking pace. The road was narrow anyway, and strewn with fallen branches. The man swerved and almost skidded to avoid a massive tree-trunk which had crashed right across their path, its roots gouging up the concrete, its branches like ungainly arms flung up to break its fall. They could only pass it by driving on the verge, and, even then, its long dark tentacles scraped along the paintwork, knocked against the windows, as if calling out for help. They bumped down on the road again, the car bucking like a panicked horse as a squall of even stronger wind hit it with full force. Leaves and twigs were hailing down around them, thudding on the roof, tall trunks swaying on the near side of the road, as if they were mere flimsy fronds of fern. The man suddenly wrenched the steering wheel to avoid a heavy-duty dustbin rumbling down the road and right towards them, spewing tins and papers from its mouth.

He laughed, a crazy chuckling sound, shrill and almost girlish. She laughed herself, just to be polite; then found the laugh was real, shaking through her diaphragm, hurting in her chest. This was how it should be – everything stirred up, solid things dissolving: boats upturned on pavements, trees hurled roots-to-sky. The evening she'd left home, it had been so calm, deceitful; not a breath of wind, just icing-sugar moonlight and stagey love-song stars. And the next day equally false – a coyly sunny morning with talk of Indian summers; people in their shirt-sleeves, licking ice-creams in the street. At last, nature had caught up and was expressing all its fury and its shock. Why should she be frightened? She had felt like that herself, felt like that inside: would have roared and raged and rampaged if she'd been a Force 12 wind with her parents' house to blast.

She rubbed the window with her sleeve, peered out through the glass. The road was mulched with leaves now, as if they were driving across a forest floor in some ancient fairy tale, or perhaps one in a dream, since the 'forest' seemed to plunge and writhe; strange shapes lowering in the gloom, then a cannonade of tangled twigs blocking any vision as it strafed against the windscreen. She could smell the ripe dank odour of crushed and bleeding leaves, hear sudden booming thuds as new branches thundered down. They could be killed at any moment; had already seen a Volvo buckled by a tree-trunk, a twisted wreck trapped beneath the foliage. It had been driverless, in fact, a parked abandoned car, but it could be their turn next. Yet she wasn't scared at all now, almost revelled in the danger, longed to shout out 'Harder!' to the lashing pounding wind.

She shut her eyes a moment, hung on to the door. She was a child of eight or nine again, riding on a ghost train in a rough and raucous fairground they had discovered one bank holiday – the sense of dizzy motion as they'd hurtled round the track, cobwebs brushing their bare arms, spectres looming up in the sticky threshing darkness, then vanishing to sudden howls and whinings. She squinted through her lashes. They were, in fact, driving very slowly, but there was still the sense of speed, the same exciting feeling of being shut up on their own, with things coming at them, threatening, then veering off again; the same uncanny noises and patchy, shifting light. The street lamps were all dead, and though the headlights lit up frequent casualties – trees fallen, leaning, smashed – their dark and massy branches seemed to leach away the light, make the darkness darker. The ghost-train ride had lasted just five minutes, seemed more like an hour. It was the same with this brief drive. A mile or so of easy road had been spun out to infinity, become a test of courage. The tiny car was rocking on its springs, tugged and shaken by sudden savage blasts, blown along like a puny paper carton.

She laughed again, out loud. The man joined in, as if they were sharing some huge private joke – nature's joke, which only she and he could understand. Their two breaths and the heater's were fugging up the car, bonding them in some way. It was so long since she'd sat close to someone, shared the same small space, apart from the sick mouse in the kitchen, the sea-gulls on the porch. She glanced outside again. The road was slowly widening, houses looming up one side, as at last they reached the outskirts of the town, a darkened town, still without its street lights. The man jammed on his brakes, as they saw a knot of people huddled in their nightclothes beside the wreckage of a bungalow. Their flickering torches cast grotesque shadows on gaping roof and blown-out wall. She could see right into the bedroom – a rumpled lacy coverlet on the still-warm double bed, a pile of bricks and mortar on the fluffy bedside rug. Her parents had a rug like that, even the same colour. She drew her breath in sharply, sat absolutely motionless. The man scrabbled at his door, about to offer help, only shrugged back in again as a police car sirened past, followed by an

13

ambulance. Even when the sirens stopped, she could still hear them shrilling in her head; see her mother on a stretcher, her pale face even paler, her bossy fussing figure quiet at last.

The man drove jerkily away, letting out a hail of words, as if he needed to express his sense of shock. The words were simply noise to her, answered with her own noise. Why was life so complicated? Couldn't things have been arranged so that people spoke one simple basic language, or belonged to just one gender, or had fewer complex body-parts, or minds which could tell truth from lies, or mothers who were real? She stared out through the windscreen, wishing they could just turn back, or had lost their eyes, their feelings. Other cars were now converging, their acrid yellow headlights showing up a scene of total chaos. They had nagged her for untidiness at home, but here everything was messed, convulsed, on some gigantic scale: scaffolding collapsed, lamp-posts snapped like matchsticks, the entire roof peeled off a block of flats, as if someone had removed it with a can-opener. Gaps everywhere – gaps in walls, in windows, gaps in lines of trees or rows of terraced houses; stout fencing hacked to firewood, a large imposing caravan toppled like a toy, shop windows open to the street, selling only rubble.

The man was almost panicking, slowing down, half-stopping, then lurching on again, muttering and groaning to himself. He drove towards a woman wrapped in an old eiderdown and sitting in the gutter; was stopped before he reached her, flagged down by the police.

'You can't go that way, sir. The road's completely blocked. I suggest you go back home. We're trying to clear the streets.'

The man blustered, shouted, failed to understand. She understood too well: go back home. Impossible. She tried to hide her face, had been hiding from policemen for twenty-seven days. It was time she went to ground again, said goodbye and thank you to her driver. He had done what she had wanted, brought her into town, to light and peace and safety – except all three had broken down. She waited till the police car slid away, then tugged his sleeve, pointed through the window, made a stopping sign. She doubted he could see it in the dark, since, instead of stopping, he veered sharply to the right. The chaos was increasing; two ambulances nosing down the road now, sirens blaring out again, garish blue lights flashing. He turned into a side-street to avoid them, crunched across a tide of fallen debris, then pulled up outside a small hotel, which looked relatively unharmed, though three elderly guests in dressing-gowns were shivering in the doorway, one sobbing and hysterical. She opened the car door, tried

14

to dart away, but the man was already round her side, trying to coax her up the steps of the hotel.

She shoved him off, bolted down the narrow road, dived behind a wall, crouched there, out of breath. She could see him sidling up to her in the shabby hotel bedroom, turning back the faded yellow candlewick; hear his guttural noises as he climbed on top of her; flabby folds of stomach dripping on her midriff, blue nylon sheets clammy with his sweat. The scene went blank at that point. She wasn't sure what happened next, had no direct experience. One boy had lain on top of her, a boy called Ian she'd met on a computer course, who had coaxed her to his bedsit for a drink, though she had found herself not sipping beer or coffee, but lying on his sofa-bed with her skirt up round her waist. Suddenly she'd panicked, changed her mind, fought him off, pretending she felt sick. The same queasiness was rippling through her stomach now, as she tried to quiet her breathing, make herself invisible. Sex was everywhere – in magazines, on bookstalls, in doctors' waiting-rooms, in novels, films and videos, but that didn't make it easier – *worse*, in fact – because she seemed to be the only prude, the only prissy innocent.

Maybe she'd misjudged the man. He might only have meant to help, been offering her a bed alone, or a meal or warmth or shelter. She didn't want a bed or meal; only craved for light – proper light, morning light, not those flaring storm-lamps, or callous torches flushing out trapped victims. She checked her watch, astonished it was only four A.M. According to her internal clock, several nights had passed; time pulled out and out like strudel pastry, yet now contracted back again. So how kill the hours till morning? There were no all-night cafés open, no bustling bars or night-clubs. That was why she'd settled here when she'd first run away from home, relieved to find a stopping-place so stagnant and anonymous, a small and dying South Coast town which discouraged tourists with its drab shops, shingly beaches, dearth of entertainments, and where nobody would find her, no one even care; three hundred and fifty miles away from angry, frantic parents. She had planned to flee still further, maybe run into the sea and be swallowed up and drowned, or run across the Channel and keep on going until she reached the South of France. But she hadn't had the money or the strength.

She eased up from the ground, crept on down the road, tense and on her guard still, in case the man was loitering, though no one seemed to follow save the wind. She turned a shadowy corner, almost trod on something – a corpse, a female corpse, stiffly dead, but smiling, its breasts completely bare, its lower limbs swathed in dirty velvet. She stared in horror, then realised it was plastic; a fashion dummy, blasted from a store, its coy smile only painted, taut nipples pointing skywards. She broke into a run, pounded on, despite the wind, despite the ruts and hazards in the road; kept tripping, stumbling, dazed by blinding headlamps, then plunged again in darkness. Everything was jumbled: light and dark, noise and eerie silences; urgent sirens, panting cars, then deserted ghostly alleyways, sudden cold and void. She faltered to a stop, uncertain where she was. Shops and homes had thinned now, but she could just make out the dark bulk of a church looming to her left. She limped towards it, and suddenly a passing car illuminated the letters on a poster in the porch: 'AND UNDERNEATH ARE THE EVERLASTING ARMS'. The car turned the corner and the poster blanked to nothing, but she had transferred it to her head. She liked the words, could see the arms, like huge and feathered wings, spread out beneath the broken world, soothing it, supporting it.

She groped towards the porch, pushed the heavy door. It resisted her, refused her. Why were churches so often locked, when they were meant to offer shelter, described as sanctuaries? She had sometimes tried to visit one, out of simple curiosity, but rarely found it open, even in the daytime. Her parents weren't religious, hadn't included Sunday services in their bustling full-packed timetable, which had worked its way through ballet classes, Brownies, piano lessons, tennis coaching, stroke-improvement classes at the local swimming baths, and scores of joyless sessions at the ice rink, which had ended with a gashed and bleeding leg. Her legs were throbbing now, as if remembering the pain; her feet hurting in their thin unpadded trainers. She would have to stop and rest, and at least she'd found a windbreak. She crouched down in the porch, right beneath the poster, with its wildly generous promise, which was probably the most colossal lie of all. Yet she wanted to believe it, yearned for arms beneath her, for words like 'everlasting'. She stretched out on the bare and dirty wood, turned it into wings, snug supportive wings, a mother's arms, storm-proofed and secure.

2

Jane ran, and kept on running, ran through high brick walls and tangled hedges, ran through foaming waves and wasn't wet, ran through panes of glass and wasn't cut. She pounded to the winning-post, woke up, bewildered by the stillness, the fact she couldn't hear the sea; then suddenly remembered where she was. The wind had dropped, at last, but it was still raw and spooky-dark, the moon fretting the grey tombstones which seemed to have edged up closer to the porch, moved nearer to the church while she'd been sleeping. The damp cold must have woken her, the hard uneven floor. Her feet had lost their feeling, her limbs were stiff and cramped. She pushed her sleeve back, squinted at the illuminated figures of her watch. Still only half past five. It wasn't just the weather which was chaotic and disturbed, but time as well. Someone must have tampered with it, reset the cosmic clock. She never remembered any night lasting quite so long. She felt grubby and dishevelled, as if she'd been out for days and days, taking part in some endless pointless route-march, scheduled always for the dark.

She eased up to her feet, tried the door again. Still locked. Perhaps locked churches had no power, couldn't save themselves. This one had been struck – or at least its gravestones had – two pinioned by a fallen tree, the marble angel next to them lopsided with one wing. Despite his disability, he was still smiling, pointing Godwards; pale moonlight pockmarking his skin, rippling his white hair. Jane edged on down the path, past a carnage of torpedoed flowers – a recent corpse's 'floral tributes' mangled to a pulp. She picked up a headless stalk, thorns jabbing at her fingers. Roses always moralised, tried to teach you that scent and gorgeous colour had a price; the more beautiful the blooms, the sharper the thorns. The day she'd left, their garden had been cruel with them, crimson bullies

17

out-shouting all the other flowers. She could still smell them three days later, when the only smells were paraffin and brine. Had the storm struck Shrepton this time, smashed her mother's hybrid teas in their mulched and weeded beds? She dodged behind a bush, could see a torch flashing along the south wall of the church; someone examining the stonework, peering at the windows. It must be the vicar, worried by the storm, checking any damage to his church. The only vicar she'd ever met was the one who came twice-yearly to their school, a boyish bouncy type, who tried to make religion sound jolly and good fun, as if he were a Redcoat in some Jesus brand of Butlin's. She shrank away instinctively, back towards the gate, stopped before she reached it. A vicar might be useful, not stern like the police, but someone trained to help, trusted to keep confidences. She was desperate for a job; her money almost gone now, her few old clothes inadequate for winter. She'd been nervous about applying for a post, scared of all the questions and the grillings; feared someone in authority might try to send her home, even though she was officially an adult and had every legal right to work at what she wanted, live exactly where she chose. Her parents were bound to have alerted the police, given them her photograph to circulate, so that if she entered any dole office or job centre, she'd be recognised, tracked down. But a vicar would be different, might know of some more casual job which she could do for cash in hand, so that she wouldn't be entangled in tax demands, officialdom.

She crept back to the church. The torch had disappeared now; no sign of life at all. She followed the wall round to the far side of the church, a sallow wash of moonlight jaundicing the stone, showing up a small side-door, overhung by ivy. She pushed aside the tangled noose, tried the rusty handle, falling forward suddenly as it yielded to her pressure and she found herself inside. She paused a moment, awed. The church looked larger than it had from the outside, shadowy stone arches soaring up beyond her, glints and gleams of moonlight seeping through the dark stained glass, revealing ghostly figures, highlighting saints' haloes, angels' outstretched wings. The darkness was gradated now, deep pools of it in corners, dappling into silver where the moon could gain an entrance, but mostly sombre black. No solid shapes or lines; walls and roof-beams indistinct, a blur of pews, a looming bulk of pulpit. She stood silent where she was, aware of all the smells – the rotting scent of overripe chrysanthemums, the odour of old stone, the subtle smell of candle-wax all but snuffed by the fondant breath of freesias wafting from a ledge above her head. She could hardly hear the wind

18

now. The solid walls had blocked it out, reduced it to a drone. She edged into the centre aisle, between two broad-shouldered pillars, felt the darkness drift and clog around her, as if she were groping through black smoke.

'Is that you, Anthony?'

The deep male voice boomeranged towards her, reverberated back again. So the vicar was still there, skulking in the shadows. She'd assumed he'd gone back home, and, anyway, it now seemed quite impossible to discuss employment prospects with him at half past five on a bruised and broken morning in an empty, unlit church. She backed away, banged her shin on something, stooped down to rub it, wincing. 'No, it's not,' she stammered. 'I'm sorry I disturbed you. I'm just going, actually.'

She was answered by his torch, which suddenly stabbed on again, a huge round eye blinding and transfixing her, so that she couldn't move at all. She tried to shade her eyes. The torch had extinguished everything save its own insistent beam, a fierce searchlight swooping closer, as his footsteps shocked the cold stone floor, stopped a yard or two in front of her. Still she couldn't see him, only feel his own eyes drilling through her body, until she was reduced to shred and sawdust, vital pieces of herself just shavings on the ground. She collapsed into a pew, bent to rub her leg again, felt the bruise swelling like an egg.

'Are you all right?' he asked, not waiting for her answer. 'There's a total black-out between here and Portsmouth. The entire network's broken down. I heard it on the news. They're saying it's the most savage storm on record since the great hurricane of 1703.'

His voice was strong, well-modulated, what she'd call a blue-chip voice, fattened on good food and wine, good breeding and good schools. His coat looked fattened, too – what she could make out of it – a bulky coat, padded at the shoulders, as if to lend him force and weight. Vicars should be poor, she thought, carpenters and fishermen. She turned to leave, wishing she could beg his torch, or that he would offer it himself. His house was probably just next door, whereas she had miles to trudge.

'You local?' he asked tersely, as if he'd read her mind.

'Er, no.'

'On a bike or . . . ?'

'Walking.'

'I wouldn't recommend it, not until it's light, at least. You'd better hang around.'

Men were always dominant – fathers, vicars, teachers, bosses.

She'd learnt not to react, to keep silent, seem submissive. He couldn't hear her anyway. A car had drowned his own voice, headlamps sweeping past the window, imprinting his dark shadow gigantic on the wall, her own shadow swamped in his. She stole a nervous look at him, as both shadows ebbed to nothing. He was small, in fact, in terms of simple stature, though his voice, his clothes, his presence, seemed to expand to fill the church. Perhaps all vicars were like that. They must need great charisma to thunder from the pulpit, lay down the moral law; must feel self-important with God as their immediate boss and a soaring church as office.

He turned abruptly on his heel, as if bored with her, or restless, started striding back the way he'd come, towards the dark west end. She stood dithering in the aisle, tempted to escape now, yet attracted by his torch, by the fact he was a minister, someone in control, perhaps even with some influence on things like storms, disasters. She followed him uncertainly, stumbling in the gloom as she watched the beam in front of her light up fleeting details in the church – a sudden splash of colour from a green and purple hassock, a spiky candelabra, doubled by its shadow, some exotic speckled leaves bulking out a formal flower arrangement. He stopped beside a marble font, tilting back his head so that he could scan the whole tall window, flashed his torch up and down the glass. 'Can *you* see any damage?'

She frowned, screwed up her eyes, couldn't make out much at all, except a jigsaw of vague shapes, some darker and receding, some lighter, leaping forward, though none with any certain form or colour.

'We had a lot of problems fixing this west window. The stone-work's not too brilliant, and it's weakest at this end. I was tossing all damned night, listening to the wind, and imagining that glass just a pile of shattered fragments on the floor.' He refocused the torch, peered intently upwards. She glanced at him instead. He was as undefined as the figures in the glass – no colour in his eyes or clothes, no outline to his features. Yet she imagined he'd be dark: stern brown hair and eyes, to match his strong brown voice.

'The saddle-bars seem to be intact, thank Christ, and none of the glass has blown out.'

She tensed at that 'thank Christ', disliked the thought of godmen trying to be trendy, tossing in a 'damned' or two to show what sports they were. She turned away, leaned against the font, ran her hand across its pregnant underbelly, which felt smooth and clammy-cold.

'The whole window was destroyed in the last war, and they asked me to replace it. It was my first commission, actually – caused me more sheer bloody heartache than anything else I've ever done, even windows twice the size.'

She stared at him, bewildered. Vicars preached sermons, didn't make their own stained glass. 'So you're not the vicar?'

'God, no! I'm an artist.'

'You mean, you . . . you *made* that window?'

'Yes.'

He made the 'yes' so matter-of-fact, he could have been talking about a piece of minor carpentry, some odd ledge or bookshelf he'd rigged up in his home, not a thirty-foot-high window, intricate with shapes, which dominated the entire west end of the church. How it was created she had no idea at all. She had never really thought about stained glass. It was simply there, like trees were there – something she took for granted without bothering to question. And if her parents took her out, it would be a day-trip to a wildlife park or motor museum, rather than a cultural tour involving art or architecture.

The artist was still peering at his window, concentrating now on the lower right-hand corner, which looked a dirty leaden grey, but might in fact be peacock blue, or the red of flames or rubies. She tried to see the window with his eyes, envied him the fact he knew its colours, didn't need to wait for sunrise.

'I was bloody lucky really to have my first commission almost on my doorstep, instead of having to flog five hundred miles or more to some godforsaken village in the wilds. I was friendly with the vicar, who liked the panels I'd just done for a stained-glass competition, and he put my name forward for the job – not that it helped, when it came to the crunch. The PCC hated my design, wanted all the symbols made more obvious. They're total bloody philistines as far as modern art's concerned, run a mile from anything that's not tamely figurative.'

Jane didn't dare reply, knew nothing about modern art herself. And who or what was the PCC? She'd never heard of them.

'All we could agree on was the theme – the Seven Gifts of the Holy Ghost. But of course those fogies wanted Fortitude to be an angel with a flaming sword and Wisdom a Greek goddess with a scroll.'

She mumbled something vague, hoped he'd change the subject. The Seven Gifts of the Holy Ghost were as much a mystery to her as the PCC, or saddle-bars.

'I made that window a hundred years ago, but I'm still having problems now. A different set of philistines, but the same crass literal-mindedness. Though the donor's got more sense, thank God. In fact, it was because she liked my style so much that she commissioned me to do another window – that one over there.' He flung his arm out, gestured to the darkness. 'It's the first time ever I've been asked to do two windows in the same church.'

'You mean, people just commission windows like . . . like . . . ?' She groped for an analogy. 'Like ordering a birthday cake, or a McDonald's takeaway?'

He laughed. 'If they've got several thousand pounds to spare, and a hell of a lot of staying-power and patience. It's over a year now since Isobel first approached me, and the window's hardly started. Most of that time was spent going cap in hand, first to the vicar – a new one with no taste – then to that decrepit bunch who call themselves the Council, and after arguing the toss with them over every footling detail, we then had scores of new objections from the Diocesan Advisory Committee – another set of know-alls who see themselves as gods. The theme of this new window's Resurrection. I'm beginning to feel I'll need it personally, if and when the window's ever finished.'

Jane was still gazing at the glass above her head, amazed he could have made it, that anyone could make it. How and where did he begin, or ever reach so high? 'Will it be as big as this one?'

'Not so tall, but wider. It's a two-light window this time. Want to take a look at it?' He swept along the side-aisle, walking far too fast for her, as if he were perpetually in a hurry, chafing at Diocesan Committees, or girls who tripped and blundered in the dark. Her other leg was bruised now, though she didn't stop to check it. She could feel his impatience twitching through the church, as he stood on the south side, already lighting up the drab glass with his torch.

'It's plain glass here, you see, which should make things a bit simpler. If it was a question of replacing some smirking nineteenth-century saint or saccharine madonna, all hell would be let loose, especially if the donor was the worthy great-great-grandfather of the chairman of the Council.'

Jane glanced around her nervously, as if the Council might be present, concealed behind the pillars, but recording these impertinences. His voice still seemed too aggressive for a church, his manner too offhand. She recalled the words of gentle hymns they'd sung at school assemblies, humble deferential words which flattered and cajoled. Wasn't that the proper language for God's house?

'Isobel specially wanted a window on the south side. It gets a warmer light, you see, which gives the glass more life. That's probably psychologically important to her. Her husband was an enlightened man himself, and the window's a memorial to him, even a way of resurrecting him, I suspect. He died pretty nastily in a pile-up on the motorway. Ironical for a surgeon who spent his life patching up other helpless wrecks.'

Jane said nothing for a moment. It seemed disrespectful to make some trite remark, yet she almost envied the dead surgeon – to be that honoured, that exalted. 'Gosh! I'd love a window when I die – to sort of make myself immortal.'

'Well, you'd better start saving for it now. Something on this scale would set you back a good twenty thousand pounds. Or probably ten times that, if you live another sixty years.'

She grimaced in the dark, didn't want money mixed up with immortality; had no intention of living sixty years. Old age was worse than death. She'd watched it at first hand. 'I hate the thought of death. Just some horrid little plot in a faceless crematorium, and being burnt in a microwave with hordes of other bodies, and your ashes all mixed up with other people's, and the undertaker grabbing back your coffin so he can re-use it for another corpse, and . . .'

'I'm surprised you've thought so much about it at such a tender age.'

She bristled silently. Why did people always assume that because you were still young, you were casual, superficial, didn't dwell on serious things? Even as a kid of eight, she'd been anxious about dying.

'What are you, seventeen?'

'Eighteen,' she said fiercely. 'Eighteen and a half.' The half was an invention. She'd been eighteen just a month ago, celebrated with a big and showy birthday party, a present from her parents – the worst evening of her life. She was suddenly transported back – piano, drums and saxophone clashing in her head, the dance-floor tipping sideways as Uncle Peter's whisky breath blasted in her face; his hot hand on her back, his seesaw voice belching out those crazy lethal questions.

'What?' she said. 'I didn't hear.' The artist had stepped closer, his voice fused with Uncle Peter's. She tried to disentangle them, smash up the whole party, as it had broken up in fact: guests shouting, sobbing, quarrelling, or sneaking out embarrassed to their cars.

'I just asked what you were doing out at such an unearthly hour?'

She wished he wouldn't question her. It made her feel uneasy, as if he already knew the answers, and was seeing if she lied. He had guessed her age within a year, yet they could barely see each other.

Did he have some secret powers? She couldn't tell his own age, not even the rough decade. She'd like to ask him outright, but that was not allowed. One rule for the young again. Anyway, he was still awaiting her reply. She mumbled something fatuous about not being able to sleep, edged a step away.

'Name?'

She didn't answer. He made it sound so rude, as if he were a sergeant-major; she servile, on parade. Or was he merely saving words, saving time again? Her nails were digging in her palms, in an effort not to snap. Sharp, like thorns. 'Rose,' she muttered suddenly.

'Rose? Your name?'

'Mm.'

'Pretty.'

She could be pretty in the dark, could be almost anything – exotic, foreign, even royal or titled. She no longer had a name or an identity, so why not ditch the Jane and snub her parents? If they had called her something pretty in the first place, she might have grown to fit it. Rose was rather beautiful, so the artist had approved. Artists all loved beauty, and artists were as rare as vicars – rarer, actually. She had never met one in her life, not a proper one. Miss Mason had taught art at school, but she was very ordinary, wore anoraks and Hush Puppies, made lumpy garish collages out of silver foil and scraps of felt, not Resurrection windows.

'Rose,' she said again, trying to conjure up a surname which would harmonise and match it, impress him equally. She could feel her hair rippling down her back, twining into ringlets, her pale eyes flashing into black, her too-wide mouth a rosebud. 'Could *I* commission a window – I mean, just because I wanted to, not for any husband or bereavement?'

'If you've got the cash, why not? What sort of work d'you do?'

She paused, relieved he didn't presume she was a schoolgirl, but reluctant to reveal her lack of role. 'I'm . . . er . . . working out my future at the moment.'

'I envy you.'

She glanced at him, perplexed. He'd sounded almost bitter, had switched the torch off, subsided in a pew. Darkness closed around them both, she standing in the aisle still, he sitting, shoulders hunched. She looked up in surprise at the faint cough of a lighter, its blue flame biting through the gloom, exposing his dark face; the dead point of a cigarette igniting, deepening, dwindling to a tiny glow of red. Smoking in a church? It seemed a desecration, an insult to his window, to the church's congregation, its coffined dead outside. She also felt excluded. He hadn't asked if *she* smoked. Rude again, demeaning, as if he'd dismissed her as too young for any vices.

The smell of smoke was quashing all the church smells, reminding her of death again – crematorium chimneys, cancer of the lung. He turned the torch back on, propped it on the seat beside him, used its light to scrabble through his pockets, draw out a scrap of paper which he bent into an ashtray. Her eyes tracked along the torch-beam to a swathe of dull grey floor, the fallen petals of some small red flower like blood-stains on the stone. The paving was uneven; the tattered pennant above it all but crumbling into dust. That was all she'd be herself in another sixty years or so – dust and ashes in an urn, a rose-bush in a garden of remembrance. She shrugged, sat down, chose the pew in front so she needn't see him smoking, could restore the church its dignity and power. She looked up at the altar, the huge window poised above it, so dense with wings she felt it might take off. The moon was pressing close to it, stencilling in its shapes, not in their true colours, but in shades of yellow-grey. She could even make out some pale letters: 'GLORIA IN EXCELSIS DEO', running round the border of a halo.

She shut her eyes, so she could concentrate on glory – a whole vast congregation joining in a service – triumphant music, rich embroidered vestments, lilies, incense, choir. Great to have a faith, to conquer age and death; to be martyred even, die for something, burn for some huge cause, so you could rise above the hurts and disillusion. Jobs were so banal – the few she'd tried, or read about – withering in offices, decaying at some desk. They had tried to talk her into doing a degree, but university was only school without the rules – or different rules and even longer hours. She had yearned to work for some ideal, but ideals kept disappearing when you tried to track them down, and her stint at the Old People's Home had been mostly bedpans, bedsores. You spent so long growing up, reaching double figures, fretting through your teens, waiting, hoping, fantasising, then landed up as computer-fodder serving a machine – worse, landed up as nothing, a question mark, a riddle.

They had done Keats at school, for A-level. 'Beauty is truth, truth beauty.' Okay for *him* to say it, but try saying it yourself to parents or headmasters, and you were called immature, or arty, living in a dream-world.

'That is all ye know on earth, and all ye need to know.' A blatant lie on Keats's part. You had to know scores of other things – algebra, biology, how to use a database, how to set out your CV when you hadn't really got one yet, how to seem intelligent at interviews, appear delighted by the prospect of just four weeks off a year and a subsidised canteen; how to build another life when your first one had been smashed.

She let her eyes drift open, saw feathered wings again. Did angels have CVs, or long vacations? Did they worry, feel alone? She heard a sudden noise behind her, turned round to see the artist rising from his pew, re-buttoning his coat.

'Well,' he said, shaking the now feeble torch, to jerk it back to life. 'Now I've checked my window, I'd better check my studio. You'll be all right here, will you, on your own?'

'Mm,' she answered vaguely, feeling somehow disappointed. She was back to Jane again – plain, of no importance, not a commissioner of windows, not a savage sultry Rose.

'It'll be light in half an hour. In fact, I think the sky's lightening even now – just the palest glimmer.'

She shook her head, had almost stopped believing there was such a thing as daylight. She could see the sun lying smashed and mangled on some lonely narrow road, a victim of the storm.

'*Ciao* then,' called the artist, already halfway down the aisle, his footsteps seeming to play it like an organ, as the whole church boomed around him.

' 'Bye,' she muttered, as she slumped back on the seat. He hadn't even given her his name.

3

'Christopher,' he said, as he slowed to check his right of way at a set of blinded traffic lights.

'Not Chris?'

'No, Christopher. No shortenings. It means bearer of Christ, which I rather like.'

'But you just said you didn't believe in Christ.' It had shocked her, that remark. How could an artist making windows for a church be atheist, agnostic?

'I said I didn't believe in *God*. You can't not believe in Christ. He's a historical fact – well, Jesus is, anyway. As for Saviours and Messiahs, that's something else entirely. Are you a believer, Rose?'

Jane tensed. Every time he used that 'Rose', she felt pleasure mixed with guilt, knew she ought to put him right, yet every time she didn't, the name seemed more her own, changing her, inspiring her, paying out her parents. 'I believe in believing,' she began uncertainly. 'At least, I think I do. I'm sure it makes you better, gives you causes and ideals, but . . .' She shifted in the passenger-seat, gazed up at the horizon – a forest of Scots pines with hardly a single branch left, just naked stumps picked clean by last night's gale. It was so hard to find the right thing to believe in, something huge enough. Her parents put their faith in petty things like punctuality, tidiness, and vague but pompous concepts such as Unselfishness and Honesty, which always had capital letters, but didn't actually prevent them telling strings of small white lies, or refusing to give money to the homeless, on the grounds that it encouraged layabouts. They also believed in Education, which meant their only child must go to university, to reflect credit on them, move them up a notch or two in status, since they hadn't been themselves.

'Anyway, he was said to be a giant.'

27

'Who?' she asked, streaking back from Shrepton.

'Saint Christopher.' His mouth relaxed into a grin, which then expanded to a laugh. She was glad he could take a joke against himself. He was barely five foot six, which gave him four good inches over her, but was still short for a man. She'd been fazed altogether to see him in the light. He had returned to the church as its clock was striking seven, pounded down the path, scattering 'damns' and 'blasts', having only realised when he was halfway to his studio that he'd left the place unlocked, which meant at risk from vandals. He'd been surprised to find her there still, now wandering in the graveyard, offered her a lift. The lift was still in progress, a slow and dangerous drive, negotiating road-blocks, crawling round dead cars, their mangled bodies flattened by fallen trees and buildings. Only in the last half-mile had she felt confident enough to ask his name. But they'd been discussing other things, important vital things which sprang naturally from the carnage all round them; and he hadn't sounded patronising, or made her feel she was too young or inexperienced to have opinions and ideas.

She still couldn't tell his own age, though he was far older than she'd thought. She had been disappointed somehow to see he had grey hair – not greying, total grey. Yet it was thick assertive hair, standing up like the crest of some exotic bird above his lean lined face. The dark eyes she'd envisaged were lighter than her own, a different shade from hers, more steel in them than sky. She glanced down at his hands, gripped tightly on the steering-wheel; not the slim artistic fingers she'd imagined, but workman's hands, blunt with dirty nails. They didn't match the rest of him: the expensive camel coat and fine grey cords, the fastidious-looking features – narrow nose, neat mouth – the tidy brows, good teeth.

Her gaze moved to her own hands, down further to her creased and grubby tracksuit. He must have found her disappointing in his turn, once the light exposed her, revealed her as a drab and windblown Rose. Just as well she hadn't got a mirror. She hardly dared imagine what she looked like, hadn't combed her hair or washed her face for what felt like a week. She was worried she might even smell – of paraffin, or mouse-droppings, or maybe of the sea. The last few lonely nomad weeks had left their imprint on her, removed her from the sterile world of bubble-bath and hairspray.

He had asked her where she lived, in fact, and she'd had to lie, think quickly, had blurted out the name of a small village several miles away.

'That's not far from my studio. I can drop you at your door, but we'd better stop and check my roof first. There's a rather dodgy patch right bang in the middle, which might well have sprung a leak.'

She skewed round to the window, as if to turn her back on him, at least symbolically. This was the second stranger she had met in just one night, landed in a car with. Could she trust him any more than that oily chuckling foreigner who'd tried to lure her up the steps of his hotel? At least it was now daylight and they had no language barrier, and anyway she longed to see his studio, felt important and excited to be conversing with an artist, one who sounded famous, who had even written books, given public lectures, made a gigantic modern window for a new church in Los Angeles when he was only in his twenties. She needn't stay for long, just a lightning tour of everything, then scat. He'd be bored with her, in any case, if she tried to hang around, must be used to cultured people who could talk his language, ask the right deep questions.

He had turned off the main road, along a narrow winding track, so thick with leaves and branches the car crunched and crackled over them, complaining sometimes, shuddering, throwing up cascades of mud from treacherous hidden puddles. She felt worried for the car, now smirched with mud and grime, but extremely tidy inside; the shelf beneath the glove-compartment neatly stacked with map-books, the back shelf clear and clean, a car-rug folded four-square on the leather seat behind her. It could have been her father's fussy Ford, except the make was very different; one she didn't recognise, with a long body, lowish snout, and walnut panelling inside, instead of fake-grained plastic. She'd have thought a stained-glass artist would have driven something workmanlike – an estate car or a van, and that she'd have been sitting in a cluttered mess, with tools and things around her.

'No wonder Saint Christopher was demoted,' his namesake muttered grimly as they passed a Ford Fiesta crippled in the ditch, one door hanging open, a child's blue-patterned sweater trailing in the mud. 'He's meant to be the patron saint of travellers. Or perhaps he was just overstretched last night.'

Jane shut her eyes, so she needn't see the sweater, or that pathetic piece of knitting still anchored to its needles, but flung into the ditch. 'Why was he demoted?'

The artist shrugged. 'A mistake, in my opinion. We lost Saint George as well. Just the Church trying to be rational, whereas the whole point of religion is its appeal to the irrational. In medieval times, Messrs Christopher and George were both in the Top Twenty, both included in the list of 'Holy Helpers', who were rather like our

29

wonder-drugs – a group of fourteen saints famous for their potency in serious diseases, and probably far less dangerous than modern chemicals.' He rummaged for a cigarette, lit it from a lighter concealed in the front panel. 'I wouldn't mind betting that people owe a damn sight more to Christopher than they do to penicillin. He's reputed to have cured everything from snake bite to the plague. Most medieval churches had a picture of him right opposite the door, so that everyone who entered would be protected from fire, water, tempest, plague and sudden death. Perhaps I ought to have him in my studio, instead of calling in a builder for the roof. Hey, you'd better keep your fingers crossed. We're here.'

She crossed them superstitiously, looked out at what appeared to be a large deserted barn, divorced from other buildings or a farmhouse; its strong walls stoutly boarded, its old roof furred with moss. The narrow tree-lined road had opened out to a vista of bare fields, combed in neat brown furrows, the pale sky vast beyond them, its curdled clouds glinting where the sun was breaking through. The dawn light had been grudging up till now. Both trees and town had hemmed her in, the car itself had blinkered and restricted her. She struggled with the door, couldn't find the handle, wound the window down instead, gulped lungfuls of sheer space, breathed in light and air, inhaled the cold November smell of raw morning and ripe leaves. The artist slammed his own door, didn't help her out, started exclaiming at the tide of debris blown in by the storm, which fringed the barn like some untidy garden planted randomly with empty cans and boxes, dirty tattered papers, plastic bottles, a mauled and bloody bird. 'Okay?' he called, not looking back, but picking his slow way between the litter.

She nodded, clambered out at last, wincing at the shock of cold which stabbed right through her clothes, contrasted with the stale fug of the car. She turned up her coat collar, ran to catch him up, stumbling on a plank of wood spiked with rusty nails.

'Careful, or you'll break your neck. Hell! It'll take me half a day to clear this shambles. The roof looks fine from here, but God knows what it's like inside. Come in.'

She couldn't see at all at first. He was standing in the way. Then he moved, dived sidewards, and the huge dramatic window which filled one end of the barn suddenly jolted into view, colours shouting at her – blazing scarlet, smouldering purple, fierce electric blue, yellow like a dandelion, so sharp it set her teeth on edge. She moved a few steps nearer, still reeling from its impact, realised she was looking at three panels of stained glass – tall explosive panels which magnetised the room, drew the eye towards them, almost bludgeoned it with colour. The reds were dominant, rowdy restless reds in what she'd thought were abstract shapes, until they suddenly transmuted into birds – birds flying at her, spiralling, swooping, plunging down. She had never seen such creatures, some ferocious bloody species with jagged wings, cruel talons; other smaller tawny birds flapping up beneath them from a tangled overgrowth. The panel on the right was not yet quite complete, and the trees outside were showing through the gaps, their bronzed and yellowed foliage jumbling all the images, adding still more rich confusion.

She kept staring, mesmerised. One bird's elongated head thrust right across the panel, like a spear or a javelin, flung into mid-air. Another's neck was bent back on itself, in such a tortured posture she almost felt its pain. The sky was represented by scraps and shards of blue; not a tranquil summer sky, but a threatening one, crisscrossed with black lines. Her eyes were hurting from the clash of violent purples, the grind of red on blue. She turned away, saw more birds: drawings, paintings, sketches, tacked all round the walls. Some she recognised – eagles, falcons, herons, doves – others were fantastic, birds from myth or nightmare; many daubed with colour, a few just whirling lines.

She longed to make some comment, find words intense and keen enough for the boldness of the glass, but the only ones which came to her seemed timid and subdued. 'It's . . . it's huge,' she mumbled lamely, as she gazed up at the roof-beams, aware that she was copping out by shifting her attention to the lofty room itself. When he had talked about his studio, she'd imagined somewhere poky, an attic or a garret, not this hangar of a building, whose steep-pitched gabled roof made it look another church.

'It needs to be when you're working on this scale.' Christopher was prowling round the room, looking out for breakages or leaks, though she couldn't see a trace of any damage. 'The larger the better, so you can get as much glass as possible up against the light. My first studio was tiddly – well, just a room at home, in fact. I found it so frustrating. It was rather like working in a coal cellar. You could only see a fraction of the window at any one time.'

She had assumed he made the windows in the church itself, felt a total ignoramus, longed to ask a tidal wave of questions, but was scared they'd sound so basic he would dismiss her as a fool. She moved into a swatch of sun, the dull blue of her winter coat immediately lightening into summer. Even so, she felt lumpen in comparison with the blaze and slam of colour which had drawn her

31

back again. She stood closer to the window now, crouching down, then peering up, to try to scan it all; aware of greater detail in the panels – some sections streaked and variegated with amazing marbled mottlings like wine-stains, sunbursts, tortoiseshell, or the rainbow bloom on pigeons' breasts or puddles. She pulled her coat off, threw it on a chair, felt hot from flaming scarlets, drunk on claret reds. How could glass be so transformed from the boring stuff of window-panes or milk bottles?

There was more glass in the wooden racks which ran down one long wall, and were divided into sections, each labelled with its colour and graded into sizes – sheets and stacks and slabs of glass, but which all looked dour and dead. Could it be the same glass as that glowing in his panels? How had he transformed it, made it come alive? The labels on the racks didn't seem to match their contents – the glass-sheets dull and dusty, sometimes broken pieces, or just motley strips and scraps; the names themselves poetic: streaky gold pink, seedy ruby, flashed amber, reamy white. She touched a sheet of pink, shuddering at the sharpness of its edges, one corner snicked and jagged. The studio seemed dangerous altogether – sharp-toothed saws hanging naked on the walls, savage-looking unsheathed knives laid out on a table, a murky jar of acid labelled 'POISONOUS', a large box crammed with glass fragments, each a small discarded knife itself. Yet it was also very orderly – all the brushes marshalled into sizes, and standing to attention in a battalion of old coffee tins; jars of paint lined up in tidy rows; tools and rulers, screws and nails, in separate drawers and boxes; the high walls newly whitewashed, the wooden floor well scrubbed.

She turned back to look for Christopher, found he'd disappeared, then heard a rush of water from a cistern just outside. She, too, needed the bathroom, desperately, in fact. She darted out to find it, pushed the door in front of her, glimpsed a cooker, not a toilet. She backed away, collided with the artist who was just entering the kitchen, still wearing his thick camel coat, as if he couldn't spare the time to take it off.

'I'm . . . looking for the loo,' she said, cursed herself for blushing. She had turned into an awkward adolescent who couldn't mention simple natural functions without squirming, going red.

'Just there.'

She was glad to lock the door, let her flush subside, only hoped he couldn't hear as she emptied her full bladder; had a strange uneasy feeling he was standing right outside. She washed her face and hands, peered into the mirror, surprised to find she looked nothing like she'd feared – not the dishevelled grubby wreck she had kept seeing in her mind. Her cheeks were very pink still, which made her eyes look brighter, and though her hair was tousled, it wasn't unattractive, seemed thicker tangled up like that, as if some arty hairdresser had spent several skilful hours on it to produce the natural look. She opened the bathroom cabinet which hung above the basin, feeling like a spy as she found indigestion mixture, senna tablets, cough linctus, shampoo for sensitive hair. She also found a toothbrush, gave her teeth a brief but guilty scrub; knew it was a crime to use someone else's toothbrush, or go through strangers' cupboards. She pushed her jersey up, tried to spray her underarms with Deodorant For Men. The smell was powerful, an uncompromising reek of spice and musk. Now he'd know she'd stolen it, know that she'd been snooping. She grabbed the disinfectant bottle from its niche behind the toilet, dabbed a little on her skin, prayed the two strong odours would counteract each other. She lingered for a moment more, to calm herself, let the smells disperse; admired the unusual toilet seat, carved from dark unpolished wood, with knots in it and markings.

She emerged, at last, still nervous, but relieved to see he was not outside the door. She found him in the kitchen, mopping up water from the fridge – a narrow compact kitchen, tightly snugly organised like the galley on a schooner; more birds tacked all round the walls, violent ones again.

'Are the birds for your church window?' she asked, pausing in the doorway.

'Christ, no! Anthony wouldn't give them house-room.'

'Who's Anthony?'

'The vicar. Though he thinks he's God, actually, or perhaps God's elder brother. I'm starving, Rose. Are you? We can't have proper breakfast. I never normally eat it here, so I haven't got eggs or even cornflakes. And the power's still off, so I can't make toast. How about smoked salmon? There's a packet in the freezer here which has started to defrost. We'd better eat it up. I can thaw it on the oil-heater.'

She loathed smoked salmon, had only had it once, almost retched on its slimy texture, its salty raw-fish taste. 'I'm not hungry,' she remarked, as her stomach gave a loud protesting rumble.

'It sounds as if you're ravenous.'

She was. She hadn't eaten anything since tea the day before, and that had been just soup again, a brand called Poacher's Broth with speckly bits and pieces floating on the top – scraps of fur, of feather? She longed to tear into a whole large loaf of bread, something plain and filling, which she could cram into her mouth, not wait for sluggish oil-stoves, or toy with fancy fish. He was, in fact, getting out some bread now, but thin-sliced in a wrapper, not the farmhouse loaf she'd pictured, with its crisp and floury crust. He spread two flimsy slices with some low-fat butter substitute, portioned them one each. She glanced at his flat stomach, had presumed he was the thin type – naturally, as she was – but perhaps he had to struggle with his weight. The fridge looked sadly bare. She glimpsed a 'Gourmet Meal-for-One', with a picture on the packet of a salmon steak in an unlikely shade of pink, nestling on a bed of snow-white rice. Eagles on his kitchen walls, salmon in the fridge. He was fiddling with the other salmon, spearing out the still half-frozen slices, pausing for a moment to push back his heavy coat sleeves.

'We could always have some figs with it,' he murmured.

'Figs?' She associated figs with constipation – liquid in a bottle – recalled the senna tablets in the bathroom. Perhaps his bowels were dozy, or plain stubborn.

'Why not? Apple sauce with pork, gooseberries with mackerel . . . I've got an ancient fig tree in the garden. It's the first time in a dozen years the fruit has ever ripened. All other years, they've just stayed small and hard. But we had such an incredible summer – nineteen thousand hours of sunshine, here on the South Coast. That's the official figure, Rose, from January to now, which means it's the sunniest year on record.'

She climbed up on a stool, still eating breakfast in her head, grilled bacon with the loaf now, two fried and buttery eggs. 'We seem to be breaking all the records. The coldest January, I think they said, followed by the hottest spring and summer, then the worst storm just last night, and . . .'

'That reminds me – perhaps I *haven't* got a fig tree. I was so relieved about the roof, I never thought to check.' He was already through the door, striding down a passage to an exit at the back. She followed, screwing up her eyes against the sun, which was setting fire to russet leaves, kindling late chrysanthemums. He had made a patch of garden just behind the barn, with a rustic bench, a table, a square of pavement edged with plants and shrubs, and one twisted and distorted tree supported by the wall.

'Good God! Yesterday that tree had all its leaves, and was loaded down with figs. Yet this is meant to be a sheltered spot, protected from the wind.'

The branches were now bare, save for two last bravely clinging figs, and a single leaf fluttering near the trunk. Its other leaves and fruit were smashed beneath it, or scattered round the garden, some figs split right open, revealing fleshy pink insides. He began to gather up the whole ones, stuffing his coat-pockets until he was bulging either side. 'It's funny, really. Things always seem most fruitful just before they're kiboshed. I've noticed it before. I had this exotic flowering bush which went down in the last storm, and its flowers had never been more lush that year, some the size of tea-plates.'

Jane said nothing. Nature seemed so cruel, not just decimating bushes, but fattening them up first, then gloating at the loss.

'We could have breakfast out here,' Christopher suggested, retrieving one last fig. 'It's so bright it's unbelievable. Or would you be too cold?'

'No,' she said, shivering. 'I'll go and fetch my coat.'

'I'll get it. I've got to light the oil-stove. At least we'd avoid the stink of paraffin outside. I loathe the smell, don't you?'

'Yes,' she said with feeling, wondering if her cottage was just a pile of boards now, her precious oil-lamp engulfed beneath the rubble. Thank God she'd brought her duffel-bag, which at least meant she had a ten-pound note and her most vital bits and pieces.

'I won't be long. You sunbathe. Hey, talking of records, where d'you think is the sunniest place on earth?'

'Timbuktu.' She picked a name at random, like a rabbit from a hat.

'Clever girl! You're just a bit far west. The Eastern Sahara gets an average of four thousand three hundred hours of sun a year.'

She tried to picture the Sahara – sand and sand and sand – swaying phantom date-palms, long-lashed humpy camels. She sat down on the bench, which felt damp and splintery, gazed out at the horizon, the Sahara's dusty yellow moistening into the brown of patchwork fields; misty blue beyond them, which could be haze, or sea. The clouds were wispy, furrowed, so dazzling where the sun broke through, she had to look away. She closed her eyes, felt the sun scarlet on her lids, as fierce as the geraniums bleeding in their shattered pots beneath the table legs. She ought to leave, and couldn't; felt hypnotised by colour, the colour in this garden, the colour in the studio. Yet despite the sun, her hands were stiff with cold. Her coat had not materialised. Perhaps he'd forgotten all about it, got distracted in the kitchen, or was trying to boil a kettle on the oil-stove. Tea would be quite wonderful – a pint of something sweet and hot, to warm her from inside.

Still he didn't come. She paced around the garden, to stir her circulation, calm her fretful mind. He was probably bored with her

35

already, had started work, dismissed her, thought better of his offer of smoked salmon in the sun. She jumped a flowerbed, dived back through the door. She'd tell him she was late for something, had to leave immediately. She wrinkled up her nose at the stench of paraffin, seemed to taste it in her mouth as she walked towards the studio, stopped outside the door. She could hear him on the phone, his voice quite different from the controlled and faintly ironic one he'd used to her so far. It sounded almost shrill now, querulous, vindictive.

'I said *no*, Anne, and I mean no. For Christ's sake, can't you . . . ?'

She slunk back to the garden, sank down on the bench again, pulled off a geranium leaf, tore it into pieces. She removed a second one, twirled it in her fingers. The edge was brown and withered, the centre vivid green. Things dying while they bloomed.

'Your coat,' a voice said suddenly, a controlled ironic voice. 'I've also brought a picnic rug, since this is something of a picnic.' He tossed it on the bench beside her, went back to fetch the food. 'Sorry I was such an age. That oil-stove takes for ever. Right, shift that table up a bit and I'll put the tray down there.'

He handed her a plate, a precious-looking antique one with painted birds and flowers; a knife and fork with delicate pearl handles. The figs were quite transformed. He'd arranged them on a silver dish, with their own crenellated glossy leaves spread beneath them like a doily.

'I've squeezed some orange juice. I'm afraid the oranges were rather old and shrivelled – some I had a month ago when I was working on a still-life.' He passed her a small tumbler, a heavy cut-glass one, which sparkled in the sun. Everything looked elegant, as if he had turned an offbeat breakfast into a minor work of art. She took a sip of juice. It tasted strange – stale and slightly brackish, little flecks of sediment adhering to her tongue. She bit into a fig, to take away the taste, didn't like that either. It was too sickly-sweet and pulpy, seemed to ooze and slobber in her mouth, as if she'd swallowed something alive but decomposing. The inside looked obscene, pink and swollen seeds dribbling sticky juices.

'Good?' he asked, piling several on his own plate.

'Mm.'

'Have another. And eat them with the salmon. The two tastes complement each other and the colours look quite stunning.'

She chose the smallest fig, the thinnest slice of salmon, spent as long as possible cutting them in pieces, then pushed them round her plate, made a show of munching bread, wishing there was more of it. 'The . . . plates are really lovely.'

'I got them in an auction twenty years ago.'

'Did you choose them for the birds?'

'No. Birds meant nothing then.' He cut a fig in quarters, and then again in halves, ate with great finesse, laying down his knife and fork between each small but dainty mouthful. 'Or perhaps I'm wrong. Now I come to think of it, I've always been a bit obsessed with birds. In fact, as a kid, I was terrified of feathers – not ghosts or creepy-crawlies, but harmless bloody feathers.' He dabbed his mouth with a napkin, removed a smear of juice. 'Yet I always wanted to fly. There was this high brick wall at school. It was strictly out of bounds, to tell the truth, but I must have climbed it almost every day. I'd stand right on the top and jump into the air, expecting to take off. I broke my ankle once, and my knees were so damn scarred they looked like patchwork. It's funny, though, it's never left me, that longing to wing off.' They both looked up instinctively as a plover suddenly flapped up from the grass and seemed to vault into the sky, soaring higher, higher, until it was a dot, a speck, and gone.

Jane shaded her eyes to protect them from the sun, kept gazing up at the gold-fringed rags of cloud. She longed to fly herself, though she'd never even realised it till now. It was as if he'd put it into words for her, that yearning to escape, to rise above the ordinary, leap into another higher sphere. Perhaps they should climb up on the barn together and jump off into space – not fall and break their ankles, but pierce the clouds like plovers.

'Are you all right? You've eaten almost nothing.'

She crammed salmon in her mouth, wincing at the taste – raw fish tinged with paraffin. 'I never eat much breakfast.'

'This is lunch.'

'But it's only eight o'clock.'

'Yes, but we've both been up for hours. What happened to you, by the way? You never quite explained why you were sheltering in St Mark's. Was your roof blown in, or . . . ?'

'Yes.'

'Christ! Poor kid. What are you going to do? D'you live alone, or with your parents?'

'No.'

'No what?'

'No parents.'

'What d'you mean, "no parents"?'

'They're . . . dead.'

He put his knife and fork down, seemed to shrink away from her. 'What, killed last night? Surely you can't . . .'

37

'No, killed last month.'

'But that's terrible. What happened?'

'I don't want to talk about it.'

'Okay, I understand.' He pushed his plate away, a frown-line cutting deep between his eyebrows. 'I'm sorry, though, I've been rambling on about everything and anything, and you must be feeling devastated.'

'It's all right. I've . . . recovered. We weren't that close, in fact.'

'One's always close to parents. Dangerously close.'

'Are your parents still alive?' *His* parents were much safer.

'My father is. He's eighty-six. And still thinks he's Lord Byron.' She smiled. 'Is he an artist too?'

'No. A patent officer.'

'What's that?'

'You'd have to ask him. I've never been quite sure myself. Hell! I'm getting cold, are you?'

'Yes, frozen.' She was actually quite warm now, snugged inside her duffel-coat, with the tartan rug spread across her knees. But if they went inside she'd be excused from fish and figs, perhaps excused from questions. 'Anyway, I ought to get a move on.' Christopher forked in a last mouthful of smoked salmon, then stacked the plates, returned them to the tray. 'I've got a meeting with the glaziers at ten, and the roads will be impossible. This client's a real pain, always fussing over something. He's worried now about how we'll fix the panels, though we've been over it a good three times already. He's built this huge indoor conservatory – well, more a leisure-centre, with a pool and a jacuzzi, and exercise-machines, and a whole jungle of exotic plants.'

'You mean, your red birds are for him?'

'Yes. He suggested fish, at first, but fish were too damned obvious. And I've been longing for an excuse to do some birds – something on a decent scale, for once – and he wanted a whole wall of glass, so I just had to push for birds.'

She ground a piece of broken flowerpot underneath her heel, heard it crush to dust. Those birds were very special, shouldn't be entrusted to some fussy fat-cat health-freak. She could see the client in her mind – an overweight and balding prat, determined to be fit, sweating on his exercise-bike in a vulgar satin tracksuit, with brand names on his chest and shoes, and a comic baseball cap.

'I've done another separate panel – a sort of variation on a theme. It's for a stained-glass exhibition they're holding at the RIBA next month – an important international one.'

38

Jane replaced her tumbler on the tray. More initials which meant nothing. 'What, birds again, you mean?'

'Just one this time – and trapped inside a room.'

She grimaced. 'I hate it when they're trapped – the way they flap and panic, see the trees outside the window, and imagine they're flying off to freedom and fresh air, instead of smashing into glass.'

'That's exactly what attracted me – the sense of movement, yet confinement.'

Jane stood up, pushed the rug aside. 'Would you let me see it?'

'I'm afraid it's stored away, packed up in a crate, ready for its journey up to London. I did it several months ago, as a trial-run for the leisure-centre. The bird's the same species, you might say, but there's much more of a feeling of an enclosed and claustrophobic space.' He cupped his hands together, as if they, too, trapped a bird. 'Right – you ready? I'll drop you on the way. No – hell! – I'd quite forgotten. I can't drop you at a roofless house. Look, you'd better ring the police or something, or get on to the social services. You need help, you know, with no parents and no home. Haven't you got friends, or a grandma or an aunt or . . . ? Here, use my phone. It's portable, so it should be working still.'

'No, really. It's all right.'

'But you said your . . .'

'It's not that bad. Only a section of the roof's gone – quite a small bit, actually.' She was shattered by the ease with which these lies were tripping out – a new and instant talent, which seemed to come quite naturally, though it was bound to lead to trouble. If he drove her to the village she had mentioned, she'd have to point him out her house – one with just a bit of roof gone, and impoverished enough for a girl without a job. And if he knew the village well, then any house she picked on might belong to friends of his, land her in more tangles, reveal her as a sham. She trailed him to the kitchen, tried to play for time, moved over to the sink so that she could start washing up the plates.

'No, leave that,' he protested. 'There's no hot water anyway.'

She mooched back to the garden, brought in the picnic rug, folded it, refolded it. 'Where does your client live?' she asked at last.

'A mile or two from Lewes. Why?'

'Could you drop me there instead? I've got a . . . friend in Lewes, who'll probably put me up.'

'If *her* house isn't roofless. Or is the friend a him?'

She was blushing once again, though she had no idea why. Most girls had a boyfriend. She'd read in a survey in a women's magazine that the average number of sexual partners for girls of her own age was seven and a half. She hadn't even had the half, unless you could count Ian. 'No, *her*,' she said. 'Jane.'

'My mother was called Jane.'

'Really?'

'Yes.' He grimaced. 'Right, I'll just give Adrian a buzz, to make sure his precious leisure-centre is still standing in one piece. Got your things?'

She nodded, hadn't any things, except her tatty duffel-bag, still slung across her shoulder. Most of what she owned was three hundred and fifty miles away. Was the Shrepton house still standing in one piece? Should she phone to check, disguise her voice, pretend to be a stranger?

The artist reappeared, with a folder and a holdall, and easing on a pair of grey suede gloves. 'Okay, Rose, we're off. Or d'you want to ring your friend before we leave, tell her that you're coming?'

'No,' she answered slowly, turning back for one last look at his frenzied headstrong birds. 'Jane's always liked surprises.'

4

'You're his daughter, aren't you?'

'*No.*'

'I'm sorry. I thought he said . . . Look, do sit down, and do excuse the mess. It's like a fridge in here. That's the worst of being all-electric. The heating's off, the fax is off, the computer and the copier are phut, and I can't even offer you a cup of tea or coffee.'

'It's okay, I've got champagne.' Jane sipped it gingerly. She'd only had it once or twice before, at special birthday parties, and this brand was much drier, seemed to have more bubbles, which tickled up her nose, exploded down her throat.

'Lucky thing! No one offered me any. Are they celebrating something?'

Jane shrugged, then shook her head, was totally confused. She'd met half a dozen people in just the last ten minutes, muddled all their names. Sally, was it, the girl now looking after her? She glanced up at the blonded hair, the purple varnished nails, the tight black silky skirt, rucked right above her knees; then down at her own stained and grubby tracksuit. Charitable of Sally to mistake her for an artist's daughter, rather than a tramp. Christopher hadn't introduced her beyond a muttered 'Rose'. It was his client, Adrian, who had taken her coat, offered her champagne, attached names to all the faces – balding fatso Adrian, whom she'd pictured in his sports gear, dripping sweat and wealth, and who'd turned out to be a skinny, rather solemn man, still only in his twenties, dressed utterly conventionally in grey trousers and white shirt, and looking almost shabby. She was astonished to be sitting there at all, in a seventeenth-century manor house with a dozen acres of landscaped grounds and an Aston Martin in the stables.

Just half a mile from Lewes, she'd suddenly blurted out that her friend had moved away – she'd only just remembered – stupid of her, crazy, but . . . Her fear had built throughout the drive, fear of being dropped off in a strange and lonely town. She had lost her former courage, as if an hour or two of normal conversation and one shared (uneaten) meal had made her realise how much she had missed company, how scared she was of soldiering on alone. Knives and forks and napkins had sapped her resolution – the sight of chairs and tables, cooker, fridge and phone. How could she return to an orange-box, a camping spoon, the slap of waves on shingle? The artist had seemed peeved, driven on in silence after one coldly curt remark. 'Well, you'll have to come with me, then. It's too late to take you back, with the roads as bad as this.' Jane put her glass down, wincing as she remembered his sharp tone.

'Want a magazine?' Sally tossed her *Cosmopolitan*. 'Read your stars or something. I must make three quick calls.'

Jane turned to the horoscopes, scanned the page for Libra. 'With the sun passing through your own birth-sign until the middle of the month, you will be very much preoccupied with intensely personal issues, and with contemplating changes which . . .'

'Shit! The battery's run down. That's our last phone gone, which means no work today at all. Perhaps I shouldn't even have bothered coming in.'

'What *is* your job exactly?' Jane glanced down at her mother's stars – turmoil forecast, loss.

'I'm Adrian's P.A.'

Jane was none the wiser. She'd been surprised to find the old brick house doubled as an office, that the downstairs rooms held fax machines, computers, fleets of sleek cream phones, as well as antique furniture, elegant *chaises longues*, ancient gold-framed portraits on the walls. Even Sally's modest room was an eccentric mix of new and old – the latest business hardware ranged across an antique desk, with a bow front, lion's claw legs; two clomping metal filing cabinets dwarfing a graceful bureau with exquisite painted roundels set into its fine-grained polished wood. Sally herself looked somewhat out of place, her fuchsia lipstick and fake Jean Harlow hair too blatant for the sombre panelled walls. The two other men who worked there had also seemed mismatched with their surroundings – one in Levis and a sweatshirt, one in coloured braces, and both obviously disturbing the wigged and powdered worthies who sneered from their gold frames. They and Adrian himself were all well under thirty. How could they have achieved so much so early, or own so many things? In just half a dozen years would she have got as far, be driving a snazzy sports car with her initials on the number-plate, or sitting at a desk with a solar-powered gold-plated miniature oil derrick as her latest office toy? All she wanted at the moment was the loo. Her bladder seemed irritable this morning, constantly nudging her and griping. Sally was repairing a chipped nail, applying base-coat, varnish, Quick-Seal, in swift and skilled succession.

'Excuse me asking, but could I use your toilet?'

' 'Course. Just wait a tick till this has dried and I'll take you there myself. Our usual one has flooded, so we're using Adrian's, and it's quite a little trek.'

So he had his private loo. She was surprised to find it small and almost spartan – no gold-plated toilet seats or portraits on the walls. Sally waited in the passage, to show her the way back. The house was spacious, winding, easy to get lost in.

'Want to see the chapel while we're here?' Sally paused outside a panelled door in the stretch of gloomy corridor which led back to the offices.

'Chapel? In a house?'

'Yes. Some of these old places had their own private chapels, dating from way back. This one's got some history, yards of it, apparently, but don't ask me for the details. I've always hated history – all those dreary battles, and kings with the same names, so you muddle all the Georges and the Henrys. Damn! I've smudged my varnish.' She let go of the door-handle as if it were red-hot, inspected her spoilt nail. 'Actually, the previous owners turned it into a billiard room, but Adrian changed it back, had it re-whatsited – I can't think of the word.' Sally pushed the door, gestured to a tall and dim-lit room, with an intricate carved roof, a simple slab of altar, three rows of plain wood chairs. 'He comes here every lunch-time, when we're all out at the pub – I mean, kneels and really prays. Weird, isn't it? He never drinks, you know, like normal bosses do. I mean, the guy I worked for prior to this could knock back a whole bottle of scotch in an average working day.'

Jane gazed round at the dark oak walls, the frieze of sculpted angels high above them; the wooden floor, well-worn from pious feet. 'Mind if I go in?'

'No, help yourself. It gives me the creeps, quite frankly. It's so dark and sort of dreary.'

Jane liked the gloom, which made it other-worldly, lent an air of grave conspiracy, so she could imagine Christians hiding from their persecutors – heroic Papist martyrs, or brave beleaguered Protestants. She wondered whether Adrian was C of E or Catholic, or some odd

43

sect of his own. He seemed eccentric altogether – splurging a cool million on an ostentatious house, yet praying every lunch-time on his own; ordering stained glass for a leisure-centre, rather than his chapel. These windows were all plain – narrow pointed lancets, screened by funereal evergreens which blocked the light and view. She walked up to the altar, wished she were alone, so she could kneel like Adrian. It must be odd to pray. She had never really tried. It seemed a skill, like poetry, which you admired in other people, but could never hope to quite bring off yourself.

'So *there* you are! I've been searching everywhere.'

She swung round at the deep male voice, saw the artist at the door, champagne glass in one hand, someone else's khaki scarf knotted round his neck. He had taken off his coat, at last, looked strangely different without his cashmere armour – less impressive, narrower, yet also somehow younger – his figure almost boyish beneath the ageing face.

'Adrian wants you, Sally. That Greek chap's just arrived. They're waiting in the library.'

Jane made a move to follow, was stopped by Christopher. 'Could I have a word, Rose?' He leant against the window, took a quick swill of his drink. 'Look, Adrian's just suggested offering you a job.'

'A job? But I'm not trained. I mean, I did a week's computer course, but it was absolutely basic, and my typing's the two-finger stuff.'

'Not that sort of job, just cleaning and what-have-you. A skivvy, you might call it. I told him absolutely no.'

She stared at him, affronted. How dare he make decisions for her? A cleaning job would suit her fine – well, tide her over anyway, till she had decided on her life's work. Skivvy was a loaded word, suggested exploitation, whereas everyone she'd met so far had been extremely kind and friendly, hadn't put her down. It could be quite exciting – to work in an old manor house, with a chapel and a library, a brand-new leisure-centre.

'He was only offering out of pity. He asked me who you were, so I told him very briefly that you'd lost your house and parents. Adrian's a softie. He just can't help himself. He'd offer Jack the Ripper a full share in the profits, if he suspected he was down on his luck.'

'So I'm on a par with Jack the Ripper, am I?' She stalked out of the chapel, voice indistinct with fury, stampeded down the passage. Christopher caught up with her, grabbed her by the wrist.

'Of course I didn't mean that. Can't you take a joke? I merely felt a charring job would be demeaning for you, wrong.'

'You don't know anything about me.' She shook his hand off, pulled away.

'I know you're intelligent and spirited, and have views on lots of things – unusual views, which prove you've got a brain. Why waste your life and talents scrubbing floors?'

She stopped, confused, still wary. Did he really care what happened to her, truly think her talented? 'But it could be quite a help. I mean, I need a job, and . . .'

'Not this job you don't.'

'But why?'

'Look, Adrian's going to speak to you about it. I'd rather you said no. Okay?'

She didn't answer. He was like her bossy father, giving orders with no reasons. No wonder Sally had thought she was his daughter – granddaughter, more likely. Now she was close up to him, she could see the sapless texture of his skin, an old man's skin, an old man's heavy-handedness. The bit about her talents was simply empty flattery. The truth was more unpleasant. He didn't want her hanging round, was bored with her already, a lame duck and a loser, who might irritate his client, prove herself a pest.

'Anyway, I really ought to leave now. We'll just say goodbye to Adrian, then I'll drop you back at your place, and, if you like, we'll discuss jobs on the way. I've got a few ideas.'

She stumped on down the passage. She could imagine his ideas – ideas like her father's: university, followed by a safe prestigious job, or maybe something phoney like Advertising, or designing cans of beans, which could be trumped up as 'artistic', but was really meaningless and shallow.

Adrian wasn't in his office. They found him by the swimming pool, showing round a swarthy man in an oyster-coloured suit, whose three-dimensional eyebrows jutted like twin thickets above his dank-pool eyes. Jane glanced at him perfunctorily, dazed by her surroundings, which claimed her full attention – her first sight of the leisure-centre, which had only been a word as yet. She hadn't realised how large it was, how elegant, exotic. The pool wasn't just boringly rectangular, like a municipal swimming bath, but shaped more like a natural lake, with tree-sized plants jungling all around it; more plants in the octagonal conservatory which opened out one end, and was bright with pinks and purples – begonias, hibiscus, and some fantastic flowers with violet-coloured trumpets. All the walls were glass, so that the trees and garden outside seemed part of the interior, and were reflected several times – in the dazzling rippled surface of the water, in the gleaming floor and translucent mirror tiles. Everything was shimmering in the eager morning sun, which was like some special light-effect laid on by the architects, to deepen all the colours, provide tiger-stripes of shadow. The stretch of dappled lawn outside led the eye horizonwards, then cajoled it back inside again as grass drowned in turquoise water.

Jane moved towards the real lawn, from its reflection in the pool. Christopher had rushed to join the glaziers, who were up the other end, the younger one balanced on a ladder, calling down measurements to the stout chap at the bottom, who was scribbling on a pad. She felt too shy to follow, couldn't speak their language, nor anybody's here. She could see two gardeners sweeping leaves outside, a third carting off a fallen limb from a majestic spreading cedar. Apart from that one victim, there seemed very little damage from the storm. Was that what they were celebrating – or was champagne just Adrian's substitute for morning tea or coffee when the electricity was off? He was uncorking a new bottle, offering it to his guest, who had now sauntered down to speak to Christopher.

Once he'd filled both glasses, Adrian excused himself, loped between the tubs of plants to join her. His face was small and sallow beneath the dark-rimmed glasses, the eyes themselves a faded gentle blue. 'Christopher told you about the job, did he? How d'you feel about it?'

'I . . . I'm still not sure what sort of job it is.'

'Oh, a bit of everything – cleaning, running errands, helping Sally, maybe, when she's up to her eyes; even giving me a hand. We'd call you our Girl Friday.'

His smile was very genuine. She saw it light his eyes first, before it reached his mouth. She liked this man instinctively, his soft unruffled voice, the floppy sandy hair, which her mother would deplore as too long and unhygienic. She also liked the term Girl Friday, which suggested adventure and excitement. Man Friday had been saved from cannibals, helped Crusoe fight cruelty and evil. And today was even Friday, which seemed significant.

'We'd need to talk money first, of course. The old girl who cleans at present is on a pretty basic rate, but you'd be doing more than her, so we could bump that up a bit. Poor soul, she's getting gaga, which is really why I need you. I did advertise last week, in fact, but the only takers so far have been an Irish alcoholic and an ex-mental patient Jesus-freak who told me I was saved. It's difficult to get good help round here, when there are so many jobs in Brighton and we're off the beaten track.'

46

Jane chewed her thumb, considering. It sounded plausible enough. Was he really just a softie, doing her a favour, or could she turn the tables and prove a help to him? She'd noticed dust on all the furniture, a vase of dying freesias, several gold-framed paintings stacked against the wall, as if no one had found time to put them up. She could take a pride in making this house beautiful, could transform that splendid chapel – wax the floor, load the place with flowers. Why should Christopher restrict her, interfere at all? It was Adrian's decision, Adrian's home and job. She could just as well have answered his advertisement, come here independently without a chaperone.

'I know charring sounds a drag, Rose, but we can probably find you plenty else to do, and we're a really friendly bunch here, almost like a family. I try to keep things quite informal and . . .'

'It's not a drag – far from it. I'd really like the job.' Nice to join a family, replace her own lost home, even acquire some elder siblings. That man in the red braces – she had liked the look of him – a tall man with a face like Keats; a face she'd often studied in her Complete Collected Works, with its dramatic dark-lit portrait at the front. 'It's just that . . .'

'What?'

'Oh, nothing.' She might even get a place to live – not a grand room in the house, of course – that would be presumptuous, but she had noticed several outbuildings: stables, sheds and lean-tos; surely somewhere she could camp. 'Look, if I did say yes, could I start immediately – say Monday?'

'No problem. This morning, if you like. In fact, if you really want to get stuck in straight away, you could start by clearing up these empty glasses and watering the plants.' Adrian had taken off his spectacles and was polishing them abstractedly on a crumpled off-white handkerchief. His eyes looked weak without them, blinking in the light, like prisoners who'd been let out of their cells. 'And no questions asked if you want to finish up the bubbly.' He grinned, pushed back his limp fair hair, which was now falling in his eyes. She returned his smile, which seemed to make them two conspirators. She knew she could get on with him, that he wouldn't nag or hassle, or be on her back continually. Yet . . .

'Well, what d'you say?'

She paused a second, glanced up at the artist, who was standing on his own now, fumbling for a cigarette, half of him in shadow, half stippled by the sun. His scarf had fallen to the floor and was lying like a limp discarded chrysalis. His face looked grey and tired, no longer the smiling vibrant mask he had assumed since ten o'clock, but a naked face, shocking in its sadness. She looked away immediately, feeling almost guilty, as if she had burst into a private room, stumbled on some secret she had no right to know or guess. She could see his scarlet birds again – tortured birds, flying into void, some with empty eye-sockets, others tragically distorted like avian thalidomides.

'Well?' repeated Adrian, the first note of irritation jarring his soft voice.

She tried to drive the birds away, could feel their scarlet plumage scalding in her cheeks. 'I . . . I'm afraid I can't. Not now.'

'Well, Monday then. Can you make it nine o'clock?'

'No,' she said. 'I'm sorry.'

Christopher broke into a run, streaked across the shingle, right down to the sea's edge, sidestepping and dodging as the breakers rolled towards him, foamed around his ankles. Jane panted to keep up with him, surprised at his agility, the speed with which he moved, as if he'd once been a champion sprinter and was still in daily training. The sea looked weary in comparison; had spent its force last night and was now torpidly recovering. Those leaden waves had reached forty feet and higher, if the reports could be believed. They had been listening to the radio as they'd driven back from Adrian's; taken a detour to the beach to check the latest bulletins: 'The Grand Hotel in Seathorpe collapsing like a pack of cards; a twenty-storey block of luxury modern flats twisted like a corkscrew.' This lonely stretch of promenade was more or less deserted – no grand hotels or flats at all, no gang of council workers sent out to clear the shambles, no stray dog or beachcomber. Even the usual raucous sea-birds seemed to have completely disappeared, as if the storm had sucked them up, hoovered the whole sky, left no trace of their corpses. Other corpses had been hurled across the shingle, relics of dismembered boats; one whole but dented craft all but buried in the stones. All along the promenade, benches had been overturned, or blown away like driftwood. 'BEACH HUTS FOR HIRE', a notice said, but no one could hire these. The once neat and whitewashed row had collapsed into a waste of flattened boards; personal possessions glinting from the wreckage: a plump steel kettle, a plastic picnic set, a child's toy pick-up truck.

'This storm came out of nowhere,' the reporter had announced. She had tried to block her ears. It was too much like her life – a shock and devastation springing out of nowhere at a jolly birthday party, no hint of it before, no warning, preparation. She stopped a moment, shivering, gazed eastwards down the coast to where she guessed her own beach was, just two miles away. Her house had probably fallen like those huts. She would have to go and check, kept putting off the moment, relieved to follow Christopher when he'd suggested reconnoitring, so long as the havoc they were viewing was not on her own doorstep. She was lagging far behind now, feet aching from the drag and shift of stones, while the artist seemed to leap them, zigzagging and circling, as if he'd been fitted with a powerful private motor.

'Wait!' she called, but her words were blown away. The wind was pestering still – flapping at her coat, tangling her long hair – irritable and restless, rather than savage like last night. She crossed a bare patch on the beach, where the wind had hurled the shingle right up on the promenade. They had seen it earlier – piled-up drifts of pebbles, huddled close together, as if each small stone had fled to seek asylum with its brothers against the anger of a wild rampaging father.

'Can we go back?' she shouted, suddenly jumping up on a ledge of rock, and forcing her tired voice to outsmart the wind, outboom the rhythmic threshing of the waves.

The artist heard her this time, waved a jaunty hand, started plunging back towards her, throwing up the shingle like a high-stepping spirited horse. His mood had changed completely. She had first noticed in the car, when he'd been humming some triumphal tune against the background of disasters on the news. She presumed he must be drunk. Just as they were leaving, that foreign man had asked to have a word with him, and they'd sat closeted together in Adrian's private office, probably knocking back champagne.

'You seem pretty high.'

'I am.' He grinned. 'I've got a new commission – well, maybe – cross your fingers. Of course, there's always many a slip, etcetera, especially on big jobs. In fact, I wasn't going to tell you, or say a word to anyone till it's absolutely certain. I suppose I'm superstitious that way. But I've got a sort of hunch that this one's going to happen.' He stooped to pick up a shell, inspected it a moment before skimming it away. 'You know that dapper Greek chap I was talking to at Adrian's – well, he's putting up the cash for a huge new Civic Centre, bang in the middle of Manchester. Stanton Martin's the architect. He's a one-off, Rose, a visionary. I never thought I'd get the chance to work with him, especially on a scheme like this. The plans are almost finalised, and they include a whole vast wall of coloured glass – eight hundred square feet of it. Apparently Adrian told his Greek friend that I was just the man to do it, so Dimitri went to see my work – flogged all

49

over London looking at my stuff, even drove to Swansea, to see my . . .'

She was amazed that a new commission could so utterly transform him, change his voice and disposition, even alter his physique. There was colour in his cheeks now, his eyes looked bluer, brighter; his whole body more elastic. He was even speaking differently – faster, more staccato, with many of his sentences left hanging or in embryo, while he spawned a brood of new ones. She couldn't always follow him, and the people he was mentioning meant absolutely nothing to her. Even the architect, whom he was still praising to the skies and had called a household name, could have been a brain surgeon, or an astrophysicist, for all she'd ever heard of him. She felt depressed by her own ignorance, ashamed of her resentment. Okay for *him* to gloat. He was famous, in demand, had work for several years ahead. She hadn't even a charring job, or, come to that, a bed.

'He said he'll arrange for me to visit Stanton's office, to discuss details with the great man himself. He knows my work already, and apparently Dimitri put my name forward at least a month ago, though quite unknown to me. Trust Adrian to be so bloody secretive.'

She forced excitement in her voice as she offered congratulations, though feared it lacked conviction. She had always found it difficult to try to mesh with someone whose mood was totally different from her own; was scared of sounding phoney, or letting her dejection tarnish their high spirits. It had happened with her friend at school – curvaceous Helen Turner, engaged at seventeen, besottedly in love, while her own experience of love was gleaned mainly from the *Oxford Anthology of Romantic Poetry and Prose*.

They were now drawing near to the outskirts of the town, walking high up on the promenade rather than floundering in the stones. The artist paused for breath, touched her shoulder lightly. 'Tired?' he asked. 'You're flagging.'

'No', she lied. 'I'm fine.' At least he seemed concerned, had slowed his pace to suit her, even found some chocolate, which he insisted on her eating, without claiming his half-share. She sucked a fragment off her tooth, glanced up at a notice posted on the promenade: 'In case of distress at sea, dial 999 and ask for coastguard'. The phone was just behind them, vandalised, hacked out of its socket, the receiver dangling helplessly. No coastguard, no connections.

'What does Adrian do?' she asked. Her thoughts kept turning to him, not to Dimitri or his architect. It must be nearly lunch-time. Was he in his chapel, praying – maybe even praying for her? She doubted anyone had prayed for her in her eighteen years of life. She'd never had godparents, never been baptised.

'He's in futures.'

She wondered what they were, rather liked the sound of them. She was looking for a future, now her past had proved a fraud.

'You know, betting on currencies and commodities – all that sort of thing.'

She didn't know, decided not to ask. She must already seem so ignorant – all these worlds she'd never heard of, skills she'd never have.

They trudged on past the Continental Night Club, which had long ago closed down; Henri's Ice Cream Parlour, boarded up for winter; the derelict crazy-golf course, glistening in the sun. She felt angry with that sun, the callous way it shone on grief and carnage, like someone laughing at a funeral, or dressing up in party clothes. The sky was postcard blue, as if feigning innocence, denying any knowledge of last night's horror-scenes. 'It's cold,' she said, turning up her collar.

'I'm boiling. Here, have my gloves. They'll help.'

She stopped to put them on. The fingers were too long, the fronts clammy from his hands, a moist and private warmth she felt she shouldn't share. He used the pause to light a cigarette, back turned to the wind, both hands cupped round his lighter, as if he were whispering some secret to it. They stood a moment side by side – two cars run out of fuel – he drained by his excitement, she exhausted from the walk. He suddenly leaned forward, removed a burr clinging to her coat. She shrank back instantly. The gesture seemed intrusive – too intimate, possessive.

'So your parents are both dead, Rose?'

'Yes,' she said. 'I told you.'

'That doesn't mean it's true.'

'So you're saying I'm a liar.' She ran ahead, away from him, tripping on a broken slab of pavement. He lunged forward, stopped her falling, retrieved her chocolate wrapper with its last two squares of wholenut, restored it to her carefully, as if she were a child.

'People often have to lie. I respect that, actually.'

She bit, hard, into a hazelnut, crunched it in her teeth. 'Why should I be lying?'

'I don't know.' He shrugged. 'I've got this sort of gut feeling that your story isn't true. It's been nagging at me ever since you told me.'

'Well, I'm sorry, but it *is* true. They died a month ago.' She tossed

51

her chocolate wrapper in the overflowing litter-bin, tried to throw her guilt away, as well – guilt not just about the lies, but about murdering her parents. It was tempting fate to say they'd died, might bring down retribution. She didn't want them harmed; simply preferred to keep away from them, cut all ties, all contact. In that sense, they were dead – dead to her, at least.

The artist ground his cigarette out, after just a few brief puffs, as if he were trying to cut down, or perhaps control his irritation by stubbing it to shreds. 'So what exactly did they die of?'

'Nothing.'

'What's that supposed to mean?'

'I can't explain.' She traced a pattern on the pavement with her shoe. The silence felt oppressive, almost dangerous. 'Okay,' she mumbled finally. 'You're right. They're still alive. It's just – well – complicated.'

'So are you.' He met her eyes a moment, seemed to gaze right through them into the inside of her head, glimpse the muddle and confusion there. 'Race you to that kiosk,' he said suddenly.

She broke into a gallop, careering down the promenade, spurring herself on as she heard his steps pounding close behind her. She had to win this time, made a last wild effort, collapsed against the kiosk, gasping, out of breath.

'I won, I won! There should have been a prize.'

'There is.' He drew out a small pebble from his inside jacket pocket. 'A magic stone.'

'Why magic?'

'Perhaps you need some magic.'

She took the stone, which was smooth and cool and rounded like a tiny weighty egg, grey mottlings on its Bournville brown, one gnat-sized dent marring its perfection. She transferred it to her own pocket, kept her hand closed over it. 'Hey! Look at all those people!'

They had walked into an excited mob jostling on the promenade, and gawping at a shattered row of houses. The roofs had all blown in, bare wood joists showing through like bones; their frail and spindly balconies no match for last night's wind. The crowds were swarming round like sightseers, pointing and exclaiming, picking up souvenirs, even taking photographs. Some were in the gardens, trampling the bruised grass, spying on the obscene and private contents of an upturned rubbish bin – fishbones, dirty nappies, dented yogurt pots, a half-gnawed chunk of breadcrumbed cod, a man's stained underpants. Two rival dogs were rooting in a Kentucky Fried

52

Chicken box; several children playing on the creaking crippled remnants of a once-sturdy garden shed. Jane followed, almost mesmerised, touched the frame beneath a missing window, which felt jagged and uneven, like the socket of a badly extracted tooth, root fragments still embedded in the gum. Her hand groped to her own mouth, as if surprised to find it unscathed – not bleeding, not inflamed.

'Rose! Come out of there.'

She could have been his dog, the high-handed way he called her – that mangy mongrel by the fence now sniffing at a pile of greasy rags. Yet she obeyed him none the less, trailing down the promenade a step or two behind him, back towards the car. He glanced across his shoulder at the still milling, jabbering throng. 'Listen to those hypocrites! They're all wailing, "Oh, how tragic," yet secretly they're thrilled.'

'Thrilled? What for?'

'Because they're safe, of course – alive and whole and gloating while the other poor sods perished. They say nineteen people died last night, and hundreds more were injured. Yet even those who suffered see themselves as heroes. It's rather like the war. There's an excitement in destruction. Can't you feel it?'

'No,' she snapped. 'I can't. Maybe they're relieved – that's only natural, surely, but why should they be gloating?'

'Why not? We're all two-faced at heart. I mean, even with our friends we sometimes feel a curious sort of pleasure when one of them's in trouble – a certain secret relish that it's them instead of us; or maybe worse than that – maybe just a basic satisfaction at someone else's crisis.'

'That's horrible.'

'It's true.'

'Speak for yourself. Not everyone's so callous.' She knew it sounded rude, but she had to contradict him, insist that he was wrong.

'More than you imagine. You've only got to listen to the news – all that wild adrenalin pumping out on almost every channel – excited breathless voices like the ones they use for Cup Finals, a new high each time the body-count goes up.'

'It's *not* like that. It's . . .' Jane tried to quash the voices she was hearing in her head; those explosive hyped-up voices they had switched on in the car, trumpeting disaster.

'Why deny it? Except everybody tries to, as if we can't face our real nature. And yet we're all turned on by tidal waves or earthquakes,

53

or great storms like last night's, because those so-called acts of God express a violence we're familiar with, a violence in ourselves.'

'Are *you* excited by it, then?'

He frowned, considering. 'Any force as huge as that has got to be exhilarating – the force of nature, the force of art. And of course it has its plus side. I mean, think of the Romantics. Man's response to the sublime has left some bloody marvellous landmarks – Turner's violent storms at sea, Wordsworth's lowering mountains, crashing cataracts. And even a disaster can be salutary, if it shakes us up, out of our complacency, our fixed and timid view of things. But basically, it comes down to deliverance. We preen because we're spared, still alive to tell the tale.'

'That's . . . somehow not enough.'

'It has to be. It's all there is.'

'I don't want it to be all.'

He laughed. 'Nor do most, I reckon. You're in good company. Why else should human beings invent all their different gods, their other worlds and afterlives, except to kid themselves the world is safe and cosy, and that they're never going to die, or if they do, they'll wake up somewhere else – somewhere everlasting and pretty damned near perfect?'

'*I* don't believe all that.'

'I bet you wish you did, though. Religion's very useful. It must help a lot to have rituals to enact, or to turn the sun and wind into gods you can disarm, or lay on harvest festivals to propitiate Mother Nature and prevent her blighting all your crops next year. The only problem is it doesn't take account of chaos, which is a new science in itself these days. I expect you've heard of the "butterfly effect".' He skirted a pile of roof-tiles, lying raw and splintered on the ground.

'No.' She shook her head.

'Well, they say the flapping of a butterfly's wings can change the world's whole weather – and I'm not exaggerating – just one tiny puny butterfly, maybe several thousand miles away. What happens is some minuscule disturbance swells and amplifies until it's large enough to set off a great hurricane or avalanche. And why that's so significant is that it means we can't be in control. Even where we understand the so-called laws of nature, things can still be unpredictable – maybe always and for ever, and necessarily.'

'Yes,' said Jane. 'I know.' She could hear a chain-saw whining from a garden, sounding like the screaming wind of yesterday. She tried to block it out, erase the whole last month; said nothing more until they reached the car. Christopher unlocked the door, removed a paper carton from the bonnet. 'Shall I drop you back at your place?'

She didn't answer, could see a tiny butterfly flapping its jewelled wings above her cottage, an avalanche of shingle suddenly rearing up and interring the whole beach.

'Or doesn't it exist – a fiction like your parents' death? Oh, come on, Rose, don't scowl – that was meant to be a joke. The problem is I must get down to work. It's half past twelve already, and with this new commission looming, I'm beginning to realise what a lot there is to finish before I can clear the decks.'

'Well, don't add me to your burden then. I'll just stay here, in town. I . . . . I've got some things to do.'

'I doubt if you can do much with everything kaput.' He snapped his fingers, as if dismissing the whole town. 'Look, kid, you said you needed a job. Why not come and work for me?'

'*You?*'

'Don't look so horrified. I'm not an ogre, am I?'

'No, but . . .'

'You seemed pretty keen on Adrian's job. What's the difference?'

'You mean, it's a job like his – cleaning, tidying up?'

'More or less.'

She kicked out at the kerb. How dare he tell her a charring job would demean her, waste her talents, then offer one himself, and one with fewer perks – no swimming pool or chapel, no young and lively colleagues? And the way he'd called her 'kid' – so condescending, arrogant, as if she were a grubby brat in kindergarten. 'Skivvying,' she muttered, repeating his own word.

'What?'

She shook her head, avoided his stern eye.

He was leaning on the car now, playing with his car-keys, jingling them from hand to hand. 'There are scores of things you could do around the studio. It would really help me out.'

I bet it would, she thought. Adrian had told her how hard it was to get domestic help, since he was off the beaten track. Christopher must find it even harder. His barn was in the wilds, miles from any transport. He was probably pretty desperate for a cleaner, had stopped her taking Adrian's job so he could employ her as a char himself, then churned out all that stuff about her talents. She would hardly utilise her talents scrubbing floors for him any more than scrubbing them for Adrian.

'In fact, you could probably even help me with the glass. I'm going to be so busy I could do with an assistant.'

'But I know absolutely nothing about glass.'

'You'll learn. I imagine you could pick things up extremely fast and easily.'

Flattery again, she thought, jabbing her scuffed trainer up and down the kerb. How could someone totally untrained in art work as his assistant? He'd lure her there with far-fetched hopes, then keep her washing coffee cups. Okay, she needed work, but not that sort of work, slaving for one arrogant man, with no other scope or company. And anyway, it wouldn't solve her problem of finding somewhere she could live.

'I'm sorry, but I need a live-in job.'

'No problem. The studio has a mezzanine floor you probably didn't notice. There's a bed up there and storage space for clothes, and you've already seen my kitchen and . . .'

She stared at him aghast. Surely he couldn't be suggesting that she move in and share his pad? It was totally impossible – to shack up with a stranger much older than her father.

He dropped his keys, retrieved them, hooked the key-ring on one finger. 'I get in at eight most mornings – sometimes even earlier the days my wife's away. But if you want to have a lie-in, that's okay with me. I won't prise you out of bed. We could fix office hours from nine to four or five.'

'But I thought you . . .' She backed away, bewildered. She'd assumed his studio was home, that he lived there, on his own; didn't treat it like an office, didn't have a wife.

Suddenly, he opened the door, plumped into the driver's seat, leaned across to unlock the other side. 'Well?' he said. 'You coming?'

She shook her head, still needled by the words 'my wife' – two tiny harmless casual words, which had somehow stirred up sediment from the bottom of her mind, set up angry ripples, like a stone flung in a pond.

'But I can't leave you here alone, if you've nowhere else to go.'

'I'm . . . I'm all right.'

'Okay. Please yourself.' He jerked the car away, waved briefly from the window as he punished the accelerator, revved from nought to burn.

'Goodbye,' she called, though he couldn't hear, had already turned the corner, left only his exhaust behind, a blast of dirty smoke. She stood rigid where she was, still breathing in his fumes. Why shouldn't he be married? What was it to her? True, he'd seemed an obvious bachelor, prowling on his own in the middle of the night;

never saying 'we', like married people tended to; keeping toiletries and toothbrush in the studio, not to mention 'meals-for-one'. But why should it affect her? She didn't want his job, need never see him in her life again. What she had to do now was hike back to her cottage, assess the damage, and decide on her next move, try to build a future.

She slumped down on the kerb. She wouldn't mind a wife herself, someone supportive and devoted who could share that shadowy future; help to build and shape it. Everyone was married, or in cosy twos like Noah's Ark, safe from the great Flood – all her friends from school now coupled up with boyfriends, or using that smug 'we'. She'd never had a special friend, not of either sex. There was probably something wrong with her – one of those strange animals cast out by the tribe. She peered down at the puddle in the gutter, tried to see herself reflected. She looked blurred and insubstantial, her features trembling slightly in the water, as if scared, or very cold. She *was* cold, cold all over, and also starving hungry. All she'd eaten since six o'clock last night was half a fig, a mouthful of smoked salmon, and one small bar of chocolate. She pressed her hands against her stomach, surprised it wasn't rumbling. She would starve in grim reality if she didn't get a job. Wasn't she being inconsistent, cutting off her nose to spite her face? She had wanted Adrian's charring job, so why not Christopher's? She couldn't work it out, was too obsessed with food still – pizzas oozing melted cheese, hamburgers so huge they stopped your mouth.

She closed her eyes, saw the artist striding from his studio, setting down a loaded tray on the table in the garden – not for her, but for his wife. The wife kept changing – first blonde, then dark and sultry, then auburn with green eyes – but always wildly beautiful. She heard his deep impatient voice rapping out a name.

'*Rose!*'

That couldn't be his wife's name. She probably had a long name – something elegant, exotic – Clarissa, Ariadne.

'Rose, I want my gloves.'

She jumped, looked up, saw the artist's classy car snorting there in front of her, the nearside door flung open, as he leant across the empty seat, reached out an impatient arm.

'You haven't lost them, have you? They're a very special pair.'

She glanced down at her hands – bare and freezing hands, blue-tinged around the fingernails.

'I saw you take them off. Which probably means you've dropped them on the promenade. We'll never find them now, with all those trippers out in force.'

She stumbled to her feet, rummaged in her pocket, drew out the grey suede gloves, coldly limp and squashed now.

'Thanks,' he said, stretching right across to take them, then gesturing to the passenger-seat. 'Get in.'

5

Jane switched on the light, stared straight into the private parts of a gigantic fallen oak, its roots lifted like a woman's skirt, shamefully exposing a writhe of tangled tubes, a dark hole at its base. She felt like a voyeur as her eyes tracked down the hole, recoiling from its texture, the ooze of sticky sap seeping from the middle, like dark half-clotted blood. There were more trees all around her – blighted trees, blasted trees – as if the storm had come inside. It had been difficult to sleep with them surrounding her – scores of lowering canvases stacked against the wall, or hung, unframed, on three sides of the mezzanine. They were all signed CHS – aggressive black initials in the bottom right-hand corner. Christopher Harville-Shaw. She had seen his name written on the fly-leaf of a book; hadn't realised that he painted, as well as made stained glass. She skewed her head and shoulders round, so she could see the two large paintings hung above the bed. They had haunted her all night – trees like human figures, but horribly dismembered, one split from neck to knee. He must have used the last two great storms, turned horror into art; feasted on it, drawn from it, dipped his brush in carnage. She nestled back beneath the duvet. It frightened her to look at things uprooted.

She hugged her arms around her chest, surprised to feel it silky-smooth, and not bulked out with jerseys. Christopher had lent her a pair of his pyjamas, a real silk pair in midnight blue which he had dug out of a drawer and tossed across as casually as if they'd been a painting-rag, although the label looked exotic and was printed in Italian. Strange, the feel of silk – the way it lapped your body, clung to every curve. She tried to imagine Christopher's body beneath that same blue silk; could see his chest and shoulders – narrow, probably hairy, judging by his hands; his stomach hard and flat. Then her mind went blank. There was a gap between his belly and his knees, a disturbing gap, a judder of uneasiness.

She turned over on her back, turfed him out of bed, but he still threatened from the wall, compelling her attention in a scorched and cratered landscape, one lone bird flapping from the stubble, a charred and maimed survivor. She couldn't get away from him. Although he'd left yesterday, at tea-time, driven home, said goodbye till Monday, told her he was going to stay in Oxfordshire, he was still warped and woofed in the very stuff and fabric of the studio – his scarlet birds below her on the glass-screens, his work on every wall, his smell still in her nostrils, his voice reverberating, and now his blue-silk tentacles clinging round her body.

He had also found a dressing-gown, striped maroon and gold, with Chinese hieroglyphics on the pocket, and a pair of mule-type slippers which were far too big for her and slipped off instead of on. She couldn't understand why he kept nightwear there at all, or had bothered setting up a bedroom when he claimed to sleep at home. He even had a double bed, an expensive-looking one with a thick well-padded mattress, not just some old divan. Perhaps he used it as a guest-room when his own house got too full. He was bound to have a lot of friends – all those names he'd mentioned – important wealthy clients, famous architects.

She pulled the duvet right beneath her chin, liked the way it moulded to her body, moved when she did, followed all her fidgets; so different from that heap of heavy rugs she'd got used to in the cottage – dirty rugs which prickled, and either trapped her with their weight, or fell off altogether if she tossed and turned too much. It was like a minor miracle to have these things restored – bedsprings underneath her, instead of a lumpy fifth-hand mattress rolled out on the floor; clean and painted walls; switches which obeyed her, electric everything. The power had come back on last night, announced by the newsreader with a whoop of satisfaction, a euphoria she'd shared. Her own particular power-cut had lasted not just sixteen hours, but twenty-eight long days. Now she'd been delivered from it, her dilapidated beach-shack seemed like something in a nightmare – unreal and terrifying. Perhaps she'd make some tea, to celebrate, enjoy the buzz of switching on a fast electric kettle, instead of boiling stubborn water on a temperamental Primus stove; relish the omnipotence of snapping every light on – striplights in the kitchen, spotlights in the studio, instant light-up mirrors in the bathroom.

She rolled swiftly out of bed, slipped on the silky dressing-gown, feet groping for the slippers, then stood leaning on the balcony, peering down at the studio below. She had been almost scared at first, to be so high up, with such a plunging drop, as if she were living in a tree-house or in the rigging of a ship. Both above her and beneath her was a dim and shadowy no-man's-land; the roof-beams lost in darkness; the studio a blur of murky shapes. Just this slice of upper gallery was clearly lit, defined. It was an exciting place to sleep, the sort of den or hideaway she would have relished as a child – that sense of being in command, high up, on her own, and also unassailable – cocooned, enclosed, cut off from the nagging world below. And her mother would have hated it, complained about the difficulties of heating it and cleaning it; damned the narrow staircase as dangerous to life and limb.

She suddenly rummaged in her duffel-bag for the small framed snapshot she had brought with her from Shrepton. She could hardly understand now why she had scooped it from the mantelpiece and squeezed it in her bag, on her way out through the sitting-room. She was leaving home, wasn't she, breaking all last ties, so why should she want a photo of her parents? It wasn't even a good one. Both of them were frowning, her father looking down, so that his eyes had disappeared, her mother's perm and mouth too tightly set. She stared at it a moment, then shoved it in a drawer, face-down. Better to forget them, treat them as the strangers they'd become. She had found another refuge and should be revelling in the fact, brewing up that pot of tea, wolfing down some food.

She took the steep steps slowly, hampered by her mules, flip-flapped to the kitchen, flicked every switch she could – lights, heater, kettle, toaster, hob – just to see them glowing, just to prove her power. She checked the clock – ten to six – more than time for breakfast. She'd still eaten almost nothing since that bowl of Poacher's Broth, which seemed so long ago now, it could have been pre-history. Christopher hadn't mentioned eating, the whole long afternoon, had seemed totally absorbed in checking through his books on modern architecture – especially Stanton Martin's – sublimely unconcerned with paltry things like meals. And she herself had somehow lost her appetite, troubled by the fact that she'd returned with him so tamely, like a puppet in his power, even accepted a job she'd vowed she didn't want. By the time he left, having instructed her to help herself to anything she fancied in the kitchen, she was too tired to eat at all; obeyed her flagging body which was urging 'sleep' instead.

Now she felt ravenous as she hunted through his cupboards, which were bare of any basics such as coffee, tea-bags, milk or cheese. She nosed out some coarse black tea-leaves, which she spooned into the pot, then topped with boiling water. She poured an inch to try. The tea looked very pale, with a dark sludge at the bottom, and a strangely scented taste, like incense mixed with cheap cologne. She preferred her own Typhoo.

All she found to eat was one small tin of crabmeat and a jar of garlic paté. Neither seemed quite suitable for breakfast. The 'Gourmet Meal-for-One' she had better save for lunch, which left plain brown bread and butter – well, bread and low-fat spread. She could turn it into toast this time, upgrade it with some strawberry jam, which she discovered in the fridge. It seemed a strange place to keep strawberry jam, until she realised it was sugarless, a special brand for diabetics. *Was* he diabetic, or simply obsessional about his weight? Or perhaps his wife cooked hugely fattening meals for him, so he preferred to pick and nibble when working on his own.

That wife kept bursting in – surprising her, confusing her – always plump, voluptuous, sometimes naked as a pink blancmange. Was that the reason she'd changed her mind, said yes to Christopher's job – because she was jealous of a wife? She grabbed hot bread from the toaster, crammed it down her throat, so furious with the thought she was glad to scorch her mouth. The whole thing was pretty crazy. She'd be absolutely useless to him – couldn't type, couldn't drive, knew nothing about art. She could hardly spend all day all week cleaning just three rooms, or cooking meals he clearly didn't want. She couldn't even shop for him, stock up his fridge and larder, not without the car. So why had he employed her, and why had she said yes?

She padded into the studio, still chewing flabby toast, switched on the main light. It was those scarlet birds which magnetised her, kept tugging at her mind, yet she could hardly even see them now. They died without the daylight, faded into sombre shapes, lost their sap and life-blood. How extraordinary stained glass was – to possess that force and fervour once the sun had risen, yet dwindle into impotence at dusk. She touched a gaping beak, a fragmented flaunting tail; envied him his skills, his ability to lose himself in total concentration. She had watched him yesterday, his whole mind and verve and energy focused on a wall of coloured glass, which didn't yet exist except as challenge. She had seen him rough the shape out, sketch his first ideas, feeling totally superfluous herself. He had offered her a job, yet appeared to forget that she was there, as if he'd already gone to Manchester and was weighing up the site, or was deep in consultation with the architect.

She rooted in the waste-bin for a crumpled piece of paper, smoothed it out, laid it on the table where he'd sat sketching yesterday – a sturdy scrubbed-pine table at the far side of the room, which stood beneath a tall but narrow window. She turned the long-necked lamp on, found herself a pencil, then tried to draw her own bird. It came out stiff and stupid, a stuffed bird or a caged bird, with no vigour in its wings. She made another start, but was distracted by a noise, the faintest drone and buzzing just above her head. She looked up from her paper, saw a good two dozen wasps crawling up the outside of the window, attracted by the strong beam of the lamp – frantic wasps, weaving round in circles; flailing, jostling, slipping down the pane. Each time a tiny body slumped, another seemed to take its place; wasps fighting for more window-space, crawling over each other's heaving backs; transparent wings vibrating, shiny stripey bodies throbbing and pulsating. Jane watched them, fascinated, startled by their energy, their determination to achieve a hopeless task – to fly through a closed window, penetrate a pane of solid glass.

However frequently they fell, they'd doggedly return, as if desperate for the light, bewitched by it, sucked in by it; feelers waving valiantly, as they flapped and lurched and staggered. Were these the same two dozen, or were there thousands more outside, a whole universe of wasps, with her the only human; this one small lamp the only source of light? She peered out at the darkness, aware of the surrounding fields, spreading cold and desolate for miles, the waste of sea beyond them, the black and lowering sky. These wasps were homeless, shelterless, driven in by cold and dark to grovel at her window. She realised she was like a god, could accomplish the impossible, end their hopeless flounderings and release them into warmth and light. She kicked her chair back, reached across the table, tried to ram the window open. It felt reluctant, stiff with age, but she kept resolutely pushing, falling forward suddenly as it yielded to her pressure.

The wasps poured in, triumphant, swooped towards the lamp, others venturing further to the spotlights on the roof-beams, lunging in a manic dance; the shadows of their bodies like daubs of grey-blue paint, splattering and rippling the white walls. She could feel their wild exhilaration pulsing through her own body, as if she shared their sense of purpose, and had joined their spiralling dance, skittering and reeling from lamp to lamp to lamp. Yet they were risking death in aiming for the light. Several of them had already hit the bulb, wings sizzling in the heat, the faint smell of singeing in the air, the plop of falling bodies. More swarmed through the window, like replacements in a battle, stirring up clouds of dust as they circled round the lampshade. She realised only now that the studio was full of dust, not spotless as it seemed before, spruced and scoured by Christopher. It was as if the wasps had found him out, revealed the private dirt, the layers of rebel dust still lurking on the roof-beams, on countless hidden ledges and secret nooks and crevices.

She slammed her pencil hard against the table, angry with the intruders, angry with herself for allowing them inside. They were threatening Christopher's order, disturbing his whole studio, and he had told her to be careful, warned her very sternly that there was a lot of valuable stuff around – dangerous stuff as well. Before he'd finally engaged her, he had suddenly seemed anxious about taking on a stranger, and had started barking questions at her like a heavy-handed father: did she smoke, did she drink, did she have a boyfriend, could he trust her not to use the place as a doss-house for her friends? What he hadn't thought of asking was whether she was fool enough to let in not her boyfriends (who were non-existent anyway), but a plague of footling wasps.

Well, she would have to get them out again – and fast. She turned off all the lights, opened the window as wide as it would go, counting slowly up to sixty in the dark. She switched just one small light back on, to check they'd disappeared. A frantic buzzing swarm seemed to spring to life from nowhere and zoom towards the bulb. Again, she snuffed the light out, waited for ten minutes, shivering in the wintry draught knifing from the window. Surely they would leave now, with nothing to attract them; a raw and clammy dankness creeping through the studio from the pre-dawn cold outside.

Her fingers fumbled for the light-switch, pouncing on it fiercely, about to cry, 'I've won. They've gone!' They hadn't gone, resurrected instantly, as if the blazing lamp were a magic source of life. So long as she sat quietly in the dark, they would seem to die, or disappear, but one weak shaft of light brought an immediate buzz and whirring as they flurried to embrace it. She rolled her dangling sleeves back, seized her piece of paper, folded it in three, swatted at them wildly, flapping with her other hand. A sudden stab of scarlet pain lasered through her arm. She dropped the paper, stared at the red mark, already swelling quite dramatically just below the elbow. She limped into the kitchen, hand across her mouth, to stop herself from crying. She mustn't fall apart because they'd stung her, but fight back, pay them out. She remembered seeing wasp-killer when she'd

64

been riffling through the cupboards. She grabbed it from the shelf, flipping off her slippers as she ran back to the studio, and switching all the lights on, so she that could see what she was doing.

A cloud of wasps besieged the room immediately, zigzagging in dizzy arcs towards every source of light. She followed with her aerosol, finger on the trigger, darting round in circles, spraying them relentlessly. Yet their numbers seemed still greater, rather than diminished, or were they simply doubled by their convulsive restless shadows, projected on the walls like some speeded-up picture-show borrowed from a dream? She focused on just two or three, mercilessly dousing them until at last they fell; their limp and powdered bodies now silent on the floor. She pursued another cluster, aiming very steadily, despite the pain and throbbing in her arm. Soon, small white-shrouded corpses littered the whole floor; more bodies on the table, on the cutting-bench, the worktops. She slumped down on a chair. The aerosol was empty now, and both her feet were cut and sore from tiny shards of glass, which, like the dust, coated the whole studio, though she hadn't been aware of it before.

'There's an excitement in destruction,' Christopher had claimed, and she had tried to close her ears. Yet now she had experienced it herself – felt an almost gloating relish in wreaking her revenge, a hateful sense of triumph as she'd stunned each tiny body. She rubbed her eyes impatiently. No point sitting crying. The murderer must dispose of all her corpses.

She went to find a dustpan – and some aspirin – grimacing at the reek of acrid chemicals which was choking from the studio, tickling up her nostrils like a sneeze that wouldn't come. That smell might linger all weekend, prevent her hushing up her crime. She flung open all the windows, and then the doors as well. The place was freezing cold now, but better that than the artist's accusations. She could always bundle up in the chunky Shetland sweater she'd seen stuffed in his top drawer. She dragged upstairs to fetch it, yanking the drawer open, removing not the sweater, but her parents' photograph. She sank down on the bed with it, touched the two pale faces. Were they really frowning, or simply squinting in the sun?

'Dad,' she said, out loud, imploring him to raise his eyes. Were they searching for her, missing her, driven to distraction by worry and remorse, or merely continuing their calm well-ordered lives?

She watched her tears splash on to the photo, run down her father's cheeks. If only he would cry for her, prove he cared that much. She had refused to cry herself, the whole month she'd been away, but now she was weeping for the mess she'd made – not just the wasps, but because she'd lost a home again. It was the little things she missed – that precious goodnight ritual she had taken more or less for granted every single night for eighteen years – the curtains drawn, the blankets tucked around her, her father's scratchy boisterous kiss, her mother's more restrained one; both her parents solid and assured. She missed that more than anything – more than meals or company, more than roof and walls. She stretched out full-length on the bed, the photograph beside her, sharing the same pillow.

'Goodnight,' she said to no one, aware that it was morning, and pulled the duvet right across her head.

6

Jane flung off the duvet. She could hear a car drawing up outside, scrunching into the stretch of pitted wasteland just beside the barn. Christopher! She leapt up out of bed, grabbed a sweater, dropped it, dived towards the stairs, dithered back again. Should she hide, or brave him? He must have come to spy on her, only pretended that he'd be away in Oxfordshire. What was it he'd said? – some boastful fabrication about spending all weekend with friends who owned a water-mill – and how he'd see her in the studio, up and dressed and ready, at nine A.M. on Monday. She peered down at her watch. It was nine o'clock exactly, but Saturday, not Monday, and she was neither dressed nor ready. She hadn't swept the wasps up, nor even washed her breakfast things; and the place was like a fridge. She'd left all the doors and windows open, and then dropped off to sleep, risking burglary and break-in, damage to the artist's precious glass. He'd be absolutely furious, and could she really blame him? She had no excuse at all, except those aspirins must have knocked her out, so that she'd totally forgotten the mess and stink downstairs. She skittered to the door again, wondering why he'd not come in, not erupted up the stairs, cursing her and shouting. She could hear the engine grumbling still, as if he was sitting in the car outside, setting her a trap, waiting till she blundered down, guilty and dishevelled.

She crept back to the window, the one high tiny window which looked out over the road; climbed up on a chair, so that she could see his face, judge his mood and temper. It wasn't his sleek car, but a different one entirely – a smaller squatter model, a comic-looking toy car in a scatty shade of sunshine-yellow, with a snub nose in the front and its offside light splintered at the back. The driver's seat was empty, the door left gaping open, the ignition not switched off. She could hear no footsteps underneath the gallery, so whoever

67

owned it hadn't ventured in yet. Suddenly she glimpsed a figure emerging from the garden at the back – a woman, not a man – a plump curvaceous woman with a tousled skein of auburn hair bouncing on one shoulder. The wife! It must be her – not quite as she'd imagined, but undoubtedly voluptuous, and if not young and beautiful, then statuesque and striking, and looking far more arty than the artist did himself. Perhaps Christopher had sent her as a more subtle form of spy, or had she come as a Samaritan, to invite her husband's 'skivvy' for a home-cooked lunch or dinner? She'd ditch the invitation once she saw the mess; was already edging through the door with a wary apprehension, as if prepared for an encounter with a burglar or a thug.

'Who's there?' the woman called, her anxious voice now rising from the studio below, a voice which matched the artist's, urbane and thoroughbred.

Jane tore off her pyjamas, climbed into her tracksuit, not bothering with bra and pants, just heaving up the bottoms, struggling with the fiddly zippered top. Mrs Harville-Shaw mustn't find her naked, or dressed in men's pyjamas. She might be shocked in any case – angry and astonished to find a stranger sleeping in her husband's bed, and a female one at that. Perhaps he hadn't told his wife he'd hired a new assistant. Perhaps he'd gone to Oxfordshire alone, without his wife, not thinking for a moment she might drop in at the barn. Perhaps, perhaps, perhaps. She knew absolutely nothing about either of the Harville-Shaws, except she was scared of both of them. She tied her laces, finger-combed her hair, crept slowly down the stairs – one step, one step, like a child, wishing she would never reach the bottom.

She paused a moment four steps up, looking at the wife, who was nervously examining the widely opened window, and hadn't heard her yet. She seemed too big for Christopher, a tall well-covered woman with too much of everything – a generous mass of hair, a soft bolster of a bosom, big eyes, big hands and feet; even several layers of clothing which looked curiously mismatched – a flowing poppied skirt worn with both a tee shirt and a knobbly knitted waistcoat, then a man's severe tweed jacket buttoned over the top. Jane had a sudden image of the two in bed together – the wife rising like a yeasty loaf, swelling and expanding till Christopher was lost in dough, its soft pale yielding stickiness smothering his body, erasing its sharp lines. She jumped the last four steps, landing with a thud, to announce that she was there. She could no longer bear the tension of waiting to be found, waiting to be reprimanded.

68

'Look, I'm sorry. I can explain, honestly. I had to let these wasps out. I mean, I had to let the smell out. I just didn't know I . . . I'd . . .' The words stuttered to a halt. She could hear herself sounding quite inane. She was thrown by Mrs Harville-Shaw, who had swung across the studio towards her, and was now standing very close. Her scent was sweet and heady, a jumble of conflicting flowers – honeysuckle, jasmine, lily of the valley – suppressing the last lingering trace of wasp-killer. Her eyes were greenish-grey, with little flecks of blue in them, as if they couldn't quite decide which colour they should settle for, and had hedged their bets with snicks and streaks of each. She was older than she'd seemed at first, the flesh slack around her chin, the auburn hair scrawled with grey; wiry wilful wavy hair which tendrilled from its plait, escaped in eager spirals.

'Who are you?' she asked simply, unbuttoning her jacket – or was it Christopher's jacket, an older shabbier version of the tweedy one he was wearing yesterday?

'I'm . . . er . . . working for your husband.'

'My husband?'

'Yes.'

'My husband's dead.'

'Dead?' Jane slumped back to the staircase, leaned against it, stunned. Images of accidents were bloodying her head – horrific ghastly pile-ups on the motorway to Wantage, maimed and mangled bodies, twisted wrecks of cars . . .

'What's wrong? You're white as a sheet. There must be some mistake. He died fourteen months ago. It was in the papers, on the news. Everybody knew.'

'Fourteen months ago?' Jane pulled herself to standing, cleared her throat, which still felt blocked and choked. 'Then you're not his wife.'

'Whose wife? I'm getting muddled.'

'Christopher's.'

The woman laughed, an immoderate sort of laugh, which shook her heavy breasts, seemed to billow through her layers of clothes, remained sparkling in her eyes even when it rippled to a stop. 'I'm afraid he wouldn't have me. And I must admit I'm surprised to find you here. Christopher's a loner, at least as far as work's concerned. What sort of work are you doing for him?'

'I'm not too sure. I haven't really started yet.'

'Are you an art student or something?'

'No.'

'So you're not helping with the glass?'

69

'Well, he did say he might train me, but . . .' Jane broke off, suddenly uneasy. The woman was tugging at a button on her jacket, twisting it and twisting it on its fragile loop of thread. 'I'm just here to help him generally,' she mumbled. 'A Girl Friday, you might say.' Adrian's term. She should have taken Adrian's job. It would have been simpler altogether. The woman was still torturing her button, still looking at her anxiously, almost with resentment; or was she just imagining that? Could she be another stained-glass artist, someone who had tried – and failed – to work with Christopher herself? 'Look, I'm just a sort of char, that's all – the lowest of the low.'

The woman suddenly reached a hand out, a warm and plumpish hand, with chipped varnish on the nails, a Band-Aid round one thumb. 'I'm sure you're not a char, my love. You look far too bright for that. Though judging by the mess in here, the place does need clearing up. How on earth did all the wasps get in? I thought wasps died in the winter, or hibernated or something. But forget about the wasps. I still don't know your name. Mine's Isobel – Isobel Mackenzie.' She gestured to her chest, as if she'd pinned a name-tag there, before letting spill another rush of words.

'Christopher's making a memorial window for my late husband. In fact, he'll kill me if he finds me here. He hates his clients coming to the studio, though I'm really a good friend. Still, friend or no, he won't let me interfere, says you can't judge a window till it's actually *in situ*, and he hasn't even started on it yet. Of course, we've done all the preliminaries, like getting the design through all those wretched councils and what-have-you, but he's so busy always, isn't he? Anyway, I wasn't trying to snoop. I just made a little detour on my way back from Communion. I was more worried, actually. I mean, that dreadful storm last night, and I knew he was away, and perhaps hadn't had a chance to check the place for damage. He's gone to see this architect in Wantage – or was it Chadlington? D'you find you're always muddling names – place-names more than people's? The architect is Julian – that I do remember – and he's got this quaint old water-mill, which he converted himself, way back in the sixties. Gosh! Forgive me rambling on like this. It must seem frightfully rude. Though I suspect it's simply nerves, you know. I was scared there'd been a break-in, when I saw the door wide open, and I'm still recovering from the shock.'

'I'm sorry. That was my fault.' Jane started to explain, though she was recovering herself. This couldn't be the donor Christopher had mentioned – the surgeon's wife she'd pictured as a pious gawky matron, impeccably turned out in a quiet-toned Jaeger suit, and what

70

was called 'good' jewellery, with a distant chilly manner, like their doctor's wife at home. Isobel's jewellery was the flash flamboyant kind – a hoopla of gold bangles on one wrist, dramatic dangly earrings which quivered when she moved, a brooch shaped like a lizard with sparkling eyes far greener than her own. And shouldn't widows dress in black, or at least not those dizzy poppies, whose ripe and juicy red seemed more suited to a disco than to mourning?

'It's a wonder you weren't stung, my love.'

'I was.' Jane pushed back her sleeve, gestured to her forearm which had puffed up to twice its size.

'Poor child! That needs attention. Come into the kitchen.' She took Jane's other arm, coaxed her through the door, stopped a moment just outside, heavy bracelets jangling. 'So what's your name? I still don't know it, do I?'

Jane paused, longed to give her real name, not to start the lies again. But this woman was the artist's friend and client, so she didn't have much choice, would have to stick to Rose.

'Oh, what a pretty name! And my favourite flower, of course. I suppose everybody's favourite. It's a wonder roses don't get quite big-headed. Now, you sit there, and I'll see what I can find to help that sting. They say ice is very good – and bicarbonate of soda. Though I doubt if Christopher's got that. Well, at least he's got some ice. Here, put this towel underneath, so we don't get you all wet. That's it. Now just relax. Lean back against that cupboard and take a few deep breaths. You look very pale, you know. Has Christopher been working you too hard? I'm sure he doesn't mean to, but he tends to get so utterly absorbed in things, he simply doesn't realise that other normal people need a break. Actually, I really rather warm to that. Enthusiasm's so rare. Well, perhaps it isn't when you're young, but at Christopher's and my age . . . Now, how's the sting?'

Jane nodded, couldn't speak.

'Better? Good. Let's have a little look at it. Gosh! It does seem fearfully swollen. Is it wasps which leave their stings behind – or is that only bees? I can't remember, can you? Perhaps I ought to suck it anyway. My daughter had a bee-sting when she was just a tot of five – a bad one on her leg – and I sucked it out immediately, and all the pain and inflammation disappeared like magic. Odd how little things like that pop back into your mind. I haven't given it a thought for almost twenty years, but you remind me of her, Rose – I mean, when she was a child.'

'I . . . I'm not a child.'

' 'Course you're not. But you've got that gorgeous child's hair

– you know, long and straight and natural. Rowan had it too, and almost exactly the same colour – sort of autumn brown I suppose you'd call it, wouldn't you? I'm afraid she's had it cut now – cropped and layered and shingled – or whatever it is they do in these top salons. Of course I told her it looked lovely – I didn't want to hurt her. She's such a dear, and was so excited anyway to have been to this John-Michael, or whatever he was called, but to tell the truth, I was really quite upset. I know it sounds stupid, but it was like losing the child part of her, which I'd had for all those years. D'you follow what I mean?'

Jane nodded, understood.

'Good. Now how about that sting? I'd take you to the doctor's, but he isn't there on Saturday. Mind you, if it's still inflamed on Monday, I think I'd better give him a ring, make you an appointment. It's not wise to neglect these things. Look, I'll pull this other stool up, and if you just roll your sleeve back right above the elbow, I'll have a go at sucking it, okay? Relax – you're very tense, you know. I promise I won't hurt you. Why not shut your eyes, go into another world? I used to tell my children that, if they'd hurt themselves or couldn't get to sleep or something. In fact, we had our own invented world – a very small and peaceful one, full of things called Pondles, which were green and soft and kind.' She laughed, a husky laugh, which seemed to come not from her larynx, but from some laugh-box deep inside her. 'Ridiculous! Except Rowan seemed to like it. Oh dear, I must stop reminiscing. I don't know what's got into me. A lot of good I'd be if you'd just had a heart attack, instead of a wasp-sting. You'd be dead and gone by now. Right, first aid coming up.'

Jane shut her eyes, tried to slip into another world, as the woman had suggested, but it wasn't small and peaceful, rather vast and hot and feverish, throbbing like her sting. Isobel felt dangerously close. She had taken off her jacket, and despite her layers of other clothes, she seemed naked and exposed, her ample breasts so near now she would probably squash against them if she moved a fraction forward. The tail of hair was tickling on her knee; the scent of flowers cloying, almost nauseous, and there were other much more intimate smells – a whiff of musky talcum powder from warm perspiring flesh – the private secret Isobel now open to her, flaunted.

The woman's lips were on her arm, nuzzling the bare skin, sucking with a gentle tugging pressure. The sting still hurt, yet the sucking seemed to soothe it – pain and pleasure fused, so she couldn't disentangle them. And suddenly, unsettlingly, Christopher was there as well, Isobel sucking *his* bare arm, their two warm bodies touching. They seemed familiar with each other, hands knowing where to go, their silence charged, provocative, not tense and scared as hers was. She felt excluded, strangely jealous. They had so much more in common than she would ever have with either of them – both roughly the same age, both confident and cultured, achievers in the world. Had they actually slept together, shared not just plans for windows, but mouths and beds and bodies? She longed to swap with Isobel, to be full-lipped and heavy-breasted, with a mass of tumbling hair, to be at ease in her own body, relaxed with someone else's.

Irritably, she shook her head, as if to dislodge her envious thoughts, tried to blank out everything but the steady lulling suction on her arm, the disquieting sensation of cool lips on burning sting, the strange contrast between tension and abandon. She was losing all her boundaries, sinking down, dissolving, being taken over, cared for, lost in someone else. She let her breath out in a rush, hardly aware that she'd been holding it so long, uncrossed her legs, unclenched her rigid hands. No need to be so wary, close her body off, or crave to be an adult, someone's sensual mistress. She must just lean back and relax, as Isobel had told her; become a child again, a child of five, like Rowan, with long straight natural hair in a gorgeous autumn brown; Isobel's young daughter. Strange to have a mother so different from her own. Yet mothers should be plump – warm and soft and open – all curves and flesh, not angles; and have tousled messy hair, instead of tight and prissy perms; and invent small and peaceful worlds which didn't let you down; and should talk too much, pour out words like milk. She recalled some other words – peaceful words, deceitful words – couldn't quite remember where she'd heard them. 'And underneath are the everlasting arms.'

She suddenly slammed up, yanked her arm away.

'What on earth's the matter, Rose?' Isobel reached out to right the trembling chair, which had tipped back from the impact. 'I didn't hurt you, did I?'

'N . . . no.'

'Look, if the sting's that bad, we ought to call the doctor. He'll come out for emergencies. I'll go and ring him now.'

'*No.*'

'Well, how about some aspirin? You may be in a state of shock. Some people do react like that to stings.'

'It's not the sting. It's . . .'

'It's what, my love?'

'Don't call me that.' Jane turned to face the wall, tugged her sleeve down roughly. 'You're not my mother. I haven't got a mother.'

Isobel stood anxious at the door. 'I'm sorry, Rose, I don't quite understand. What happened to . . . ?'

'You couldn't understand.' Jane's voice was muffled, choked. 'No one could, not unless they'd . . . Look, forget it, please. I'd rather not discuss it. I swore I'd never say a word – never, never, never – not to anyone.'

'Look, I don't know what the problem is, but it's sometimes a bit easier to tell things to a stranger, someone who's objective, hasn't got an axe to grind. Couldn't you trust me enough to . . . ?'

'No.'

'Okay. That's fair enough. I don't want to probe. There's nothing worse than people interfering. Tell you what, why not come back home with me and we'll have a bite of breakfast?'

Jane shook her head. 'Not hungry.'

'Well, a nice hot cup of tea.'

'I've got to clear the wasps up.'

'That won't take a tick. I'll do it while you fetch your coat.'

'No.'

'Forgive me, I'm intruding. And you're probably right, you know. It's sometimes better just to be alone. When my husband died, I spent whole days on my own, and it helped more than constant sympathy or people rallying round.' She paused a moment, lost in thought – or mourning – then returned the ice-trays to the fridge, mopped up a drool of water. 'Let me put this room to rights, then I'll get out of your way. But if there's anything you need, my dear, or you simply want a chat, ring me on this number.' She scrawled it on a Kleenex which she fished out from her sleeve, left it on the worktop, underneath a cup. 'And you'd better watch that arm of yours. In fact, why not rest it now? Pop upstairs and have a little zizz.'

'Yes,' said Jane. 'I will.'

She dawdled up the stairs, flopped down on the bed, heard Isobel below her, moving to and fro, broom rasping on the floorboards. She listened for the door to close, heard it click, at last; heard the woman's slip-on shoes scuffling down the path outside; the slam of a car door. Thank God, she thought, as she sagged back on the duvet. She had to be alone, had to keep apart, must steel herself to silence, not be tempted to confide. It wasn't safe to trust people. They would only let you down, turn out completely differently from what you dared to hope. She was officially an adult now, shouldn't need a mother, or a mother-substitute, must learn to cope without one, forget her dreams and nightmares which all seemed to feature mothers – faceless mothers, wombless mothers, mothers without arms.

74

She shrugged and chewed her hair, one long strand of it wound round and round her fingers, as she waited for the car to pull away. At last, she heard the gruff snort of the engine, a complaining grind of gears. Her sting was hurting badly. She rolled her sleeve back, closed her eyes, felt the woman's mouth again, sucking it and soothing; smelt her potent mother's smell, the smell of warmth and honey. She dashed to the small window, jumped up on a chair, rammed the stiff frame open, shouting desperately: 'Wait! Don't go. Come back.'

Isobel couldn't hear her, her attention on the wheel, the uneven rutted driveway. Jane banged against the glass, willed her to look up; kept yelling, waving, hammering. Suddenly, the car stopped with a slam and squeal of brakes.

Jane subsided on the bed again, nursing her bruised fists, counting stairs as Isobel walked up. Fifteen. Sixteen. Seventeen. The door opened with a creak. Neither of them spoke. Isobel joined her on the bed, sitting cross-legged like a child, her voluminous skirt bellying round her knees, her hands and hair and jewellery now completely still, as if they'd been injected with a tranquilliser. The silence did feel tranquil – healing, very safe. Difficult to break it, maybe downright dangerous. Jane heard her voice sounding strange and shaky, seeming to speak against her will, to come from miles away.

'I . . . I've never been bereaved myself, but it probably feels a bit the same. And it happened really recently, not fourteen months ago.' She groped her hand out, touched one flamboyant poppy. 'Promise not to say anything, not until I've finished.'

'Promise.'

A bird flapped past the window, wheeled heavily away; a muffled lorry rumbled in the distance. Isobel sat so silent she could have been a painting, a canvas on the wall, though still too bright and vibrant to be one of Christopher's. Jane clasped both her hands together, fingers tightly locked, eyes fixed on the floor. 'It happened at my party,' she said slowly, very slowly; each word costing, hurting. 'My eighteenth birthday party.'

7

'So now if you'll all raise your glasses and drink a toast to the birthday girl.'

Jane was suddenly clamped tight against her Uncle Peter's chest, felt his beard prickling on her lips, his hot hands clammy on her naked stretch of back. Everyone was calling out her name, glasses clinking, cameras flashing, congratulations rising all around her, a triumphant roll of drums as the band played 'Happy Birthday'. She pulled away, cheeks flaming, bewildered by the curdled heave of colours, the blur of jostling bodies; tried to focus on her parents as the two most solid people there. They were standing just beside her – her father stiff and polished, her mother in a cooling shade of green, her docile hair still tightly crimped despite the heat and crush. Her own hair must be limp by now, had shrugged off the joint efforts of Liz and Prue at Snippers. She could feel it hanging heavy down her back – everything too heavy: the gold chain round her throat, the matching gold-loop earrings; the blusher and foundation which her mother had insisted on because she looked so pale; the smile which seemed to paralyse her face.

She ought to say a word of thanks, but her mouth felt dry and scratchy, and the phrase came out inaudible. She cleared her throat, forced her voice to work. 'Thank you,' she said shyly. 'Thank you all for coming.' It wasn't hypocritical. She was glad now that they'd come, had made her so important, marked her eighteenth birthday, her new status as an adult. At first, she'd set her face against any celebration, scared of people noticing that she hadn't got a boyfriend, or saying she looked young – eighteen in actual years, maybe, but not in poise or style. Her parents had seemed crestfallen. They'd been planning a big party, budgeting for months – secretly, excitedly, intending to surprise her – checking up on venues, sounding out hotels. 'Hotels?' she'd cried, appalled, when at last they shared their plans with her. If she had to mark the date at all, then why not just a simple meal – a few friends round the table in the safety of her home, her mother's chicken casserole, perhaps a special cake?

'But there are people we must ask. The Frasers, for example – they'll expect a proper do. And the Holdsworths and the Collinses, and that girl you met in Wales, and all the friends who've had you to their own parties, and and and and and . . .'

She was overruled, outnumbered; bombastic Uncle Peter joining in as well, wanting something grander still, buying her a party dress to match his own ideas – a backless one in taffeta with a full and flouncy skirt. The skirt swished with every move, was rustling now as she stepped towards the table to cut her birthday cake: eighteen tiny candle-flames flickering and guttering, hot against her face as she stooped to blow them out. She took a big breath in, expelled it in a rush. The guests let out a cheer, which turned into a groan. Two candles were still burning, only sixteen dead. Frantically she snuffed the final two. Too late. A second breath always meant bad luck. She tried to make a joke about her lack of puff, ignore the tiny snick of fear fretting through her head. Stupid to believe in luck. Life was just beginning – that's what all the oldies said – sometimes said it bitterly, as if they hadn't lived themselves yet.

She inserted the huge knife, felt it jib at hard white icing, plunge through oily marzipan. She wished the cake was pink or blue, not white. It seemed too like a wedding cake, and there wasn't any groom, no other hand but hers clinging to that ivory-handled knife. Strange to feel alone amidst sixty-seven guests. She glanced back at her parents, longed to dash towards them, hide her head in her mother's silky skirts, beg to be picked up and put to bed.

Hours to go till bedtime. More white-aproned waitresses had materialised from nowhere and were refilling glasses, passing round the cake. Guests crowded up to talk to her – faces, faces, faces – Rita with her hair swept up and earrings shaped like small giraffes; portly Uncle Colin waving a cigar, punctuating all his words with smoke; Andy scoffing chocolate mousse, a swirl of cream moustaching his top lip; anorexic Emma flirting with a celery stick, which looked pale and limp and skinny like her arms. Everybody talking, interrupting, arguing; sudden yelps of laughter, the phut of burst balloons, boom-di-boom-di-boom-di from the band. She tried to answer everyone at once, turn in six directions, recharge her wilting smile.

'Love the dress.'

'It's hot.'

'Hot? There's next to nothing of it. You women do complain.'

'So what do you plan to do now, dear? College is it, next?'

'Well, I thought I'd . . .'

'Hey! You can't strip off like that, Sue, not in public, anyway. Jane won't like it, will you, Jane? Here – have some more champagne to cool you down.'

'No thanks. I'd better not. I'm seeing stars already. Mac put Southern Comfort in my Coke.'

'Jane, you look sensational! Last time we saw you, you were thirteen and a half, and swore you'd never wear lipstick in your life.'

She tried to laugh, recall it. A few other long-lost relatives had clucked about her dress, or told her how she'd grown. She *hadn't* grown – or not enough. She should be five foot six at least, and acres more sophisticated. She had tried to smoke and loathed it, didn't like the taste of gin, had no real future plans, and couldn't sort out what she felt about all those burning issues which other people championed with total fierce conviction, while she weighed up all the arguments on each and every side, and ended up believing, doing nothing.

'Come and dance then, gorgeous. It's time you let your hair down.'

Andy took her hand, swept her on to the floor, improvised some wild dance of his own, half a war-dance, half flamenco. His energy ignited her, seemed to blow away her shyness, banish introspection, as she tried to copy him. She could feel her skirt and petticoats flaring out around her, Andy's laughing twirling body galvanising hers.

'You're a fantastic mover, Janey!' She flushed with pleasure, not just at the compliment, but because he'd called her Janey. It sounded affectionate, endearing, and he was quite the most attractive man in the whole crowded spinning room – Sarah's boyfriend, actually, though she no longer even envied Sarah tonight. She had received so many compliments herself – gorgeous, dishy, elegant, sensational, fantastic, good enough to eat. They couldn't all be lying, so perhaps she'd really changed, woken up more beautiful, left Plain Jane behind. It could be a good omen, a new start in her life. She stood panting for a moment while Andy tied his shoe, glancing round the stately room with its fluted pillars, ruched and tasselled curtains. All this just for her – the bowls of hothouse flowers, the trifles, salads, soufflés; the band, the splendid cake. And every single person here had turned up in her honour. Shouldn't she be flattered, not carping at her parents because they'd done things grandly, judged her worth a splash? She let Andy spin her round again, collapsing in his arms, as the band pumped out a final dizzy cadence.

'And now a few traditional numbers for the older generation, so wake up, Dad – Mum's waiting.' The dapper little band-leader swivelled back to his glitzy baby-grand, which exploded in a storm of trills, before launching into 'Stardust'. Andy booed and jeered, while a whooping Uncle Peter dived between the bodies, claimed her for a foxtrot.

'I'm not sure I can do it,' she said, stalling. She'd been to ballroom dancing classes – her mother had insisted – but they'd never got much further than the quickstep and the waltz. And, anyway, he'd severed her from Andy, who was now prancing up to Sarah, bowing low, so he could inspect her daring cleavage.

''Course you can,' boomed Peter, who hardly seemed to notice when she trod on both his feet, moved left and slightly sidewards whilst he lurched right and front. He'd been knocking back the drink, his face as flushed as hers was, and with no help from any rouge.

'Cracking party isn't it?' She nodded, dodged his breath – a strong down-wind of whisky-flavoured nicotine. He was so different from her father, despite the fact they looked alike – two grey-haired grey-eyed brothers with only eighteen months between them. Her father neither smoked nor swore, drank only wine, and rarely; believed in work and discipline, while Peter loafed about, living off past triumphs; his sole targets for the present forty Rothman's King-Size and half a bottle of Black and White each day. They'd had a row last week. She wasn't meant to know, but she had heard the two sharp voices rising to her bedroom, shattering her sleep; a final slam as Peter cannoned out. In the morning, she had tried to quiz her mother for the facts.

'It was nothing, dear – just a silly tiff. Peter and your father have never hit it off. It goes back to their childhood. I suspect he's jealous, actually. Granny always favoured Alec.'

The face was looming close again, dark shadow on the chin, a spider's web of broken veins embroidering the nose. 'So what presents did you get, Jane? Besides my dress, of course. It looks terrific, doesn't it?'

'Yes,' she said, wincing as his size-ten foot landed on her fragile patent sandal.

'And what did Mum and Dad cough up?'

'A cheque – a really big one, and this gold chain . . .' She gestured to her neck. 'Daddy gave me that, and . . .'

'I'd have thought they might have given you something else. And I don't mean just a present.'

'Well, they paid for all this party – the cake and the champagne, and all the food and drink and stuff.'

'So they bloody should! They're your parents, aren't they? Aren't they?' he repeated. He staggered, tried to right himself, clutched out at a potted palm. 'That's the question, isn't it?'

'I'm sorry, I don't follow.'

'No, I don't expect you do, Jane. Forget cheques and silly trinkets. They owe you something else – your birthright, you might say. I told them bloody years ago, and I was hammering home the point again last week – but would they listen? – no!'

Jane tried to block his voice out, dismiss the sudden frisson of uneasiness she couldn't quite explain. Her Uncle Peter had always been a problem. Her parents seemed on edge with him, almost on their guard. Admittedly he'd worked abroad for years, so they saw him very rarely, but he'd returned to live in England just this last July, and even now they preferred to keep their distance, despite his frequent phone-calls. When he phoned, he always spoke to her; had been her fan since childhood – phoning, writing, even from abroad; sending lavish presents, or showering her with compliments long-distance.

'What I'm asking, Jane, my duck, is whether your dear beloved parents sat down with you last night and had a little talk – shall we say a little heart to heart?'

'I don't know what you're talking about.'

''Course you don't. That's their fault, isn't it? You don't know bloody anything, poor kid.' Uncle Peter hiccoughed. 'Beg your pardon, Jane dear. I never could take marzipan.'

'Look, why don't we sit down?'

'What, and lose you to some whippersnapper? I've been trying all the evening to get you on your own, and now you're giving me the push.'

'I'm *not*, Uncle Peter. It's just that . . .' It was difficult to hear him, difficult to speak. They kept bumping into people, other skilful couples who'd actually learnt to do the foxtrot, could even keep in time and avoid each other's feet. She was reeling out apologies all round her, like the coloured party streamers now tangling round everybody's shoes; alternating 'sorrys' with brief embarrassed laughs, wishing Uncle Peter would shift his sweaty hand.

'Anyway, I want a little talk with you. If your parents haven't got the guts, then I feel it's up to me. It's my duty, Jane, my duty as . . .

Hey, is this still the bloody foxtrot, or have they changed the beat? That Liberace fellow should be pensioned out to grass.' He backed into a pillar, thumped it with a friendly fist, before seizing hold of her again and jigging to his left. 'Your mother was quite wrong, you know, hushing it all up. I told her so in no uncertain terms. Alec had more sense, but she overruled him, didn't she – turned on the old waterworks and swore us all to secrecy. He could have married anyone, your father, but – no – Amy was the one. She never liked me, Jane, my pet, and d'you want to know for why? A clear case of the little green-eyed monster. I was closer to your father than she would ever be – yes, even seven thousand miles away. But that's not the question, is it? What I'm trying to say, Jane, is you're grown up now, an adult, which means you've got your rights.' He stopped to mop his face, pulling out a teaspoon from his pocket, as well as a white handkerchief. 'Now, how did that get there? They'll say I've pinched the silver next.' His laugh suddenly aborted, turned into a grimace, as he gripped her wrist, too hard. 'Look, maybe you should talk to them yourself; ask them a few really basic questions like . . .' He leaned right forward, snickered in her ear – ' "Who's my mother, Mummy? Who's my father, Dad?" '

'Excuse me,' someone said.

'Get away,' said Peter. 'I'm dancing with the birthday girl, and anyway we're just right bang in the middle of a really . . .'

'Sorry, mate, this is an Excuse-Me, so you have to give her up. You've hogged her half the evening as it is.'

Jane was passed from hand to hand, hardly hearing anything save Uncle Peter's insinuating voice still hissing in her ear, spelling out those two quite senseless questions: 'Who's my mother, Mummy? Who's my . . . ?'

'What's up, Jane? You look shell-shocked.' Her cousin, David, six foot three and freckled, his rebellious ginger hair teaming oddly with his dark and tidy brows.

'Er, nothing. Where's my mother?'

'No idea. Hey, come back! You can't run off like that. I've hardly said a word to you all evening.' She let herself be led into the quickstep. At least Cousin Dave could dance, and he talked enough for both of them. She answered 'yes' and 'no', trying to discount the churning in her stomach, that sinking seasick feeling, as if she were tossing in a tiny boat in the middle of a storm. She mustn't take her Uncle Peter seriously. He was pissed, that's all, merely making trouble, spouting gibberish. *In vino veritas*, a voice nagged in her head. She tried to keep the rhythm, stumbled, almost fell.

81

She couldn't hear the music, only pounding waves crashing round her boat.

'Excuse me, Dave.'

Her father's voice, her father's hand in hers; his neat grey hair and sober stripes replacing David's copper curls and exotic purple shirt.

'It's time I asked my gorgeous daughter for a dance. How're you doing, darling?'

'F . . . fine.' How strange he seemed, like someone in a dream, blurred and out of focus, close to her, yet distant.

'The party's going marvellously. Even Mummy's let herself relax. Just look at her!'

Jane looked. Her mother had just ventured on to the dance-floor and was attempting a cross between flamenco and the twist; her silky skirt whirling round and up, a lacy inch of petticoat showing underneath it, her flushed cheeks shiny-moist.

'I don't think I've ever seen your mother quite so lively, not even at . . .'

'Daddy?'

'What?'

'I . . . I want to talk to you.'

'We're talking, aren't we, darling! Steady! You almost came a cropper then. You haven't overdone the drinks, have you? You know I warned you not to mix the . . .'

'Who's my father, Dad?'

'I beg your pardon?'

'Who's my father?'

'What in God's name are you . . . ?'

He never said 'in God's name', must obviously be thrown; eyes nervous now and blinking, slack lips mouthing nothing, his whole face slipping, as if his usual tight control had only been a mask, which someone had snatched off.

'And who's my mother, Dad?' She watched him pause and swallow, try to change his voice, make it bluff and jocular, force his mouth to smile.

'Well, that's a daft question!' He gestured to his right, picking up the beat again, waltzing round to Amy. 'There she bloody is.'

Don't swear, she begged him silently, don't stutter, stumble, bluster, fake that awful laugh. It only proves there's something wrong, that Uncle Peter wasn't simply plastered – frightening Uncle Peter, who had suddenly returned, butting through the dancers and hiccoughing 'Excuse me,' to her father.

'No, I *won't* excuse you.'

Jane excused herself instead, pulled free from her father and darted to an alcove in the lounge; heard vindictive clashing voices rising from the dance-floor, her mother joining in now, another woman sobbing; the band belting out 'Some Enchanted Evening'. She closed her eyes a moment – longed to close her ears – saw two tiny mocking candle-flames still dancing on the cake. Bad luck. She wasn't sure exactly what had happened, but it was far worse than just bad luck.

'Want a drink?' asked Mac, looming up in front of her. 'I've got this Southern Comfort – my own wee private tipple.'

'Yes,' she said. 'A double.'

'So who *is* my real mother, then?' The words felt strange, grotesque. What did 'real' mean anyway – missing, vanished, lost?

'Now listen, Jane, it's far too late to . . .' Yes, she thought, it *is* too late – years and years too late, like Uncle Peter said. He had known she was adopted since she was a baby in her pram. Everyone had known – her parents' friends, their relatives – everyone but her. She'd been totally deceived, her whole life a lie, a fraud. She could hardly take it in. There were gaping holes, deep shadows, where there'd once been solid facts; everything important negated and confused. She'd tried pressing for more details, but her parents kept on stalling, making lame excuses, plugging the black void with sham-pink candy-floss.

'You're very overwrought, darling. I think you need to rest. It's not a good idea to discuss things late at night.'

Jane glanced up at the clock above the dead and chilly hearth. Three A.M. – a nothing time, neither night nor morning. Nothing, like herself. She'd been suddenly wiped out, the person she assumed she was, the daughter of her parents. She stared at them, bewildered. She had always thought she'd looked like them – small-boned like her mother, with the same blue but dark-lashed eyes; her father's dead-straight hair, which had been the same mid-brown as hers once, judging by the photographs; even his full mouth. Had she just imagined it, made bonds where there were none? They seemed strangers now, or foreigners; two unknown hostile people dressed in drooping party clothes, sitting in a living-room she had once believed was home. Even the room itself had changed; no longer snug and comfortable, but coldly stiff and grim. And those photos on the mantelpiece, they were wrong as well, now – not a mother with her baby, one she'd given birth to, carried in her body, but a cuckoo child, a substitute.

83

She kicked her chair back angrily, slumped down on the floor. 'Why couldn't you have *told* me? I feel completely . . .' She broke off, half-ashamed, gagging on the words, which all sounded too extreme – betrayed, shattered, bitter, panicked, overwhelmed. 'Uncle Peter said you couldn't have children yourself. Shouldn't I have known that, known I wasn't yours?'

She saw her mother flinch, her face still set and tense, pale beneath its tattered mask of make-up. 'Let's leave Peter out of this. He's behaved very irresponsibly, ruined the whole party.'

'Ruined my whole life, you mean.'

Her father reached across to take her hand. 'Now, don't be silly, darling. You're getting the whole thing out of proportion. Nothing's really changed at all. We're still your parents – legally, emotionally, in every single way except . . .'

'Except the most important way.' Jane shook off his hand, hugged her arms around her chest, as if to stop herself unravelling.

'That's *not* important, darling – not to us.'

'I don't believe you. It can't be not important. You're just lying to yourselves, like you've lied to me all these years and years.'

'We never lied, Jane – never.' Her mother now, voice shrill, hands twisted, taut, together. 'We decided very carefully that it would be better not to tell you – best for *you*, and kindest.'

Jane smoothed her crumpled skirt. That too was a lie. They'd been thinking of themselves, didn't want the world to know they couldn't have a child. It had all come out in public – yes, right there on the dance-floor – Peter and her father confronting one another, blurting out private shameful secrets; old hurts and quarrels flooding back; her mother frantic, floundering, trying to hush them up, mutter sweet inanities, spray rose-scented deodorant on a raging forest fire.

Jane tugged off her earrings, rubbed her aching head. The Southern Comfort hadn't helped, only made her queasy. She was surprised by her own voice – the fury in it, vehemence, when she felt so tired, defeated. 'So if Peter hadn't let it slip, you'd have kept me in the dark until I *died*. You're meant to tell adopted children when they're barely more than babies, before they can even understand the words, I know. Anne Mathieson's adopted, and she said her parents told her when she was still in nappies.'

'And what was the good of that, dear, if she couldn't understand?'

'She could! She got the feel of it, the sense of trust, of openness, of people not deceiving her, trying to pass her off as . . .'

'Look, you must believe us, darling, we did it for your good.'

Her father sounded panicky, his usual neat and tidy hair ruffled and unkempt, one foot tapping nervously, as if all his dammed-up tension had drained into that leg. She felt a sudden pang of pity for him, tried to calm her voice, accept what he was saying. Of course they were her parents; had fed and clothed and cared for her, supported her and listened; done all the things that parents should and did. She mustn't think of blood-ties, or genes or wombs or childbirth, inheritance, conception; must dismiss them as irrelevant. Except she knew that was a lie as well. All those things were vitally important, things that people died for, which gave them their identity, their origins and ancestry, the whole history and foundations of their life.

She stared down at her hands, small hands like her mother's – or so she'd always thought. How could she have never guessed, somehow known instinctively, or been told by someone else, a friend or a relation? Except her clever plotting parents had stage-managed even that; had moved away from the county they were married in, the net of close relations, the prying street of neighbours, and come up north to Shrepton, when she was still a tiny baby. They must have felt they'd be safer in the north, removed from all the questions, the idle speculations, the chance that someone, sometime, might whisper in her ear. Strange it hadn't happened long before this evening – at a Christmas get-together, or a christening or a wedding, when they'd been forced to brave the relatives, or return to their home ground. But now she came to think of it, the occasions had been few. On the whole, they had lived apart, just the cosy three of them, good at finding reasons why relations couldn't visit, or which prevented them travelling south themselves.

She leant against her chair-seat, back aching, head still thick. 'Did . . . does Granny know?' she asked.

'No.'

'Yes.'

The two voices overlapped. Her mother flushed; her father cleared his throat. 'You know how ill she is, darling, and eighty-six next birthday. She gets muddled anyway.'

Jane ignored his bluff, eased one chafing shoe. 'Except she's not my grandma, is she?' A great hole had opened up. Who was her real mother, her first and secret family? Was she a 'mistake'? Did she have a father – one who'd cared and wanted her, or was she just the product of some brief and sordid grope? 'Look, you've got to tell me who I am – who my mother is – was. I mean, is she even still alive?'

The silence seemed to scream, close tighter tighter round them, like a shroud. Their refusal to answer was surely a bad sign. Were they trying to hide some scandal – a mother who was criminal, or not right in the head? She might have those genes herself, be the daughter of a moron or a murderer. 'I've a right to know, haven't I? Uncle Peter said so, said I had to ask you, and if you won't tell me, *he* will.'

Her father suddenly jumped up, thumped his fist against the mantelpiece. 'I told you this would happen, Amy. I warned you from the start.'

'So now you're blaming me.'

'Yes, I am. It was absolutely crazy to try to keep it from her.'

'Why did you agree, then?'

'Because you went on and on and on until I did. You were bloody near hysterical.'

'I've never been hysterical. That's a downright lie. Do you honestly imagine that anyone hysterical would ever get a baby in the first place? They vetted us for years – those snooping bossy social workers – every word we said put under their microscopes, in case it proved we were cruel or lax or stupid. Of course it made me nervous. Can't you understand that?'

'I was there as well, you realise, but I suppose I didn't count. You always made me feel that, if you really want to know. It was *your* baby, wasn't it, never mine as well – your bloody pain and purgatory. All right, I'm not complaining. It was a lousy time for both of us, but that's not the point I'm making. We should have told her later, when things had quietened down and . . .'

'I'm tired,' said Jane. 'I'm going to bed. Okay?'

No one seemed to hear her, so she slunk towards the door, shambled up the stairs, still listening to their voices rising from below, accusing angry voices. She closed her bedroom door, hung her dress neatly on a hanger, removed her shoes, lined them up together in her wardrobe, placed the gold chain in its box, her tights back in their cellophane. She had always been untidy, a disappointment to them, not the child they wanted – the precise and careful daughter they would have obviously preferred. She folded back the counterpane as smoothly as she could, picked up her rag doll – the one she'd had since babyhood, the one made by her grandma – laid it face down on the floor.

It was time she slept alone.

8

'Did you leave that night?' asked Isobel.

'No,' said Jane. 'The next. I hadn't planned to leave at all, or thought it out or anything. But they wouldn't talk, you see. Daddy said my mother had gone down with a bad migraine, and he felt it wasn't fair to discuss things on his own. She stayed in bed all Sunday, pretending to be ill. It was just another cop-out.'

'Hard for her, as well, though.'

Jane shrugged. 'I suppose so. But I mean, the way she just avoided me and . . .' She heard her voice falter like a tired horse at a jump; eased away from Isobel, who had her arm around her — a hot and heavy arm which had been bolstering her for half an hour, helping her continue with the story. She mustn't mustn't cry again; had managed not to all that festering Sunday. 'It was really odd, you know,' she said, slapping at her wasp-sting to try to stop it throbbing. 'I was sort of numb inside, as if I'd died or shrivelled up. I couldn't cry, or even shout, or stand up to my father. We had this gruesome Sunday lunch together, just the two of us, pretending we were hungry, and talking about dahlias and next year's summer holiday. And then I found myself creeping out at midnight — except it wasn't me at all, but someone cool and callous, who had no qualms about upsetting them, or fears about the future — no feelings whatsoever. I was just a robot, really.'

'Poor robot,' whispered Isobel.

'No, don't be sorry for me. It only makes it worse.' Jane jumped down from the bed, let out a sudden laugh. 'Dahlias — I ask you! My whole life blown to bits and Daddy's into slug-killers.' She leaned against the balcony, hands gripping the top rail. 'I suppose you think I'm stupid, leaving home like that. I'm not sure why I did it now, except I was so shocked and shaken up, I just had to be alone. And once I reached the station, I got this crazy feeling that I had to go on running to the other end of England, maybe even go abroad. It seemed terribly important that I put some space between us – miles and miles, if possible – so I could think things out, decide on what I'd do.' She jabbed one foot with the other, clawed her sting again. 'I took my passport with me and all my birthday money, felt the further I could get from them, the safer I would be, and if I could only cross the Channel, then the sea would cut me off, cover up my traces, like footsteps on a beach. That's also why I avoided the south-west. My parents came from there originally, before they moved up north, you see, so I was scared they might alert the Bridgwater police, who'd check on any relatives and somehow hunt me down.'

Jane wiped her clammy hands, always felt a tug of fear when she thought of the police. 'Okay, you disapprove – I can see it on your face – but how could I have stayed there, gone on living with them as if things were just the same, or do what they were hoping and simply scoop the problem up like a lump of nasty dog's mess, chuck it in the dustbin and slam the lid on tight? I felt like an intruder in the house, there on false pretences.'

'Adoption's not like that, Rose. You're legally their child and . . .'

'That's what Daddy said. And my mother tried to tell me she was more "real" than my real mother, which is just a load of claptrap.'

'Well, I do know what she . . . '

'I'd actually asked her sometimes about my birth and everything – where she had me, was it painful, all that sort of stuff – and she was always very vague, or tried to change the subject, so I assumed she was embarrassed. She hates talking about bodies, or anything too personal. But now I've got this feeling that I wasn't born at all, just bought from some department-store, like a sofa, or a teapot.' Jane swung back to Isobel, crouched down by the bed. 'Look, how could she have lied to me like that?'

'People do lie, sadly. Out of fear, or shame, or . . .'

'You seem to be on *her* side.'

'No, I'm not. Of course I'm not. I'm just trying to see her point of view as well.' Isobel seemed shaken, gnawing on her thumbnail, forehead creased, hands taut. 'And I do realise how upset you feel, and probably very angry. Perhaps you even ran away to punish them a bit?'

'What d'you mean? They were punishing *me* – Daddy in particular. I mind about him most, you know. He's always been quite strict with me, laid the law down, told me what to do, but I knew he really loved me, and I had this sort of feeling that he and I were allies, ganging up on Mummy. Now I find it's just the opposite. They were in cahoots and . . .' Her stomach rumbled suddenly, a shameful plaintive gurgling, which swamped her final words.

'Was that you or me?'

'Me.' Jane clutched her midriff, blushing.

'You sound as if you're hungry.'

'Yes. Absolutely starving.'

Isobel peered down at her watch, a cheap one on a plastic strap, which looked as if it had been issued free with a gallon of Shell oil; contrasted strangely with her expensive antique rings. 'Good grief! Is that the time? Rowan's popping over with half a dozen chums and I promised I'd be there to cook them brunch. Come and join the party. I know she'd love to meet you, and once we've got some food inside us, you and me can sit and really talk. I think we need to, don't you? That's quite some shock you've had.'

'It's odd – I feel much better now, as if it didn't actually happen, not to me, at least, but was just some crazy story I watched on television.'

'I felt like that when Tom died. In fact, I laughed instead of cried at first, when they said there'd been a crash.'

Jane eased up to her feet. 'Do you still dream about it?'

'Yes. In colour. Always red.'

'So do I, but black and white – well, sort of ghostly grey, like no-man's-land, or . . .' A second growling rumble whinnied from her stomach.

'Food,' insisted Isobel, shaking out her skirt and collecting up stray hairpins from the bed. 'That's number one priority. Fancy kedgeree?'

'Mum, you're ruining that rice. It's gone all wet and soggy.'

'Give it time, my darling, and the water will boil off.'

'Time! It's been stewing for at least an hour already.'

'It's brown rice, which needs longer. Anyway, I've got to boil the eggs.'

'I'll do those,' Jane offered.

'No, you're the guest.'

'The invalid,' laughed Mark.

Jane flushed. Mark was studying medicine, and had attended to her wasp-sting, bound up her right arm, as much to stop her scratching it as to demonstrate his skills. He was Gill's fiancé, and Lisa was his sister, and the tall man in the purple cords was Rowan's next-door neighbour, and Neville was her boyfriend (curly hair and glasses), and the plump girl with a pony-tail was Kathy with a K. She'd got them straight, at last. They had burst in like an army, talking all at once, scattering the cats, setting off the boxer who was still barking in the garden; hugging her and Isobel with equal warmth and vigour, as if she were Rowan's younger sister, not a stranger and an interloper. Now they'd trooped off to the games-room for a table-tennis tournament, though nobody had eaten yet, just downed two rounds of coffee and one small bag of crisps. Only Mark and Rowan had stayed behind with Isobel. Mark was washing up, working through a pile of dirty dishes, which looked as if they'd accumulated over several days – or weeks. He washed up like a juggler, tossing plates and cups about, sculpting shapes from bubbles, or suddenly whirling round to recount some anecdote.

The whole kitchen seemed alive. Every gadget and utensil appeared to have leapt out of the cupboards, or erupted from the drawers, and were now jumbled on the worktops, each fighting for more space. The eight-foot-long pine table was all but lost beneath a stack of books and records, the remains of last night's supper, and a tide of folded washing – a twitching ginger cat curled up on the topmost sheets and shirts. Isobel was slicing bread, hacking off thick slices with jagged crumbly edges. Everything looked fattened up – the yeasty loaf, the portly cat, the plump cushions on the tubby chairs, the paunchy scarlet teapot, Isobel herself. She was nothing like her daughter. Rowan was much stiller, sitting at the table squeezing oranges for juice, her movements small and deft, whilst her mother rattled around her, beating sauces, stirring pots; her clothes and hair and jewellery jangling, bouncing, rippling, as she dived from sink to stove. Rowan's hair was short and neat, moulded to her head; her figure slim and spare, her quiet hands bare of rings or flashy bangles. Her most unusual feature was her eyes, eyes the tawny colour of a lion's, though nothing else about her seemed predatory or wild. She had a lion on her sweater, a fuzzy one with a stick-up mane made of loops of yellow wool, and a bashful red-wool smile.

Jane went to sit beside her, feeling more and more uncomfortable about the state of her own clothes. Her tracksuit was disgusting – creased and stained and sweaty – and she had nothing underneath it; had dragged it on in panic, when faced with what she thought was Christopher's wife.

'I . . . I think I'd better go and have a wash. I still smell of that foul wasp-killer.'

Isobel dipped a finger in the saucepan, grimaced as she burnt herself. 'Yes, pop upstairs. The water's nice and hot. Rowan will go with you, won't you, darling? Find Rose what she needs.'

Rowan led the way, pausing in the hall to remove a rubber bone from the gold-toned Persian rug. The house, like Isobel herself, was a disconcerting mixture of the tasteful and the garish. The living-room was furnished with graceful antique chairs; a nylon-covered sun-lounger plonked incongruously between them. The impressive grand piano had been used as a repository for tools, toys, sweets, knitting, even a hot water bottle. The pictures on the walls ranged from traditional gold-framed still-lifes to painful writhing abstracts, and one peculiar collage made from shells and torn-up bus tickets. Every room seemed over-stuffed, as if Isobel's possessions had mated with each other, and produced more hybrid offspring – ornaments and sculptures, photographs and silver cups, pouffes and rugs and cushions, grinning china dogs. Even the garden had crept in, clearly reluctant to remain within its boundaries outside. There were seed-trays in the study, and half a bag of compost; a broken-handled trug-basket reclining on a chair.

Jane glanced in at the doors again, as they walked on down the hall. Their sitting-room at home seemed naked in comparison – just a chintzy three-piece suite, *circa* 1980, and one print, of Van Gogh's *Sunflowers*. This house breathed Art and Culture, both with capitals, and she felt a shade uneasy, as if she'd entered a new world, and didn't know the signposts. That bronze bust on a plinth, for instance, and spiky metal sculpture – were they priceless modern art, or Isobel's own handiwork? She'd no idea, and dared not ask, for fear of revealing what a dunce she was.

Upstairs was much less daunting, though even on the landing there were several modern paintings – one she seemed to recognise: a charred and arid landscape, daubed in murky pigments. 'Is that Christopher's?' she asked.

'Yes,' said Rowan, frowning. 'I hate the way he always makes things ugly. I mean that's actually a beauty-spot, just a mile or two from here, a place which people flock to, because the view's so glorious, yet he has to go and spoil it.'

Jane said nothing. The picture magnetised her, seemed to draw her in to the sweep of barren hill. She wouldn't call it ugly – oppressive maybe, violent, but also grand and solemn.

'He did a portrait of my mother about fifteen years ago, made her look quite hideous when she was still young and rather stunning.'

'I couldn't see it, could I?'

Rowan shrugged, pushed the door in front of her, which opened to reveal an unmade double bed, a cluttered dressing table, and at least a dozen pictures jostling on the walls. The portrait was the largest; dark and deeply shadowed, save for the gold flame of the hair.

'It's almost cruel, I'd say – the way he's made the flesh so slack, and sort of hacked her into pieces.' Rowan turned her back, dismissing it, started sorting out her mother's clothes, which had been left jumbled on the bed. Jane stayed where she was, gazing at the face, a fragmented face exploding from its frame; the veins like knotted ropes which seemed to serpent from her hands, give them writhing life and power; one breast half-suggested, then lost in teasing shadow. She tried to check the likeness, but it was difficult to concentrate. Other painful images were fighting in her mind – Christopher and Isobel closeted together while he explored his willing subject, probing her and penetrating; the artist and his sitter intimate, familiar, bonded by the portrait, fused in it and merged. So he had known her fifteen years or more. She could never rival that, would never be the subject of an expensive formal portrait.

'You seem pretty taken with it.' Rowan shook out a patchwork skirt, returned it to the wardrobe.

'Well, it's got your mother's energy.'

'Energy! She looks more or less demented. I think what it really shows is Christopher's attitude to women. He's got to put them down, make them vile and loathsome. Not that I'm surprised. He's already gone through several wives, which is always a bad sign.'

'Several?' Jane swung round.

'Anne's the third, and I think the only reason *she* stays is she's so busy with her own career she hardly sees him anyway. You'd think he'd quieten down a bit now he's an old age pensioner.'

'A *what*?'

'Well, jolly nearly, anyway. He must be coming up to sixty.'

'He . . . he doesn't look it.' Jane leant against the wall, light-headed suddenly. It must be simple hunger. What was it to her that the artist was a fossil, a man older than her father, who'd chucked two wives on the scrap-heap? 'Look, I . . . I'd better have that wash.'

'Gosh – sorry! I should be showing you the bathroom, not my mother's art collection. Why not use the basin here, though? The bathroom's such a mess. I'll fetch you a clean towel.'

'I couldn't borrow an old sweater, could I? This tracksuit's really filthy. I came out in a hurry, and . . . '

'Yeah, 'course. I'll dig one out.'

Rowan padded back with two towels, an emerald sweater, and a pair of hot-pink dungarees. 'I've brought you these, as well. They're my favourites, actually, though they must be ten years old. Mum bought them as a present for me in the Portobello Road, when I was a horrid spotty schoolgirl with no clothes except my gym-slip.'

Jane mouthed her thanks, blinking at the colours.

'If they're a bit too long, you can roll the bottoms up. And do help yourself to talcum or anything you need. It's all there on the dressing table.'

'But won't your mother mind if I monopolise her room?'

'Mind? Of course she won't. Anyway, she's busy. Mum's a super cook – except for rice, I suppose, which she always seems to murder – but she likes to take her time. If she invites you round for breakfast, expect your eggs and bacon at half past twelve, or one, and if she calls it brunch' – Rowan grinned and shrugged – 'we'll probably eat by tea-time. Don't rush, anyway. I'll wait for you downstairs.'

'Thanks,' said Jane, then went to run some water, glancing at the unmade bed – sheets crumpled, slightly grubby, both pillows on the floor. She could well imagine Isobel tossing through the night, active even in her sleep, churning up the bedclothes, flinging pillows right and left as she threshed in scarlet dreams. What had Tom been like – the surgeon, the dead husband – vivacious, like his wife, or a quiet unruffled foil to her? There were photos of him everywhere – a tall and bony man, with a fringe of boyish hair, which contrasted with his wrinkled face, his worn and veiny hands. It must have been difficult for Rowan to have had her father die when she was only in her twenties. She felt a certain bond with her. They had both lost something vital, someone irreplaceable, except Rowan had a mother still, and a brother two years younger, who also featured widely in the photographs downstairs. All those smiling snapshots of brothers, fathers, kith and kin, were genuine in Rowan's case, not sham, as in her own.

She picked up the wedding photo standing on the dressing table – a slimmer shyer Isobel beaming at a young unwrinkled Tom. She tried to picture them in bed together, the first night of their honeymoon; Isobel's warm willing flesh melting into Tom's – except it wasn't Tom, but Christopher – an ardent violent Christopher, reaching out to Isobel, paint-stained hands grazing down her back, mouth open and . . .

She splashed cold water on her face, tried to kick the artist out from Rowan's mother's bed. It was clear Rowan didn't like him. Could that be a danger-sign, mean that Isobel and Christopher had in fact been closer than they should? She unzipped her tracksuit-top, scoured her neck and shoulders. Who cared anyway? Why should she upset herself about a man of nearly sixty who was obviously quite past it? She finished washing, sprayed herself from half a dozen bottles – deodorant and skin-tonic, and at least four brands of scent – then pulled on the green jersey, the showy dungarees. She had never worn such brilliant boastful colours, normally tried to lose herself in grey or brown or navy. She fastened the wide belt, examined her appearance in the mirror. She looked older somehow, wilder, a daring sort of girl, artistic and bohemian, who might well be the assistant to a famous stained-glass artist – one still in his thirties, who had never married, ever, and was waiting for a soul-mate.

She strode back to the kitchen, wishing she had green suede boots like Lisa's, instead of grubby trainers. Isobel was on the phone, alone, plumped down in a chair, shoes kicked off, skirt rucked up, spewing words in torrents, only pausing now and then to chew a wedge of orange, or mop juice from her chin. The brunch seemed quite forgotten. The gases were all off, the table still not laid. Only the cats and dog were eating – a tabby on the worktop licking butter from a plate; the boxer and the ginger tom gulping down some scraps. Isobel suddenly looked up, saw Jane at the door, startled to her feet, clutching the receiver.

'Rowan!'

'No, it's Jane.'

'*Who?*'

'Er, Rose.'

'Rose! You really threw me. You looked exactly like my daughter when she was just about fifteen. It was like jolting back ten years. Yes, I'm sorry, Eve, I'm here still, but I'd better ring off now. These poor loves are all starving, and . . . Rose, pop through to the sitting-room. The others are in there. Tell them nosh in fifteen minutes. Yes, Eve, of course I'll see her, only . . .'

Jane paused outside the sitting-room, too shaken to go in. Isobel had called her Rowan, and she herself had forgotten she was Rose. How confusing it all was. She had been wondering for a month now what her real names were – the name that she'd been given as soon as she was born; the surname of her mother – or father, if she had one. 'Rose,' she kept reiterating, before she joined the party and forgot herself again. 'Rose, Rose, Rose, Rose, Rose.' She liked the name, would stick with it – her third name in eighteen years.

'Rose!' the others all exclaimed, as they praised her change of outfit, told her she looked fabulous.

'Wow!' grinned Mark. 'You're blinding us. I'll have to get my sunglasses.' He was sprawling on the floor, squeezed up to make room

for her, yanked two cushions down for her to sit on. She didn't need
to talk much, since his red-haired sister, Lisa, was recounting a long
story about her other, younger brother, who had been expelled from
public school, then set up a market-stall with a cousin aged sixteen.
Brother, sister, cousin – how casual it all sounded. Normal for most
people to have siblings and real families. Maybe she did, too – rebel
brothers, red-haired sisters, just waiting to be found. She glanced
down at her emerald sleeve clashing with the pink knee underneath
it. Could that be really her? Perhaps her mother was an artist, who'd
worn flamboyant clothes herself, had a house stuffed full of sculptures, with portraits on the walls. The artist-mother swelled, filled
her head, the room. She'd had so many mothers in just the last short
month – countesses and raddled slags, teenage drop-outs, pop stars.

'What d'you do?' asked Kathy, leaning down to offer her some
nuts. 'For your job, I mean.'

'I work for a stained-glass artist,' she said, what she hoped was
nonchalantly. Maybe art was in her genes, and she would reveal some
natural flair, prove indispensable.

'You've met him, Kath,' said Rowan, pulling at a loose thread
on her sweater. 'You know, Mum's friend – Christopher Harville-
Shaw.'

There was a sudden awkward silence. Kathy cleared her throat;
Rowan peered intently at her hands, as if she were reading something
printed on them, which required her total concentration. Jane shifted
on the floor. Was there some mystery about Christopher – something
he'd done wrong? She crammed in more cashews, choking down
a spurt of anger, as well as just the nuts. What right had they to
judge him? None of *them* could make a stained-glass window, or
create red birds which ripped right through your mind. She reported
Isobel's message about food in fifteen minutes, deliberately changing
the subject before she lost her cool.

'Multiply by four,' said Rowan, uncurling from her chair. 'We'd
better have a drink, to fill the hole.' She rummaged in the sideboard,
juggling several bottles. 'There's not a lot of choice – a tiddly bit of
gin, some sherry which looks past it, one measure of Jack Daniels,
and something called Kahlua.'

'I'll have that,' said Mark.

'What is it – a liqueur?'

'Yes, Mexican, I think. Sort of coffee-flavoured, and pretty strong,
as far as I remember. I had some, once, in Acapulco.'

Rowan filled a glass and sniffed it, nodding her approval. 'Some
for you as well, Rose?' Jane paused. She never touched liqueurs, had

been warned since she was twelve or so about the dangers of strong drink. 'Yes,' she said. 'Why not?'

'Let's have some music, too,' said Gill, joining Rowan at the sideboard, and annexing the gin. 'Has your Mum got any records?'

'Only symphonies and stuff. Or there might be some of Hadley's. I'm not sure if he took them when he moved out to his flat. If you rifle through that cupboard there, you might dig out something interesting.'

Jane gulped her dark liqueur, which set her throat on fire; the first innocuous coffee-tang followed by a scorching searing aftertaste. She felt strangely hot already, as if the fireball of her wasp-sting had affected her whole body. Perhaps she had a temperature, or was sickening for some virus. Wasn't brandy medicinal, so why not Kahlua?

Gill had found a record, put it on full volume. The whole room seemed to tremble. Jane could feel the carpet shaking underneath her, the ornaments and sculptures shuddering on their ledges – or was it her own body, pulsing from the sting? Somebody was speaking to her, but she couldn't make the words out. 'Yes,' she said uncertainly. Safer to say yes, to hold on tight, not let herself unravel.

'What's the record?' Neville yelled above the din.

'Glen Miller's Swinging Big Band,' Gill bellowed back, thumping out the rhythm on her thigh. 'It was either that, or Verdi's Requiem.'

'Let's dance,' said Lisa, springing up and grabbing hold of Neville.

'Dance? You must be joking. It's not even lunch-time yet.'

'Who cares? I'm feeling bouncy. And that rhythm's really great. Come on, you old fogies! I'm your compère for "Come Dancing".'

The man in purple corduroys whisked Jane to her feet, pushed the chairs and sofa back, then clutched her to his chest; elbows out, head tilted. 'We're Gavin and Sharon and we both live in Southend. We've been dancing seven years together and our hobbies are canaries and . . .'

Jane tried to force a laugh. He'd been drinking the Jack Daniels, exhaled it in her face as he hummed a boom-boom descant to the band. She stumbled suddenly, felt Uncle Peter's sweaty hand groping her bare back; could smell his whisky breath, mixed up in her mind with the sweet and poisonous taste of Southern Comfort. She closed her eyes a moment, dizzy and disoriented. The music was the same – dangerous whining saxophone, angry pounding drums.

'Excuse me,' someone said. It sounded like her own voice. She was trying to pull away, escape her Uncle Peter, leave that wild hotel room, the sixty-seven guests; but the dance-floor slowly somersaulted, and she was swaying, tipping, plunging down to meet it.

9

'Better?' Christopher enquired, hardly bothering to look up from his desk.

'Yes,' said Jane. 'I'm sorry.'

'What are you sorry for?'

'Well, fainting, being ill, not turning up on Monday.'

'You can't help being ill.'

'No,' she said, though she still somehow felt responsible. After all, she had let the wasps in.

'Isobel was worried, said you had a temperature. Are you sure you should be up?'

She nodded. 'It was just a sort of freak thing. The doctor said a sting can do that sometimes, affect you like an allergy, make you feverish.' She suddenly looked up, realised what was missing. 'Hey,' she said, swinging past him to the window. 'What's happened to the birds?'

'They flew away,' said Christopher.

She stared. The whole studio looked different; lighter altogether, without the fiery panels masking the main window, yet somehow also barren, as if someone had undressed it, removed its fancy clothes. A presence had been lost, the sense of speed and vigour, the almost dizzy motion of threshing beaks and wings, the whip and snap of scarlet.

He smiled at her shocked face. 'Don't worry, they'll be back. I packed them off to be fired. I usually do my own firing – and it's a damned sight cheaper, actually – but I'm getting really pushed for time, and it'll save at least a week. Fortunately, my fee for that commission was rather on the high side. Not that Adrian seemed to mind.' He laughed, stubbed out his Marlboro. 'I reckoned if he can make five hundred grand from one hiccough on the stock market, or a flicker of his screen, then he's hardly going to fret about a minor bill like mine.'

Jane gazed out at the sweep of fields which had been blocked from view till now. It seemed wrong to mix up money with stained glass. Oh, she knew it was his livelihood and he had to earn his bread (or maybe his smoked salmon), but she disliked his mocking tone, his suggestion he could rook the rich. He must be pretty rich himself, what she'd call top-drawer. He always looked well-heeled, even now, in working clothes – jeans and husky sweater. Did men of sixty still wear jeans, or had Rowan been exaggerating, adding on a decade merely to insult him?

He was poking at his fag-end, as if he regretted having put it out, or hoped it might revive. 'This Civic Centre job is going to be the big one, Rose, so I need to free my time and energies for that.'

'But what about the window?' Isobel's commission. Isobel had nursed her, cooked her meals the last few days, even bought her clothes. She didn't want Tom's window pushed out in the cold.

'I'm working on the preliminaries now, hope to finish it by the end of March. I've been in touch with Anthony – the vicar – discussed my plans with him, and we both agreed that Easter would be the ideal time for the dedication ceremony. I mean, it fits the Resurrection theme, and has all the connotations of new life, rebirth and so on. The only disadvantage is that Easter's very early, and what with Christmas in between, I'll have to get my skates on, and I'm definitely going to need some extra help.'

'You mean, you're hiring an assistant?' Jane tried to keep her voice cool; sound casual and offhand.

'I've got one.' His voice was cool as well; his attention on his work again.

She dragged back to his desk, stood level with his shoulder. He must have fixed it up while she'd been away at Isobel's, taken advantage of her absence and her illness. Or maybe Isobel had phoned him, changed his mind, given him the same long and rambling spiel she'd received herself last night: how she was basically unsuited to the job, and could hardly help an artist when she was totally untrained, might even prove a hindrance. She had listened in glum silence, wondering why the older woman was trying to warn her off. Was it genuine concern, or grudging envy?

'Where is she?' she asked coldly, glancing round the studio. Her rival was bound to be a female – some skilful fellow artist, voluptuous and enchanting, working tête-à-tête with Christopher, while she returned to camping out, jobless and a nomad.

'Here.' He touched her arm. 'Take your coat off, Rose, and that extraordinary new outfit you're wearing underneath it, and be back down here in five minutes flat in your oldest working-clothes.'

She rocketed to the bedroom, returned in Rowan's jeans and a cardigan of Isobel's, found the artist tearing off the wrappings from a tall and bulky parcel. 'Right,' he said, pushing back his sweater sleeves, and revealing forearms tangled with dark hairs. 'I'd like your help tacking up these cartoons on the wall.'

'What cartoons?' she asked, already baffled.

He hauled a roll of paper from the parcel – stout white paper, tightly furled and standing four foot high. 'This is a cartoon. It doesn't mean a comic strip' – he grinned – 'but a photographic blow-up of my original design. When you make a window, you start with your design, or sketch, which is your blueprint, so to speak, and which you draw to scale, in colour – say, an inch to a foot. Then you get it blown up to the full size of the window, and from that you make your cutline.'

She tried to concentrate. What she was seeing in her mind was not a photographic blow-up, but the strip of bare brown flesh which had appeared between his sweater and his low-slung hipster jeans, when he'd leant towards the parcel – just an inch of naked back, which somehow made her nervous. She wished he had more clothes on – a vest, a coat, a suit of armour – something to protect her from the idea of his nakedness – those dark hairs on his forearms now sprouting on his chest, even creeping down his stomach . . .

'You also need the cartoon to trace important details on the glass – say a face, or an inscription, or a fold of drapery.' Christopher was opening up a stepladder, a tall one with a wooden platform-top; shinned swiftly up it, one arm round the roll. She was surprised by his agility, the way he seemed so little hampered by his load.

'You have to work in sections with a window so damned big. This is the main middle section, which I'm going to pin just here – not too high, otherwise it's difficult to reach. Can you foot the ladder while I lean across? That's it. We'll start with the left-hand light, and then tack up the right one. Now, I want you to tell me if it's absolutely straight, Rose – no dipping down to one side.' He pinned the top two corners, then let the roll unfurl. 'Pass me some more drawing pins. They're down there on that ledge.'

She dropped a scattering on the floor, clumsy from sheer nerves. If she was to work as his assistant, then she had to prove herself, and this was her first trial. It was hardly any test of skill to hold a ladder steady, but any minute now, he might faze her with some daunting task.

He dismounted from the ladder, moved it over a foot or two, to fix the right-hand light, then clambered down a second time, still eyeing the cartoon, but stepping slowly backwards, so he could view it at a distance. She followed both his steps and eyes, stopping with a sense of shock as the blur of random lines suddenly transformed into a figure. The lines had meant little to her while she'd been standing right up close – just a jumbled disarray of shapes she couldn't quite decipher. Now a powerful soaring creature, half-human and half-bird, seemed to scorch up to the sky; streaming hair uplifted, wings of feathered steel. Its bottom half was missing, and it was sliced off at the forehead, but even so, the effect was overwhelming. The studio was once again alive – electrified, dynamic.

'The Resurrection Angel,' Christopher informed her, his whole attention fixed on the cartoon. 'It's quite a challenge nowadays to make an angel convincing, avoid those sickly stereotypes the Victorians went in for, poncing in their nighties or mooning over lilies. I've tried to catch the essence of an angel, refine it down, remember it's a spirit – something higher than mere man, a sacred intermediary between this world and the next.' Jane was startled by his tone. He sounded like a devout committed godman, not the atheist and cynic he had claimed to be before. How could he believe in angels, or in another higher world, when he'd dismissed such things the day they'd met as childish wishful thinking? Yet his Angel was so supercharged, it compelled belief, demanded it; seemed indeed a spirit with more power than its creator.

'What happens at the top?' she asked. 'Do you have clouds or sky or . . . ?'

'I'll show you on the sketch,' he said, tugging open the middle drawer of a sturdy wooden chest, and bringing out a drawing mounted on black card.

She could see the whole design now – his Resurrection Angel complete with feet and forehead, but in glowing jewel-like colours, and looking like a miniature compared with its huge copy on the wall. The word 'sketch' seemed far too casual for this careful detailed drawing, enclosed in a two-light window shape, complete with tracery. It looked a work of art itself, the Angel's potency undimmed, despite its modest size.

'The sketch is really crucial,' Christopher was saying. 'All your ideas and energy go into the design, whereas the glass itself just interprets those ideas. And you keep it handy right through the whole process, refer to it continually, because you can never see the whole of the window all at the same time – at least, not when you're working on this scale.' He handed her the drawing – reluctantly, she sensed, as if he feared to lose control of it. 'The whole project stands or falls on this design. It's how you present your window in the first place, not just to the donor, but to all those crass committees, who may try to modify it, or even turn it down. Frankly, I won't compromise. I have to do what I know and feel is right, and if the philistines don't like it, they can . . .' He made a hostile gesture, to fill in for the words; continued talking, now pacing up and down.

'But you're still constrained by other things – especially the architecture itself. St Mark's is fifteenth-century, and it's always rather tricky trying to fit a modern window into a building so much older; match the ancient with the new. And the south side has its own particular problems. The light's most changeable that side, and also most intense, which affects your choice of colour. Too much red or yellow and the whole thing looks too hot – maybe even crude.' He glanced back at his sketch again, as if rechecking his decisions. 'I've used mainly blues and greens, which I feel are right symbolically. Blue's a spiritual colour, which gives the feel of sky and space, suggests heaven and a higher world; and green's for Resurrection – spring, rebirth, and so on.'

'How long did it take?' Jane asked, admiring the gradation from a perky lichen green beneath the angel's feet to a streaky slatey hazy blue, which finally misted into the white and gold of heaven. 'I mean just to do the sketch?'

'Only a couple of weeks of actual drawing, but a heck of a lot of thinking out beforehand. I kept it sort of simmering in my head, pushing images around, or mulling over colours, when I was in the bath, or driving, or cutting glass for someone else's job. I sometimes even dreamed about it. One night, I saw the Angel in a dream, which gave me the idea of having it break across both lights. That provides a sort of jolt, you see, unifies the window, draws both sides together.'

'The Angel's like a bird,' said Jane, examining the wings, which seemed to lift off as she watched.

'Yes, deliberately. Birds are symbols of the soul – and spirits again, spirits of the air, the spirit freed from the body, so it can soar up into heaven, and therefore very apt in Tom's case. And, like angels, they're commuters between this world and the next. In fact, they're sometimes used as messengers of angels. I tried to fuse the two – create a bird with a human face, and with hair as well as wings. Birds are such intense things. They have a very high body temperature, as high as a hundred and ten degrees, and amazingly fast heart-rates, especially when they're flying – over a thousand beats a minute for a small bird like a tit, and double that for a humming-bird, which is really quite incredible.' The artist seemed intense himself, speaking with a vehemence he never used in normal conversation. Did he identify with birds – their vitality and speed, the way they fought for space and freedom, fought against enclosure or any clipping of their wings; always vibrating with alarm and nervous energy? She compared her own quiet father, whose safe job in insurance was something passive and routine, never galvanised him, roused him, and who lived tamely in his cage at home, content with seed and water, and a few simple plastic toys.

'I've put three small birds down here, as well.' Christopher leant over, pointed to the border at the bottom of the sketch, beneath the Angel's feet. 'They're all resurrection symbols – the phoenix because it rises from the ashes; the eagle which renews its plumage by flying up to the sun, and the dove holding out a palm branch, which means victory over death.'

Jane couldn't really recognise the species. They'd been simplified, abstracted, only made explicit by their emblems – the fire, the sun, the palm. She was beginning to feel a total ignoramus; had never understood before how much thought and knowledge went into stained glass. Up till now, it had been nothing really more for her than a few stuffy saints in simple standard colours.

'The birds relate to Tom, as well,' Christopher explained. 'The phoenix stands for mercy and compassion, because it won't eat any living thing, or even tread on grass or plants. The eagle is said to have dominion over all the other birds, and so represents authority and power, and the dove is peace and gentleness. Thomas was a gentle soul, active in the peace movement, but also had the power and skills of a top-rank medico. He was also maddeningly untidy, rather mean with money, and hopeless with his kids. But since the window's in his honour, we only stress his good points.' He laughed, fumbled for his cigarettes, which were squashed in his back pocket. 'I took the eagle from the surgeons' coat of arms. It's the crest of their Royal College, so it's relevant twice over. Isobel suggested the serpent twined round a staff, which is the symbol of medicine in general, and is also included on the surgeons' coat of arms, but I didn't want the thing to get too cluttered. Mind you, I've done enough serpents in my time. They're symbols of so many things in so many different cultures, you could write a damned great book about it.'

He leant back against the wall, exhaled a curl of smoke as he studied his cartoon again. 'I'm still not happy with the face. It's not quite strong enough. Sometimes, when you get your sketch enlarged, a few details just don't seem to work. Perhaps I'll have another bash at it before I make my cutline.' He suddenly turned to look at her, eyes full on her face, his Marlboro drooling ash as he appraised her hair and features. 'I'll use you as my model, Rose. You've got good bones, and the sort of hair an angel would be proud of.'

She flushed right to that hair. 'But I look a mess, and I'm wearing my old clothes and . . .'

'Never mind your clothes. It's your eyes I'm more concerned with. I like the way your eyebrows sit. Eyebrows are important, even for an angel. Move nearer to the window, please, and sit sideways to it, could you, so your face is half in shadow. No, don't drop your head like that. Look straight at me, okay?'

He went to fetch his sketch-book, pulled a stool up close to her, stared at her intently before making his first marks. All her imperfections seemed to swell and shout; the mole on her right cheek, the tiny spot which had erupted on her chin last night and now seemed hot and huge; the split ends on her hair, which needed trimming. And yet he'd praised her hair, praised her bones, her eyebrows. She felt suddenly important. The Angel-bird would have her face. She'd be included in the window, turned into a spirit, a messenger between two worlds.

She tried to sit as still as possible, make her expression worthy of an angel; not fret at Christopher's scrutiny, but simply look right through him, as if she were gazing into heaven. He didn't say a word, just kept on drawing vigorously and swiftly, his charcoal squeaking on the paper, one piece even snapping. She was aware of a new bond between them – he duplicating her, in charcoal – or perhaps even recreating her, like God. She had his whole attention now, and the silence in the studio seemed to emphasise the importance of the project; make it almost spiritual, as if they were both in church, or involved in some strange rite.

'That'll do,' he said, at last, laying down his pad and squinting up at the cartoon. 'I may need to have another shot, but these will get me started.' He went to fetch tubes of paint and brushes, while she examined her own face, surprised by it, yet flattered. Although he'd caught her likeness, he had transformed her mood and character, made her both more strange and more exciting; exaggerated all her basic features – her full mouth gaping wide, her deep-set eyes looking haunted and half-lost beneath jutting jagged brows; her hair alive, electric.

Christopher was swarming up the ladder, setting down his painting things on its sturdy platform-top. 'This may take some time, Rose. I want to change the hair, as well. Hair like yours is rare. I should have met you earlier, when I was grappling with my original design.' He leaned down to touch the hair, pick up one long strand. She stood rigid and embarrassed, uncertain what to do. Was this just another part of his artistic scrutiny, a closer reappraisal of the shade and length and texture of her hair, or an advance she should rebuff? She felt chained to him by the fetters of her hair, chained by something else – something much less tangible, which both baffled and alarmed her. He gave her hair a final teasing tug, then let it go, at last. 'While I'm working, I'd like you to start clearing away the glass. I left it around deliberately, so you'd get the hang of handling it, and learn where all the different pieces go.'

'But won't you need it for the window?'

'Maybe some of it, but I've ordered new glass, chosen it specifically. Choosing the right glass is all part of the job – and a vitally important part. Anyway, I like to clear my studio before I start on a new job. It's essential to be disciplined when you're working in stained glass. It's a very dusty, bitty sort of process – chaotic, you might say – so you have to keep things orderly and tidy, so you can lay your hands on exactly what you want.'

Jane said nothing. He sounded like her father. She was scared she'd let him down, also frightened of the glass itself; worried that she'd break it, or even cut herself. It was all around the studio – large sheets propped against the walls, smaller bits and pieces lying on the worktops, fragments crushed to powder, or ground into the floor.

The artist prowled down from the ladder, seized a sheet himself, as if too impatient to wait for her to start; calling out instructions as he returned it to its rack. 'Any whole or half-sheets put back in these racks. They're all marked with their colours, but if you're not sure about a certain shade, then ask. The smaller offcuts go into these boxes, again sorted into colours. And all the really tiddly bits, just sweep up with a brush and dump in here – which is what we call the cullet box. I suggest you wear a pair of gloves until you're more used to handling glass.'

He tossed a scrap of blue glass in the box, then turned his back, started rooting through a cupboard. 'Come here,' he ordered curtly, as if he were summoning his dog. She approached him apprehensively, flinched away as he reached his arms towards her. He had already touched her hair; was he trying now to grope her? She blushed at her mistake, as she realised he was holding out an apron, merely endeavouring to tie it round her middle. Even so, his hands felt very intimate, lingering too long as they fumbled at her waist. 'That will help to keep you clean,' he said. 'Your clothes get really grubby working with stained glass, and you'll find the fragments creep in everywhere – down your nails, in your hair, even in your shoes.'

He was still standing very close to her, the prickle of his sweater seeming to chafe against her body, though she wasn't actually touching it. She tried to edge away, felt disturbed and threatened somehow, as if he were dangerous like the glass. Did he really need her there as his assistant? Isobel had told her he never worked with anyone on principle; preferred to concentrate alone, without noise or interruptions; resented any invasion of his privacy. So why had he invited her to live, as well as work there, and why had she returned? After all, Isobel had offered her a bed, urged her to stay longer, promised she would help her find another, more appropriate job. Yet she had somehow felt suspicious of the older woman's motives; feared she wanted the artist for herself.

'Right,' she said. 'I'll make a start.' That provided an excuse for her to move, though he followed, with a pair of gloves, and a few final points about sorting tints and colours, and how she must hold them to the light to see them clearly.

'Don't look so terrified. The stuff won't bite, you know. You need to just relax with it.'

'Okay,' she said, wishing that were easier; wondering why she felt so tense; why he had that strange effect on her – a mixture of excitement, agitation, and sheer nerves. She pulled on the leather gloves, tried to fix her whole attention on the racks. She'd run through all their names first, then try to check the colours against the sheets of glass inside. The names themselves were strange, chalked in red above each rack – spoilt ruby, copper ruby, and something called streaky gold ruby, which was a vivid blue and fuchsia shade, with no gold in it at all. Even the whites, which she would have expected to be simple, confused her with their intricate varieties – warm white, cold white, seedy white and reamy white, green-blue-white, white opal. She admired their subtle shades – the palest, most ethereal tints of green or grey or amethyst, which seemed to fade still further when she held them to the light, so they were transformed to ghostly pearl, or watered silk.

She began to move the largest sheets, handling them as boldly as she dared, though forced to pause each time, as she tried to judge their colour, decide on where they went. She glanced across at Christopher, who was now standing on the stepladder, reaching halfway up the wall, repainting the face on the cartoon. He wasn't checking up on her, seemed to trust her totally, apparently unworried about his precious costly glass. She liked the fact they were working as a team; must aim to copy his own drive and dedication, somehow make him proud of her, surprise him with her skills, and also prove to Isobel that she'd been wrong, wrong, wrong, wrong, wrong.

She started sorting all the smaller pieces, collecting them together, so that she could grade them into colours; surprised by their odd shapes, their veined and rippled textures; some like hazy cloud forms, some like swirling rivers. She felt almost like a child, who'd been entrusted with a new expensive toy – the same sense of gloating pleasure tinged with apprehension, for fear she'd break or spoil it. She hated throwing out the fragments, which, despite their tiny size, still seemed too rare and lustrous to toss into a rubbish box. She dithered for some time over a small but very chunky piece in a dazzling pinkish red, which appeared to glow and smoulder, as if she'd snatched it from the embers of a fire.

'Christopher,' she called.

'Mm?' he said, not looking round, his head tilted at an angle as he reached up to paint the hair.

'I don't know where to put this bit. There's nothing else quite like it, either in the boxes or the racks.' She stood beneath the ladder, held it up to him.

'You deserve a medal!' he exclaimed, leaning down to look. 'I've been searching for that piece for months. It's a bit of streaky gold-pink, the most expensive glass you can buy. I got it from this amazing chap who'd been working in stained glass since the age of twelve or so, and eventually took over from his father. I knew him pretty well, and when he died at ninety-three, his son allowed me first refusal on all his stocks of glass. I bought some really choice pieces at half the trade price. This particular piece is probably Edwardian.' Christopher shifted on the ladder, so he could hold it to the light. 'See how thick it is? That makes the colour richer and more concentrated – so delicious I could eat it.' He laughed, raised it to his mouth, pretended to be chewing.

Jane realised from the growlings in her stomach that it must be well past lunch-time. Would lunch be scraps of glass – red for meat-course, pink for pink blancmange, washed down with dirty paint-water? The artist's mind seemed far from food. 'It's like the inside of a rose,' he said, still fixated on his jewel of glass. 'You know, those damned great damask roses which are so intense in colour they seem to be alive and almost hot. Hey! I've just had an idea.' He grabbed his brush again, turned back to his cartoon, started changing some small detail in the border.

'What are you doing?' Jane was trying to watch, but his arm obscured her vision.

'I'm going to put you in the window – not just your face, your name.'

'What name?' asked Jane, confused; moving round, so she could get a better view.

'Well, Rose, of course. I've got these little blobs of colour dotted round the border, but I'll turn them into roses in your honour. It'll be a private thing between us. As far as Isobel's concerned, they'll be just another symbol – and, actually, they'll fit extremely well. I mean, roses have always been associated with eternal life – lush and blooming in a perfect endless spring. The Romans used to plant them in their funerary gardens for just that very reason, or scatter them on graves.' He squeezed more paint from his tubes of black and white, dabbing at his palette, mixing with his brush. 'And their thorns are meant to signify pain and wounds and blood, which all tie in well with Tom's job as a surgeon. But as far as we're concerned, Rose, they'll be there for you – your emblem – and a pretty potent one; the flower of love, of feminine perfection, the flower most praised by poets, artists, writers, mystics, lovers – and my own small way of making you immortal.'

Jane turned away to hide her face, which must match the blushing glass. Was he teasing her, or mocking, or could he mean it seriously? She struggled for a moment between elation, pride and guilt – guilt because she wasn't Rose. Writers, artists, mystics, lovers, hadn't deigned to mention Jane. Should she own up now before he worked a sham into the glass? He might be really furious if he found out later on, realised she'd deceived him, that her name meant 'plain', not feminine perfection. 'Christopher, there's something I should . . .'

'Pass the sketch up, can you, Rose. I need to check the top part of the border.'

She went to fetch it for him, checking it herself first, noting that the little dots of colour went all around the outside of the window, to form a lively abstract border. If he changed them into roses, her emblem would sing out, define the two tall lights. And if the Angel had her face and hair, then it would almost be her window. Isobel might be putting up the cash, but was that really as important as serving as the model? Why shouldn't she be Rose? She had chosen it herself, and Christopher could render it official. It could even be a new start in her life. Isobel had urged her to phone her parents, tell them she was safe; even consider going home to try to make her peace with them. Far better to stay here and be made immortal in a window. Stained glass endured for centuries, defying wind and weather, whereas everything she had left behind was precarious and crumbling, likely to capsize.

'Thanks, Rose,' the artist muttered, as she handed him the sketch, and she stood a moment, silent, as if to accept her formal christening, while he drew a second rose-shape, a rough but robust-looking flower with a splint of thorns supporting it.

'I suppose it's the paradox of roses which has always fascinated people – I mean, a flower of such great beauty on a savage thorny stem. It's a bit like light and darkness, or joy and suffering – one pointing up the other.' He outlined one last leaf, then flicked the water off his brush, spattering the floor. 'Saint Ambrose claimed that before the Fall, roses had no thorns, and it was only Adam's sin which put them there.'

'D'you think there really was a Fall?' Jane reached up to take the brushes from him, helped him put his paints away.

'Oh, yes – no doubt about it. Man's a fallen creature. Maybe not the apple and the serpent, but some other foul temptation in another squandered paradise. Mind you, it gives me quite a kick to think we're fallen angels. I'd rather be a Lucifer than some unfallen bloody drone. Right, can you do your ladder bit again – hold it nice and steady while I pin my cutline on top of the cartoon.'

She wondered what a cutline was. He always assumed she was familiar with the terms; seemed to take it as read that anybody reasonably intelligent could make a stained-glass window, or at least understand the processes. He darted to a corner of the studio, returned with a tall roll of what looked like tracing paper, and as he climbed the ladder with it and let it hang down from the wall, she noticed that the outline of the window-shape had been drawn in on the paper, plus a series of thick lines running horizontally across it.

'What are those?' she asked, pointing to the lines, which had been ruled in bold black pencil, every foot or so.

'They indicate where the saddle-bars will go.' He saw her frown, shrugged a shade impatiently as he realised she was none the wiser, maybe even more confused. 'Saddle-bars are metal supports which go across the inside of the window, and are drilled into the stonework on each side. The glass panels are tied to them with short lengths of copper wire, which are soldered to the leads, then twisted tightly round the bars to hold them in position. They stop the glass from blowing out, or buckling.' He paused to ram a pin in, hard, sucked his smarting thumb. 'Stained-glass windows are always made in sections, each panel roughly three feet high. It goes back to the Middle Ages, when everything was based on what a man could handle comfortably. The same holds good today, of course. You couldn't lug a ten-foot panel up a ladder or a scaffold.' He sweated down his own ladder, stood a pace or two away from it, eyes fixed on his cutline.

'I always rather enjoy this bit, and in one way you could say it's the most crucial stage of all. I've got to think out how to break the window down, decide where I want my leadlines, then trace them on this paper. It's important that I get it right, because, apart from defining the images, and giving tension to the whole design, it's the leads which hold the window together. I also use the cutline when I come to cut all the individual glass-shapes. And, later on, the glaziers use it too, when they're leading up the panels. It's their guide as well, you see, helps them position everything exactly in its place.'

She didn't see, decided to admit it. 'Look, I'm sorry to be thick, Christopher, but I'm getting rather muddled. I'm still not really sure what a cutline is – or leadlines, come to that.'

'Okay,' he said, leaning back against the ladder. 'Let's start at Isobel's front door. Remember that glass-picture she's got set in to the upper half – that tiny autumn landscape with the sunburst?'

Jane nodded, liked the picture. It seemed appropriate for Isobel to have a cheerful yellow sun blazing on her threshold, regardless of the rain or gloom beyond it.

'In the building trade, that sort of thing is known as leaded lights, but in fact it's a basic stained-glass window, and you'll see them all around the place, in pubs and public libraries, and in hundreds of private houses, from Victorian times right through to the thirties.' Christopher was fiddling with the pin-box. His hands seemed always restless, unless they were busy with a cigarette or paintbrush. 'Next time you're at Isobel's, look closely at her door, and you'll see the picture's been made up of lots of little pieces of different coloured glass, held together with strips of lead – rather like a mosaic, except the leads are actually part of the design. And because those leads are so important, you need to mark them on the cutline, so that they outline the shape of each separate piece of glass. It's quite a tricky process, since you have to think out several things at once. I mean, every piece must be manageable in size, so it fits into the kiln, and has no awkward curves or angles, which are difficult to cut. And of course you're considering scale and colour, not only in themselves, but in relation to the building, and the setting as a whole. And then you have to decide whether you want a leadline to break across a form, rather than define it, and what width of lead you'll use. I'll show you in a moment, when I've made a few decisions as to exactly where I want my leads.'

He swept out to the kitchen, returned with two large cans. 'Want a beer?' he offered, ripping them both open, so that they frothed across his hands.

'Thanks,' she said, wincing at the bitter taste, as she copied him by drinking from the can. She would have preferred a chicken sandwich, or, better still, the late but lavish lunches she'd enjoyed at Isobel's. Every meal at the Mackenzies' had seemed a wild amalgam of breakfast, dinner, tea – eggs served up with chocolate cake, pork chops after muesli. She smiled as she remembered.

'You look pleased with life.'

'Yes,' she said, 'I am.' Her own words startled her. Why should she be pleased with life when she was a runaway, a stray, her whole world overturned? Yet it no longer seemed to matter quite so much. This studio was now her base, and Christopher her mentor – or almost more her team-mate as they stood swilling beer together, like two relaxed and equal colleagues. She felt happy in his studio, liked its mood and atmosphere: the faint and subtle smells of linseed oil and dust; the way the winter sunlight fell in bars across the floor; the browns and greys of barren fields surrounding it, contrasting with the coloured glass inside. And each week she'd get her pay, which was a huge relief when she'd been faced with the grim prospect of slow starvation or begging on the streets. The pay was only basic, but it was cash in hand, which would save her from officialdom, and she had bed and board thrown in. She also liked the fact that she was learning, moving beyond her parents' way of seeing things myopically, with no long-distance view. Christopher's keen vision swept angels from the sky, penetrated sunbursts. He was still glancing at his cutline, gesturing with his beer-can as he talked.

'When I first started working in stained glass, the leads seemed horribly frustrating, a real constraint which tied me down, but I gradually found a way of using them expressively, not just to allow a change of colour, but so they'd play a part themselves in the whole impact of the window, make it more active, more alive.' He drained the last few drops of bitter, wiped his mouth. 'You see, any stained-glass artist worth the name is aiming at a sense of spontaneity, despite the technical restraints. The images mustn't look inert, or imprisoned in the window, but should move as the light moves, one flowing into the other.' He tossed his beer-can in the bin, fussed back to his cutline, as if he already regretted having wasted four whole minutes; busied himself with flattening out the bottom, repositioning the pins. 'It'll take me a good week or more to make this pair of cutlines, and it's no good trying to rush it. Stained glass is a slow, laborious business, with several distinct stages. You have to take each one in turn, submit to the rhythm of that particular process, give it all it needs in terms of time and patience. It's a different thing entirely when you're working on a canvas. I've known some artists who can knock off a small landscape in an hour, but any two–light window will take at least three months, and double that if you include the whole design stage. And yet it must look fresh and vigorous, not laboured.'

Jane glanced up at his back. Laboured was the last word she would use. Everything he did seemed energetic, lively – even now, his movements deft and quick. He looked boyish from behind; his slim hips outlined by the jeans, his hair stubborn in its thickness, as if it had obstinately refused to thin or disappear, as most men's seemed to do once they had passed the age of fifty. He adjusted one last pin, jumped down from the ladder.

'It's funny, really, most modern ways of making things have speeded up dramatically, yet stained glass has hardly changed at all since the twelfth and thirteenth centuries. They didn't use a paper cutline, or have fast efficient kilns like ours, but almost all the other processes were just the same as now. In fact, if a medieval glazier were to stroll in here, he'd probably feel perfectly at home. Though he might be rather envious of my carbon-wheel glass-cutter, ask if he could swap it for his rough and ready grozing iron.' He laughed, strolled down to the sink, to empty out his paint-water, rinse his dirty brushes.

Jane glanced round at the door, as if she half-expected some thirteenth-century craftsman to come barging in, sleeves rolled up, to help. She sincerely hoped he wouldn't. That was *her* prerogative, and she was jealous of her role. She watched the artist sorting through his pencils, sharpening one or two, selecting a clean rubber, about to start his tracing.

'While I'm doing this,' he said, 'you can clean the screens, scrape off all the plasticine, and give them a good wash. Then after that, perhaps you'd do some phoning for me. I'd like you to get on to the photographers and tell them . . . Damn! Who's that at the door? They'll break the bell if they lean on it like that. Go and see, will you, Rose, and unless it's anyone important, say I'm out – okay?'

The doorbell pealed a third time. Jane felt strangely nervous as she walked out to the passage. Would she come face to face with some smug medieval glazier, or Mrs Harville-Shaw, or a policeman sent by Isobel to march her back to Shrepton?

The man whistling on the doorstep was neither medieval nor a bobby, but a burly balding hunk in twentieth-century jeans. 'I've brought the glass,' he barked, cocking his thumb at his Transit van which was panting just outside. 'If the guv'nor's in, could he give me a hand?'

She rushed back in to Christopher, who didn't even stop his drawing. 'They've been quick,' he commented. 'I wasn't expecting a delivery till Friday at the soonest. Good job we had a clear-up.' He climbed down from the ladder, sauntered to the door, pencil in his hand still, as he nodded at the driver. 'My assistant here will help you,' he said, gesturing to Jane. 'Just bring the glass right into the studio and stack it round the walls. Okay, Rose, can you supervise?'

'Of course,' she said, flushed from Bass and pleasure, and accompanying the driver to his van. Christopher had called her his assistant, told the world – or at least one weighty member of it – that she was officially his helper. Isobel was wrong again – there was masses she could do – clean screens, stack glass, supervise deliveries, phone photographers. Best of all, she had a role and purpose; was involved in a project which might endure for a millennium, when petty things like parents were long since dead and gone.

'You an artist, too, then?' The driver started unroping the glass, which was stacked vertically, on end, with corrugated card between each sheet.

She didn't answer. He wouldn't understand. She might not be an artist – yet – but she'd become model, symbol, helpmate, pupil, all in one brief morning.

IO

'I'd divorce any man who played Birtwistle in my house.'

'Come off it, Viv, he's one of Britain's most celebrated composers.'

'Sez you, John.'

'Sez the music critics of *The Times*, the *Independent*, *Music Weekly*,
the *Sunday* . . .'

'Oh, shut up, you two. You've been bickering all evening. Adrian,
can't you split them up?'

'Okay. Anything for peace. Christopher, be a sport and sit next
to lovely Viv, and John move down next to Rose. In fact, let's all
change places, then we can chat to different people. They did that at
a dinner party I went to just last week – swapped seats every course.
I got quite dizzy in the end, but it did mean I'd talked to everyone
by the time we reached the After-Eights.'

'Does that imply you're sick of me?' the woman next to Adrian
enquired, a sharp-faced almost-blonde, with a mask of heavy make-
up, which was creasing as she pouted.

Jane recoiled at Adrian's whinny of denial. He seemed a different
Adrian from the one she had met the morning of the storm – more
ingratiating, smarmy. True, he was the host and must keep his guests
contented, but she didn't like the change in him. Christopher had
changed, as well – not the intense and serious artist she had got to
know these last ten days, but a show-off and a chauvinist, talking
far too loudly, dropping names and forks, picking pointless quarrels.
She wasn't sorry when he jumped up from his seat, and John Howard
took his place. She had hardly said a word to John as yet, just noted
his plain English name, which didn't fit his exotic foreign looks –
jutting powerful eyebrows blacker than his hair; hair so long it hid
his ears, trickled over his mulberry velvet jacket.

Everyone looked elegant, almost overdressed, or perhaps she was just too casual in a plain black skirt of Rowan's and a stripey sort of jerkin thing which Isobel had found her in what she called her 'Bits Box'. Christopher hadn't warned her that the dinner would be formal, or that there'd be so many guests – all chic and cultured socialites, who'd already cantered through a series of intimidating subjects, including the use (or abuse?) of percussion in Lutoslawski's latest work; the acceleration of Porsches as compared with BMWs; whether fourth-generation computers would eclipse the human brain, and why La Clusaz was a washout as a superior ski resort. She had not contributed anything so far, though it hardly seemed to matter, since everybody else was so busy interrupting, they hadn't time to notice her own silent ignorance. John now turned to face her, one hand on her chair-seat, as if to prevent her from escaping, even shifting his left thigh so it nudged against her own.

'So what's your line of business, Rose?'

'I'm Christopher's assistant.' It was easier to say now. Not only had she practised it a dozen times this evening, but she also felt more claim to it; had been working really hard for him, if not exactly on the glass, then on scores of other things. She'd also received her first week's pay – double what he had originally agreed. He'd told her she deserved it, and to regard it as a bonus, which she would get for extra hours.

'Good God! You must be brave,' John drawled.

'Why?' she asked him coldly, trying to edge her leg away. She had already defended Christopher from two or three attacks, one from a woman now flirting with him openly, a fashion buyer called Felice, whose cleavage seemed to plunge down to her navel. She wondered how his wife coped, and what she might be feeling if she were sitting at this table – which she should in fact have been, if she hadn't just departed for New York. She herself had been invited as a stopgap – a second best, a stand-in. The harsh names seemed to fit. Mrs Harville-Shaw would wear designer clothes, drive a BMW (with Lutoslawski on the stereo, and a computer in the dashboard), go skiing every winter in the most fashionable resorts, and recognise what pheasant was, when it was put in front of her.

She herself had been baffled by the taste, embarrassed by the fiddly bones; had still eaten only half of it, hardly touched the Château Montrose 1969, which the others had all praised, comparing it with wines they'd drunk in a host of different restaurants, countries, continents, as if all they ever did was jet-set from one dinner to the next. And yet they all had high-powered jobs, worked hours as long as Adrian's. So how did they find the energy to build empires, play the stock market, sit through strident symphonies, lay down vintage wines? Life had never seemed so complex back in Shrepton. Her parents' friends aimed lower – put their modest savings in the Halifax, chose Scarborough for their holidays or windy Whitley Bay, splashed out on Sainsbury's Liebfraumilch, if friends came round to dine. She mopped up port and chestnut sauce, felt a sudden longing for her mother's plain meat-loaf, their sturdy kitchen table with its well-ironed gingham cloth, the bossy clock which tick-tocked from the primrose-painted wall. Adrian's walls were panelled, hung with frowning portraits, the huge mahogany table laid with heavy silver; everything expensive and oppressive.

John Howard was still quizzing her – had she been to art school, did she live in Lewes, how had she grown her hair so long, and did she peg it out to dry? She tried to match his jokey tone; relieved when Rupert's penetrating baritone cut across her own voice, as he hollered down to Christopher at the far end of the table.

'I thought stained glass was dead,' he said. 'A lost art, you might say.'

'Not at all,' said Christopher. 'It's had almost a renaissance since the war, especially in America and Europe. There've been some pretty exciting projects in the States – stained glass not just in churches, but in restaurants, airports, private homes and offices. I'm not saying it's all good – some is bloody terrible – but at least it means the art's alive and kicking. In Washington, they've even got a Space Window, which commemorates man's landing on the moon, and includes a tiny chip of moon-rock which the astronauts brought back with them, and is meant to be several thousand million years old.'

'What, they've got that in a restaurant?' Rupert interjected.

'No,' the artist laughed. 'The Episcopal Cathedral.'

'It doesn't sound quite the thing for a church.'

'Why not? The theme of the window is actually infinity – the vastness of space and man's puniness in God's universe. Anyway, in one sense, the subject's immaterial. In fact, what's interesting to me is how non-religious artists like Léger and Matisse created stained-glass windows which are so profoundly spiritual. Léger was an atheist, and he said he hoped that unbelievers would be moved by his work as much as actual church-goers. And Matisse designed his Vence windows with the aim of cheering those who walked into the chapel, hoping they'd feel comforted, relieved of all their burdens. You could say art is our religion now. I remember John Updike remarking to me once that he went to the Museum of Modern Art to pray.'

'That's crap,' said Viv, pausing with a parsnip on her fork. 'Art's big business. What was it those Japs paid for Van Gogh's *Portrait of Dr Gachet* – eighty million dollars? – which makes even top Picassos look a snip.'

'Eighty-two point five million,' Christopher corrected. 'And they described that as – I quote – "quite cheap". It works out as roughly a hundred and forty thousand dollars per square inch.'

'Yes, but you're buying immortality,' Claire demurred, dabbing spilt wine off her dress. 'Which is what religion used to offer.'

'Tell that to the Japanese!' Viv bit off the top of her roast parsnip, as if decapitating a Jap. 'They're buying up the art market, like they're buying up the world, and investment's the key word, not bankrupt immortality. The paintings themselves are pretty incidental. They're just manipulating money, dabbling in a market which is a playground for rich speculators. I don't know whether you realise, Claire, but some-times they don't even *see* the bloody canvases, except on video. They're recorded on computer disks and faxed to Tokyo, where the fat cats watch them on TV, like they're share-reports or something, then phone their bids to London or New York. And they're all offered instant credit, so that even billionaires can buy their paintings on the never-never, as if a Van Gogh were a three-piece suite, or a Renoir a new dishwasher.'

'You're completely out of date, Viv,' John protested. 'The market has collapsed now and no one's buying a damned thing.'

'Of course it hasn't collapsed,' Rupert contradicted, crumpling up his napkin. 'It's simply marking time. Things could be entirely different in another year or two. Great pictures tend to come on to the market when great prices tempt them out. A seller mightn't bother for a mere ten or fifteen million, but a hundred million will change his mind miraculously.'

'Art's always been commercial,' Christopher remarked. 'I mean, even in medieval times, cathedrals were a status symbol, cities vying with each other to build the biggest and the best. And all the kings and barons showering money on them, in the hope they'd save their souls, which is just another kind of self-concern. But that doesn't mean they're not spiritual as well. I mean, take the Abbot Suger. He always comes across to me as something of a vain man, even had himself depicted in one of the new windows he commissioned for his church in 1135, but he was also potty about light and art and beauty. He said he wanted his stained glass to lift man to a higher world, so that the light flooding through the glass would be a symbol of divine light.'

Jane glanced across at Christopher, surprised. His voice and mood had changed now that he was expounding his own subject – his tone no longer querulous, but passionate, involved. She had never even heard of Abbot Suger, but the artist was still lauding him as a visionary, a mystic, someone who'd experienced the transcendental quality of light. He made him sound a colleague or a friend, yet if he'd been commissioning glass in 1135, then they were divorced from one another by more than eight whole centuries.

'Glass was seen as magical, almost as divine, because it started off as the lowest of the elements, something base like earth or sand, but was transformed to something spiritual, something you looked through, as much as at, and which transmitted light – or God, or Life, or Spirit.' The artist used his fork to gesture, pointing upwards, as if indicating heaven. 'They believed it could cause visions, and maybe they were right. Last time I was in Chartres, I had this extraordinary sensation in the cathedral of being transported to another world, like Suger; removed from my own body by the sheer impact of the glass.'

'How much had you been drinking?' Felice asked with a malicious little grin.

'It was seven in the morning,' the artist countered sharply. 'The cathedral had just opened and I was the only person there. The light was filtering through the east end, but it was still basically quite dark inside, with just this amazing glow and dazzle from the glass. I actually found that I was praying, quite naturally and . . .'

'To the God you don't believe in,' Viv objected.

Christopher nodded vigorously. 'Yes. Why not? Belief is neither here nor there. Art's as much a mystery as religion is itself. We can't grasp either one. Inspiration, revelation, visions, mysticism, even creativity – who the hell can really understand them, let alone define them? The artist *is* a god, in one sense, creating out of nothing.'

'The Almighty Harville-Shaw,' mocked Viv, snapping a small pheasant bone which she had picked up in her fingers. 'Who's also a big hypocrite. Last time we were talking, you were breathing fire and flames about the evils of religion; how it had caused more wars and conflict than almost any other force, and . . .'

'That's organised religion,' the artist interrupted. 'And I stick to what I said. You can hardly get away from it, for fuck's sake, if you read the papers or the history books – Catholics gutting Protestants, Hindus bashing Muslims, martyrs charring to a frizzle, crusades and holy wars. I watched a programme just last week about this city in Colombia which has the highest murder rate in the world – some poor sod slashed to ribbons every hour or two. And yet they're said to be devout religious people, especially the pious hit-men and the ultra-Catholic drug barons, who call their local Virgin the patron saint of drug dealers, and spend their time praying on their knees, when they're not lobbing bombs or blowing up the courthouses.'

'You can't take Colombia as typical,' Anne-Marie put in. 'It's a huge problem in itself, and . . .'

'I'm not. Nothing's ever "typical". Anyway, the word religion means so many things. It's like sex, in that respect – one word trying to cover for a whole variety of disparate experiences, and also both have got their darker side – even perverted, you might say. I mean, take the Crucifixion. If that's not pathological, I don't know what is – the Place of Skulls, the betrayal for hard cash, the mock purple robes, the thieves and gambling soldiers, the broken legs and bleeding wounds, the hallucinating women mooning over a stinking corpse. All that's pretty sick, you know, yet it's the central bloody image of our basic Christian culture – bloody in all senses.'

'Look, I object', said Adrian.

'I know you do, old chap. We've been over this before, and we'll never see eye to eye, when you're a paid-up Christian, and I'm a . . .'

'Yes, what *are* you?' Colin butted in, a skinny man, with lank black hair, but an expensive pin-striped suit. 'Let's hear it from the horse's mouth.'

'Well, first of all, I loathe all "-ists" and "-isms" – Marxist, Papist, atheist, any bloody "ist" at all. Who can ever be that sure? The older I get, the less I know anything for certain.'

'You surprise me,' Felice griped. 'You always seem to be laying down the law.'

Jane stabbed a roast potato with her knife, angry for the artist. Why did everyone attack him? He had talked to her in private about his beliefs, or lack of them, and she'd been impressed, and even moved. He had made the point that people's needs and longings went far beyond their ability to meet them; that most fundamental questions stayed unanswered, unresolved; that man invented gods to fill the gap – sometimes loving Father Gods, who then went on to torture them. She knew that even now he was speaking very seriously, tackling crucial subjects, but his tone was somehow wrong. He sounded too cocksure, was hogging all the limelight, not letting other people put their oar in. When they'd talked alone, he had let her see his pain and vulnerability; even admitted that he envied those with faith – the sort of fervent and unquestioning faith which had built the great cathedrals. 'Faith and hope,' he'd said with almost longing. 'The two great gifts you can't produce to order.' Then he'd explained that Gothic architecture was not just a simple matter of a change of building-style, but an explosion of the human spirit, a new adventurous outlook, which symbolised escape from the constraints of the Dark Ages. She had remembered that particularly, because it seemed to have some relevance to her own new life and prospects, her own escape from sham parental ties.

He was so different from her parents, brought such fire and feeling to all the things he cared about; whereas they dismissed most subjects in a prissy phrase or two, especially any dangerous ones, which must be instantly defused. She wished these friends of Adrian could see him as he was, see his other side – that time he'd told her broodingly that maybe the whole universe was sacred – nature and creation not separate from the divine, but expressing and including it. Did she dare remind him, say a word herself? It was surely time she made some contribution, repaid her host for the prawn and lobster soufflé, the exotic winey pheasant. She cleared her throat, clung on to her knife and fork, as if to give herself more weight. 'Yes, but what about . . . ?'

'Let's get back to art,' boomed Rupert from the other end.

She subsided into silence, didn't have much choice. She knew even less about art than she did about religion, could only reproduce the views she'd heard from Christopher. She sometimes felt uneasy that art should matter quite so much, when half the world was starving. How could people justify splurging eighty-two million dollars on one single smallish portrait, rather than put an end to famine in the whole of the Third World? Yet who was she to talk? She hadn't sent a penny to Save the Children or Oxfam. She pushed away her pheasant, seeing in her mind those scraggy haunted kids in the advertisements, holding out their begging-bowls with stick-arms and hopeless eyes. The talk ebbed and flowed around her – galleries and prices, fakes and restorations; art as self-expression, art as self-indulgence, art as therapy, investment, religion, propaganda.

'There's a link with sex again,' Christopher insisted. 'I mean, both art and sexuality take us out of our normal common sphere, shake us up, hurl us a bit higher, give us a small taste of something immortal or ecstatic.'

'You should be in Pseuds' Corner, Chris,' Viv exclaimed acerbically. 'I've never heard such crap.'

'The name's Christopher, in fact.'

'Oh, go to hell! I've no patience with these phoney claims for sex. It's become our new religion now, yet everyone's quite well aware it's just an animal and earthy thing.'

'I disagree,' said Christopher. 'What's wrong with our society is that we've turned sex into an industry, made it purely recreation, which is also a big business. And before that, it was procreation, which is just as bad – or worse. Sex must be more than that – a way of breaking out, not just from ourselves, our usual tight controls, but from other people's boundaries, experiencing unity, communion.'

'Christopher, you make me sick! You're so unbearably pretentious. In fact, I'm going to move – I can't stand any more. Felice, be an angel and swap with me.'

Jane watched the thin and sallow Viv change places with voluptuous doe-eyed Felice. She and Christopher made an all too handsome pair, offsetting one another; Felice's brilliant emerald contrasting with the artist's sombre black. He was dressed all in black tonight; looked elegant, dramatic, in a stylish corduroy suit, black silk shirt, and deep plum velvet tie. Jane glanced from him to Adrian. The two couldn't be more different – Adrian's myopic eyes peering wanly through thick glasses, his boring navy suit already creased and seeming slightly big for him, as if he'd nicked it from a messy elder brother. Yet she still felt somehow drawn to him – his air of boyish shyness, the way he ate so sloppily like a nervous scatty kid, spilling gravy down his shirt, dropping flakes of bread-roll in his wine. She wished she could sit next to him, dismiss his dozen guests, chat simply and sincerely on her own.

The general talk was now on sex and violence, which made her feel uneasy, as well as just embarrassed. She wondered why the two were yoked together. You never said 'sex and sport' or 'sex and meditation'. *Was* sex often violent, even between apparently loving couples? She'd no idea at all. She glanced from one face to the other, as if trying to find out. Everybody present had been to bed with someone else – everyone but her. That was fairly obvious from their attitudes, their tone. Had it made them different, hurled them a bit higher, as Christopher had claimed, removed them from the normal common sphere?

She let her eyes linger on the artist, who was deep in conversation with his neighbour, and so unconscious of her scrutiny. She was imagining him in bed with all three wives – not separately – together; aware that she was blushing as the pictures grew more vivid in her mind. Before she met the artist, she had never been so blatant. If she'd thought of sex at all, it was fuzzily and vaguely, like out-of-focus snapshots in blurry black and white. But recently those childish snaps had changed to video – dramatic adult movies in flagrant Technicolor. She couldn't understand it. She was living

121

very chastely in the studio. Christopher had made no real advances – just touched her hand occasionally, or caught her by the hair; teased her sometimes, called her Rosabella if she was bemoaning some small pimple, or her lack of curls and curves. But he had never propositioned her, never asked her out; rarely lingered on beyond five or six o'clock, but returned to his own pad.

Yet, even when he'd left for home, she was aware of him, obsessed by him, found herself lying hot and sleepless, thinking of his wife – or wives – not just curious idle thoughts, but jealous and resentful ones, like those she was experiencing now, as she watched his hand slide slowly down Felice's naked throat, pretending to admire her amber beads. He'd never touched *her* neck like that, but then she didn't have a cleavage, or unusual antique jewellery, or a designer dress so daring it revealed more than it hid.

'I hear you've got a panel in the "New Horizons In Glass" exhibition at the RIBA.' Felice's voice was husky, a sensuous suggestive voice, more suited to the bedroom than the dining-room.

'Yes. How did you know?' The artist's tone matched hers, as if they were discussing something intimate, not a public exhibition.

'Alan Younger told me. He's exhibiting himself.'

'So are you coming to the private view?'

'No. The rotter says he's been limited to just a dozen guests, and by the time he'd included all his hangers-on and family, there wasn't room for friends.'

'Well, come as *my* guest, Felice.'

Jane forced her eyes away, started forking in mange-tout, now cold and almost slimy. She disliked their soggy texture, but it seemed rude to leave them on her plate, as well as half her pheasant – as insensitive and rude as Christopher was being. He had invited a mere stranger to the private view, while excluding his assistant. She had seen the invitations – including one at Isobel's – made her interest crystal-clear, yet had still not been included. He was exhibiting his scarlet bird, the one trapped inside a room, which was doubly trapped in a packing-crate in the shed just off the studio, waiting to be taken up to London. There were still three weeks to go till the exhibition opened, but if he started asking every casual female he encountered in that time, there would be no room left for her.

'You're very quiet,' John Howard smiled.

'I'm sorry. I'm . . . still eating.'

'Most of us do both at once.'

She tried to animate her face, match his breezy laugh; tensed in shock as his hot and clammy hand suddenly landed on her thigh, as if he wished to change the sex-talk still smirching round the table into practical reality. She stared down at her plate, her whole body braced and rigid. How could she remove the hand without offending him? He was one of Adrian's clients, an almost-billionaire, who bought up thriving businesses as casually as other men bought beer or razor blades. If she drew attention to the hand, she might embarrass Adrian, anger Christopher. She took a sip of wine to hide her face, moved her leg a fraction; felt his hand grip tighter as she tried to edge away. The hand began to flutter; stroke slowly, slowly, up and down her thigh, squeezing it, exploring. She gulped more wine, could feel the claret burning in her throat, flooding down her body to the thigh, which seemed to scorch and sweat, sticking her and John together. She used her own hand to try to nudge his off, but he caught the hand and snared it, started fondling that as well.

She fixed her eyes firmly on the table, dared not look around her. People might be watching, not just the other guests, but the three young girls whom Adrian had hired to cook the meal, and who kept trooping in and out with plates of extra vegetables, new supplies of wine. They had made her feel self-conscious from the start, since they were roughly her own age, yet were waiting on her, serving her, as if she were just as grand and monied as the other, older guests. She'd felt she should jump up and join them in the kitchen, get stuck in to the washing-up, or help them with the cooking. One was hovering right behind her, offering petits pois. She had completely lost her appetite, but she took a generous spoonful, since it provided an excuse to tug her hand free, then kept it busy pronging up tiny fiddly peas. She swallowed the first mouthful, then turned to speak to Colin, who was sitting on her other side, asked him what he did – anything to distract herself from those hot intrusive fingers.

'I'm afraid I'm a rather dull accountant in a very boring firm. Though perhaps I was a pirate in another earlier life. Or maybe an astronomer – a biggie like Copernicus. I'm reading this fantastic book . . .'

She tried to concentrate. John's own thigh was pressing close to hers, his expensive calfskin shoe wooing her cheap canvas one. She glanced desperately at Christopher, but he was totally oblivious, flirting still with Felice, drinking from her glass, offering her a cigarette, despite the fact that the others were all eating. Lighting it involved them in a ritual, he leaning over close again, peering down her dress; the lighter held too long, their twin smokes wreathing, fusing; joining them together in a hot and filmy haze. Felice touched his cheek, to thank him for the light, kept her finger on his face, coquettishly, possessively. Jane crammed her mouth with peas, to stop herself from shouting out, laying claim to Christopher herself. He wasn't hers, though, was he? If anyone had claim on him, it was Mrs Harville-Shaw the Third, who was now winging far away from him in BA's Business Class.

Yes, she too was a businesswoman – not the artist she had once imagined – though apart from her position as Marketing Director for a multinational food company, she knew very little else about enigmatic Anne. She had tried to pump Isobel, who had dismissed the famous wife as 'not my type, but basically okay'. Jane had clothed her in a dozen different forms – darkly plain and angular, or a well-upholstered blonde; a seductive soft-voiced siren, or a nagging harridan. Though if she were genuinely seductive, then why should her husband be making such a play for Felice the instant she was gone?

She watched him dribble claret from his glass into Felice's, as if he were feeding her his life-blood. Jane snatched up her own wine, drained it in a gulp. Who cared about him, anyway? He had more or less ignored her the whole evening, courted all the other women, his eyes scrutinising their faces with the passion of a painter, taking in their figures. They'd been attacking him at first, aggressive and condemnatory, but now they seemed his fans; even prickly Viv trying to prise him free from Felice, firing jokes and flatteries down his end of the table. Jane suddenly resented his energy and wit, his refusal to be tired, or behave with more restraint. He was at least three times her age, so why should he be firing on all cylinders, wowing all the females, when she herself felt jaded; even at this moment longing to excuse herself, creep away to bed? Adrian had disappeared already, summoned to the phone, but that was strictly business. There were still hours to go till bedtime – pudding, cheese and coffee to be served; liqueurs in the drawing-room, after-dinner talk.

'You're quite a greedy girl, you know,' John Howard said admiringly, as she continued to stuff in peas and cold mange-tout. He lingered on the 'greedy', made it sound provocative, not an insult, but a compliment – one she didn't want. He himself was eating with one hand, his other hand still busy. 'I'm very glad to find a fellow gourmet. Food's my second-favourite pastime.'

She pushed her plate away, relieved to see the serving girls were now clearing off the dishes, bringing in dessert. There were several different puddings – chocolate soufflé, strawberry mousse, meringues, and lemon sorbet – all frilled and swagged with rosettes of whipped cream.

'Great! Some of each for me,' said John, relinquishing his plate at last.

'None for me,' said Jane.

'What, are you trying to show me up?' smirked John, turning to the waitress. 'Some of each for both of us.'

She could hardly contradict him, when the girl had already heaped her plate with chocolate, pink and white, then whooshed on more whipped cream. A second waitress filled her glass with a new golden-coloured wine. She tried the wine, found it sweet and sickly; started ploughing through her puddings, more to occupy herself, shut her off from John, than from any sense of pleasure in their taste. She was more aware of smells, in fact – the insistent reek of garlic, which still lingered from the main course; John's heavy cloying aftershave, which mingled spice and musk; his claret-breath as he leaned suddenly towards her, scooped a swirl of soufflé from her lip. His finger on her open mouth felt intimate and dangerous. Surely Christopher would notice – intervene, object? No. Christopher was holding forth to Felice, wooing her with words now, as well as wine and touch. Jane took a gulp of wine herself, kept both hands round her glass. The heavy fluted crystal would anchor her, at least; though she was nervously aware that her bladder would complain soon, and she'd have to find the loo. Yet how could she get up, interrupt the dinner, make herself the focus of attention? Almost better to endure John's trespassing hand. She was amazed by his persistence, his basic bloody cheek. He must realise she disliked the hand, yet those feverish fingers were fiddling with her skirt-hem, even daring to slip under it.

'No!' she muttered, as fiercely as she dared.

'You like it,' John purred softly, as his hand explored the texture of her tights, inched slowly, damply upwards.

'I *don't.*' She could see Viv staring at them. Their mutual whispering must sound most suspicious, as if they were conducting a flirtation *sotto voce*. 'Get off,' she mouthed, spooning in iced sorbet, in the hope that it might cool her down, reduce the burning scarlet of her cheeks. John appeared oblivious, merely offered her more sorbet from his own plate.

'Greedy guts!' he teased. 'I've never seen anyone eat with such sheer gusto. And even when you hold your glass, you're almost making love to it.' His hand had reached her crotch now, was moving in and down.

'Excuse me,' she said cuttingly. 'But I'm afraid I need the bathroom.' She kicked her chair back, bolted for the door.

★   ★   ★

She stayed longer in the toilet than she needed, scrubbing her right hand, the one that John had fondled, as if to scour him from her body and her mind. She reapplied her lipstick, which she had eaten off with dinner, then walked slowly back along the panelled corridor. Adrian had six loos in his house – or so he'd been joking to his guests – but she'd deliberately chosen the one she'd used before, the morning of the storm, the one nearest to the chapel. She paused now outside the chapel door, pushed it open cautiously, saw Adrian inside, kneeling on the bare wood floor, a few feet from the altar. He immediately swung round, stopped her from escaping.

'Come in,' he smiled, rising from his knees. 'I'm just grabbing a quick breather after a pretty hairy phone-call.'

Jane said nothing. It seemed an offbeat way to use a chapel. He made it sound like a jacuzzi, or a gym – somewhere to refresh the flagging businessman.

'I'm sure God understands. I often feel He's a sort of Chairman of the Board Himself – making all the big decisions, and making them long-term; hiring, firing, doling out rewards or raps . . . Here,' he said, gesturing to a chair. 'Sit down and grab a bit of hush yourself. They won't miss us for five minutes.'

He closed his eyes, sank back on his knees, appeared perfectly at ease praying with her there, though she herself felt awkward, as if she'd come across him doing something shameful. How odd it was that full-frontal flagrant sex seemed more normal and acceptable in the relaxed and casual nineties than silent private prayer. She shifted on her chair, admiring his ability to kneel absolutely motionless, to change gear so emphatically from this world to the next. Yet she also felt put down, banished like an alien from that other, higher world; and wishing he'd communicate with her, instead of God. Perhaps it was her lot in life to be ignored by men – at least the ones she liked. She tried to pray herself, found she was addressing not God, but Christopher; begging him to listen, to ditch that devious Felice and concentrate on *her*, restore her to his favour.

Adrian eased up from the floor, at last, his casual jokey tone contrasting with his previous prayerful silence. 'Well, I suppose we'd better wander back, or they'll imagine we've eloped together. Though, if I'm absolutely truthful, I'm not too madly keen on these occasions. And I suspect you're not enjoying it any more than I am. Perhaps it wasn't fair to ask you, especially so late on, but . . .'

'Oh, no,' she said, embarrassed. 'I was actually quite flattered.'

'Good,' he smiled. 'Things always get more lively when

126

Christopher's a guest. Though I find it rather a pain when he keeps attacking my religion.'

She mumbled some reply, felt disloyal discussing Christopher when he was unable to defend himself.

'As far as I'm concerned, Rose, faith's a very personal thing – like one's physical appearance, or one's family, or kids, which it's bad manners to disparage.'

Jane glanced up at the angels sculpted in dark wood, tame impassive angels, compared with Christopher's. 'I'm sure he doesn't mean it to be rude. In fact, I wouldn't be surprised if he once had a faith himself, but lost it or . . .' She broke off in confusion, surprised by her own words. She had no proof of that at all, except he seemed to know so much about religion; appeared as much at ease with angels as if he'd been to art school with them; could talk about the Holy Ghost like other people talked about the milkman.

'The problem is,' said Adrian, pausing at the chapel door. 'You can't choose to believe. It's a bit like love, in that respect. You can't fall in love to order, or make people love you back.'

Jane shivered suddenly as she stepped from the warm chapel into the dark and draughty passage. Adrian was right. Love was an elusive gift you could neither buy nor beg – the love of one's own mother, who might kick you from your cradle, pass you to a stranger, like a useless piece of jumble. Or the love of someone you admired, who could ignore you all the evening. She continued down the corridor, following Adrian's blue back. How strange it was that he'd said the same as Christopher – that you can't believe to order – when the two appeared so different on matters of belief: Adrian a devout committed Christian; Christopher agnostic, still baffled, searching, open to all views.

The phone was shrilling once again as they approached the offices. 'I'm afraid I'd better pick that up.' Adrian dived towards his desk. 'It's probably Tokyo. Make my excuses, will you, Rose – tell them I'll be back in just a tick.'

She nodded, guessed the tick might well be half an hour; lingered for a moment beside the small framed coloured etching by Chagall – Adrian's new baby, which he had shown them when they first arrived, describing how he'd outbid all the dealers. He clearly had no problem coughing up the cash for it. Christopher had told her that in Adrian's line of business, a typical transaction was worth a cool ten million dollars, and he could rake in a million profit on just one single deal. Yet what was the point of earning all that loot, when you never had the leisure to enjoy it? Adrian worked round the clock; had very little social life, apart from occasional dinner parties; often got up in the night to phone his contacts in Japan; didn't smoke or drink or dance, and had used his ironically named leisure-centre a mere half-dozen times. Money ruled him like a tyrant, so Christopher had pointed out, never allowed him to let up or even delegate. And there was always the real danger of losing everything – not just his precious millions, but his house, his car, his nerve. She was surprised he clung to such a risky job; even more surprised that a man who seemed so mild and easy-going (and had boasted he was lousy at maths) could somehow be a sharp hard-headed speculator.

She mooched towards the dining-room, reluctant to go in; could hear Christopher pontificating before she'd even reached the door; Felice's contralto embroidering his baritone with admiring interjections in a lower minor key. She had defended him from Adrian's attack, yet here he was holding forth again, using his opinions as a form of crass seduction; Anne-Marie now adding her own descant, as he spouted some irreverent view to tantalise her.

She stopped a moment, dithered, then doubled back the way she'd come. He wouldn't miss her for another few brief minutes; probably hadn't even noticed she had gone – not with all that heady competition. And if John Howard was concerned at where she'd wandered off to, then let him try his groping on some other willing thigh.

She slipped out through the side door to the garden, the warm fug of the house giving way to raw and shadowed gloom; the smell of rotting leaves replacing that of expensive hothouse flowers. She wandered down the path, shoulders hunched against the cold; could hear the party chatter spilling from the dining-room, whose bright-lit windows spangled the dank grass. Even here, she couldn't escape the artist; his laugh whooshing like a firework from the table to the sky. She looked up at the sky, the new moon so frail and puny it appeared to have fallen on its back, and was waiting for its mother to pick it up and comfort it; the stars faint and far away, as if they belonged to that strange higher world which Adrian could enter, but which was locked and barred to her. She walked on to the chapel, its windows dark, mysterious, the tall evergreens surrounding it seeming to point straight up to God. She could hear the stealthy breathing of a bonfire, its charred remains sighing into ash, its final smouldering flicker contrasting with the blackly torpid laurels. She stood, chilled and undecided, between the chapel and the dining-room – one silent, dark, ethereal, the other bright and raucous. The path divided at that point, so there were other, harder choices. Did she press on further still, to the dim uncertain stretches of the unlit, unknown garden, or return to the safe house?

A second, louder firework suddenly exploded from the windows
– the artist's laugh, now sparking like a Catherine wheel, some
woman's shriller giggle spinning round and round with it.

Jane turned her back, walked on.

'You were very quiet,' the artist said, as he drove, too fast, along
winding country lanes. 'You hardly said a word. And it wasn't
exactly polite, you know, to disappear like that.'

'I'm surprised you even noticed.'

'What's that supposed to mean, Rose?'

Jane declined to answer, peered out of the window at the rush of
blurred black fields. The silence felt uncomfortable, like a bad smell
in the car which they were both trying to ignore.

'Tired?' he asked, at last.

'A bit.'

'Or sulking?'

'No.'

'Good. I can't stand girls who sulk.'

'I can't stand men who . . .'

'What?'

'It doesn't matter.'

'Yes, it does. What were you going to say?'

'Nothing. I'm just tired.'

'You said you weren't tired.'

'Did I?'

'Yes. We'll be back in a few minutes. You'd better go to bed.'

'I shall.'

'I don't feel tired at all – wide awake, in fact. I think I'll do a bit
of work before I drive on home.'

'Work – at two in the morning?'

'Mm. I've had a rather good idea for the Civic Centre job, and I
want to get it down. I've had it on my mind all evening.'

'Really? You surprise me.'

'You surprise me, too – the new sarcastic Rose.'

'I'm not sarcastic.'

'No?'

'No.'

They drove in edgy silence until they reached the barn. As soon as
they got in, Christopher whipped off his tie, removed his corduroy
jacket, then prowled around the studio, pouncing on odd papers, or
rearranging shelves, as if he had to have things tidy before he dared
disturb his mind with what might be a chaotic new idea. At last, he

rolled his shirt-sleeves up, pinned a sheet of paper to the wall, started drawing standing up; crude black shapes in charcoal flowing from his hand.

'Goodnight, then,' Jane said curtly, feeling totally dispensable as she moved towards the staircase.

'Goodnight.'

He didn't even bother to turn round, despite the fact that she lingered on the stairs, then stood stiffly on the balcony watching him still drawing. Was he deliberately rejecting her, or capping sulks with sulks, or so absorbed in his new project that he was blithely unaware he was being rude or thoughtless? She plumped down on the bed, peeled off her jerkin top, paused a moment nervously before unhooking her thin bra. She sat shielding her bare breasts, frightened he could see them; though he was at least twelve feet below her, and had his back turned anyway. She reached out for the jerkin, dragged it on again, over her bare skin. It felt wrong to start undressing with Christopher still there. But how long might he stay? All night, and then all Sunday? Perhaps he wouldn't drive back home at all, but just continue working there till Monday, ignoring boring things like sleep and meals. Yet she herself felt desperate for sleep – faint from too much wine, smudged around the edges, as if some official with a giant eraser had begun to rub her out.

She lay back on the bed. She could sleep in all her clothes, just shut her eyes, let go. Why worry over Christopher, when he seemed utterly oblivious of anything beyond his precious project? She wormed beneath the duvet, rearranged the pillows, frowning at the light. She was used to total darkness when she slept, not this distracting mix of glare and shadow intruding from his Anglepoise. She was also used to total silence, which was broken now by the faint insistent rasping of the charcoal, the artist's shifts or steps, the sudden small explosion of a match. She tried to shut them out – after all, they were only muted noises, not blatant bangs or crashes. Yet their stealthy faintness seemed to make them worse, because she was straining to interpret them, guess what he was doing.

She turned on her right side, tugging at her skirt, which had tangled around her legs and felt uncomfortably tight. The rasping noise had stopped. Had he finished drawing? She half-sat up, wondering if she would hear him walking out; hear a splutter from his car as he switched on the ignition. No – just the splash of liquid in a glass. So he was tippling again, when he was already over the limit. She flopped back on the bed. Why not simply blank him out, count sheep, or try deep-breathing? Fourteen, fifteen, sixteen. The sheep all had his face, a mane of coarse grey hair instead of soft white wool. She tried lying on her front next, which at least obscured the light; tried imagining a beach scene, a peaceful stretch of sea and sand, to calm her down, relax her. But somebody was lounging on the beach – the artist in his swimming trunks, naked to his navel, and just lighting up a Marlboro. She could hear him coughing from the smoke, a hoarse and hacking smoker's cough, rising from below.

She flung the duvet back, cannoned down the stairs. 'Do you have to cough as loud as that? I'm trying to get to sleep.'

He turned round in surprise, as if he'd totally forgotten her; fighting the cough, trying to suppress it with a draught of something amber in a glass.

'And why are you still drinking? You were pretty well tanked up when you drove us back, could have killed us both.' She was appalled by her own words, even as she rapped them out. How had she dared speak to him like that, adopt the tone of a nagging scolding mother, when he was so much older, and accountable to no one?

He didn't say a word, just refilled his glass, turned back to his drawing. She stood battling with a confusion of emotions – anger still, resentment; embarrassment and shame, especially when she realised that the bottle he'd just poured contained apple juice, not whisky.

'Look, I'm sorry,' she murmured, at last breaking the taut silence. 'I'm tired, that's all, and . . .'

The artist paused, slumped down on a stool, charcoal in his hand still. 'Yes, Isobel keeps telling me you're tired, accuses me of working you too hard.'

'That's crazy – and a lie. I never said a word to her.'

'Didn't you?'

She blushed. 'Well, I did just mention that we started very early in the mornings. But only because she brought the subject up. She was telling me how bad she was first thing, and how she was basically a night-person who liked lying in till noon.'

'And you told her you're the same?'

'No. I'm not. I didn't.'

He suddenly lunged forward, ripped his sheet of paper from the wall, as if her anger were infectious, and he had caught it now himself. He crumpled up the drawing, tossed it in the waste-bin. 'Rubbish!' he said tersely, reaching for his cigarettes.

She wasn't sure whether the 'Rubbish!' was directed at his work, or a contemptuous comment on her last remark; felt more and more uncomfortable as he stood motionless beside her, his cigarette unlit. 'Look, I . . . I'd better go to bed.'

He appeared not to have heard her, kept staring at the floor, his face strained and almost ugly, as if he were tuned in to some private grief impenetrable to her. At last, he spoke, straightening up, fumbling for his matches. 'You don't have to work here, Rose, you know. You can always go back home. No – you can't. You haven't got a home.' His mood had changed, cruelly, unaccountably, as he gave a mocking laugh.

'What d'you mean?' she countered, on her guard immediately.

'The almost little orphan,' he said sardonically.

'That's not fair!' she shouted. 'Wait till I see Isobel. I'll kill her! I'll . . . She'd no right to tell you anything. She promised on her honour she wouldn't say a word.' Suddenly she was crying, noisily and messily; tears sluicing down her face; sniffing, gasping, trying to use her knuckles as a handkerchief. 'I can't bear the thought she told you, when I trusted her and everything. Everybody lies. You just can't . . .'

'Rose, I don't know what you're talking about. Isobel hasn't said a word to me about your private life – not a single word. All she rattles on about is how she's worried you're anaemic and do I feed you properly. I told her you feed me.' He grinned. 'Come on – no more tears. Dry your eyes on something, and I'll take you up to bed.' He reached for an old paint-rag, wiped her eyes himself. 'Damn!' he said. 'I'm not much good at this. Now you've got a green-streaked face.'

She used her fists to shift the streaks, let herself be led upstairs, feet faltering on the steps, which seemed steeper and more treacherous than usual. He dived ahead, started straightening up the duvet, as if desperate for some order in the chaos. She could see he was embarrassed, trying to do in deeds what he couldn't say in words; picking up her shoes, removing clothes and papers from the floor. 'Where are your pyjamas, Rose?'

She rummaged in the bed, unearthed his own blue silk ones.

'You're not still wearing those old things? They're only fit for cleaning rags.'

'I like them.'

'Do you?'

'Yes.'

He paused. 'Because they're mine?'

'Yes.'

The silence seemed to tauten for a moment. Something had been said, some barrier dismantled, in four brief casual words. The artist started talking, to cover up his lapse, talking loudly, swiftly, whilst he fussed with the pyjamas. 'Well, you'd better put them on then. At least they'll be more comfortable. Does that thing zip or button? Christ! Women's clothes are complicated. I don't know how you manage. That's it. Tug it off.'

They were both sitting on the bed, she naked now above the waist. She didn't shield her breasts this time, and he didn't shift his eyes. Endless breathless minutes seemed to pant and lumber by, while she felt his gaze scorching her bare skin.

At last, he reached to touch the breasts, tentatively, as if expecting a repulse, or frightened they might break, like glass. Jane sat very still. His hands felt rough against her flesh, a labourer's hands, calloused from his work. He was rubbing one hard thumb across her nipple; then cupping her whole breast, squeezing it and stroking. She was surprised she felt such fear – fear of pleasure, as much as fear of pain; fear of men – all men. 'No,' she said uncertainly. He didn't seem to hear, had suddenly leaned forward to kiss the breast, take it in his mouth. She was startled, apprehensive, yet she liked the new experience of a man's head on her chest, the strange sensation of his lips around her nipple, pulling very gently; his coarse grey hair prickling on her skin. She touched the hair, held on to it; surprised at how the tingling in her breasts seemed to have set off other feelings she couldn't quite define. She was alarmed by her own body, which felt more real and solid than it ever had before; not blurred and half-erased now, but insistent and intrigued. It might disgrace her, overwhelm her, if she didn't keep control. Christopher had talked about control, claimed that sex must snap it, breach barriers and boundaries, but did she want them smashed? She tried to cover up her breasts again, reclaim them for herself.

'What's the matter, darling? Am I hurting?'

'N . . . no.' He'd called her 'darling'. She was no longer silly child or backward pupil; no longer just employee, or menial assistant. Half a minute's kissing of her breasts had somehow upped her status. She touched his hand a moment, as if in recognition, and he picked up both their hands, held them to his mouth, started grazing gently with his teeth, nibbling all her fingers, then his own. The teeth were sharp, and dangerous, and again she tensed, instinctively, edged away a little.

'Just relax,' he whispered. 'It's rather like the glass – nothing to be scared of.'

'I *am* scared.'

'Don't be. We'll take it very slowly.'

He kissed her mouth; his lips so soft and careful she could barely

133

even feel them; then moving to her eyelids, fluttering across them, lapping down her neck, almost to her breasts again, teasingly, frustratingly; then back up to her ears, his tongue exploring all their crevices, flicking round the lobes. She had been kissed before, by Ian, and by another inexperienced boy who'd asked her to a disco once, but those kisses had been brief and rough, just crude mouth clamped on mouth. This was very different. The artist's tongue was circling her right palm, licking slowly but insistently up towards each fingertip, then down between the fingers. The ripples seemed to spread through her whole body. She lay back on the bed, closed her eyes a moment, didn't want to see what he was doing. When she opened them again, his upper half was naked, like her own; his tanned and muscly chest grizzled with coarse hair, his nipples pinkish-brown and defined by darker circles. She felt both curious and bashful, frightened and elated. They were equals now, both stripped down to the skin, though he seemed a stranger, almost; not the refined and well-dressed artist armoured in his clothes, but someone much more animal, who had shed his silk and cashmere. Yet this was still the man who had created those red birds, produced a soaring Angel who would trumpet up to heaven for the next few hundred years, defying death, decay.

She almost wished she could transform him to an angel, change him into Spirit, so she wouldn't feel so threatened by his hot and heavy body, now pressed against her own. If only she could lose herself; relax, as he had urged her, lie back in all senses, experience that taste of immortality he had mentioned earlier on. But she was still on edge, still jumpy, still unnerved by all the other things he had told her previously – the violence he'd appeared to relish, the morning of the storm. Sex and violence. She tried to block the phrase out, as he kissed her mouth, her throat. One hand was groping down towards her skirt-band, fumbling for the fastening.

'Just move a fraction, darling, and help me with this zip. Hell! The damned thing's stuck.'

She pushed his hand away, turned on her left side, so she was lying on the zip. 'You said we'd take things slowly. Let's just kiss and . . .' She swallowed her last words. Perhaps it was unfair to him to lie there with her skirt on; clammy nylon tights encasing her whole lower half, but she felt better with them on, safer doing things by halves. She seemed split in two all ways – half naked and half clothed; half willing and half wary; half woman and half stupid clueless child.

'Okay – no rush,' he smiled, though the smile seemed forced, and false, and she could detect a hint of irritation in his voice. He was not a patient man, never did things slowly. Despite his words, he had already pulled her round to face him and climbed on top again; was moving much more wildly, regardless of their clothes; his body grinding into hers, so that the rough cord of his trousers chafed and rubbed her crotch. She felt swamped by him, invaded, and it was difficult to breathe now, with his mouth on hers as well; no longer cautious, teasing, but fretting at her lips, compelling them to open, then inserting his swift tongue. She gagged, half-choked, then jerked her head back sharply.

'Rose, I've got to have you.' He was tugging at his belt, his face intent, contorted; his whole force and concentration directed at her body, as if there were no reality beyond it. She heard a rabbit's high-pitched scream stun the sleeping fields outside; could suddenly see her mother in bed with Christopher – not Amy, but her real mother, bludgeoned by his body, begging him to stop. That's how she'd been born – a mistake, a crazy impulse, a one-night stand, with no forethought, no precautions. This man could be her father – literally and tragically, if, eighteen years ago, he had seduced some other helpless girl, pestered and insisted, despite her fears, her lack of all protection. She jack-knifed up and backwards, severed their two bodies, as if she'd slashed them with a scalpel.

He sank back on his heels, his trousers half-undone, a drool of slow saliva hanging from his lip; hugged his arms across his chest, clearly trying to contain himself, prevent his body or his temper from flaring up, losing all control.

'I'm sorry,' she said shakily. 'It's just that . . .' She could feel herself blushing as she tried to get the words out. 'I'm not on the Pill, or anything. I know I should have said before, but I didn't really think we'd . . .'

'Look, that's not a problem, Rose – okay?' He put his arm around her, seemed ashamed of his impatience now, and aiming to appease her, get back close again.

'What d'you mean?' The arm felt damp and hot.

'What I say. It's not a problem. You won't get pregnant – not with me.'

'But . . .'

'Can't we do without the "buts"?' *No*, she felt like shouting. Probably all men tried to kid you, promise they'd pull out, as Ian had sworn to do, in fact – though they had never got that far, thank God. She dared not take the risk, or believe what could be lies, without probing, checking up. 'Do you mean you've had that . . . operation?'

'The snip? No thanks.' He grimaced. 'I wouldn't let them near me.'

'Well, what then?'

He erupted from the bed, stalked on to the balcony, hitching up his trousers, standing with his back to her, shoulders hunched and tense. 'I can't have kids – okay?'

'What d'you . . .?'

'Do I have to spell it out?' His voice suddenly crescendoed, the words hitting her like stones. 'I'm sterile, barren – call it what you like.'

She ducked away, as if dodging further blows; cursed herself for asking. Whatever could she say; how defuse his bitter tone, his air of damaged pride? At last, he spoke himself, back still turned and rigid.

'Forgive me if I shouted, Rose. It's not a subject I find easy to discuss. For years I blamed my wife, tried to pass the buck. But when I married for the second time, Veronica had children of her own, so I could hardly lay the fault at her door. She'd had three by her first husband, without the slightest problem, but drew a blank with me.'

'Look, I'm sorry, honestly. I never would have asked if . . .'

'Hell!' he griped. 'I need a cigarette, and I've left the bloody things downstairs.' He slouched towards the door, shambled down the staircase, still buttoning up his shirt. She slipped on her own top again, heard a match strike angrily from somewhere far below. She understood his feelings. He had made himself look small, and that was unforgivable for a man of modest stature, who was immodest in ambition. She prayed that he would come back up, so they could sit and talk, confide. He had told her his own secret, so she could match it with her own, prevent Isobel forestalling her, maybe telling it all wrong. Up till now, she had deliberately concealed the fact of her adoption, the details of her life, fobbed him off with fictions or evasions; had somehow always feared his scorn or pity; even suspected he might play the heavy-handed father, and insist she went back home. But things felt different now. He had permitted her to see that he was vulnerable, and she could do the same. She stood leaning over the balcony, willing him to catch her eye, resume their conversation, sound less curt and fractious. He was collecting up his jacket, turning off the lamp, stood a moment in the gloom, jingling his car keys, whistling some harsh tune.

'Rose,' he called, at last, looking up and frowning when he realised she was watching him. 'I think I'll push off home. I'm feeling really knackered.' He didn't even wait for her reply, mumbled a goodnight as he scorched towards the door. She heard it slam, listened to the car coughing like its owner, then fading to a drone.

She stooped down to the floor. He had left his tie behind, his deep plum velvet tie with its chic Parisian label. She stood stroking its soft plush, remembering his own hands lapping down her breasts. She suddenly yanked her top off, touched the breasts herself, copying his movements, the way his thumbs had chafed, disturbing yet exciting her. Why had it gone wrong? She felt guilty and embarrassed, yet furious as well – guilty for allowing him to touch her in the first place, embarrassed that she'd stopped him, made him look a fool; angry at his obstinacy, his sheer pig-headed pride. Yet she was also still aroused, couldn't settle, couldn't sleep, couldn't think of anything but Christopher's bare body; the feel of him on top of her – that strange and frightening part of him which seemed alive in its own right, thrusting out between his legs, like a bully and a rebel, not under his control. She had also glimpsed his pubic hair as he'd eased down his tight cords, and was still obsessively preoccupied with that flash of almost-black – completely different from the grey hair on his head – springier and younger, yet somehow also threatening.

She took off her skirt and tights, removed her flimsy pants, stood looking in the mirror. She suddenly wanted him to see her – all of her, and naked – her own curly pubic thatch, her deep and secret navel which she'd used for storing beads in, when she was a kid of six or so; even the scar on her left thigh where she had fallen off her bike.

She sprawled back on the bed, both hands on her body, as if Christopher were with her still, stroking and admiring. She tried to kick the anger out, the embarrassment, the guilt; obliterate the last bit of the evening, keep only the quiet careful part, when he had treated her like glass; erase his curt admission that he was sterile and infertile. She hated those two words – words connected with her parents now, with failure and deception. He was nothing like her parents; could never be described as barren, not when his creations enlivened the whole studio. She remembered Uncle Peter's scorn for his brother's 'lack of balls' – a phrase she'd found quite loathsome, and which had made her see her father as inferior, castrated. She had somehow blamed her parents for failing to conceive, so, if she was consistent, then she should also blame the artist.

She rubbed her eyes, exhausted; couldn't sort her feelings out. They were too confused, too complex, and she was aching now for sleep. She crawled beneath the duvet, switched off the bedside lamp. She was still a child, in one sense, still a retarded gauche eighteen-year-old who didn't know what sex was – not the practical reality. She should have brought her rag-doll, stuffed it in her duffel-bag the night she fled from Shrepton, so she could sleep with that, instead. She tried to make herself a child – a genuine small kid, happy in its innocence, rather than ashamed and muddled up. She imagined herself as six again, sleeping in the tree-house she'd never actually had. She could feel it rocking gently in the branches of an elm, hear the sparrows twittering just outside its windows, and then a louder noise – the thrum of a car-engine suddenly fading into nothing, the slamming of a door.

'Rose?' a voice called nervously – the artist's voice, which rarely sounded anything but confident, cocksure. 'Are you still awake?'

II

'"Awake thou that sleepest",' Isobel recited. 'It's got quite a ring, hasn't it?'

'Yes,' said Jane, uncertainly, peering over her shoulder at the ancient yellowed Bible, open on the table at St Paul's letter to the Ephesians.

'I wanted the whole verse, but Christopher objected – said there wasn't room.' Isobel stood up, rolling out the words as she darted to the stove to save her grapefruit marmalade from burning. '"Awake thou that sleepest and arise from the dead, and Christ shall give thee light." I thought that last bit would be really rather apt – have a literal meaning, as well as a symbolic one, in the sense of light flooding through the glass – but Christopher said no, complained it was too obvious, and that something short and snappy would be more effective anyway.' Isobel stirred the saucepan vigorously, slopping molten marmalade over the already crusted hob. 'Actually, I suspect it's more a personal thing and he's just not keen on doing long inscriptions. Lettering's a tedious job, and not all that creative, so it's probably not his forte. I didn't argue, Rose. What's the point? You never win with Christopher.'

No, thought Jane, you don't. She sat chopping up more grapefruit for the second batch of marmalade, trying to stop her mind from returning to last night. 'Isobel,' she said, at last, putting down her knife, so that she could concentrate on a rather different question she hoped would not offend. 'Do you really believe that Tom will – you know – wake?'

'You mean rise from the dead? Well, yes, of course I do. What's the point of a Resurrection window if you don't believe in resurrection – not just Christ's, but everyone's?'

'I wish I could believe it,' Jane remarked, reflecting on her own mother, who might have died herself, so that she'd never get to meet her or find out who she was. If she believed in resurrection, they could all three be reunited – herself, her absent mother, her lost departed father.

'You can,' said Isobel.

'Not without a faith.' Jane resumed her chopping, hacking through the tough and knobbly skins.

'Faith's extremely simple,' Isobel affirmed. 'What you believe *is* actually the truth – becomes true, if you like. It's as if the universe fulfils your expectations, gives you what you want.'

'But surely that's just cheating – avoiding all the evidence and swallowing fairy tales.'

'What "evidence"?' asked Isobel. 'Nothing's really proved, you know. Even in science, there's no final certain proof. So-called facts are always changing. I mean, it was a highly respected fact, once, that the world was flat, or the sun went round the earth.' She tried a taste of marmalade, blowing on the spoon first, to try to cool it down. 'Hadley's reading physics at Southampton University, and he says that "real" reality is nothing like our picture of it. We see everything so partially and dimly that our facts are just distortions. And even the top physicists are divided among themselves. Some are militant atheists, while a few regard the laws of physics as expressions of the will of God.'

'So how can *you* be sure, then – I mean, even if top scientists don't know?'

'I go about it in a completely different way, Rose, regard meaning and imagination as every bit as valid as scientific proof. If you insist on proving everything, you lose all mystery, the whole world of the spirit. You can't see ghosts or angels.'

'So you believe in ghosts, as well?'

'Oh, yes.' Isobel made them sound as tangible as cats – the ginger tom and slinky tabby female now rubbing against her legs. 'Those lines from the inscription – "Awake thou that sleepest" – don't just apply to death, but to our whole half-baked dozy state of being only half-alive, unaware of higher things, or of the fact that time is circular, so nothing's ever really lost, and no one ever "dies" in any ultimate sense.'

Jane removed a shower of pips from one over-fertile grapefruit. Would she ever sort such mysteries out herself? The adults in her life to date had never made things quite so strange or complex. Facts were facts at school, especially in the sciences, and her parents seemed to view the world as rational, simple, solid – rather like their simple solid home. 'But you can't believe to order,' she objected, now quoting Adrian, since she was getting lost herself.

' 'Course you can,' said Isobel. 'Except "order"'s the wrong word. You have to just let go, surrender your control, trust that God will meet your faith, and that the universe will give you what you need.'

Jane said nothing. The words 'let go' had set up nervous ripples, returned her thoughts to Christopher, and sex. And the whole idea of trusting seemed more hazardous, since her parents had deceived her. Even now, she felt some deep suspicion of what Isobel was saying. It all seemed far too rosy, too simplistic.

'You're free to choose, you see, my love. You can choose to think you die and rot, or you can choose to know eternity. So why not choose the better one? Faith's good for you, like vitamins.' Isobel strolled back to the table, one cat beneath her arm, the tabby mewing anxiously behind her. 'Do you know what William Tyndale said – the man who wrote this version of the Bible – "Faith maketh a man glad, lusty, and cheerful, and true-hearted unto God and to all creatures." I always like that "lusty". I think it just means healthy, but it sounds slightly naughty, doesn't it?' She plumped down on her chair again, both cats on her lap. 'As far as I'm concerned, there's no such thing as misplaced faith – or false hope, for that matter. Either you're hopeful or you're not. The very definition of hope is that it's hopeful. And hope's like faith, in that they both have good results. I mean, they've shown you can cure cancer now by hoping and believing you'll get better – whereas if you think you're going to die, you die.'

'Sometimes you die anyway,' said Jane.

'Good gracious, Rose, you are a gloomy girl today. What's wrong?'

'I'm tired.'

'Still tired? I told you last time you were working far too hard.'

She blushed. 'It's not work, not at all. I was just out late, at a party.' She tried to change the subject, made an observation about the tabby's ragged ear; didn't want a flood of awkward questions about where the party was, or who had asked her. It had been bad enough this morning, when Isobel had come to fetch her, found her still in bed at noon – though fortunately alone. She had invented some excuse about a disturbed and restless night; hadn't breathed a word about going out with Christopher; was still extremely cautious about admitting her involvement with the artist, especially as it had developed since last night. She'd just been thoroughly relieved that Christopher had left at dawn, and wasn't lying there beside her; had totally forgotten her standing invitation to spend every Sunday at Windy Hollow House. She had jumped at the idea when Isobel first mentioned it, since weekends could be lonely, and she always felt relaxed in the Mackenzies' friendly home, but she was now beginning to realise there could be complications, if Christopher decided to break his weekend purdah.

Isobel leaned forward, eased the knife and grapefruit from her hand. 'That's enough, Rose, honestly. If you go on chopping fruit at such a rate, we'll finish up with twenty tons of marmalade. Let's just flop today. It's so rare to have a Sunday with no one dropping in – no meals to cook, no family – so we ought to make the most of it. We'll have cheese on toast on trays for tea, take things really easy. In fact, why not pop up to my bedroom and have a little zizz.'

'Oh, no.' Jane knew what might well happen if she climbed into that double bed – more playbacks of last night, more taunting naked pictures, more longings, shame, resentment. 'It's not that kind of tiredness. More a sort of hangover.' Not from wine, she brooded – though she had drunk more than usual – but a hangover from Christopher; her head still thick with him, her breasts still flushed and tingling, her mind dizzy, woozy, fuddled, and in turmoil.

'Well, how about a walk, then, to blow away the cobwebs? Byron would like that.'

'Okay,' said Jane, getting up to fetch the boxer's lead. They had never had a dog at home, only three small goldfish, and, once, a peevish rabbit. She was already fond of Byron – a sloppy, dribbling madcap, who had been purchased as a guard-dog, but who worshipped all mankind, including muggers, rapists, burglars, gunmen, thugs.

Isobel dug her out some wellingtons, pulling woollen khaki knee-socks over her own purple patterned tights. Her clothes always looked confused, as if she had started off by dressing up for some formal fancy occasion, then changed her mind and dragged on something casual, and lastly added one more layer, as if to harmonise the two. Today she wore a ruffled chiffon blouse over a baggy tweedy skirt, and a long-line knitted cardigan in a bossy shade of scarlet, which shouted at the purple, but matched her strawberry earrings. Jane's wardrobe was now equally capricious, since Isobel had given her a whole plethora of clothes – throw-outs from the Bits Box, cast-offs from her family (male as well as female), and also brand-new outfits which she claimed she'd bought dirt-cheap.

Isobel stirred the saucepan one last time, turned the gas to simmer, locked the garden doors, then fought off Byron's kisses as she tried to fix the lead. 'Right, beach or woods?' she asked.

'Woods,' said Jane. She felt too fragile to face the pounding waves, the wide-awake sea-wind, which would bluster and oppress. The woods would offer quiet and shade, especially on this wan November Sunday, which seemed to mark the change from glossy golden autumn to grey and gloomy winter; the trees half-bare and shivering, the sky leaden, overcast. She walked in silence for a while, letting Isobel divert her with a long and complicated tale about their next-door neighbour's eldest brother's wife. She tried to stop her thoughts from doubling back to Christopher, though she knew she had to ask a vital question; kept rehearsing it, rephrasing it; finally jumped in when the talk had turned to babies. 'Has Christopher got children?' she asked, nonchalantly and casually, as if the thought had just occurred to her.

'Christopher? Oh no.'

'What, from none of his three wives?'

'Well, his second wife had three – all girls – but they were by her first husband.'

'Did they ever live with him?'

Isobel shook her head. 'They were more or less grown up by then, and I don't think darling Christopher's all that keen on teenagers – or on toddlers either, for that matter.'

'Is that why he didn't have them – I mean, he decided from the start he didn't want a family?'

'I've no idea. I've never liked to ask, to tell the truth. Mind you, a lot of creative artists aren't that keen on kids. They're kids themselves, in one way, and need a lot of nannying. I suppose they see their creations as their children.'

Jane stooped down to find a stick for Byron. So she knew something Isobel did not – something private, intimate, which the artist had confided to her, and her alone. But was it really true? Part of her still didn't quite believe him. Or perhaps she didn't want to. It was important he was fertile, not just in his work, but fertile in all ways. She had seen him fathering children in her stupid secret fantasies – children with his strengths, his skills, her features, her long hair. She flung the stick with all her force, started running after it herself, Byron overtaking her in a tangle of six legs.

'You've revived!' smiled Isobel, panting to catch up, breasts and bracelets shaking, hair tumbling from its pins.

'Hey, Isobel?' said Jane, out of breath herself as she ran another circle, then doubled back with Byron at her heels.

'What now?'

'Is it common to be . . . barren?' She wished there was some other word. 'Childless' wouldn't do. You could choose to be childless, deliberately avoid conceiving, as the artist might have done. 'I mean, like my parents were?'

'Pretty common, yes. One in ten, I think they say, and that's men as well as women. I remember the first time I got pregnant, the man assured me I was safe; told me he'd had cancer as a child, which had left him *hors de combat*, as it were. Less than five weeks later, I was sicking up my breakfast every morning.'

Jane stopped dead in her tracks, swung round to face Isobel, forcing her to stop as well. 'What do you mean, the first time you got pregnant?'

'I had a child at seventeen,' said Isobel. Her voice was soft, impassive.

'So where was Tom?' Jane plunged on down the path, tried to make her own voice sound less sharp and angry. She had heard the touching story of Isobel's young life – but a completely different version, which contradicted this one. Rowan had reported that her parents had been childhood sweethearts who'd lived in the same village and been destined for each other almost from the kindergarten. So why had Isobel betrayed her almost-husband?

'Oh, Tom was there all right.' Isobel struggled to keep up. 'All of twenty-one, and already terribly committed to his medicine. My father was a doctor – so was his – and we'd been paired off since our childhood, in a sense; all the aunties clucking "Wouldn't it be nice if . . .", and "They've always been so close, those two, got so much in common", and "How lovely for both families", and all that sort of stuff. I was very fond of Tom, in fact, and we did have lots in common, but I was only just a kid, Rose, and dying to sail round the world, or cross the Gobi desert on a camel, not just settle down and be a wife.' Isobel ducked to avoid an overhanging branch, snapping off a beech twig as she passed, breaking it in pieces, as if to punctuate her story. 'I suppose the other guy was lying when he claimed that we'd be safe, but I realise now I probably wanted to get pregnant, so I wouldn't have to marry. It was a sort of mad rebellion against my devout and happy family, who saw no other option for their dear devoted daughter than a nice conventional wedding, with an engagement notice in *The Times* and half a dozen bridesmaids in pink satin.'

'Why are you *telling* me all this?' Jane was almost shouting, running on ahead again; didn't want to hear, didn't want another happy family revealed as just a sham. She stumbled on a tree-root, hobbled to a standstill. 'Let's go back,' she muttered. 'The path's all wet and muddy, and now I've hurt my leg.'

'You'd better rest it for a minute. Here, sit down on this log.' Isobel patted the rough bark, coaxed Jane down beside her. 'I'm telling you all this, Rose, because I hoped it might be helpful.'

Jane said nothing. 'Helpful' seemed hardly the right word. The last thing that she wanted was more scandal, more dark secrets, more devious mothers who weren't what they appeared. She edged away uneasily as the older woman tried to squeeze her arm, Byron nudging close the other side, all dribble and devotion.

'Look, wait a minute, darling. You don't quite understand. This is something rather vital which I've been brooding on for days, included in my prayers each night. I agonised for ages before finally deciding that perhaps it was my duty to share my story with you. I'm just sorry if I took you by surprise. I planned it all quite differently, intended to ease into the subject very sort of gradually, instead of blurting it all out like that. I suppose I was embarrassed.' She frowned, pulled off her gloves, started chewing one cold finger. 'I've never told another soul, you see, not in all these years – not even my own children.'

'Well, there's no need to tell me.'

'Perhaps there *is* a need, Rose.'

'What d'you mean?'

Isobel reached forward, wiped a gob of dirty froth from Byron's lower jaw, stayed crouching down beside the dog, back still turned to Jane. 'I had my child adopted,' she said slowly.

Byron filled the silence – panting, frisking, charging round in circles, laying hopeful sticks at both their feet. Jane ignored both dog and sticks. 'I see,' she muttered coldly. 'And that's supposed to cheer me up?'

'It's supposed to show you that even loving, decent mothers who want their babies desperately can still be pressured into giving them away.'

'You *didn't* want your baby,' Jane retorted, kicking at the log. She dared not voice the fury she was feeling: that devoutly Christian Isobel should conceive a child almost as a ruse, to avoid another problem, rebel against her parents. She pushed Byron's slobbering mouth away, envying him his simple boisterous happiness.

'I did, Rose. The instant she was born I knew she was the most beautiful important thing I'd . . .'

'So why didn't you hang on to her – sod the stupid pressures and stick out for what you wanted?'

'At seventeen?'

'So what? I'm only a year older, and I wouldn't give my child away.'

'It's entirely different now, Rose. You just can't imagine what it was like in the late fifties, *and* in small-town America.'

'America?'

'Yes. I ran off to the States as soon as I realised I was pregnant. Well, maybe "ran off"'s the wrong word. It was all officially arranged, all above board, so to speak. I told my loving family I'd decided that I needed a bit more time and space before I settled down – maybe an au pair job abroad – and once they'd recovered from the shock, they actually helped me fix it up, though of course they'd no idea there was a much worse shock I'd totally concealed. It was really quite amazing that my father didn't twig. I mean, there he was – a doctor – and me with bloated breasts and morning sickness . . .' Isobel shook her head, incredulous, plumped back on the log. 'Though I suppose he was just blinkered, in a way. The scandals and seductions happened to his patients, or to poor benighted working girls, not to his own chaste and cosseted daughter. Anyway, he had this friend in Wernersville, Pennsylvania, a neurologist with three young kids, who jumped at the thought of a docile English nanny who was only asking bed and board and a bit of pocket money. The trouble is, she wasn't all that docile, and had planned to do a bunk the minute her bulge showed, simply go to ground. Unfortunately, he . . .'

'Isobel, my . . . my leg hurts.'

'Well, perhaps you've sprained your ankle. You'd better take your boot off, and let me have a look.'

'No, it's not as bad as that. I'd just like to go home.'

'Home where?'

Jane paused. If she went back to the studio, the artist might appear again. With no Mrs Harville-Shaw to tether him to Sunday tea or chores, he might come round to apologise, or try to change her mind. However much she chafed at it, she was still tied to Isobel. 'Er, back to your place, if that's all right with you.'

'Yes, fine. I'd like to pop some things round to Avril in the village, but that won't take me long, and you can curl up on the sofa and watch the Sunday film.'

'Okay.' The rubber boots were slipping, chafing at the heel. Jane longed to kick them off, remove every single article which had come from Isobel, shed her like a skin. How could it be right to conceive a child as she had – so casually, impulsively, with the father just a cypher – or worse, a rat, a liar? Had her own father been like that, or her mother fallen pregnant just to avoid some other guy, or to spite her loving family? She picked another stick up, not for Byron this time, but to slash the tangled undergrowth, swiping at the bushes as she passed them.

'Rose . . .'

'Mm?'

'Look, I know you're angry with me, but . . .'

'I'm not.'

'Well, a little bit upset, then. The problem is if you refuse to let me finish, then there's no real point or purpose in me telling you the story in the first place.' Isobel was talking faster now, as if determined to continue, despite the fact that another group of walkers were now bearing down towards them – a family with three small boys, two muddy panting spaniels. She smiled and nodded as they passed, then resumed her flood of words. 'I fought to keep my baby, Rose, did everything I could – ran away, lived on Seven-Up and cornflakes, took the only jobs available – washing dishes in the evening, and shampooing hair by day; finally caught a really bad infection, and landed up in a so-called Christian refuge, where they branded me a foreigner as well as a fallen woman. They made me feel a monster for condemning my own child to what they saw as a life of shame and poverty, instead of giving her the chance of two prosperous settled parents who could remove that label "bastard" – which to them was worse than "leper". In the end, I couldn't stand the guilt, so I signed the papers, signed my child away.' Isobel paused at last, as if marking her child's loss with half a minute's silence. Jane slowed to match her amble, but refused to comment, refused to say a word, just continued thwacking bushes with her stick.

'I never found out where she went, could never get in touch with her, never even knew if she was healthy. It was as if she'd died, in one sense, though of course she was very much alive in my mind and thoughts and longings. For a while, I was absolutely obsessed with babies. Any one I saw could be my Angela. I'd called her that deliberately, to undo all the stigma, turn her into an angel. It was also Tom's own mother's name, and I was still in love with Tom, you see – returned to him, eventually – and married him.'

In love, thought Jane ironically. You deceive a man, dishonour him, then claim to be in love. She stopped to swat a silver birch, a ghostly-white and slender bride, hemmed in by lowering oaks – a deceitful tree whose bark was scaly-rough, its fair skin pocked and mottled, when you peered a little closer. 'Did you ever tell him?' she asked, frowning.

'No.'

They both walked on, in silence; even Byron seeming chastened now, padding sluggishly behind them, instead of bounding on in front.

'I realise that was wrong, Rose – a betrayal, if you like. I suppose I was a coward. I was frightened that I'd lose him – lose everything, in fact. And if my family found out . . .' She left the sentence hanging, as if the thought of their reaction – the recrimination, horror – was too painful to be voiced. 'They were already fearfully upset that I'd left their friends in Wernersville, and in most suspicious circumstances. I had to keep on lying, even in my letters, invent absurd excuses, make up stories, reasons, fabricate addresses every time I wrote to them; pretend I'd got the travelling bug and itched to see the whole of Pennsylvania, and then the whole East Coast. I'd never lied, Rose, never, and suddenly I'd become an expert at it – a truly fallen woman, as far as my own standards were concerned. But when I finally went home, they were so relieved to see me, so delighted I was fit and well, and seemed just the same old Isobel, that I simply didn't have the heart to churn them all up again, or let them know how much I'd changed, and I couldn't bear the thought of hurting Tom . . .'

'So you had your six pink satin bridesmaids and your notice in *The Times*?'

'Eight bridesmaids, actually, in yellow-sprigged organza.'

Jane didn't smile, just flung her stick away. 'So your husband never really knew you – not the real you?'

'That's a bit extreme, Rose. I was only hiding one thing in my life.'

'A pretty whopping thing, though.'

'Well, I tried to justify it, decided I must start again, put all that behind me. I'd confessed to God, and confided in my vicar, who was a very holy and compassionate man, and talked about forgiveness – the sort that lets the past go, allows you a clean slate. And I vowed I'd make it up to Tom all our married life. I mean, even now, I suppose the memorial window's like a sort of reparation.' Jane tried to close her ears. She didn't want the artist's precious window ensnared in this whole sham; its theme of Resurrection twisted and distorted to fit a child who'd vanished, a child whose very birth insulted Tom. She stopped to remove the tentacles of a trailing thorny bramble, which were clutching at her sleeve.

Isobel picked a last lone blackberry, linked her arm through Jane's.

'Look, we're going off the point. I only told you the whole saga so you'd understand how loved and wanted babies sometimes come to be adopted. I know you said how sad you felt that your own mother had rejected you, but maybe she was . . .'

'Could we end this conversation?' Jane interrupted rudely. She couldn't really understand her anger. Isobel had tried to help – that was crystal clear. And it must have been an ordeal for her to rake up the whole scandal, face her pain and loss again, admit all her deficiencies to someone more or less a stranger who might rat on her, betray her, recount the sorry story to the artist, or to Rowan. Isobel had trusted her, implicitly and totally, so why was she not grateful, or even reassured?

She unlatched her arm, thrust both her hands deep into her pockets, plodded on dejectedly, trying not to think of her own mother, whom Isobel unwittingly had murdered. She simply hadn't realised that a natural mother could be kept in such gross ignorance, never told the name or whereabouts of her child's adoptive parents, so that child and mother were not just separated, but dead to one another. Did that still happen nowadays? She splashed fiercely through a puddle, mud spattering her boots. Secretly, naïvely, she'd been imagining wild reunions with the mother who had borne her. On the days she didn't fear her dead (or mad, or sick, or criminal), she saw her searching frantically for her lost but longed-for daughter, about to track her down, hold her in her arms, tell her how she'd missed her, bitterly regretted having given her away. Isobel had killed that hope, destroyed that precious meeting; had also killed the myth of her own straightforward happy family – she and Tom devoted, no skeletons in cupboards, no sordid complications. Why were adults' lives so messy – the artist shamed and bitter because he couldn't father children; Isobel's whole marriage built on a deception, and her own adoptive parents feeding her with lies for eighteen years?

'Oh, look!' said Isobel. 'A hawk.'

Jane glanced up to where Isobel was pointing, saw a proud brown bird circling in the sky, mobbed by a black crow, who kept jostling it, attacking.

'That beastly crow will kill it!' Jane exclaimed.

'No. He's defending his own patch, trying to drive it off, that's all.'

'But I thought hawks were the real bullies, with vicious claws and talons.'

'Crows are bigger, though, and they won't stand competition.'

Jane watched the brute black body dive-bombing and harassing, listened to the hoarsely guttural cry. She turned away, couldn't face such unreasonable aggression. Her own was bad enough.

'Make yourself some tea while I'm at Avril's,' Isobel said, smoothing back a strand of Jane's long hair. 'And there's fruit cake in the tin, and a new loaf in the larder. Remember what I told you, Rose, it's your home now as much as mine, so do help yourself to anything you want.'

'Thanks,' said Jane, ashamed. Isobel was kind, generous to a fault, a truly loving giving mother. Yet . . .

She tripped and almost fell. The light was fading now, though it was only four o'clock; dusk blurring all the outlines, smoking up between the trees, like fog. The woods looked strangely threatening in the gloom: ivy choking anorexic birches, bare trunks split and splintered, damaged in the recent storm, whole limbs torn off, rotting where they lay.

'Nearly home,' said Isobel, fastening Byron's leash.

'Yes,' lied Jane, as they crossed the road, walked the last few weary yards to Windy Hollow House.

'I love you,' the man whispered, his eyes intense, seductive, as he sank back on the bed.

'I love you, too.' The woman seemed to merge into his chest-hair, as the shot discreetly faded, replaced by pounding breakers, prurient violins.

Jane switched to ITV. Sex was so uncomplicated in those old romantic movies. Bodies simply fused – no belts, or stubborn zips, no messy contraception, no fears or guilts or hang-ups. It should have been like that when Christopher returned last night – just a sinking-fusing-merging to the strains of Paganini. It had started off that way – her lying on the bed in nothing but her bracelet, listening to his footsteps throbbing up the stairs; determined to relax this time, simply offer him her body. And, instead, she'd panicked right at the last moment, thrown her clothes on as he strode into the bedroom; somehow needed to be covered – no, not just covered, steel-clad – armoured totally against him.

All her fears had snowballed – not just fear of pregnancy, but fear of sex itself: all those gruesome articles linking it with AIDS; commercials showing coffins, programmes featuring people who had died from just one single casual fling. Yet how could she discuss it without offending him, or sounding so neurotic he wouldn't want her anyway? He wasn't in the mood at all for cool and quiet discussion; seemed fevered and on heat, driven by some force beyond his own control; used his voice only for cajoling, his lips for stopping hers. She had let him kiss her, let him take her top off, even felt herself responding when he'd moved his slow but urgent mouth from her throat down to her navel; flurry and excitement now curdling with the fear. Then suddenly she'd stalled; freezing, as she had before, when he tried to take her skirt off, irrationally afraid of going any further, being naked in all senses, exposed to him and open.

She reached out for the box of sweets, unwrapped a chocolate hazelnut. Was it so irrational? After all, Isobel had found herself in trouble by being too impulsive and too trusting, and *her* affair had been way back in the fifties, before AIDS was even heard of. She sagged back in her chair. Isobel's confession still seemed to weigh her down – all its implications: lies again, and loss; things not what they seemed; daughter ripped from mother, wife deceiving husband.

She moved the sweet towards her mouth, left it still untasted as she crunched not the tiny hazelnut, but a sudden bitter overwhelming thought. Had that rat, that lying bastard, who'd fathered fatherless Angela been Christopher himself? It wasn't that impossible. He and Isobel had known each other years, had been living in the same small incestuous stretch of southern England for almost half a century. And wouldn't it explain Isobel's interest in the artist, her strange obsessive mixture of resentment and attraction? It could be just his line to claim to be infertile every time he met a girl he fancied. Or perhaps he'd honestly believed it, then discovered he was wrong. Or maybe Isobel had spared him, never breathed a word about their casual mutual child. Angela Harville-Shaw. She tried the name out, substituted Jane, instead, then Rose. Rose Harville-Shaw sounded best of all; could be wife or daughter.

She fretted to the window, peered out at the drive, to see if there was any sign of Isobel returning. She must question her again, ask her more about her lover – how old he'd been, where he'd lived, how and when she'd met him. The drive was empty, save for shadows – nervous trembling shadows which looked as restless and uncertain as she felt. Isobel was playing Lady Bountiful, visiting a pensioner who was housebound with arthritis. Isobel the Good; Christopher the Bad. Labels could mislead. Yet Isobel *was* bountiful – genuinely warm-hearted, while Christopher was moody, churlish, impatient and offhand. And, despite her anger and resentment, she somehow loved them both; had become intimately involved with both, in just the last few hours. Both had entrusted her with their private shameful secrets; both had called her 'darling', which had jolted.

She switched channels once again, back to the old movie; the two smiling sated lovers now sipping pink champagne. Of course they'd never get a hangover – or AIDS. The Keats Ode she'd done for A-level suddenly buzzed into her head. She had known it off by heart then, could still remember most of it.

> 'All breathing human passion far above,
> That leaves a heart high-sorrowful and cloyed,
> A burning forehead, and a parching tongue.'

Keats understood so well. Her head still burned from Christopher, her tongue felt raw and swollen; whereas the lovers in the film looked totally unscathed – the woman's perfect make-up still triumphantly in place, her hair as neat as Amy's when she'd just walked out of Snippers. She longed for life to be like that – a light romantic comedy with a simple happy ending.

'Darling,' breathed the goddess on the screen. 'I'm going to have our baby.'

'Mum!' called someone else, a loud impatient yodelling voice, preceded by the slamming of two doors, and a fusillade from Byron.

Jane swung round as a tall untidy man with reddish hair burst in through the door, loaded down with two bulging plastic carrier-bags, a dress-suit on a hanger, and a pile of files and books. 'Hi!' he said, stretching out a hand which didn't reach her, then collapsing on the sofa and off-loading his possessions on the floor.

'Hi,' she echoed shyly, comparing the high forehead, the almost girlish mouth and ragged thatch of hair with their copy on the mantelpiece – Hadley, grinning sheepishly at an out-of-focus camera. She glanced back at the clearer lines of the flesh-and-blood duplicate, now sprawling with his feet up on the couch. Even without the photograph, she would have recognised immediately that this was Isobel's son. They shared the same colouring, the same wayward wavy hair, the same eyes which changed from grey to green, according to the light; and though Hadley was much thinner, he, too, had a plumpish face, clumsy hands and feet, and several layers of disparate clothes, bulking out his slim and rangy figure.

He fumbled for the chocolates, stuffed three into his mouth at once. 'I'm Hadley, by the way,' he said, pausing in his chewing, and pushing Byron off his dress-suit, which the dog was using as a rug.

'Yes,' she said. 'I know.'

'Oh, sorry. Have we met before? I sometimes get quite muddled.

Mum knows so many people, and I'm not home that much these days. Where *is* Mum, by the way?'

'She's out, visiting a lady in the village.'

'What, that dreadful Mrs Brooking, with the cats?'

'No, someone called Avril, with arthritis.'

'Never heard of her. Look, I'm frightfully sorry, but I don't know your name, either.'

'It's okay,' said Jane, glancing at his hands, which were large and freckled and dusted with fair hair. 'We've never met. I'm Rose.'

'Rose!' He spun the name out, his voice rising with new interest. 'I've heard a lot about you.'

'Oh, dear.'

'No, all good stuff, I promise. Mum's raved about you on the phone. You're a stained-glass artist, aren't you?'

'Well, I only . . .'

'Don't you work for Christopher – his new assistant, Mum said?'

'No, not quite his assis . . .'

'What d'you think about this window – the one he's making for her? I'm not sure I approve. It's costing nearly twenty grand, and when you think what you could do with all that cash – really make some difference not just to a fusty church with a dozen dear old souls shuffling in on Sundays to show off their best hats and sing a jolly hymn or two, but to some real human problem. The homeless, for example.' He swung his legs down, as if to emphasise his point; Byron leaping up as well, his doggy face expectant, hoping for a second walk. 'There must be several thousand dossers sleeping rough in London every night. Well, if Mum used her spare money on the soup-run, instead of . . . Byron, *down*! You're hurting.' He pushed the boxer's paw off, an insistent paw nudging at his chest. 'Well, maybe not the soup-run – Mum's not into tramps – but some single-parent family or something. I mean, she could really change their life, maybe even . . .'

Jane switched the movie off. It was difficult to concentrate with the lovers' wild endearments panting through Hadley's talk of tramps. He had veered off on a tangent now about how he'd left the church, and was trying to see if he could harmonise the quantum revolution with the idea of reincarnation. They seemed to have moved extraordinarily quickly from their first brief mumbled 'Hi's to what she'd call deep water; dispensed with the preliminaries, the painless trivialities which started off most normal conversations.

153

Hadley clearly shared not just his mother's colouring, but her gift of spinning words.

'If you believe in reincarnation, Rose, you could say it doesn't matter what you suffer in a life or two, because there are always several more to come, and maybe dossers are quite lucky compared with cockroaches or stag beetles, or things which just get trampled underfoot, but that's a cop-out, don't you think?' He scratched roughly at his ankle, pushing up his trouser-leg and delving down his woolly scarlet sock. 'I'm sorry to bang on about the homeless, but it's not just tramps, you realise. There are crowds of kids still only in their teens camping out in cardboard boxes, or injecting drugs and rooting round old waste-bins for their nosh. Now surely you can't tell me it's more important for the nation to splurge its money on a new Turner for the Tate rather than get out and feed the hungry.'

'Well, no, but . . .' Jane broke off. She had used much the same arguments herself, and Christopher had shot her down, even called her facile, trotting out tired clichés with no real understanding of either art or economics. She could hardly take that caustic line with Hadley, so she tried cobbling up some brief defence, largely cribbed from Christopher, though lacking his high tone. 'But maybe people *need* art,' she began. 'I mean, just as much as food, especially nowadays when all the stress is put on things like hand-outs and the dole, and no one seems to think in terms of man's other higher needs, or ask if . . .'

'You try and tell some starving bum about his higher needs, or fob him off with a still-life of three apples and a lemon, when he's crying out for good red meat.' Hadley removed his denim jacket, to reveal an orange sweatshirt with 'Flamingos Do It On One Leg' printed on the front.

'But a lot of people have got their good red meat.' The Mackenzies, for example. Jane's voice petered out as she watched Hadley suck the strawberry cream from chocolate number seven. She doubted he'd been hungry in his life, and wasn't it just a fraction hypocritical for him to champion the homeless, when he'd lived since pampered babyhood in a plush six-bedroomed house, overstuffed with treasures? He should move a few dossers or drug-injecting teens into his own empty room upstairs; an extensive room with a view of the large garden, and his second-best stereo left casually behind. But Christopher would regard that as totally irrelevant; insist that one should argue not from individual anecdote, but from sound objective principle. His voice was always clamouring in her head, unsettling her, confusing her, making her aware that she couldn't hope to match him intellectually. It hurt to have her views dismissed as facile. But maybe most things were 'tired clichés' when you'd reached the age of sixty, heard it all before. At least Hadley saw the issues as fresh and wildly urgent. In fact, she felt more in tune with *his* line than the artist's, so why was she opposing him? Because she didn't want the Resurrection Window melted down to chicken noodle soup.

'Look,' she said, trying to see the window in her head, in the hope it might inspire her, fuel her arguments. 'The radicals used to say pull down Covent Garden or close the National Gallery, and distribute all the money to the poor. But once the poor had blown it, we'd still be left with poverty, except now we'd have no paintings and no opera, to make life seem worthwhile, or . . .' She broke off again, embarrassed. She had never been to an opera, hardly knew the names of any, and even the National Gallery was unknown territory. She must sound really phoney, paraphrasing Christopher, without either his experience, or his bold command of words.

Hadley pleated a chocolate-paper into a tiny concertina, offered it to Byron, who started whining with excitement. 'How can opera make life worthwhile when the great mass of people don't know Verdi from Neil Kinnock? Or pictures, for that matter. What difference does it make to Joe Bloggs on the dole that we've saved Poussin's *Finding of Moses* for the nation?'

Jane reached out for a toffee, to give herself a thinking-space. She had never heard of Poussin, but Christopher had claimed that it was vitally important that paintings were just *there* – as part of man's achievement, the mysterious unique creations which raised him higher than mere animals, gave him a taste of the immortal. No – that was sex wasn't it, not art? She was getting muddled, and not sure she believed it now, in any case. Her first brief taste of sex had seemed all too fiercely physical – sticking zips and probing tongues, the smell of perspiration, the taste of nicotine.

'Look at Hitler,' Hadley said, as if the Nazi Führer had just goose-stepped into the room. 'He adored Wagner, didn't he – probably played it in the gas chambers, and Goering was an art-collector, a highly cultured brute who nicked half the Renoirs from the French, and . . .'

'Yes, but that proves nothing, does it? You can't ban all art and music just because the Nazis happened to go for them. It's like banning chocolate cake because it was the Yorkshire Ripper's favourite.'

'*Was* it?' Hadley asked. 'How on earth did you know that?'

'I didn't. I just made it up. But someone told me once that evil people almost always have a sweet tooth, as if they're seeking in their diet what's missing in their character.' 'Someone' was the artist, and she was churning out his views again. His amazing store of knowledge was like an encyclopaedia in several different volumes, while her own mind was a puny *Reader's Digest*.

'Well, Hitler loved *Sachertorte*, so maybe there's some truth in it.'

'What's *Sachertorte*?' She recognised the word as German, though Hadley's pronunciation left a lot to be desired.

'Just the Viennese for chocolate cake.' He laughed. 'Actually, my father loved it, too, so that theory doesn't wash. Whatever else, my father wasn't evil.' He paused a moment, flicked back his red hair. 'You know, if I'm honest with myself, my objection to that window is probably less to do with principles, or cash, than with the fact I'm just a bit pissed off that Dad's getting all the honour of a grand memorial window, when he . . . he . . .'

'When he what?' asked Jane, to fill the awkward silence.

'Oh, nothing.' Hadley shrugged. 'It's just that Dad and I never got along too well. He was always so damned busy, never had much time for us as kids. Yet how could I complain, when he was DOING GOOD, in capitals – tending to the sick and all that stuff. Other people *needed* him, you see, more than we were meant to – or allowed to. D'you know . . .' He laughed again, shamefacedly this time. 'I sometimes almost wished I had a Nazi for a father.'

Jane shared his grin. 'A Nazi who played Wagner while he guzzled chocolate cake?' At least she knew who Wagner was. Christopher often played his hi-fi in the studio, and she had picked up names and titles, tried to match the composers to their works. Whatever her deficiencies, she was undoubtedly more knowledgeable than the Jane who'd fled from Shrepton just six weeks ago, a Jane who'd never heard of Bayreuth, and the Ring Cycle, let alone Stockhausen or Boulez.

'I'm starving,' Hadley announced, as if he'd tired at last of Hitler, Wagner and London's plague of tramps. 'I only really stopped off here to try to scrounge a meal. I'm on my way back to college. We stayed up half last night at this rather crazy ball, then crashed out at a friend's pad just fifteen miles away. I did try to phone, but nobody was in.'

'We went out for a walk.'

'Poor you! I loathe Mum's walks. They're always sort of ambles with free nature-study lessons thrown in as a bonus.'

'I didn't get the nature study.'

'No?'

'No.' Or perhaps she should say yes. Illegitimate babies could be classed as nature study. Supposing she just blurted out what Isobel had told her? 'Hey, Hadley, do you realise you're not your mother's second child, but actually her third? You've got an elder half-sister somewhere in the States.' The idea really frightened her, though she would never dream of doing it. Secrets gave you power, the power to crush, destroy; to change beliefs, relationships; outlaw love and trust.

'I suppose I could just raid the larder,' Hadley mumbled, shaking out the last sweets from the box. 'Did Mum say what's for supper?'

'Cheese on toast.'

Hadley made a face. 'We had caviare last night. And venison, and real out-of-season strawberries – huge fat luscious juicy ones almost as big as avocados.'

'No wonder you feel so bad about the starving.'

Hadley yelped with laughter. 'Yeah. I like it! Come on, Rose, let's go and do the soup-run. I'm sure Mum's got cream of caviare.'

'No,' said Jane, rooting through the larder, while Hadley sat watching, feet up on the Aga. 'Only spring vegetable, tomato, or a tin of beef and leek.'

'Spring vegetable,' chose Hadley. 'It's so damn cold outside, I like the thought of spring. They ought to make snowdrop soup, or crocus and narcissi.'

'Spring vegetable's a sham,' said Jane, thinking back to her first month as a nomad, when breakfast, lunch and supper had been soup soup soup soup soup. 'It's just coloured water with odd bits of confetti floating on the top.'

'Lots of food's a sham – especially things in boxes. The pictures on the outside look fantastic, and inside it's all ersatz. I suppose I was lucky to have Mum for nineteen years. She never buys that sort of muck. It's only since I've been a student, catering for myself, that I've realised what a con it is.'

Jane said nothing. She approved of Isobel's cooking, but not her mess and muddle. The larder was chaotic – things like oven-cleaner mixed up with rice and cornflakes; flour and sugar spilling from their bags; sticky strawberry jam smeared across the biscuit tin. She had never really thought about her own mother's tidy kitchen, her neat and well-scrubbed fridge, the regular and well-timed meals which appeared steaming on the table at the dot of one, or six; just taken them for granted. She was starving now, like Hadley; would have welcomed Amy's bacon roll, or her steak and kidney pie. She didn't know the time, had left her watch upstairs, but her parents might be sitting down to table exactly at this moment, the third chair empty, the pie too big for two of them. She could suddenly see the pie-funnel her mother always used – an elongated blackbird in ceramic, its head and neck stretched vertically, so that the gaping yellow beak appeared just above the pastry. She had loved it as a child, that surprising glimpse of glossy black when her mother cut the pie; the strange sight of a china bird standing in a pond of meat and gravy.

'What's wrong?' asked Hadley, strolling to the cupboard to find a saucepan for the soup. 'You look as if you've seen a ghost.'

She shivered. Ghosts and shadows. Her parents might well fear her dead; a corpse by now, a wraith. She really ought to contact them, as Isobel had urged; at least tell them she was safe, stop them fretting, grieving. 'Do you want cheese on toast as well?' she asked, trying to change the subject, quash the thoughts and memories churning in her mind.

'What do you mean, "as well"? You make me sound a glutton!' He grinned. 'Mum had this awful friend who always said "Milk *and* sugar?" when she poured the tea; put such stress on the "and", you felt like a pig with all four feet in the trough if you dared to ask for both.'

'Well, we could have buck rarebit – cheese on toast *and* eggs.' Jane felt gratified by Hadley's laugh. He seemed to laugh easily, enjoy her company. She was doing rather better, now; no longer the shy booby she must have seemed at Adrian's last night, but someone with opinions and rejoinders. Okay, the views weren't quite her own, but at least she wasn't sitting there in silence, or getting all tied up in knots, or blushing, as she often did with Christopher.

'What's it like, working with old Harville-Shaw?' asked Hadley, as if he'd peered into her mind, and seen the artist sitting there, taking up his residence, filling the whole space.

'Okay,' she said, jibbing at the 'old', but determined to be cool and non-committal.

'You live there, too, Mum said.'

She nodded, sprinkling powdered soup onto the panful of cold water, and cursing her hot cheeks. Now she *was* blushing, and Hadley gazing straight into her face – no, through it to her mind again, so that he could probably see the artist lying on the bed with her, kissing her bare breasts, forcing his deft tongue . . .

'Shall I make the toast?' he asked.

'Yes, please.' She turned away to hide the blush, but couldn't shift her thoughts from mouths. Did Hadley have a girlfriend, thrust his tongue between her lips, tasting what she'd eaten; swap saliva with her? She had never known a kiss could be so intimate, so . . .

'Dad always burnt the toast,' said Hadley, meditatively, sliding bread into the toaster, and breaking up the kiss. 'Regularly, each breakfast-time. Making the toast was the only thing he did around the house, his only contribution to the morning rush, yet he never seemed to really get the hang of it, not even with this automatic setting. I know it sounds dumb, Rose, but the thing I've missed most since he died is the sight of him standing rather glumly by the sink, scraping all the burnt bits off, and making so much mess, he . . .' Hadley's voice was wavering. Jane could tell he was upset; clearly missed this father who had always been too busy for him, and would now never see him graduate, or marry.

'It seemed so out of character. I mean, a surgeon's really skilful with his hands, needs split-second timing, yet there was Dad, a wizard in the operating theatre, but bungling his small chore.' He checked his own toast, still pale and barely warm. 'It's funny, I always think of Dad in terms of breakfast, slicing the top off his boiled egg, like it was a cancerous growth or something, and complaining to my mother that the knives weren't sharp enough, as if he was so used to his scalpels nothing else would do, not even for just cutting up his bacon. Mind you, we hardly ever saw him at any other time. He was rarely in for dinner – always some emergency, or meeting – and even Sunday lunch-times, the phone kept ringing all the time. It was almost a red-letter day if we still had him there for the apple pie and coffee.'

Jane sliced cheese, cracked eggs. Her own punctilious father had never missed a meal, had always had the time to mend her broken toys, help her with her homework, chauffeur her to swimming baths, or tennis courts, or parties. She had seen it as her natural right, not a rare and special privilege. She glanced at the red phone sitting on the table between the teapot and a cat. She ought to ring him now, today, not dither any longer.

'Mum's been gone for ages.' Hadley checked his watch. 'If she doesn't get a move on, I'll probably miss her altogether. I'm sorry to seem rude, Rose, but I'll have to grab my nosh and run. It's six o'clock already, and I've got a rehearsal at half eight. I'm playing Alonso in *The Tempest*. Just a student thing, but it's quite a lot of fun. Hey, why don't you come down for it? We're putting it on the first week of December, and it'd be really great to have you in the audience. It finishes by ten, so we could go out for a meal, and you could meet the cast and everything. The man playing Caliban's fantastic, should have gone to drama school instead of grafting away at dreary Economics.' He struck a pose, screwed up his face, imitating Caliban. 'Or, if you come on the last night, we always have a party – just an informal sort of knees-up in the Green Room, but if you don't mind Spanish plonk in paper cups . . . Well, what d'you say? Could you manage it, do you think?'

'Well, yes, I'm sure I can.' Jane tried to focus her attention on stirring soup, poaching eggs, finding knives and forks. She felt extremely flattered to be asked, yet also rather thrown. She hardly knew this man, yet here he was inviting her to a play, a meal, a party. And what about the problem of getting there and back, catching the last train – or maybe missing the last train, then having to explain why she wasn't in the studio for nine o'clock next morning? It felt disloyal to Christopher to agree to go at all, which was totally irrational, yet . . .

'Soup's ready,' she announced, trying to cut across her worries by tipping steaming liquid into bowls.

'Just a jiff. I've got to wash my hands. They're all over Byron's slobber.' Hadley crashed out of the kitchen, walloped up the stairs.

Jane turned the grill to low, checked the bubbling cheese, then walked slowly to the table, reached out for the phone. Her parents would be in now, always were at six o'clock on Sunday. She missed that order in her life, that safe predictability, which she'd criticised, disparaged. She suddenly longed to hear her father's voice; the special way he said her name, briskly and yet fondly, with a slight upbeat at the end, as if giving it an extra loving syllable. She picked up the receiver, dialled the code for Shrepton, then put it down again. She ought to think it out first, plan exactly what she'd say. They might be deeply shocked, or wildly angry; might even have the call traced, and come storming down to find her. No. That was quite impossible. She had checked on it already, been told that calls could not be traced unless you made them through the operator. She dialled the code again, paused for three long seconds before continuing with the number; heard its soft burr-burr, then immediately rang off. Sweat was sliding down her back, her hands clammy, almost shaking. This was quite ridiculous. Was she frightened of her parents, or reluctant to do anything which might cause still more friction? She was making far too much of it. All she had to do was simply report that she was safe, admit she wasn't ready yet to discuss things any further, but promise them she'd be in touch again. 'Okay,' she told herself. 'Here goes. And this time you're forbidden to ring off.'

She dialled the number as slowly as she could, listened to it ring and ring, crazily relieved when she assumed they must be out. Suddenly, the ringing stopped, and her father's deep but measured voice was spelling out their number. She stood paralysed with fear – longing, shock, confusion, fighting in her head. She only had to say her name. Her mouth opened like a fish. 'Jane,' she tried to say. 'It's Jane. I'm safe and well.' No sound came out at all. 'Jane,' she mouthed again, heard her father, anxious now, his fretful voice repeating 'Yes, hallo, hallo? Who is it?'

'It's . . . Jane,' she said, at last, her voice hoarse and almost gagging on the name, a name she hadn't used for weeks. 'I just wanted you to know that . . . '

'Rose!' hallooed a louder voice, resounding from the hall, and clinched by Byron's barking. 'I'm back.'

Jane slammed the phone down instantly, rushed over to the grill, tried to look totally absorbed in easing well-poached eggs on cheese on toast.

'Oh, clever girl!' said Isobel, breezing through the door. 'To have supper cooked and ready the minute I walk in.'

12

Jane snapped the piece of glass between her fingers. The scored
edges fell away, leaving a perfect shape behind – a shape she'd cut
miraculously herself. She fixed a blob of plasticine to each of its four
corners, stuck it on the glass-screen, which blocked the tall north
window. She had now cut twenty-seven pieces, in several different
shades of streaky green, which formed part of the lush landscape
beneath the angel's feet; bars of rippled emerald suggesting hills
and fields. She stood back to scrutinise them, still hardly able to
believe that she was working on a real live stained-glass window,
actually creating it with Christopher; his assistant, now, in fact as
well as name.

She glanced swiftly round the studio – glass lying on the cutting-
bench, propped against the walls; sheets and scraps of every shape
and colour. She no longer regarded it as dangerous and alien, but as
highly-strung and spirited; all the different kinds of glass possessing
their own character, like lively personalities she had come to know,
respect. Some glass was tough and obstinate, fought you when you
cut it – seedy-ruby, for example, with its gritty pitted texture; or
selenium, which was so extremely hard Christopher had refused to
let her touch it, claiming that someone of her limited experience
would find it near-impossible to cut. Other types were smooth and
acquiescent, submitting to the cutter, not making any fuss. Still others
seemed exuberant and springy, almost leapt out of your hand; or were
moody, inconsistent; breaking on a bad day, docile on a good one.
You needed to accommodate their moods, treat each separate sheet
of glass as a distinctive individual which you understood, placated.

Christopher was cutting a sheet of reamy blue, working on the
right-hand light, while she worked on the left; sharing the same
cutting-bench, though up the other end. They were even dressed

alike, both in denim jeans, she wearing an old shirt of his, the twin to his own chequered one in squares of blue and grey; their almost matching clothes seeming to symbolise their new professional bond. He joined her by the window, sticking up an oval-shape on the second, right-hand screen – the angel's face – blank as yet, unpainted. 'That's good,' he said, glancing from his own screen to her slowly-growing landscape. 'Bloody good, in fact. Funny – I always felt you'd have the knack. I've watched you doing other jobs, and you've got a basic confidence, a certain deftness with your hands. Some people make a real pig's ear even of washing up the breakfast things.'

She flushed with pleasure and surprise, had always assumed she was something of a bungler; not just basically untidy, which she'd heard a thousand times, but also rather slapdash and cack-handed. Mind you, she had never put more effort into anything, more passion, dedication, than in learning to cut glass, which she had practised all the week. The artist had been busy returning Adrian's panels to the glass-screens, sticking up each individual glass-shape, to ensure no piece was over-fired and would therefore need repainting; then taking them all down again and packing them in boxes, to be sent back to the glaziers for leading. She had used the time obsessionally – cutting, cutting, cutting – attempting every shape from simple squares and oblongs to tricky curves and circles; so determined to succeed, she had ignored her reddened knuckles, her stiff and aching hand, the Band-Aids on four fingers, bloodstains on her shirt. She had started with just scrap glass, the larger bits and pieces from the cullet-box, so that it hardly mattered really if she wasted it or spoilt it; then practised on some offcuts of white Cathedral Roll, and finally Christopher had given her a largish sheet of pale green tinted pot-metal; watched her like a hawk while she tried to cut the demanding shapes he'd drawn for her.

All her nerves had flooded back, so many admonitions resounding in her head, it seemed impossible to remember even half of them. She must hold the cutter firmly, at an angle; keep the pressure even, keep her whole hand steady, cut just within the black lines of the cutline, to allow room for the heart of the lead; mustn't press too hard, but hard enough for the cutting-wheel to bite; use her pliers to nibble away any jagged edges; always blunt the edges of each and every piece of glass the instant that she'd cut it, so it wouldn't be too dangerously sharp; and, finally, cut very economically, like a thrifty tailor determined not to waste his precious cloth.

She had hardly dared to start – the cutter sitting awkwardly between her first and second fingers, her neck tense from the strain, face creased in concentration. She had heard a gentle hiss as the cutter scored the glass, watched the sparkling silvery line biting through the surface; made sure she kept the pressure even, avoiding any jerks or skids; then doggedly continued scoring, tapping, grozing, until she finally passed Christopher an almost perfect diamond-shape.

'Not bad,' he'd muttered grudgingly, lighting up a cigarette, as if the tension had affected him as well. She'd had to cut another dozen pieces before he'd judged her 'Better', then even 'Pretty good'. Today she'd graduated. 'Bloody good' was praise indeed, but she mustn't slacken off, become careless or offhand. She was aware that he was watching her, even now, when he'd returned to the cutting-bench and was continuing with his own work. He could watch her without looking, part of his attention somehow always focused on her, ready to swoop down.

Yet she was also watching him, fascinated by the speed with which he cut, the way he made a ticklish process look absolutely simple; his obvious relish in the job; the way he kept things tidy, despite the mess and clutter, continually sweeping up the glass fragments, and always laying down his tools in exactly the same spot. She hadn't been allowed to touch his pliers. Her own were new and serviceable, whereas his pair dated right back to the forties, and more than looked their age – the first pair he'd ever had, as a student of nineteen. He had shouted when she tried to pick them up. 'Never touch those – *never!*'

She couldn't understand the note of almost-panic in his voice, as if she were threatening not the pliers, but his very past itself. He'd saved other sacred relics from his youth – many of his brushes, which were too ancient to be used now; a pair of battered marching boots from his days of National Service, and a Victorian reducing-glass which he'd been given as a present when he'd graduated from art school. He had also kept every single sketchbook – every drawing, doodle, daub, he'd ever done; the first few dating from his childhood when he was still in single figures, and that and every subsequent book stored in drawers, and indexed. His studio was something of a sanctuary, not just a simple workplace, but a museum for his exhibits, a memorial to his past.

He finished cutting a section of the halo, an awkward curve, which had needed patient grozing. She watched him blunt its sharp and jagged edges, using a second piece of glass to dull it down, scraping the two cut sides together, one against the other. Then he placed it in position on the screen, dithered for a moment, took it down again. 'I think I'll have to recut this piece – use a lighter blue. Though I

164

never like recutting. It's a bit of a bore, apart from wasting glass.' He started sorting through the racks, all the ones marked blue, scanning sheets, returning them. 'There's an old Russian proverb which says "Measure thrice, cut once." And very good sense, too. I remember some poor sod who was making a memorial window for a local church in Lewes, and didn't bother to recheck his initial measurements. He produced this pretty fearsome-looking Saint Ignatius, which was just a shade too big to fit the space. He wasn't actually there when it was fixed, so the glaziers simply sliced off seven inches, removed the saint's two feet, so he was standing on his stumps. The artist shot himself.'

Jane stopped her cutting, stared up at the screens. She could understand the suicide. After all that work and effort, to have your window wrecked, your precious angel's wings clipped . . . Their Angel's wings weren't cut yet, but its head and half its halo were in place; still looked rather strange without the painted features, just blank transparent shapes in the palest of pale blues. The only likeness she could see was in the long straight streaming hair – *her* hair – traced out on the glass-screen in black lines. She suddenly laid her cutter down, slumped back on her stool. Isobel's emotive voice was sounding in her head. 'Angela,' it murmured, lingering on the name. 'I called her that deliberately to undo all the stigma, turn her into an angel.' Could this window be a memorial not to Isobel's late husband, but to her first abandoned child? Was the resurrection Angela's, not Tom's? And had Christopher been chosen as the artist because he was the father of that baby, himself in debt to it?

'Need a rest?' asked Christopher, who was still comparing blues, holding up each one against the light.

'Yes,' she said. 'My back aches.'

'Okay, we'll break for coffee, if you'd like to put the kettle on.'

She was back in minutes, set two mugs on the bench. 'Christopher?' she said.

'Mm?' He was hardly listening, his whole attention concentrated on one small piece of glass, a fragile-looking turquoise, swirled and veined with white.

'How long have you known Isobel?'

'Oh, ages.'

'Since she was seventeen or so?'

'No, not quite as long as that.'

'Well, how long then?'

'Oh, I don't know – twenty years, maybe. Why d'you ask?'

'Just curious.' She gulped her coffee, burnt her tongue. The artist could be lying. If everybody lied, things would simply crumble. You could never build relationships, or any firm foundations to your life. Yet it was part of being human, the ability to lie – a sophisticated skill which raised man above the animals, like art. She had learnt the skill herself; was a hypocrite on top of it – castigating Isobel for hiding things from Tom, while she deceived the artist by pretending to be Rose, deliberately concealing the fact of her adoption, the details of her life.

'Just look at this blue, Rose. Heaven itself!'

She didn't look, was focusing on 'Rose' rather than on turquoise. 'I'm Jane,' she murmured silently. 'And maybe illegitimate. Which is pretty hellish, actually.' She rolled her drooping sleeves back. His shirt was much too big for her, though she liked its faintish smell – a mix of oil-paint, cigarette smoke and musky aftershave.

The artist was checking his sketch against the glass-shapes on the screen; still seemed uncertain about the exact shade of the halo. But there was nothing indecisive about his voice. He always sounded forceful and assertive, even when he talked to her about perplexity and doubt, though this time he was still concerned with colour. 'I've always gone for blue, you know. My favourite teacher used to wear it almost every day, though actually she was the one who more or less destroyed it for me. I was about eleven at the time, and she was giving us an elementary science lesson, telling us that colour is only a reflection of the light – that tomatoes, for example, aren't really red themselves, but just reflect red light. I was absolutely dumbstruck, could hardly bear to listen when she claimed there was no colour in peacocks' tails or pillar boxes, and that no colour would exist at all if there wasn't any light. Then she pointed to her dress and said that without the light it, too, would be a nothing, and so would kingfishers and sapphires, and the sky and sea and all the blues I loved. I was so upset I told her she was fibbing, and she stood me in the corner as a punishment, face turned to the wall. The wall was primrose-yellow and I just stared at it and stared at it, almost feeding on that yellow, and knowing she was wrong.'

He laughed, put down his glass-sheet, so he could stir and sip his coffee, light a cigarette. 'I suppose we always long for everything to be as simple as it looks. Once I'd studied light, at a rather later stage, I realised it was quite devilishly complicated. In fact, what we actually call light is merely just one octave of vibrations out of at least fifty others known to us, which reach us from the sun and stars. Our eyes are only open to that one single octave out of fifty, or still more. So our picture of the world is limited, distorted – "real", maybe, in one sense, but certainly not reality.' He reached out for a ginger nut, snapped it in his fingers, like a piece of just-scored glass. 'There's a whole vast range of things totally invisible, and therefore closed to us. It's funny in a way – we rely on our senses for the appearances of things, but our solid truthful senses are probably deceiving us.'

Jane cupped both hands around her mug, as if trying to cling on to something, find support and comfort. There was enough distortion in the ordinary world of families, relationships, without adding all these cosmic ambiguities. Yet even cheery Isobel had said something much the same, had cast doubt on reality, unpicked facts and certainties, as if they were little more than a paltry piece of knitting.

The artist was now rooting through a box of smaller offcuts; seemed unwilling to relax or take a rest. He held up a diamond-shape just a foot or two away from her, so she could admire the tiny bubbles in its texture. 'That greeny-blue gives me quite a lift. Strange how colours can affect your mood and spirits, work like music, almost. I always feel at home with blues, whereas most reds make me restless.'

'So you can't have been too happy doing Adrian's job?'

'No, but I didn't have you then.'

She half-choked on her biscuit. That was the first truly personal thing he had said for a whole week. When he'd returned to the studio last Monday, after their tense aborted sex two days before, he had adopted his professional role, friendly still, but distant; not made a single mention of Adrian's dinner party, nor its sequel in the bedroom. She'd been horribly on edge herself, fearing everything was spoilt, that he would refuse to let her work there any longer, be embarrassed by the whole affair – or rather non-affair. And, instead, he'd simply blanked it out, as if it hadn't happened. *He* was busy, *she* was busy, and they both worked hard, said little. Yet he was surely all too well aware of the words not said, the things not consummated, and all the week she had been expecting an attack – if not an actual physical encounter, which she feared she would fight off again, then an irritable tirade. Yet it seemed he wasn't scornful, as she'd feared. 'I didn't have you then', suggested need and intimacy, not anger. He hadn't followed the remark up, simply left it hanging. All the tiny noises seemed to stampede through the silence, the slap of mug on bench, the tinkle of a spoon.

'I . . . I like green,' she said, at last, glancing at her emerald, its jewel-like colour glowing on the light-box.

'So you should,' he countered, seeming grateful that she'd changed the subject, steered them on to safer ground. 'It's the colour of youth and hope. Though it stands for death as well as life, which is why I've used it in the window. It's something of a paradox, is green – formed from blue and yellow, heaven and earth combined.'

'I'm still a bit thrown by all these symbols,' Jane observed, brushing off what she thought were biscuit crumbs, then wincing when she found that they were glass. 'It's like I've been half-blind for years, simply unaware of them.'

'I doubt it,' Christopher replied. 'You can't avoid them, really. Symbols are basic to the human mind, arise out of our deepest hopes and fears. Every race and age and culture has produced them. I mean, bread and wine were universal symbols long before the Christian Eucharist. Bread means life and food and sharing – and even union, because of all those separate grains in just one substance. And wine is life, as well – synonymous with blood. And bread and wine together symbolise the union of feminine and masculine, solid and liquid, man and god.' He propped the sheet of glass against the wall, used his hands to gesture with – urgent restless hands which Jane felt should be tired by now. They had been cutting glass since nine, and were nicked in several places, dirty, grimed with dust, a Band-Aid round one thumb. Yet his hands seemed like the rest of him – determined, energetic, refusing to sit idle. He was pacing up and down now, as if the vigour in his words had spilled over to his body, had to be worked off.

'Even language itself is symbolic in its origin. Take poetry or drama, or even maths – the circle and the triangle are some of the oldest symbols in the world. And what do we do with triangles? Stick them on road signs to warn motorists of danger, when they stand for so much more than that – the Trinity, to start with, and I don't mean just the Christian one, but every sort of trinity – heaven, earth and man; father, mother, child; body, soul and spirit; love, truth and wisdom.' He broke off, drained his coffee. 'Back to work,' he ordered. 'If you start me on this subject, we'll never get our window cut at all.'

Jane removed the dirty mugs, washed them up immediately, replaced them in the kitchen cupboard, grinning to herself. Her parents would hardly recognise her now. Christopher had taught her in a fortnight what they'd been trying to instil for eighteen years – the importance of order and routine. She paused a moment, thinking of the Shrepton kitchen, with its spotless tidy worktops, the neat labels on each tin and jar, which Amy stencilled in herself, as if spice and tea and sugar were unsure of their identities and needed to be reassured.

She had ripped off her own label – 'daughter' – but still sometimes felt a deep sense of loss and longing; still missed tiny stupid things like her mother's knitted tea-cosy, or the egg-cups with the legs.

She wrung out the dishcloth, folded it in four, tried to cram her mother back in her own highly-polished jar – a small one with no label, and a tight well-fitting lid. She was better off with Christopher. 'Our' window, he had called it – which meant his and hers, not his and Isobel's. He could hardly be intending it as a tribute to an unknown baby, Angela, when he had told her quite specifically that it was celebrating Rose – no, more than that – making Rose immortal.

Her stupid grin was spreading as she returned to the cutting-bench, and her last small piece of green, found a triangular-shape on the cutline which it fitted more or less, then laid the glass on top. She ran through her instructions as she prepared to cut again, priming both her hand and brain. Christopher had compared it to a dentist and his drill, requiring a similar combination of pressure and control. She cut the piece as accurately as possible, then stuck it up in place; stood a moment, motionless, delighting in her landscape, her shining furrowed fields. She could hardly see the real November landscape which stretched beyond the window. The glass-screens blocked it off, together with the half-drawn thick black curtains, which the artist used to prevent the light filtering in from each side of the screens. Just two narrow strips were showing, one on either side – sombre wintry farmland in sallow greys and browns, which only served to heighten the brilliance of her greens. She had found the curtains strange at first, especially on a bright and sunny morning, but he'd explained that when he was working on a window for a church, then he liked to try to reproduce roughly the same light-conditions; using heavy curtains or tacked-up strips of card, to create the effect of the stonework round the glass, and so cut out all glare. Now she'd come to like the muted light, which seemed intimate, romantic, lapped them both in their own private snug cocoon.

The phone shrilled through the privacy, a blatant bossy ring. She cursed beneath her breath. Christopher encouraged her to take the calls, so she could fob off any time-wasters, or deal with practicalities. But sometimes she was greeted by a poncy female voice – some friend or fan or floozy who insisted on speaking to the artist, and she was then forced to listen in while he gushed or even flirted. He had picked it up himself this time, and she couldn't hear the caller's voice, though, judging by his seductive tone, it was a woman he knew well. His private life was a mystery, and she felt totally excluded from it when he jabbered on to some anonymous Presence, whom she always pictured instantly as a voluptuous doe-eyed Venus with Shakespeare's brain and the genius of Picasso. This particular Aphrodite was kind enough to keep her phone-call brief, and after three goodbyes from Christopher, Jane could concentrate again.

She selected a new sheet of flash-veridian, which varied in both thickness and in colour, from deep and almost chunky at the bottom, to paler and much thinner at the top. She checked her cutline, frowning; wasn't always certain which particular shade or texture of the glass-sheet the artist wanted where. But he had returned to work himself, and she didn't like to bother him, when he was cutting the first segment of the Angel's outstretched wing. She watched in admiration, listening to the gentle squeaky scratching of his cutter, the sudden sharp metallic tap which followed it, then the abrupt but muted snapping of the glass. The noises made a music of their own; a strange discordant music she preferred, in fact, to the angry wailing symphony he'd been playing earlier on, with its thumping drums and strident stabbing brass.

Despite his concentration, he was aware that she was stumped; laid his pliers down, and slipped round to her end of the bench, gesturing to her cutline. 'Where I've chalked DG – dark green – use this end of the glass, okay? It's a fantastic colour, isn't it? Hell! I'm sorry, Rose, I'm boring you, harping on and on about fantastic bloody colours, when maybe they don't grab you in quite the same gut way. Colour's like a drug for me, and I crave my daily fix of it. I've always been like that, you know, even as a student. Yet we hardly even touched it for the first two years at art school. We did life-drawing and plant-drawing, and drawing from the cast, but we had to work in line and tone, not colour. Then there was anatomy, perspective, composition – all extremely disciplined and highly academic, but I was dying to slap paint on something, burst into an art-shop and buy every bloody tube and pot they had!'

He cut her sheet in half for her, to make it easier to handle, blunted both cut edges. 'I suppose that's why I was attracted to stained glass. It uses light and colour so directly, and all the colours shift and change continually, according to the time of day, and what the clouds and sky are doing.'

He handed Jane her half-sheet, replaced the remainder in the rack, pausing for a moment to inspect another offcut of flash-green. 'The first time I ever went to Chartres, as a student of eighteen, I stayed in the cathedral for hours, just watching how the windows reacted to the light. It was one of those spring days when the sun keeps going in and out, so the colours changed dramatically. And different windows came to life as the sun moved round the sky – first the east end, after sunrise; then the south side, by midday; and those amazing, almost hurting blues above the west-end portal started really shouting out by latish afternoon. And then, as the sky began to redden into sunset, all the warmer colours like the rubies seemed to blaze out like a fire; then, finally, everything died down, and once the sun had set, the whole cathedral was plunged into a sort of murky twilight gloom. It was really quite a spectacle. No wonder people call stained glass the most ancient form of kinetic art there is.'

'What's kinetic art?' Jane asked, longing for his way with words, so she could make some more appropriate response to his energetic monologue.

'Art that moves – you know, mobiles or mechanical sculptures with moving parts or motors. It's from the same Greek word as cinema. Right, start with the dark green, Rose – this area I've marked. I suggest you use that end of the sheet for these oblong-shapes down here.' He returned to his own cutline, studied it a moment before picking up his own glass, positioning it on top. 'Actually, talking of the cinema, I've always thought medieval stained glass was something like a picture-show, a sort of magic panorama, or a Cecil B. De Mille extravaganza.'

'But you told Felice it was spiritual.'

'It was – a supernatural drama played out in the windows, with the faithful sitting in the gloom, transported to another world. It was several things at once, in fact – a teaching-aid for an illiterate population – what they called the Poor Man's Bible, with vivid coloured pictures instead of miles of text; a mystical experience using light and colour as a hot-line up to God, and sheer undiluted sensual thrill.' He tossed a piece of scrap glass into the cullet-box, its ringing chink sounding almost celebratory. 'Of course, the cathedrals were quite different then from how they are today. All the walls were painted, and half the sculptures too, so the whole interior was a riot of bright colour. And just think of the grand scale – vaulting soaring up a hundred and fifty feet and more, when most buildings at that time were cramped and primitive. The thirteenth-century equivalent of the man on the Clapham omnibus must have felt he'd reached the Pearly Gates already.'

He paused to light another of his Marlboros, his entire attention focused on the process, as if it were more important momentarily than any vast cathedral. He inhaled luxuriously, then blew out smoke and words. 'Those stuffy academics who write about medieval art don't always stress the sensuous side enough. It irritates me

171

sometimes, the way they try to defuse its charge, refuse to get excited, or react with any personal involvement. But then that's true of art in general – music, poetry, paintings, are all so potent, Rose, people try to tame them by shrouding them in worthy words, or inventing names or labels to pin them safely down. I suspect they're sometimes scared of art, or their own responses to it. It can arouse such extremes of feeling, set off a sort of anarchy or wildness, even a vulnerability, which can be very threatening, undermine their certainties, their settled rational view of things, make them insecure.

'Damn!' he muttered, sucking a cut finger, and whipping out his handkerchief to prevent the blood from oozing down his cutline. He went to fetch the Band-Aid, still talking as he cut a strip to size. 'I mean, look at Samuel Beckett, or Francis Bacon, or Kafka. Their view of life is terrible and painful, doesn't hide the cruelties or pointlessness, which the rest of polite society tries its hardest to deny. I suppose there's always a majority who want art to be safe – consoling and uplifting, rather than challenging, subversive, or simply very bleak. Of course, there's obviously a difference between private art and public art, but even when the work is done to order – for a patron or an institution, the Church, or state, or some such – there's still an individual voice or vision which can challenge accepted conventions and beliefs, and may well be subversive. That's why art's destroyed, Rose – one of the reasons, anyway – Puritans smashing centuries'-worth of treasures, Muslims burning books, tyrants flinging poets into jail. They may trot out high-flown arguments to justify themselves – spout reasons of security, or moral codes and creeds, but underneath there's an element of fear – fear of that whole side of man which is naked or explosive.'

Jane tried to keep her mind on cutting glass, but it kept sneaking off, reflecting on his words. Had Christopher been talking only about art, or also referring indirectly to her own fears – her fear of wildness, letting go, losing all control? She stared down at her shirt – *his* shirt – which had pressed against his naked skin, absorbed its heat and sweat. She could see him in her bed again – the bare brown chest and back, the coarse dark hair running down and down, until it was cut off by his belt; the sudden glimpse of other hair, as the belt unsnapped and he seemed to change from cultured artist to aggressive rutting stranger. She *did* feel fear – fear of anarchy and wildness, cruelty, vulnerability – all the words he'd mentioned.

'Actually, I've often felt a conflict in my own work between public art and private. I can be subjective and expressive in my paintings, but when I'm working on stained glass, especially for a church, then

I'm often saddled with a theme which may constrain me, or which I find hard to reconcile with my own personal beliefs. Though I never compromise. Why the hell should I, Rose, when there are ways of getting round it? I mean, if I'm asked to depict the sacraments, or the Trinity, or grace, they can always be interpreted in a more general and symbolical way, rather than conventionally and slavishly, following some narrow creed.'

Jane found it hard to listen to his views on artistic conflict when she was fighting her own battle between resistance and surrender, wondering which she'd choose if he removed not just her clothes but her scruples, inhibitions. She glanced at the dark bloodstains on his cutline; felt drained and almost dizzy, as if she were losing blood herself; her hand feeble on the cutter now, not pressing with its usual power and force. She was aware of him observing her, the note of irritation in his voice.

'If you find that glass too thick to cut, then start the other end – do the pieces on the cutline I've marked as medium green. No, turn it over, Rose. Don't forget, you always cut flash glass on the non-flash side, okay? You've really got to concentrate. It's my fault, probably. I'm distracting you with all this talk. Right, back to work for both of us.'

'Back to work' continued until tea-time, with just one short break for lunch – though Jane couldn't help reflecting that the word 'lunch' seemed inappropriate for two Kit-Kats, one cold sausage and a pot of instant noodles. By four o'clock, when the fading light forced them both to stop, she collapsed back in a chair, all her muscles aching, her right hand sore and stiff.

'I'm dead!' she said, examining the reddened weal between her first and second fingers, inflamed now from the pressure of the cutter.

'Well, we'd better resurrect you, or Isobel will sue me. She's right, you know – I do work you too hard.'

'I don't mind.'

'Don't you, Rose?'

She met his eyes a moment, and they seemed to strip her naked – mind as well as body, so she imagined he could see her flesh, the ferment in her head. She turned away, confused; tried to hide her awkwardness by studying the glass-screens, checking on how much they'd done since nine o'clock that morning. The artist had completed the Angel's head and shoulders, the top part of its hair, and almost one whole wing. She herself had finished off her landscape, and started on the Angel's foot. The glass they'd cut looked radiant and rich, with the subdued light filtering through it; far more sensuous and solid than the colours on the sketch. Despite her painful hand, she felt a real elation in seeing a small-scale paper sketch translated into glass. And the glass itself had changed, seemed alive now, and vibrating, as it floated in the window. All the hard slog of the day, the cumbersome procedures, cut fingers, dust and mess, had transmuted into something other-worldly – disembodied colour hovering in space.

She glanced from head and halo, on the upper right-hand light, to her landscape on the lower left; the Angel's pointed foot poised above the bars of green, as if ready to take off. The foot was not quite finished, but, even so, she'd still cut almost half as much as the artist had himself. And considering she was less than a third his age, and had absolutely none of his experience, that seemed pretty good – no, more than pretty good – it was astonishing, phenomenal.

She had helped create an Angel.

13

Jane turned the volume up to loudest, so that the rowdy rampant rock music crashed around the studio, its insistent beat thumping through the walls. Christopher would hate it, reserved his precious hi-fi system for his string quartets, his operas, his Boulez, Berio, Birtwistle. But Christopher wasn't there.

She tossed her tangled hair back, started dancing to the beat; her body twisting, circling, while her mind zoomed up to Manchester. It had been there and back a dozen times already, spying on the artist, following him all day; from the site-meeting that morning with the architect he idolised, to lunch with the contractors, and now the fund-raising reception with the mayor. She could see the swanky salon with its painted gilded ceiling, flunkeys pouring wine, silver trays of supercilious food – caviare, smoked salmon – the crush of stylish people talking art and money, the Wife in her designer-dress the centre of attention. If only Anne had been abroad, he might have taken *her*. Then she'd have been the escort sparkling at his side, the one who charmed the famous Stanton Martin, asked profound perceptive questions about the proposed new Civic Centre, met architects and sculptors, dignitaries, tycoons.

Instead, she'd been excluded, left behind like a superfluous young kid, and with nothing much to do while 'Daddy' was away. The artist had refused to let her continue cutting glass, without him there to supervise. She glanced up at the screens, which seemed blank and almost dead with no outside daylight to kindle them. They had been cutting for a week now, and the window looked an uncompleted jigsaw; some parts blank, some filled, but mostly dull and dark, save for the orange-yellow gleam of the selenium, and a shimmer from the palest of the blues. She resented breaking off when she'd just got into the swing of it, and was gaining speed each day, enjoying the real feeling of achievement.

She checked her watch. Only ten to eight. The day had lasted a century already. She was so used to being busy, to falling into bed at nine, exhausted. She wasn't tired at all now, only twitchy and frustrated, and even her energetic dancing didn't help. She skittered round the room once more, avoiding glass and furniture, feeling half-embarrassed bopping on her own; longing for a partner, someone who might change her restless mood. Perhaps they'd be dancing up in Manchester later on this evening – go on to some night spot; the artist cheek to cheek with Anne beneath the pulsing strobe-lights; exotic-coloured drinks in frosted glasses; Stanton Martin soliloquising about Art and Truth and Beauty. She skidded to a stop, turned the record off – one of Rowan's she didn't even like. Rowan had lent her a pile of books and records; Isobel bought her a small television from what she called a junk-shop. Both of them were worried about her living on her own, stuck out in the wilds with no company her age, no family, no flat-mates, not even any neighbours, no other house at all within a mile or more.

'Why not move in here?' Isobel kept urging. 'It would be company for me. And it wouldn't affect your job. I could drive you to the studio each morning, fetch you back at five.'

She'd been tempted once or twice. It would be a comfort and relief to have someone there at night, to share an evening meal, instead of spooning cold baked beans straight out of the tin; to see a friendly face at breakfast-time, or go to bed with a cat curled on her feet. But she enjoyed all that at weekends, and there was something rather special about living in the studio as well as simply working there. She felt like its custodian – the protectress and night watchman who kept it safe, prevented any harm from coming to the glass. And she liked the links with Christopher – sleeping in his bed, eating in his kitchen, using all his things – the sheets and towels which had touched his skin, the soft and pillowy duvet which had lain on top of him. And if he wanted to start early or work late, she was instantly available, not tied to other people or to meal-times. She still also had the feeling that Isobel objected to her close bond with the artist, though she had no proof of that at all. It was just an intuition, perhaps a fabrication, but, even so, it meant she kept resisting the older woman's lures.

Today she felt quite different, would have gladly stayed at Isobel's, except Isobel was out herself, had been gone the whole long day, visiting a relative in Bournemouth. She envied her her car. If only she had transport, and had passed her driving test, she could motor into town, see a film – or another human face; buy a pizza, window-shop. Isobel had lent her an old bike, which had proved extremely useful for running Christopher's errands, but she wasn't keen on riding it after dark. She prowled into the kitchen, hacked herself a lump of cheese, ate it standing up. She could see the artist's sharp white teeth crunching into canapés; hear his voice ringing out as he dazzled all the women – sophisticated women dripping jewels and culture.

She glanced down at her own rough shirt, stomped back to the studio, switched on the television, ran through all the channels: snooker, and a soap opera, a commercial for shampoo, a depressing documentary about torture and corruption in Turkish prisons. She switched off the ravaged face of a lifer in Ankara, slumped down at Christopher's desk, fiddling with his paperweight and pens. Wasn't this her chance to write that letter to her parents, the one she had been postponing for so long, the one she'd promised Isobel she'd send? She went to fetch a jersey, suddenly felt cold, as if just thinking of the letter had chilled her brain and fingers, so that she could hardly hold a pen, or work out what to say. She tucked a second sweater round her knees; didn't like to turn up all the heaters, waste fuel and money when the artist already paid her more than she was worth. She'd been saving money, actually; feeling some vague sense of dread that she couldn't rely on anyone or anything; must have some resources of her own, something to fall back on if her job were snatched away.

She took a piece of paper from the drawer, wrote the date in her neatest slowest handwriting – December 3rd. The December stopped her dead. Only three weeks now to Christmas. Could she really spend a Christmas separate from her parents? She never had before. Home and Christmas had always been synonymous: the same solemn yearly rituals, with both her mother and her father playing crucial roles – the wrapping of the presents, dressing of the tree, the cooking and the carving, the lengthy preparations which had probably started even now.

'Dearest Mum and Dad,' she wrote, then stopped. They weren't 'dearest' any longer – weren't even Mum and Dad. The letter would be full of lies. How could she explain where she was living? Her parents would be profoundly shocked to know she spent all day alone with a man a decade older than themselves, who had already tried seducing her. She could give Isobel's address, but then they'd come to find her – and would soon discover Christopher as well, unless they hauled her back immediately. She wasn't ready to return, couldn't face the turmoil, the recriminations, questions. Best to write a scant two lines, confirming she was well, but giving no address at all. She picked up the pen again. 'This is just to tell you not to worry. I'm quite all right and . . .'

Of course they'd worry. Her mother always worried, even when she'd been living safe at home. She began again on a second sheet of paper. 'I know you must be worried, but . . .' That seemed callous and offhand, especially when Isobel had pointed out that they'd be torn apart with grief and guilt, and would have no real means of tracing her, since the police were loth to help when the missing person was officially an adult, and anyway so far from her stamping-ground. She'd been relieved to hear that, yet also disappointed; somehow wanted them to track her down, even if she fled again.

She crumpled up the sheet of paper, started on a third one. 'Dearest Mum and Dad, This letter is extremely hard to write.' That was true, at least, but how should she continue? Did she have to write at all? They had heard her voice already on the phone – knew she wasn't dead. But she couldn't break her promise when Isobel had been so kind. 'Dearest Mum and Dad, I'm living with a lady who's been absolutely marvellous.' No. That would make them jealous and resentful.

She kicked her chair back, rattled up the stairs, removed her parents' photo from its hiding-place. They looked sadder now and older, seemed to be reproaching her, reminding her of the good they'd done, when she stressed only the bad. Isobel's story of her own adopted baby had made things still more complicated. Angela had been rescued from being a 'bastard' and a 'leper', from a life of insecurity, with no money and no home. Did the same apply to her, and should she therefore thank her parents, rather than resent them?

She traipsed downstairs with the photo in her hand still, glanced around the studio, wishing she could turn it into a warm and cosy sitting-room. It always seemed so bleak at night, with no carpet, no coal fire, no easy chairs or sofa. If she were back at home, she could go and call on Sarah, or phone John and Helen and suggest they met at Crispin's. She was missing all her friends, missing the local wine bar, where they often met on Saturdays; even missing Mrs Appleton, who always stopped her in the street and warned her about the dangerous rays from television. Home was more than just parents and a house; included neighbours, weather, views – even the way their milkman whistled on his rounds, or that dog which yapped and slobbered in number twenty-five, or the smell of Brylcreem curry in their local Pakistani shop. It was milder in the south, yet she almost longed to feel the cruel north wind grabbing at her hair, see the sulky rainclouds

178

pressing low on purple hills. She had tried to keep her mind off all those things, stop her thoughts from sneaking back to Shrepton; had put up a 'No Entry' sign around the whole rolling windswept county, so why was it returning there today? Maybe because the artist had gone up north himself, and she was missing him, rather than her parents and her home. Or had he *become* home, in a way, so that the studio without him was empty, pointless, bare?

She was relieved to hear the phone ring, rushed to pick it up. It was probably Isobel, reporting she was back, suggesting she came over for a meal. Two hours at the Mackenzies' would distract her from the artist; from receptions, night clubs, rumpled double beds in grand hotels.

'Hallo. *Who?* Oh, Hadley! Yes, I'm fine. And you? What, this weekend? I'm not sure if . . . Well, I suppose I could get down, but . . .'

She tried to sound coherent and decisive, not flustered, even panicked. She hadn't heard from Hadley since their one brief meeting fifteen days ago; had assumed he'd changed his mind about the play, or forgotten all about his invitation. Yet now he was phoning to give her dates and times, taking it for granted she'd be free. Well, she *was* free at weekends, so why was she still dithering?

'You see, I'm miles from any station here and there isn't any bus or . . . Your mother? Yes, I expect she would, but . . . Oh, I see. You've already asked her. Fine, then. The only other problem is . . .' she paused. What was the other problem? She couldn't quite explain it, not even to herself, except it was concerned, of course, with Christopher; the strong but subtle bond she felt between them, as if they were committed to each other, forbidden to accept all outside invitations. She could suddenly see the artist offering his wine glass to an enchanting Felice-clone, kissing her wet lips beneath the smirking cherubs on the sumptuous Town Hall ceiling. Committed? He'd already had three wives, might even now be tracking down a fourth one among the Lady Mucks of Manchester. 'It's okay,' she said to Hadley. 'Friday will be fine.'

Friday. Three short days away, and a working day on top of it. She would have to leave early to make the play in time. Suppose Christopher objected, refused to let her go? Well, she wouldn't stand for it. He wasn't her strict father; had no exclusive rights to her, and no compunction whatsoever in wooing other women. Anyway, she ought to be with people her own age. Both Isobel and Rowan had warned her it was unhealthy to live the way she did, with no normal social life, no circle of young friends. Christopher was fine as an

179

employer, but far too old for any other role. He was probably only playing with her, wheeling out his wife for all the glitzy social occasions, while treating her as a useful minor stand-in.

'Yes, sorry Hadley, I'm still here. How are you? How's the course?' She tried to leave the artist up in Manchester, concentrate on Southampton. It could be quite exciting, meeting Hadley's friends and fellow actors, attending the cast party. She was flattered that he'd phoned, glad he seemed in no hurry to ring off, but keen to hear her news. She hadn't any news, so she talked about the glass-cutting, aware that she was claiming more experience and expertise than she had in actual fact. But she liked the admiration in his voice, the way he obviously saw her as a trained and skilled professional, someone to respect.

By the time she'd said goodbye, she believed the myth herself, rushed into the kitchen, flung anything and everything into Christopher's old frying pan – cold potato, sausage, a chunk of luncheon meat, tomatoes, peas and beans. Let them choke on caviare up in the Town Hall. She would have her fry-up, her glass of sparkling apple juice, and she would be Miranda in *The Tempest* – adorable Miranda, whose name meant 'a girl to be admired' – Miss Clarke had told them that when they'd studied it at school. She'd wear her new green dress and dangly earrings, and Hadley would admire her, and if there was any sign of tempest from the artist, she would magic it away, like Prospero.

She turned the gas to low, while she sprinted to the studio, found one of Hadley's records which Rowan had entrusted to her, a group called Up and Coming, which she put on now, full volume, leaving both doors open, so it would flood into the kitchen. She had created her own night spot; was no longer even alone, had the whole cast of *The Tempest* sitting down to supper with her; Hadley on her right, playing not Alonso, but the smitten Ferdinand:

'Admired Miranda!
Indeed, the top of admiration . . .
O you,
So perfect and so peerless, are created
Of every creature's best!'

She laughed, served up her fry.

'Rose! Rose – where are you?'
Jane opened her eyes. Who the heck was Rose? She'd spent all night

as Miranda, full fathom five in dreams; Hadley dressed in green velvet doublet and hose over thin blue-silk pyjamas. She groped out for her watch, leapt up from the covers when she realised it was almost noon, and Christopher was calling from the studio. She hadn't expected him back till after lunch. He must have got up at the crack of dawn, hurtled down from Manchester at ninety miles an hour. Typical of him, though, not to lie around in bed, or waste his precious time on lazy hotel breakfasts, but hotfoot it back to work. He'd be all the more annoyed that she had overslept herself, with no late night to justify it. Where was Anne, she wondered? Had he dropped her off in London at her job; she, too, back in harness after only four hours' sleep?

She squirted herself with Eau de Rochas, as a substitute for washing, dragged on her old jeans, tore the tangles from her hair, then stumbled down the stairs.

'Look, I'm really sorry, Christopher, I just didn't . . .'

'Coffee?'

'What?'

'Do you want a coffee? You look still half-asleep.'

'I'm sorry,' she began again, then realised he was joking, not complaining. He seemed hyped up, his whole face and body animated as he swept into the kitchen, talking as he clattered cups.

'The trip was quite fantastic! Stanton and I hit it off immediately. He's a fascinating man, Rose, a strange mixture of idealist and autocrat. He believes that buildings can damage your health – depress you and destabilise you, even lead to bankruptcy for businesses, or divorce for families. He's got this vision of architecture raising up man's spirit, working like religion, almost. Yet he's a tyrant in a way, hates any opposition. If one of his staff tries to question his ideas, or change some detail of the plans, the old man will hardly listen, and there's always a huge argument before he'll ever compromise. Right, coffee coming up. Want some toast or something to go with it?'

She was amazed that he was waiting on her. It was her role to make the toast. But he seemed benevolent, expansive, as if Stanton Martin's idealism had overflowed to him.

'Have we time?'

'Time? Of course we have. I don't intend to cut today. I'm going to pop in to the art school to use their reference library. Stanton and I have decided that the panels should be figurative – female figures, mainly, to represent the arts, so I want to get some details of the Muses – Calliope and Clio and . . . ' He turned round, to touch her hair. 'Will you be my model, Rose?'

'Your model?'

'Yes. I'll need to do some studies of the female figure. It'll mean keeping still for quite a while, holding a few poses. Could you manage that?' He pressed the toaster down, went to fetch the butter from the fridge.

Jane sipped her coffee nervously. Didn't artists' models normally pose nude? She couldn't quite imagine him drawing Muses in blue jeans. 'You mean, pose with nothing on?' she asked, trying to sound impassive, unconcerned.

He nodded, spread lumps of cold hard butter on the toast, passed the plate across to her.

'None for you?' she asked, reaching for the jar of grapefruit marmalade, which she had brought from Isobel's.

'No thanks.'

She bit hard into her toast, taking out her anger on the crusts. Posing nude was clearly just a ploy, a clever way for him to coax her clothes off. He'd been foiled in his first attempt, so now he was dissembling, disguising sex as work. Did he really think she'd fall for it, that she was so pathetically naïve she couldn't see right through him? He'd just returned from a junket with his wife, had been sleeping with Anne, obviously, and now wanted some variety, something on the side. Well, she refused to play that role; be nothing more to him than some casual model whom he shagged, to provide a bit of spice.

'Well, what d'you say?'

'No.'

'What d'you mean, "no"?'

'I mean I won't pose without my . . .'

'Don't be silly, Rose. There's nothing to it. I've seen scores of naked models in my time.'

She didn't answer, just dolloped on more marmalade, trying to distract herself from the tonnage of bare female flesh weighing down her mind – all those free-and-easy models he had scrutinised in over forty years. She gulped her coffee – hot – then continued chewing silently, annoyed he wouldn't eat with her. He often made her feel a pig for suggesting that they stop for meals at all. A cigarette would do for him, or a quick bite standing up. The toast was pale and limp, as if he hadn't the patience to wait for it to brown. She remembered Hadley's story of his father always burning toast; the sadness in his voice, and sense of loss; then the way he'd wolfed his rarebit, gulped his soup; devoured a simple snack as if she'd saved him from starvation, pouring out compliments like ketchup. Isobel had found ice-cream for afters, and Hadley had demolished a whole quart, piling on whipped cream and nuts; licking maple syrup off his fingers as he rushed to fetch his bags, then zoomed off in the car. Isobel was right. She ought to be getting out much more, meeting different people.

'By the way,' she murmured, spitting out a grapefruit pip. 'I'm going out on Friday, and I'll need to leave by three-ish.'

'Where you going?'

'Just to see a friend.'

'Anyone I know?'

'Yes, Hadley, actually.'

'Hadley? When the hell did you meet Hadley?'

'At Isobel's.'

'I thought he was away at university.'

'He is. He dropped in very briefly, on his way back from a dance.'

'What, last weekend?'

'No.'

'When, then?'

'Look, is this an inquisition?' Jane wiped her mouth, pushed her plate away.

'No, I'm interested, that's all – wonder what you see in him, quite frankly. I've always thought he was a bit of a spoilt brat.'

'Oh, really?'

'Yes, really.'

The artist lit a cigarette, which helped to fill the silence, taking several puffs before he spoke again. 'Still,' he said, at last, snapping a used match in half. 'I suppose he's your own age.'

'Exactly one year older. It's quite a strange coincidence. His birthday's the same day as mine. We're both typical Librans – peaceable and gentle, but also moody and confused – up and down like yo-yos.'

'Fascinating.'

Jane ignored the irony. 'What sign are you?' she asked.

'Scorpio.'

'Oh dear.'

'Why "oh dear"?'

'Scorpions sting!'

'Only when they're goaded. They're also very loyal.' Christopher started prowling round the kitchen, tidying things, shutting drawers and cupboards, pouncing on odd crumbs. 'Look, about this modelling, Rose. It would really be a help if you agreed. I need a woman

183

with long hair, you see, but someone very young with a good firm figure, and smallish breasts which aren't floppy or low-slung.'

'Are you trying to tell me my breasts are too small?'

'No. I'm telling you you'd be ideal. I want my Muses young and fresh and beautiful – innocent, unspoiled. You're all those things.'

She was touched, despite herself; pulled between suspicion and sheer vanity. To be turned into a goddess, a Muse of Art or Poetry; stand almost twelve feet tall; grace a Civic Centre designed by a famous architect, whom some had called a genius. She glanced down at his hands, strong and compact hands, which would design and cut those Muses – saw them fumbling for Anne's breasts, groping lower, lower, to her navel, lower still, to . . . 'No,' she said. 'I'm sorry. But I just don't want to do it.'

'Okay, please yourself. I can get another model from the art school. One of my old friends teaches Fine Art there, and she'll give me a list. In fact, if I get off right away, I'll catch her in the lunch break.'

Jane slammed out of the kitchen. He had trapped her well and truly now. She could already see her rival – Lady Godiva hair, peach complexion, pert and pouty mouth, breasts as smoothly firm as the ones on marble statues. Except there was nothing marble about the sexpot's blatant poses, her sprawled and willing flesh. She mooched into the studio, stood sullen by the window. Everything seemed grey – the mean and muted light outside, the sluggish brooding clouds. The artist strode in after her, buttoning up his coat. 'Right, I'm leaving now. Perhaps you'd give this place a clean. It's looking a real mess.'

She kept her back turned, shoulders hunched. So now she'd been demoted – become the skivvy once again, instead of the professional, or the Muse. The local art school was probably packed with Muses – all young and fresh and beautiful – innocent, unspoiled. She heard the front door close, heard the artist's footsteps thudding down the path, suddenly dashed after him, raced towards the car.

'Wait, Christopher!' she shouted. 'Let me come too – oh, *please*.'

Jane walked along the corridor, a step behind the artist; the notice-boards on either side crammed with details of societies and sports clubs, meetings, marches, lectures; huge colour posters of exhi-bitions, or advertisements for rock bands. Christopher had once taught at this art school, and had already met two staff he knew, who'd immediately closed in on him – excited shouts, embraces. The Great Man returned to instant adulation. She wished she looked more worthy of him, or at least had brought a comb and lipstick, instead of dashing out in her oldest clothes, with neither bra nor coat. Was he ashamed of her, she wondered, or had he forgotten clean about her, as he chatted with his colleagues about his latest show, his latest big commission?

'Christopher!' a woman cried, a petite brunette in a multi-coloured sweater, her curly hair swept up on top, her eyes so black and lustrous they looked as if they'd been taken out and varnished.

'Serena!'

The artist moved towards her, and all Jane could see was his camel-coated back, now straining at the armpits in an enthusiastic hug. The woman finally pulled away, but reached for Christopher's two hands, clasped them in her own. She was no longer young, but skilfully made up; the wide mouth glossed with pink, the Latin eyes made larger by dramatic arcs of bronze. Jane had not been introduced, but judging by the fervour of their meeting, this must be one of Christopher's ex-mistresses – or maybe not so 'ex'. Jane tried to see her shape beneath the sweater. Was the figure slim and girlish, the breasts high-slung and firm? It was difficult to see at all, with the artist standing right up close, still handcuffed by Serena.

The two walked on up the stairs together. The other staff had disappeared, as if they had no wish to play gooseberry. Jane felt much the same herself, followed at a distance, trying not to hear their conversation.

'So how's old Blackie?'

'Old's the word! Old and very fat. She still misses you, you know. Remember that quite ghastly night when . . .' Peals of laughter, more eager reminiscences. They paused on the first landing, Jane stopping too, embarrassed.

'Oh, this is Rose,' said Christopher, seeming surprised that she was there still. 'She's working for me temporarily.'

Jane noted the 'temporarily', forced a duty smile, let her hand be shaken by Serena's. The woman's hand felt hot and damp, as if she'd just climbed out of bed – the artist's bed – after a night of . . .

'In fact, could you be an angel and look after her for half an hour? I want to dig around in the library, find some references.'

Jane jabbed her foot against the wall. 'Look after her' implied she was a child, not an equal and professional who might like to see the library for herself, even help him scan the books. Perhaps Serena would offload her in the crèche.

'Well, I'm due back in the painting studio.' Serena checked her watch, a man's one on a butch black strap which only served to emphasise her frail and slender wrist. 'Should be there already.

But if Rose has no objections to my jawing to the students about their giraffes and kangaroos . . . They're doing a project based on drawings they made at the zoo.'

'Sounds fun,' said Christopher.

Their eyes met for a moment, as if recalling other fun times, other private outings. 'See you,' said Serena, with a final intimate smile, then teetered along the passage in her high-heeled black suede boots. Jane dithered just behind her, wondering if she should speak her mind, say that she'd no wish to be nannied, and could easily amuse herself, maybe go and grab a coffee.

Too late. The door had closed behind them, Serena and herself swallowed up in noise and colour – colour on the easels, colour on the walls, colour in the students' way-out clothes. She could hardly make them out at first – just looming faces, gabbling voices, shocks of puce or scarlet. One girl had bright pink hair, sticking up on end; another sported a large red hat with ostrich feathers nodding from the brim. Some looked very ordinary, in shabby jeans like hers, or creased and dirty sweatshirts, but they faded into the background, while the extroverts leapt out. An Indian girl had made herself dramatic by painting purple zigzags on her cheeks; a five-foot-nothing redhead was plastered with stage make-up, tiny silver sequins glued all down her neck. The boys looked more like tramps, or punks, with patched and holey jeans; three or four with earrings, one in a Hawaiian shirt with paint splashed on his face. Jane felt not just shabby now, but boring, unoriginal. She tried to shrink into a corner, but Serena followed, smiling, began telling her that these were students in the first term of their foundation year, who were trying to discover what kind of artists or designers they wished to be eventually. 'Last week they were doing graphics; this week I've thrown them in the deep end of Fine Art.'

Jane tried to concentrate, though she was aware of eyes upon her, some of the male students glancing at her bra-less chest, her long and tangled hair.

'I gave them all a briefing earlier on this morning. Now I'm going to see them individually, criticise the work they've done so far. If you want to listen in, you're very welcome, or just look round on your own. Or if you'd rather sit and read . . .' She scrabbled in her bag, tossed Jane the *Independent*, then loped towards a student with earrings made from milk-bottle tops, who was painting polar bears, striping them like zebras in black and yellow ochre; working on the floor, her discarded outer clothing scattered all around her.

Jane stayed put in her corner, still felt overwhelmed, as if she'd walked into a zoo herself, to view some rare exotic species. The girl with the pink hair might have come from the flamingo cage, or flown in from the tropics; another wore a leopard print, with her talons painted black to match, and a rumbustious group of mostly boys was chattering like monkeys, one wag in particular keeping up a constant stream of banter.

'For Christ's sake, Darren!' Serena bawled impatiently. 'Let's have less yak and more work.'

Darren grinned, strolled back to his easel, stopped to talk to Jane. 'Have you come to see the course?' he asked.

'Well, not . . .'

'It's a year's hard labour, but disguised as education. Hey, come and feed my lions.'

Jane let herself be coaxed towards his canvas, tried to find the words to admire his strange brown beasts, which bore almost no relation to any lions she'd seen. Darren himself was tall and very skinny, with his dark hair in a ponytail, and baggy turquoise trousers which looked as if they'd been borrowed from a fancy-dress supplier. Her mother would have damned him as bohemian, unwashed. She giggled suddenly. She hadn't washed herself, must seem quite a tramp; no longer her parents' clean and model daughter.

'What's so funny?'

'Nothing.'

Darren frowned suspiciously, as if she were laughing at his work; began repainting one hind paw. 'Are you thinking of applying here?' he asked her.

'No, I . . .'

'I can highly recommend it. The food's lousy, the tutors waltz in when they think they will, the building's all but falling down, the art-history lectures are boring boring boring, and we all love every minute.' He laughed, revealing gappy teeth, then squirted orange paint onto his palette, brilliant glossy paint which she longed to use herself. She had never even thought of going to art school, had dropped art in the fifth form. Yet, despite Darren's mock-objections, she was tempted by the way of life – the fun, the camaraderie, the fact that these students all belonged, were committed to a course, to developing their individual skills; didn't need to earn their livings, or fret about the future yet. She was even attracted by the mess: the dirty paint-smeared walls, the floorboards barely visible beneath the tide of clutter – rolled-up coats and sweaters, knapsacks, cardboard boxes, paints and palettes, dirty rags, bottles, paper cups.

Serena was approaching them, talking to the student on their right, a strawberry-blonde in a daring crotch-length mini over stripey woollen tights. Jane listened to the phrases: 'The scale of the main image is wrong, and nothing is relating to the four sides of the canvas.' 'That red in the middle-ground is contradicting the space . . .' She felt baffled and excluded, the only one who didn't speak the language, didn't have the talents. Yet she'd shown skill in cutting glass, picked it up extremely fast, so Christopher had said.

'Can you do stained glass here?' she asked, watching Darren daub a mane on to his lion.

'No,' Serena butted in. 'Very few art schools seem to include it nowadays. They teach it up at Edinburgh and Swansea, and I think it's part of the Mural Design course at Chelsea, but nowhere else, as far as I recall. Why – are you planning to take it up?'

'I'm . . . not too sure.' Her future was so uncertain. If she embarked on a training, then she'd lose her link with Christopher, and would they take her anyway? She was bound to need an A-level in Art, which would mean going back to school, or enrolling in some college – interviews, exams, more pressures, indecision. She felt pulled so many ways, yet the strongest of the magnets was always Christopher.

He was suddenly at the door, beckoning to Serena, who hurried over, smiling. Jane could hear them whispering like two conspirators.

'Who's that?' asked Darren, swinging round to look.

'Christopher Harville-Shaw.'

'Jeez! You mean the artist?'

'Yes,' said Jane. 'He used to teach here once.'

'D'you know him then, or something?'

'Yes,' she said airily. 'I'm working for him, actually.' She enjoyed his startled look; relished it still more when the artist called her over, used her name for everyone to hear. Of course she wouldn't apply for any training. Her work with him was far too precious, and, anyway, he was training her himself. She felt superior, important, walking down the passage with him, now raised above mere students – a famous painter's friend.

Her elation was short-lived. 'Right,' he said. 'I've finished in the library. Now we'll pop into the life room. I want a word with Ben. Serena says he's using this new model, who sounds just the job for me – a seventeen-year-old dancer with hair down to her bum.' He paused outside a scuffed and paint-chipped door, held his finger to his lips. 'You mustn't make a sound, Rose. We shouldn't really interrupt the class. The models always hate it. But if we just sidle in and make ourselves invisible . . .' He opened the door, crept in on velvet feet. She followed apprehensively, surprised by the difference between this room and the painting studio – the cathedral-like silence and air of concentration; no jabbering or joking, but a sense of high solemnity.

Her eyes moved from the students to the object of their scrutiny, posed naked on a dais at the back. She blinked and shook her head. A seventeen-year-old dancer with hair down to her bum? The withered flabby body looked nearer seventy; the breasts sagging to the belly, the eyes half-lost beneath drooping heavy lids, the hair itself sparse and dirty grey. Jane felt herself recoiling. How could any woman of that age agree to take her clothes off; allow her glaring defects to be emphasised in paint? Yet she also felt compassion for the model – the pathetic plastic flip-flops on her feet, the string of cheap blue beads, child's beads from a chain-store, as if she had tried to grace her nakedness, or provide a touch of colour to counteract her dingy sallow skin. A spotlight had been rigged up just above her, its relentless beam revealing all her flaws: the swollen veins running rope-like down her legs, the mottled thighs and mangy pubic hair.

She seemed to catch Jane's eye a moment, accept the horror in it, though her own expression didn't change at all – a strange ecstatic mystic smile, as if she was aware of something higher, something no one else could see. She stood absolutely motionless, one hand on her hip, the other resting on a chair-back, the palm upturned, the fingers reaching out. Jane began to feel faint stirrings of respect. It must be very tiring to stand in that position, to remain unfazed, undistracted, by twenty pairs of eyes, to shrug off their contempt; maybe earn her living the only way she could. The pay for models was not exactly high, but at least it was a job a pensioner could do, when she was too old or frail or frowsty to be accepted as a waitress or a char.

'Rose!'

She heard the artist's hushed but urgent voice, had forgotten he was there, forgotten almost everything save the sight of that old woman, who seemed lost in her own world, despite the crowded room. Christopher was whispering to the tutor, standing with him almost at the door, and was now beckoning her over, implying they must leave. She felt a strange reluctance to drag herself away; walked only very slowly, glancing at the students as she passed them. There was no revulsion in their eyes, just complete absorption in their work. They were not judging the model as a woman, or a body, but reproducing her; each seeing something different in the figure. The frumpy wrinkled crone had somehow been transformed – not

189

glamorised, or rejuvenated, but allowed her human dignity, her gritty dogged courage. Jane realised now how brave she was – to strip completely naked before a group of students who were half a century younger, and still retain one's poise. Some had made her older still, not shrinking from her defects, but faithfully recording them, yet also re-creating her patience and resilience, her strange other-worldly smile. The woman had some aura, a sense of style and confidence, which the students had picked up, mirrored on their canvases.

'Come *on*, Rose.'

She started, tiptoed to the door, where Christopher was waiting; shut it carefully behind her.

'Are you in a dream or something?'

'No,' she said, running to catch up with him, as he strode along the passage.

'Look, you'd better have the day off, and catch up on your sleep. You don't seem quite yourself. I'll drive you back to the studio, then I'll push off home. I haven't had a chance to unpack my suitcase yet.'

'Okay,' she said disconsolately, dodging two male students who looked like terrorists in dark glasses and rough beards, and were hurtling up the stairs as she and Christopher walked down. 'What about your model?' she dared to ask, at last, once they'd reached the ground floor and were emerging through the main swing-doors.

'I'm going to phone the dancer. It's a bloody shame I missed her. Ben was expecting her today, but she had to cry off very suddenly, because a TV job came up. He says she's usually reliable, and really quite a stunner – tall and slim and fair.'

Jane said nothing, trudged in silence to the car; relieved to climb inside, escape the bitter wind which was groping her tense body beneath the skimpy sweatshirt. She turned towards the window, to distract herself by looking out, watch the townscape change to winter fields, observe the clouds smudging the grey sky as they drove towards the studio. She looked at things quite differently since she'd been working for the artist, as if he had given her his eyes, deepened her perception, so that she was aware of depths and subtleties she had previously ignored; aware of shapes and textures, of how light affected colour, or heightened mood and atmosphere; aware of his strange power to infuse a common image with solemnity, significance. Even now, she could appreciate the impact of a bloated cloud breaking up the clean line of the hill; one tiny twisted hawthorn bush prickling the vastness of the sky. He had made the world more interesting, imbued quite humble objects with a richness and distinction.

The car lumbered down the bumpy track which led on to the barn. The artist pulled up with a jolt, kept the engine running. 'Jump out,' he said, reaching for his cigarettes. 'I'll see you in the morning.'

She clambered out, but didn't close the door. 'Could you come in for a second? I want to show you something.'

'Well, make it snappy. I've a lot to do at home.'

She dived ahead, unlocked the heavy door. The studio was chilly, but she didn't stop to switch the heaters on – just removed her sweatshirt, tossed it on the floor behind her; couldn't waste vital minutes folding clothes or putting them away. She kicked her shoes off, started tugging at her belt, had it half-unbuckled, when the artist's head appeared round the door.

'What in God's name are you doing, Rose?'

She didn't answer, simply dragged her jeans down, and then her lacy pants. She shivered in his scrutiny, but refused to meet his eyes; just arranged the chair exactly as they'd had it in the life room, took up the same pose – left hand on her hip, right hand on the chair-back, palm upturned, fingers reaching out. She even made her face the same: eyes impassive, guarded; strange enigmatic smile. She didn't have the flip-flops or the cheap blue plastic beads, but the fine gold chain she always wore would help relieve her nakedness.

She could hardly feel the cold now. Her flesh was burning in his gaze, the blood flowing from her flaming cheeks like a scarlet muffler wrapped around her limbs. She had never been so nervously aware of the sheer solidity and impact of her body, which felt totally exposed, as if somebody had prised it from its shell. She longed to use her hands to hide her breasts, or turn the other way, so he couldn't see her flaunt of pubic hair. Had he noticed it was darker than her head hair, and how untidily it curled, as if in need of a strict brushing? Or was he looking at her thighs, noting that deep scar where she'd fallen off her bike?

'Rose, put your clothes back on.'

She pretended not to hear, didn't move a muscle, even held her breath; eyes fixed on a stretch of wall, smile unwavering.

'Get dressed, I said. And hurry up. You told me quite specifically you didn't want to model for me; implied I was a lecher for having even brought the subject up.'

She'd implied no such thing at all, simply thought it privately. Uncanny the way he seemed to read her mind. She had deliberately said nothing, concealed her true reactions.

'Anyway, I've found my model now. I was about to phone her, as soon as I got home.'

Still she didn't answer, tried to move her mind into another gear entirely, become a Muse, a goddess – young and fresh and beautiful – innocent, unspoiled. She must forget the individual details of her body, its scars or blemishes. Nobody was judging her. She was no longer Jane at all – no longer even Rose, but Woman, subject, model.

'Besides the fact you'll catch your death. It's freezing cold in here.'

She could feel herself not cold, but warm and live and growing, reaching twelve feet tall, until she could look down on a city, grace its art and culture.

'Rose, are you deaf, for heaven's sake?'

Not deaf, but stiff already. Posing wasn't easy. Her neck felt tense and cramped, and there was an annoying sort of itch in the middle of her back, which she had to stop herself from scratching. No – Muses didn't itch. She must transcend such petty twinges, concentrate her energies on being what he wanted, prove herself superior to that hateful dancer with her yard of yellow hair. She wished she dared to look at him, judge what he was thinking. She knew he had his coat on still, muffled up in layers, while she was stripped down to the skin – or further than the skin, since it felt as if his gaze had pierced straight through her now, so that he was peering at her bones and blood.

The silence was so total she could hear the judder of the fridge through the open kitchen door, hear the artist's breathing, which sounded heavy, even angry; the nervous way he inhaled his cigarette. She realised they were locked in some fierce battle, and that he wasn't used to losing. But why should she lose, either? He always got his own way. First, he'd wanted her to model, now he was rejecting her. Her eyes were smarting from the smoke, which increased her own annoyance. She was forced to breathe in that foul nicotine every hour of every working day; also breathe in his bad moods – his touchiness, impatience, his snappish gruff disdain. But what about her own moods? She was touchy, too; rebellious sometimes, sullen. They were alike in certain ways: both felt things far too deeply, bore grudges, cared too much.

She heard him bang an ashtray down, tensed immediately; aware she'd lost her smile, changed her whole expression, which no good professional model would surely ever do. She must hold on to that smile, keep it mystic and ecstatic, like the woman in the life room; imagine she was standing not in a cold studio, with lowering clouds outside, but on shining Mount Parnassus. Her fingers ached, but she mustn't shift or rest them. That uncomfortable right hand was deliberately reaching out to him, the only tiny part of her which could speak to him, implore him, beg him to give in.

Suddenly, he moved himself, darted to the corner and switched both heaters on, then grabbed a piece of charcoal and his sketch-book.

'Damn you, Rose!' he muttered, as he flung his coat and scarf off, pulled up a stool a yard or two in front of her, and started swiftly drawing.

14

'The strawberries for Madame?'

'No, thank you,' Jane said shyly, so shyly that the artist didn't hear.

'Yes, please,' he said. 'For both of us.'

The waiter inclined his balding head, glided to the kitchen. Jane felt nervous of him, disliked the snooty way he'd appraised them when he'd shown them to their table, as if calculating the difference in their ages, clearly disapproving.

He was back in minutes, with two floral-patterned bowls. The strawberries looked unreal – strawberries from a still-life, arranged on glossy fig leaves. She daren't imagine what they cost. Strawberries in December weren't quite the same as the glut her parents picked themselves from their local farm, in June – plebeian squashy berries, not these hothouse aristocrats. She was surprised that Christopher had ordered them at all, when neither he nor she had done justice to their second course, and had left most of their first. Was he nervous, like herself, she wondered, too churned up to eat, or worrying about his weight, even when away?

Away! She put her spoon down, her stomach churning once again, queasy from the *crème Chantilly*, brandy-flavoured, rich. She still felt it wasn't happening to her, or only in a dream. Had they really set off in the car a mere four hours ago, driven up to Lincolnshire with a suitcase in the back, she wearing her green dress – the one she'd planned to wear for Hadley's play? She took a gulp of wine, kicked Hadley from the restaurant. No good fretting any more about his injured feelings. Christopher came first.

'Good?' he asked her, scraping cream off a large berry, then forking it fastidiously in half.

'Yes, wonderful,' she said, picking up her spoon again, but wishing she could take the strawberries back with her – take all the luscious food they hadn't eaten – store it in the studio to be relished for a week or more, instead of mousetrap cheese and cold baked beans. She had never been to such a sumptuous restaurant in her life, hardly knew such haughty places existed. It looked more like a private house, with old clocks and antique furniture, a real live harpsichordist playing Handel and Scarlatti. When her parents took her out to eat, it was usually to a Berni Inn – steak and chips and musak; chirpy teenage waitresses with name-tags on their chests: Tina, Sandy, Val. Their waiter was just hovering, filling both their glasses. She imagined him with 'Sandy' on his chest, tried to hide a laugh. His face looked like the fish they'd eaten – disdainful and deep pink. What had it been called? The fish names were all new to her – monkfish and John Dory, and a whole shoal beginning with B: brill and bass and bouillabaisse; baked bream in Béarnaise sauce. The Berni Inn offered only breadcrumbed plaice. There'd been no breadcrumbs on their fish at all, but it had been swimming on a choppy sea of scallops, truffles, grapes, and served with something called a coulis, which tasted of liqueur. The vegetables came separately – not peas and greasy chips, but tiny tiny carrots, one centimetre long, still with their green frills on; corn cobs barely larger, as frail as baby's fingers; alternating discs of courgette and aubergine, and everything arranged in an overlapping pattern, as if they'd hired an artist, as well as just a chef.

'D'you know this piece?' asked Christopher, pausing with his wine glass poised, as he listened to a flurry from the harpsichord.

She shook her head, wished her answer wasn't always 'No', when he asked her if she knew things.

'It's Vivaldi's *Four Seasons*, and the chappie's playing "Winter" now, which seems appropriate.'

Instinctively, their eyes turned to the window, where a sleety snow was harassing the panes, not totally concealed by heavy velvet curtains in a sunburnt shade of brown. Inside, all was warmth – a log fire spitting in the grate, a pink blush from the lamps, steam curling from the silver soup tureen. Even the other diners appeared to give off heat – their blaze of conversation, the colours of their clothes, the afterglow of wine flaring in their cheeks and claret breath. The smells were warm and comforting: hot bread and sizzling butter, flamed brandy, rich game soup.

'I hope we're not snowed up,' the artist laughed.

She forced a smile. More complications, if they were; more lies to Isobel. She could hardly believe that one weekend away could entail so many lies. He must have lied himself, to Anne, except he already had a pretty good excuse. Officially, he'd been summoned to inspect a glass-appliqué window, which he'd made almost twenty years ago for a small modern church in Lincolnshire, and which was beginning to deteriorate – pieces of the coloured glass working loose, or even falling off. The vicar and the architect were hoping he'd remake it, or at least restore and save it, and had arranged to meet him in the church at ten o'clock next morning. She had heard about the problem a good two weeks ago, when Christopher had shrugged it off, said he simply hadn't time at present to go haring up to the back of beyond for the sake of one small window in a pretty soulless church. But things had changed since then.

'I've never known snow quite so early.' The artist gave a theatrical shiver, as if the flakes were actually falling on his head. 'Especially after such a mild November. I mean, just last week, we were exclaiming at the sun.'

Jane smoothed the damask napkin on her lap, wondered why they were talking about the weather. It was the sort of conversation her parents' friends might have. 'Chilly for this time of year . . .' 'The mildest autumn since . . .' Christopher seemed tense, his fingers clenched too tight around his glass. Was he genuinely concerned about the weather, or needled by the glances they had received since they'd come in, not just from their waiter, but from several other couples who were doubtless speculating. Father and daughter? Dirty old man with his bimbo? The couple right next door to them were both white-haired, stern-eyed, and were eating their poached turbot in almost total silence, their chief preoccupation watching Christopher's bold hand edge across the table to her own. She cursed the fact she looked so young, though she had made a special effort for this evening; larded on more make-up, coiled her hair on top, tried to add a decade.

'Coffee?' asked the waiter, who seemed to be taking a cruel pleasure in prowling within earshot, so inhibiting them both.

'No thanks. It stops me sleeping.' She flushed right to her ears; had said it without thinking. They had hardly come away to sleep. Or had they? Even now, she wasn't sure if he'd booked them separate rooms, or whether the purpose of the trip was genuinely to view the ailing window, or more to jettison her original plan of going down to Southampton. She tried to turf out Hadley once again, but already his resentful voice was cutting through the babble of the restaurant.

'But you said you'd come – you promised, Rose. And I've already arranged a bed for you in Alexandra's flat. And invited half a dozen friends for lunch on Saturday, so we could have a second party in your honour. And I've even . . .'

'A brandy for M'sieur? Madame?'

'No, thanks. Just the bill.' She watched Christopher pass his credit card across, heard him tell the waiter to add twenty per cent for service. He must have spent a fortune on the meal. Would he expect it to be paid back – and in half an hour, or less? They were only a dozen miles now from the Swan, an unpretentious country inn, owned by an old friend of his, which she presumed he'd chosen to avoid more curious stares, at least from the proprietor.

Snow slammed into their faces as they walked the few dark yards towards the car. He kissed her once they'd got inside, as if released at last from all the prohibitions he had felt throughout the meal. She was pressed against his coat, tensing in surprise as snowflakes melted from his hair, trickled down her neck. His lips were warm against her cold ones, smoky-flavoured, fierce. She was half-relieved when he let her go, switched on the ignition. If only they could drive and drive through deep black shadowland, never quite arrive; hurtle through the night with the dots of whirling blurring snow spinning in the darkness, making everything unreal. The road stretched on and on – no buildings, landmarks, houses, trees; just the hypnotic frantic dance of white on black.

She must have closed her eyes a moment, because suddenly they'd stopped, and the normal world was back – a solid red-brick inn, standing on a river, the brass carriage-lamps outside mirrored in a stretch of shimmering water; darkly clotted ivy shadowing the coloured squares of bright-lit curtained windows.

'That's it,' Christopher announced, nosing through the car park to a sheltered private courtyard at the back. 'You stay put a moment, and I'll go and tell Jonathan we're here.'

She slumped back, disappointed, wanted to sweep in on his arm, not be left behind like a parcel on the seat, while he checked the coast was clear. But she understood he had to be discreet. He was married, and well-known; couldn't risk being recognised by some art aficionado, or mischief-making gossip – which was probably why he'd chosen the wilds of Lincolnshire. She stroked her naked wedding finger. Perhaps she should have brought a ring to wear in the hotel, or would they hide away – take their meals upstairs, or sneak out to other restaurants? 'Strawberries for Madame?' 'Coffee for Madame?' Had she just imagined it, or had that waiter been deliberately provocative, increasing her shy awkwardness by stressing the 'Madame'? She peered down at her watch. It was too dark to see the time, though it felt as if the artist had been gone for hours and hours. Was he having a private pow-wow with his friend, catching up on months of news, or indulging in a secret little snigger about his teenage conquest? How often did he come here, she wondered suddenly? He seemed to know his way around, had dived straight in the back way, through a door marked 'STRICTLY PRIVATE'. Had there been other girls before her, young and fresh and beautiful – innocent, unspoiled?

She could taste fish again, nudging in her throat – fish and cream and brandy, all mixed up. Now she almost longed for mousetrap cheese, two slices on cream crackers, in the small safe tidy kitchen in the studio – no one there but her; nothing to do afterwards but watch the Friday play. Snow was fretting at the windows, dribbling down in dirty lazy rivulets. She could hardly see at all, felt imprisoned in some limbo; abandoned far from home. She was tempted to jump out and run away, pelt south again to Hadley; turn up soaking and dishevelled for the last act of the play. Or strike north and make for Shrepton; join her parents for Ovaltine and shortbread before they went to bed. Lincolnshire was more than halfway there. She could even hitch a lift, flag down some kindly lorry-driver, who'd . . .

'Rose?'

She started. Christopher was standing by the car, leaning down to let her out, his coat collar turned up, snow crusting on his hair. 'I forgot to ask Jonathan to lend me an umbrella. You'll have to make a dash for it.'

Yes, she thought, I will, and too fast for you to follow. But he was faster still, already had her arm – the suitcase in his other hand as he steered her down the path, feet slipping on the shining treacherous cobbles.

'Welcome, Rose,' said Jonathan, smiling at the door, a tall immaculate-looking man in slate-blue trousers and an exactly matching shirt; a flowered cravat around his neck, and unnaturally fair hair, which she suspected would be quite as grey as Christopher's without assistance from a bottle. She shook his proffered hand, which felt small and soft and moist, like the scallops in the restaurant. He coaxed the case from Christopher, led the way upstairs, prattling brightly on about the weather and the traffic, and those endless wretched roadworks just north of Peterborough. She wondered why he hadn't called a porter, and why they were using the back staircase (the servants' staircase, judging by its steep and narrow treads); disliked the sense of being hustled out of sight, like somebody infectious.

'Goodnight,' he said obsequiously, as he left them in a passage outside a door marked 21. 'See you in the morning.'

'Wait!' she almost shouted, as Christopher inserted the small and fiddly key. 'I'm coming down myself.' But Jonathan had disappeared already, the echo of his footsteps suddenly cut off as the artist scooped her in and closed the door.

She stopped, transfixed, saw a double bed and roses, in that order – a king-size bed, and at least six dozen roses – expensive hothouse roses, more precious than the strawberries, arranged in bowls and vases all around the room: reflected three times over in the astonished triple mirror of the dressing table. Every rose was red – tight-furled buds half-lost in swathing foliage; fuller, more exotic blooms, opening out in the heat of the two radiators; tall and thorny roses standing to attention in an exquisite cut-glass vase. She was so dazzled by the sight, she could only stare at Christopher, struck dumb by his extravagance. The strawberries had been rationed – eight scant fruits apiece – but here was a whole feast of flowers, a riot, a luxuriance.

Christopher was watching her, smiling at her face. 'Red roses for my Rose,' he said, shrugging off his coat. 'I'm afraid I couldn't rival Cleopatra. When she entertained Mark Antony, she spread the floor with roses to a depth of eighteen inches – or so the story goes.' He slipped across, to take her coat as well, helped her with the fastenings, since she seemed still mesmerised. 'Perhaps we should strew them on the bed, like the Romans used to do, sleep on scarlet petals instead of boring sheets.' He laughed, and pulled her close. 'There's a story in Seneca of a Sybarite who couldn't sleep a wink if just one single rose-petal happened to be curled. I suppose it's an earlier version of the Princess and the Pea.'

'What's a Sybarite?' she asked, cursing her own lack of style, her sheer artlessness with words. She should be pouring out her thanks to him, in a Keatsian ode, or Shakespearian pentameters, telling him how touched she was, how flattered, overwhelmed, and all she'd managed so far was to ask a futile question.

'Well, literally an inhabitant of Sybaris, but more generally a sensualist, someone who loves luxury. We'll be Sybarites tonight, Rose.' He gestured to the ice-bucket, removed his jacket before opening the champagne, the cork blasting off in a violent spurt of foam. He poured two glasses, set hers on the table between the chintzy fat armchairs, which had been arranged as a small sitting area at one end of the room. 'Sit down,' he said, 'And let's drink a toast to us.' He clinked his glass against her own. 'To Rose and Christopher – Christopher and Rose.'

She mouthed the phrase herself. Their names were linked, their glasses, fingers touching; the toast official now. But that was just the overture. They would be joined completely soon, and he would expect her to be worthy of him, worthy of the roses, the dinner, the champagne; also expect her to be blatant, repeat her wild performance of Wednesday afternoon. She could hardly understand now how she had behaved so flagrantly, actually pressing herself against him, shameless and stark naked, once he'd finished sketching her, and had laid his charcoal down. Posing nude seemed to have set off some explosion in her body, as if by drawing her, he'd changed her, unleashed a different self, abandoned, unrestrained. But he had gone the other way – aloof and unresponsive – removed himself from her embrace, unlatched her naked limbs, then told her sharply to put her clothes back on, his whole manner strangely fraught.

She'd felt humiliated, baffled, as she replaced her limp blue jeans. He had wanted her three weeks ago, yet now he was rejecting her. Had she injured his male pride by taking the initiative, or was he worried about Anne, who might be chafing back at home? Or did he simply feel the ambience was wrong; preferred a slow seductive build-up to a sudden low-key grope? She hardly knew this new romantic Christopher, who had deemed her worthy of a ten-course feast of flowers, and who contrasted most emphatically with the stern exacting artist who seemed wary of indulgence, insisted on hard work. He was a mystery to her generally, despite their weeks together – his partner on the window, but a stranger to his mind. If he didn't still desire her, then why bring her here at all, why book a double bed? In fact, he had burst into the studio the day after she'd posed for him – arrived before first light, with a letter postmarked Lincolnshire, suggested they drive up there, and stay for the weekend; leave as soon as possible, as if the deteriorating window, which he'd dismissed as just a drag, had become his top priority.

She crossed her legs, uncrossed them, fiddled with her bracelet. If only he would draw her now, so that she could feel those same sensations in her body, that new sense of flaunting confidence, as if she were indeed a goddess, an imperious Muse who could make the first bold move. But instead of picking up a pencil, he was fumbling for his lighter.

'I was going to buy you white roses,' he said, tearing off the cellophane from a new pack of cigarettes. 'I'm reading this marvellous new biography of Nijinsky, and when he was first married, he bought his wife a good two dozen roses every single day. But he insisted they were white ones. He said red roses frightened him, and he wrote in his journal that he knew his love was white, not red. Odd, that, isn't it, when red roses are the flower of love?'

She sneezed in answer, the champagne bubbles tickling up her nose. The word 'love' made her nervous. She was as inexperienced in love as she was in sex – or more so. Yet that brief four-letter word had changed the course of history, blazoned through all literature and art. She was still the philistine, responding to his gesture with a gauche and witless silence, so lost in introspection, she hadn't even thanked him for the flowers.

'They're fantastic!' she told him, gesturing round the room to all the vases; roses smiling back at her whichever way she looked. 'The most amazing thing anyone's ever done for me.'

He leaned across and kissed her in reply, a very cautious kiss this time, as if her lips might bruise or crush. 'The Romans used to put them in their wine, you know, to flavour it and scent it. We could do that with our bubbly.' He leaned across to pluck a rose from the nearest of the vases, eased its outer petals off, then floated one in each of their tall glasses.

Jane sipped her rose-champagne. It tasted just the same, but she shut her eyes, imagined a new flavour – the taste of Sybaris, Scarlatti, Nijinsky, Cleopatra – all those names he had woven through the evening, seductive stirring names. The artist was still playing with the flower, dipping it in his champagne, then sprinkling wine-drops on his tongue. 'I chose red because you're red yourself – passionate and fiery, Rose, however much you kid me you're a shy and shrinking violet. But let's try to keep things white this evening, which means slow and very gentle, like Nijinsky. He called himself a dove, you know.'

'A dove?'

'Yes. The bird of peace and innocence.'

'Well, this dove's getting hot.' She unfastened the two top buttons of her dress, could feel her heart thumping through her fingers, though not just from the heat. She had to make some gesture, some sign that she was willing. If they spun it out too slowly, as the artist seemed to want now, she might lose her nerve completely, become even more bogged down in speculations.

'It's a stunning dress,' he said, undoing the next button.

'My favourite.'

'A shame to take it off, then.'

'Yes.' She liked the rustle that the skirt made as she slid it past her knees, stood in her white waist-slip, hands across her chest. 'Aren't you hot yourself?'

'Boiling. The heating must be turned too high. Shall we go outside and cool off in the snow?'

She nodded. 'Roll naked in it, like – who was it you said?'

'I can't remember. I say too many things.'

'No, you don't.'

'So you don't wish I was the silent type?'

'I like you as you are.'

He hugged her to him suddenly, his hands reaching round to unhook her bra, peel it gently off. His shirt was silky-cool against her skin, the rough nub of his tie pressing on one breast.

'You're the shrinking violet now,' she whispered. 'Still got all your clothes on.'

'So are you going to take them off?'

She unknotted the tweed tie, forced the tiny fiddly buttons through their holes. His chest felt burning hot, heart pounding like her own. 'Listen to our hearts! They're going wild.'

'So they should.' He cupped his hand around her breast, feeling for her heart. 'Yours is even missing beats.'

'It can't be.'

'Yes, it is. I think we ought to go to bed and rest.'

She laughed, took off her tights; slid inside the covers, still wearing her lace waist-slip. Christopher turned the lights off, save for one small bedside lamp. He vanished for a moment and she heard a cistern flushing, the sound of water running in the bathroom. She should have washed herself, but she knew she mustn't move now, spoil their happy mood, that blessed sense of letting go, at last. She'd had a bath just before they left, doused herself with scent, washed her hair, smarmed on every aid she could – deodorant and hair-spray, lip gloss, hand cream, talc. Surely all those creams and potions would last a few hours more, see her through the night. She spread herself across the bed, stretching out diagonally, relishing the cool kiss of the sheets. Despite its heat, the room seemed kind and friendly, not snobby or too grand, but a homely sort of place which would help her to relax. She unfastened her gold bracelet, started pulling at her hair, shaking out the hairpins, trying to smooth it with her fingers. They were away from prying eyes now, so she'd no need to be sophisticated, or try to look a soignée twenty-five. She took another sip of her champagne, which Christopher had left beside the bed, the damask crimson petal floating on the top contrasting with the effervescent gold. The wine had helped already, softened all her edges, so she could merge and blend more easily, flow out of her body into his.

'No room for me?' he asked, gliding naked from the bathroom, a skimpy towel tied round his lower half.

'A good six or seven feet,' she flustered, moving right up to the edge and patting the expanse of crisp white sheet.

'I've kept my fig-leaf on,' he said. 'Like a shy and shrinking violet.'

'I've got mine on, too.'

'So we'll be shy together, shall we?'

'Yes.' She touched his chest, curled her fingers gently through its fur.

'Do you want the light off?'

She nodded. 'Would you mind?'

'No. It's quite exciting.' He reached out for the switch, plunged the room in darkness, and as he bent to kiss her, she heard a sudden raucous shout rising from the courtyard, echoed by a bray of drunken laughter. She tensed immediately, listened to the laughter swell, other voices joining in, then uncanny total silence; the only sound her own expectant startled breathing.

15

Jane was dreaming. Someone in the dream was stroking her and touching her, though she wasn't sure quite where. Her body felt shadowy – vague and undefined; had lost its usual boundaries. She tried to nudge the hand away, too sleepy to wake up. Her own hand closed on nothing, seemed to have no weight or strength. The stroking didn't stop. It was soothing, very soothing, slow and sensuous. Perhaps she'd simply accept it, as part of sleep, of dreaming; not push those swansdown fingers off. Everything was soft – the fluffy clouds beneath her, the drifting snow on top. Except the snow was black, not white – black velvet on her eyelids, black midnight in her mind. No, she didn't have a mind, just a blur of body, stirring slowly into life as the fingers probed more deeply, opening up some dark and secret part of her she didn't know she had.

She liked the secret feelings, yet didn't want to float up out of sleep. It must still be very late – or very early – shadow-time, nothing-time; or perhaps she'd travelled to some country where there was neither night nor morning, only twilight in between. She did remember driving – whirling white on black again, the drone of other ghostly cars, revving, swooshing past; then a sudden lurch as they braked to skirt a pothole in the road.

She half-sat up in shock, tried to push the driver off, was thrust back underneath him, wincing at the stab of pain, then jerking with his movement, picking up its rhythm, lunging back and forth in some extraordinary impetuous ride; then a judder and a strangled shout, and the driver was slumped over her, sweating, strangely quiet.

She kept her eyes closed, so as to memorise the sensations, etch them in her mind. They were nothing like she'd thought, nothing like the books said. She groped her hand between her thighs, surprised to find them slimy-wet. Her hair was tangled, one strand trapped by

Christopher, as if he'd fettered them together. She could see his face in a shaft of light filtering through the curtains; eyes shut tight, full lips clamped together, forehead tense and frowning.

'I'm sorry, Rose,' he said, at last, his voice smaller and less spirited than usual. 'That's not what I intended. Absolutely not. I don't know what it is between us, but every bloody time I've tried to . . .' His laugh was forced and awkward, and he left the sentence hanging, clearly too embarrassed to remind her of last night. 'I think I was half-asleep, just now – to start with, anyhow. I hardly even realised what was happening – until . . .'

'It's okay,' she said, wincing as he shifted, trapped a second strand of hair.

'It's not okay – far from it. I was utterly determined to make it good for you, and then I go and . . .'

'It *was* good, honestly.' How could she explain that all his slow and gentle wooing of last night had only brought her doubts and fears back, so that the more he kissed and fondled her, the more uptight she'd become. She couldn't understand it; had only slowly realised that it was affecting him, as well, so that when he finally tried to enter her, he had simply slithered out again, no longer stiff after an hour of holding back. They had finished up not making love, but pacing round the room, swapping lame excuses and apologies; he furious with himself for losing face; eyes dark-ringed with sheer fatigue – the only time she had ever seen him tired. It was a relief he'd come, at last, and come so sneakily and suddenly, she hadn't time to agonise or think. It was almost comic, in a way, though she dared not laugh, in case she hurt his feelings. He had suffered quite enough for one short night, seemed to take the whole thing so intensely, as if it wasn't merely pleasure, but some religious ritual, or vital rite of passage. Well, for her it was, of course. She had joined the adult world, passed from girlhood into womanhood, grown up with a jolt.

She glanced down at his stomach, then lower, to his thighs, amazed she had slept so soundly with a naked man beside her, sharing the same bed. Her eyes kept tracking back to the dark thatch of his pubic hair, and the pale shape just below it, which looked putty-soft and innocent, so different from the way it felt inside her. How peculiar men were. All that thrust and anguish in a bauble of pink flesh.

She tried to move her head, found herself still snared. 'Can I have my hair back, please?'

'Your what? Oh, I see. I'm sorry. I'm being a real brute today.'

'No, you're not.'

'Perhaps you like brutes, secretly.'

'Perhaps.'

He moved his hand towards her breast, stroked the palm across it, rhythmically and hard, then inched his fingers slowly, slowly lower, probing her deep navel, his touch softer now, and tantalising. She shut her eyes. All her fear had gone. She was no longer scared of being hurt, or of not meeting expectations; no longer fazed by what she didn't know. She was experienced, an adult, with an artist's sperm inside her. She still felt wet and sticky from his come, and his sly hand found that wetness; was rubbing and exciting her, where no one had ever touched her in her life. She could hear her parents' labels: 'dirty', 'private', 'dangerous', vaguely warning in her head – but her parents were quite wrong. It was no longer private, but opening up to Christopher; not dirty, but incredible, and maybe dangerous, but she craved and courted danger if it felt as good as that.

She had hardly ever touched herself, was vague about the details of what lay between her thighs, despite the plethora of sex-books which urged women to explore themselves, to use mirrors, fingers, to examine their anatomy, or give themselves more pleasure. She found such advice distasteful, if not even slightly comic, and there was always Amy's own distaste affecting her, inhibiting her; her constant presence in the house acting as a straitjacket. But her parents had been banished now, and Christopher had read those books, knew precisely what to touch, and where, and just how much crafty pressure would excite her in that spot or this, and how to subtly tantalise her by moving his slick fingers to somewhere less intense, so that she was crying out for their return, even moving her own hand down, to nudge or shove them back. She could feel her body arching up, hear her breathing loud and laboured, lungs bursting through her chest. Nothing else existed now save that vast and tiny triangle of heat and throb and fret, which had to be resolved, or she would die from the sheer build-up, from the sense of wolfish hunger. She had been waiting for this force-feed all her life – without even being aware of it – itching for this final wild release.

She shouted when it came, a shout which tore her throat, as his fingers clawed her lower down, and she was yelling, 'Stop! Oh, *stop*. You're hurting. No – don't. Go on, go on.' And there was a second rippling shudder, and her body seemed to shock up in the bed, as if sparked by an electric current.

'Wild Rose,' the artist whispered, taking back his fingers and linking them through hers, then kissing every part of her – her thighs, her stomach, nipples, throat and ears. Her ear-lobes tickled, and she laughed, which made him laugh, as well, and she thought back to the wan, tense, pacing artist of last night, amazed he could have changed so much. But then she had changed herself. She was still astonished by her body – the voracious famished feelings it had hidden and denied so long. She hugged the artist suddenly, grateful, overwhelmed. He had made her someone different, removed her from her parents' restricting prudish world. She liked the feel of his bare body, the heat of it, solidity; the way his hair was tousled and untidy, the dark shadow on his chin. She had always seen him groomed before, freshly combed and shaved. He seemed more vulnerable this morning, his body smelling warm and stale, his jaw just slightly bristly as she pressed her face to his.

'I think we'd better call that "his" and "hers",' he laughed. 'So after lunch perhaps we'll manage "ours". If you can come as violently as that, I want to be there with you, come at the same time.'

She kept her hand clasped tight in his. After lunch! She'd lived eighteen years with almost no experience of sex, and in just one day had been entered for a marathon.

'Your nipples are still standing up.' Christopher was touching them, running a soft finger in tiny teasing zigzags. 'You've got fantastic nipples, Rose, you know. They're a marvellous virgin-pink.'

'Aren't nipples all the same?'

'Good God no! They're just as different as noses are, or ears, or feet, or fingers. And they tend to darken in women who've had children. Some are really brownish, and a few go almost concave, tend to sink back into the breasts, as if they're sulking. Yours are clearly extroverts who like to be admired.' He continued with the admiration, then moved his finger just a fraction lower. 'Your little studs are hard as well.'

He traced the darker circle round her nipple, stroked the tiny nodules she hadn't even realised were there, let alone erect. How strange he knew so much about her body – far more than she herself did. She had merely lived inside it, ignoring all its subtleties, its capacity for pleasure. And up till now, it had always been a private thing – a body which she hid in clothes, locked in bathrooms, kept concealed. It seemed extraordinary to share it, open it to someone else, rip down the 'Keep Out' sign. Again, she pressed up close to him, to relish that sensation of bare warm skin on skin. Although it was an adult thrill, there was also some strange element of childish play and pleasure, as if the grown-up world with all its rules and duties, its moral prohibitions, had suddenly rolled back, and she'd found herself in a sort of sexual Disneyland, with a whoosh of new sensations. And the artist's body was one of the attractions, something to explore, something strange and even threatening, which might take her unawares again, on a roller-coaster ride. She reached her fingers out, moved them very slowly from the roughness of his chin to the bony hollow of his neck, then across to each small nipple. Odd that men had nipples. She'd have thought they might have lost them in the course of evolution, replaced them with little hooks for hanging up those notices men always seemed to wear: 'TOP DOG', 'BIG SHOT', 'BEWARE!'

'You've got little studs as well.'

'Yes – more than you have, actually, but they're crowded closer together, because we men don't have your lovely big areolas.' He fondled hers, to demonstrate, his fingers lightly grazing the darker ring which circled her pink nipple. 'It's a marvellous word that, isn't it, like the name of a goddess, or a heroine in opera. Perhaps I should have married an Areola. Areola Harville-Shaw.'

Jane tried the name herself – Rose-Areola Harville-Shaw – which was certainly more imposing than mere Anne.

The artist used the tip of his tongue to christen her areolas, then cupped them with his palms. 'They vary too, amazingly. Some are flat, some rounded, and I've even seen a cone-shaped pair, like two extra little breasts.'

'You've obviously made a study of the subject.' Jane fought a stab of jealousy, could see the artist's studio full of women with areolas – rounded ones and flat ones, some standing up like mountain peaks.

He shrugged. 'I did two years of anatomy, as well as all that life-drawing. And, God Almighty, some of those damned models weren't exactly Venuses. You get to see all sorts.'

She tried to move from naked women back to his own nipples. 'Do your studs get hard like women's do?'

'Feel.'

She nodded. 'Yes, they do.' She shut her eyes, so she could concentrate more closely on their lemon-peel nobbliness; the strange coolness of his nipple compared with his hot chest. 'D'you like your nipples being touched?'

'Mm,' he said, clamping his hand over hers, so as to make her touch them harder. 'Though most men don't, apparently. Perhaps I'm odd.'

'I like you odd.'

He kissed her, as reward. 'I envy women, actually. Their power to create makes mine look pretty puny. My first wife used to say that all art's a sort of substitute, and perhaps she had a point. D'you know, I was born two months prematurely, as if I wanted to complete myself, have some part in the whole astounding process, rather than lie around waiting for my mother to do it all herself. We're crafty, though, we males. We hide our own inadequacy with terms like penis-envy, when we're really all envying the womb. Did you ever crave a penis, Rose? I mean, maybe want your brother's, or . . . ?'

She blushed, and dodged the question. 'I didn't have a brother.'

'An only child, like me?'

'Yes,' she said, then added very casually. 'An adopted only child.'

'Adopted?'

She sat up very suddenly, both hands clenched, nails digging in her palms. Now he'd seen her naked, she must open to him emotionally, as well as simply physically, let him penetrate beyond her body, to her family, her history, her real unvarnished self. However difficult it proved, she must tell him the whole story, let it all pour out in an uncensored tide of words before she had a chance to change her mind.

He was silent when she'd finished, and she was aware of all the issues fermenting in the room – childlessness, sterility, concealment and betrayal. She tried to force a laugh. 'So I'm not sure who I am, you see.'

Still he didn't speak. She was worried that she'd hurt him, stirred up his own wounds by discussing barrenness; or made him feel deceived and even slighted because she hadn't told him sooner, had lived a lie herself. Or perhaps he was debating his own responsibilities – should he advise her to return, rejoin her parents, show them more concern?

'What's wrong?' she asked, in an attempt to break the silence.

'Nothing. I . . . I'm sorry. I mean, I realise just how bloody the whole thing must have been for you, how . . . how . . .'

He was seldom lost for words. Was he so genuinely upset for her that he couldn't find an adjective, or merely troubled on his own account? Perhaps adoption was a subject which set up dangerous ripples. Maybe Anne had wanted to adopt, when she discovered he was barren, and he'd refused point-blank. Or was it even possible that he'd been adopted as a child himself? She groped a hand out, let it feather from his stomach, down, and slowly down, between his thighs. She must change the mood and subject, try to restore the former lighter atmosphere.

'Maybe I feel penis-envy now,' she joked, amazed at her own daring as she uncoiled the bashful object of her envy; surprised again by its baby-state, its modest shrinking coyness.

Christopher made no response, but his penis compensated – seemed to swell from infancy to manhood almost instantaneously; the blue veins standing out, the tip inflamed and angry-looking, like the face of some old soak. It was ugly, yet astonishing – all that power and urgency throbbing through her fingers. She did feel envy, in a sense, longed to have some part of her which would expand in the same way, change from child to sexpot in a flash. Her breasts, for instance – why shouldn't they lie flat all day, so they didn't wobble when she ran, or hurt before her period, but simply burgeon out in bed to a startling forty inches; then, when she'd thrilled her lover with them, they'd fold down flat again? She was smiling as she thought of it, smiling as she used both hands on the distended red-faced drunk, exulting that she'd somehow got it right; that despite her inexperience and fears, she had managed to please Christopher. That wary look had left him, as the sensations from his penis seemed to reach his face, crease it in excitement; one hand clenched to match; even all his toes curled up. His voice had changed as well, become slower and more languid now; the lover, not the teacher.

'We're not meant to be doing this again till after lunch. I'm afraid my recovery rate isn't quite as speedy as it was.'

'How long?' she asked him, teasingly.

'Ten seconds! Quick, kneel up and we'll try it from the . . .'

They both jumped when the clock struck, nine rumbling chimes resounding from the courtyard.

'Christ!' said Christopher, clambering off. 'It can't be nine o'clock! I'm due to meet the vicar in an hour, and the church is twenty miles away.'

'You can't meet him like that.'

They laughed, watched his penis slowly wilt, contract from wild carouser to soft pink embryo.

'That's better,' Jane pronounced. 'Except you'd better put your loincloth on. The Reverend might not quite approve of a naked stained-glass artist.'

Christopher was already hunting through the wardrobe, cursing as he dropped a belt and tie. 'Can you ring down for some tea, Rose? I need a cup of something hot inside me before I face that winding country road, which won't be any better for the snow.'

'D'you want some toast as well?'

'I haven't time. You have breakfast when I've gone – work through the whole menu, enjoy it for the two of us.'

'But can't I come as well? I'd like to see the . . .'

'Better not. There's no point in us both rushing. You indulge yourself – loll in bed with *Country Life*, or ask Jonathan to rustle up *oeufs Bénédict* for breakfast. I won't be long anyway. And when I'm back, we'll continue where we left off.' His eyes met hers, seemed to explain in greater detail; his sensual mouth half-open, as if already kissing hers. Then he dashed into the bathroom, pulling on his shirt.

She stood at the window, watching him drive off. The snow had disappeared; a valiant winter sun sparkling on the river, two white swans gliding down towards her. Everything was busy – water rippling and reflecting, ducks plopping, diving, shaking wings and tails; coots' heads bobbing back and forth, wind ruffling reeds and rushes, self-important clouds surging overhead. A baker was delivering bread, a milkman clanking bottles. Only she was idle, gloriously idle, with nothing to do but luxuriate in bed. She longed to heave the window open, stick her head out and shout to all the world: 'I've come, I've come – and "violently", my lover said. I'm a woman and an adult, who can please an artist, thumb a penis stiff.' She craved to tell the milkman and the baker, the swans and coots and ducks; yell it up to Shrepton, to her parents and her neighbours, to the woman in the paper-shop, the Pakistani grocer. 'I've got these quite fantastic nipples – a marvellous virgin-pink, and little studs which tauten, and . . .'

The phone shrilled beside the bed, as if in answer. She picked it up, clutched her housecoat round her, somehow fearing that the caller could see the fat pink nipples, the stiffening little studs.

'Good morning, Rose,' said Jonathan. 'I was wondering what you'd like for breakfast. Christopher said you might prefer it in your room.'

'Oh yes,' she said. 'I would.' No sneering waiters then, or bossy gawping waitresses; no one calling her 'Madame' – though actually she *was* Madame, had earned the title just this morning, from her husband of one night.

'Kedgeree? Smoked haddock? Eggs any way you like. I could make you a soufflé-omelette with smoked salmon in, or chanterelles, or . . .'

Bubble and squeak, she almost said. She could see it in her mother's pan, burnt around the edges, buttery in the middle, with slices of black pudding, grilled black as their name. She didn't fancy grand food, but something filling and plebeian, with a large bowl of child's cereal to start with. Why be intimidated? Christopher had urged her to ask for what she wanted.

'C . . . could I have Sugar-Puffs, and sausages?'

'Certainly,' said Jonathan. 'And what to drink?'

She paused. Hotel coffee was always far too strong. And she'd already drunk a quart of tea – Christopher's as well as hers, since he'd rushed off after just two sips, and even then had burnt his tongue. She could suddenly see her father sitting beside her in McDonald's, both their mouths moustached with pink as they gulped down strawberry milk-shakes. Amy disapproved of milk-shakes – especially between meals – and also of McDonald's, so they had remained a secret pleasure, a delicious guilty bond between her father and herself.

'Do you do milk-shakes?' she blurted out impulsively, still clinging to her father.

'We can do anything you want.'

'Okay, a strawberry milk-shake.' She regretted it immediately. Jonathan would sneer at her, mock her childish tastes. And how could she eat breakfast with her father sitting in her head, glancing in disgust at the rumpled sheets and blankets, aware she'd been to bed with a man at least a decade older than himself? She knew he'd be appalled, yet he refused to leave the room; was eating chocolates now, picking out the strawberry creams. Strawberry was his favourite – strawberry ices, strawberry mousse. Her mother rarely ate sweets, and then only diabetic ones, which she claimed didn't make you fat, or rot your teeth. She wondered if her mother preferred diabetic sex, which didn't make you sweat, or muss your hair, didn't swell your nipples up.

Her parents seemed much closer now, not just in terms of distance – though certainly she had reduced the miles between them by driving all this way – but because she'd been describing them to Christopher, dragged them from concealment in the shadows, made them real and solid for him. Despite his wary silence, she was glad she had opened up, got it off her chest, at last, let him see the real her – or part of her, at least. She wished she could go further, force her parents to accept the truth, as well; understand the real Jane, meet the new Jane-Rose. It seemed wrong to turn back south again, having come so far towards them, rather than continue up the A1 to Newcastle, and then strike west for Shrepton. It would be easier in one way simply to turn up at their door, instead of trying to write that letter she'd abandoned twenty times, or struggling to communicate long-distance on the phone. She craved to see them, dreaded it; felt tugged between north and south, between the sham safety of her childhood and the danger of new starts. Perhaps she should take Christopher, pull up outside her dowdy house in his expensive snobby car; introduce him casually as her artist-friend, her lover. She could see her father's shocked and ashen face, hear her mother's fury; drowned it with the television, tuned to Tom and Jerry, who were fighting tooth and claw, then settled back determinedly to do what she'd been told – indulge herself in bed.

She was still watching children's television when Christopher returned, breakfast debris all around her, toast crumbs on the sheets. 'Gosh! You're back soon,' she faltered, trying to hide her milk-shake glass, with its damning ring of froth.

'Yes. The roads were almost empty, and it was much nearer than I thought. And both the vicar and the architect were very brisk and businesslike, so we didn't waste time beating about the bush.' He sat down on the bed, frowning at a congealing sausage stub. 'I'm afraid my window's had it, though. It's in a far worse state than I realised from the letter. It's as if my past is catching up with me, though it's not actually my fault. That bloody stuff I used to stick the glass down has gradually deteriorated, and now the bond is failing and pieces of the glass are dropping off.'

'Stick the glass down? What d'you mean?'

He shrugged a shade impatiently. 'Glass appliqué's a completely different technique from traditional stained glass. It's a sticking process, rather than a leading one, and there's very little formal cutting. You stick the pieces of glass – most of which are offcuts or fragments from the cullet-box – to a sheet of clear plate glass, rather like a mosaic.' He paused to rub disconsolately at a tea-stain on the counterpane. 'You use an epoxy resin, which was the cause of the whole trouble. It's gone brittle and discoloured, and begun to lose its grip, despite the manufacturer's high-flown claims. Which only goes to show that you should keep to the old traditions. The glass at Chartres has lasted seven hundred and fifty years, and may last another seven hundred, so long as it's looked after, whereas my ill-fated window is already headed for the scrapheap.' He fumbled for his cigarettes, as if he needed consolation. 'Yet, at the time, it seemed a good technique, which would release you from the leads, give you scope and freedom to be more painterly. In fact, several first-rate artists were seduced by it, as I was, and used it in good faith, but they've come unstuck – in all senses.'

'Can't you use another resin – I mean, stick the pieces back and . . . ?'

'Well, yes, we did discuss that. But it would mean stripping them all off first, and starting again from scratch, and the cost would be enormous. They're short of cash, as usual, and I simply haven't the time or inclination to do the job for peanuts. No, we decided we'd remove the thing and just plain-glaze the window, at least for the time being. It's pretty bloody depressing. I always liked that window, and it was connected with a good time in my life – had sentimental memories.'

Jane said nothing. More females, she supposed, more nipples and areolas. He'd probably had another young assistant, some sixteen-year-old siren, who'd inspired him and consoled him, modelled for him live. Part of the trouble of sleeping with a man so old was he'd lived too much, known too many women.

'Anyway, I was driving back feeling rather down, when I saw this signpost to Newark, which is actually in Nottinghamshire, and not that far from Belthorpe, where I did another window, donkey's years ago – a Saint Jerome window, complete with faithful lion. I thought we might drive over there to see it, have some lunch in the local pub, perhaps an amble round the village. It's such a perfect day. I hope you realise I laid it on specially. Blue sky and puffy clouds don't turn up on their own in the first week of December, especially when we were deep in snow last night.'

She laughed, tried to hide a twinge of disappointment. Had he totally forgotten they were meant to be continuing where they'd left off earlier on? She hadn't dressed on purpose, just had a bath, brushed her hair a hundred times, sprayed her breasts with scent. Now she felt a little spare, lolling naked on the pillows, when he was clearly chafing to get off.

'Come on, Rose. We mustn't miss this sunshine. Throw a sweater on or something, and we'll go. The views are quite fantastic, and you can see for miles and miles. If we hang about, it may cloud over.'

'But what about your breakfast?'

'I very rarely eat it. And we can have an early lunch.'

She checked her watch. It was already past eleven. She couldn't see him stopping for lunch before two-ish at the earliest. Meals came last – after work and windows. This was work, in one sense, going to see his window. He had planned it as an outing, a treat for her, diversion, but she'd have preferred to have him to herself, without Saint Jerome as a threesome – and to have him wild and naked, as he'd been when they woke up. He wasn't even looking at her, seemed oblivious of her breasts now, her areolas, her pink nipples.

'I'll wait for you downstairs, okay? I want a word with Jonathan.'

'Yes, fine,' she said flatly, slipping out of bed and hunting for her bra. The artist's clothes were all neatly hung or folded; hers strewn on the floor.

Fifteen minutes later, she joined him in reception, where he was talking with Jonathan and two other natty men. Four pairs of eyes swivelled to inspect her. She had left her hair loose, was wearing a tight sweater which made the most of what he'd called her firm and high-slung breasts. She could see the men approved; suddenly felt powerful, with a new weapon in her armoury, as if she'd broken through some barrier this morning, which had given her new status in the world.

She sauntered out to the car, the artist's arm across her shoulders, the three men strolling after them, waving them goodbye. Once outside, she was grateful for his plan. It *was* a perfect morning, cold but very clear, the sun deepening all the colours, gilding the grey water; the sky so vast and spacious it looked as if some busy giant had pulled it out and stretched it, laundered the white clouds. The roads seemed dwarfed beneath it, winding toytown roads, with wild and ragged hedgerows; an air of peace and timelessness frosted on a countryside which hadn't yet been wrenched into the age of jets or juggernauts, and which had banned transistor radios and brazen Kawasakis. The loudest noise was the screeching of a jay, soaring from a copse. They admired the flash of turquoise in its wings, its gleaming chestnut plumage.

'That's a bird which should be seen and not heard,' Christopher remarked. 'It's a pretty handsome fellow, but its voice is a disaster. It's funny how the really virtuoso singers – the nightingales and skylarks – seem always rather drab, as if God or Mother Nature refused to give them beauty as well as a good voice. By the way, did you hear about that music teacher who used a computer and a tape recorder to slow down the skylark's song – about sixteen times, I think it was, then transcribed it for the piano, and proved the bird a genius?'

'No,' she said, 'I didn't.'

'Well, he discovered that the skylark is creating music as complex and as subtle as that of Bach or Beethoven, and put together as skilfully as if a human mind was in control – actually following sonata form, with an exposition, development, and recapitulation. It almost blows the mind. I mean, larks have been around several million years before man, so they can hardly be following human rules of composition.' He swerved to avoid a rabbit, already flattened on the road. 'Apparently, the skylark sings about two hundred and fifty notes a second, which takes some believing, doesn't it? I know birds live life in the fast lane, but . . .' He was driving fast himself

215

now, bare fields flashing by, clumps of naked trees, a tall church steeple glinting, gone; restless shadows rippling on the road. 'Did you know I sign my windows with a bird?'

'No,' she said, counting no's again. Two already, and they hadn't reached the church yet.

'When I first started, I used just my initials, as I do on all my paintings, but then I met a colleague whose name was Philip Mariner, and he always signed his windows with a tiny little ship. It's called a rebus – when you use a pun or picture, to stand in for your name. Charles Kempe used a wheatsheaf, and after he teamed up with Walter Tower, they added a small tower to the centre of the sheaf. D'you know their work at all?'

She shook her head, refused to frame a third no, or to admit she'd never heard of either artist.

'Funnily enough, the first window that I ever signed with my little scarlet bird was the Saint Jerome one we're on our way to see. Christ! That window cost me, Rose. I must have had more problems with it than any other commission before or since.'

'Why? Was it glass appliqué, too?'

'No. Leaded glass. The problems came before I'd even started, not two decades later. The vicar and the PCC were both a total pain, objected to the way I'd made the figure dissolve into the background, which was the whole point of the design; even objected to the lion, because it wasn't quite the sort you'd see in London Zoo.' The artist's voice was rising as he recalled the whole controversy.

'We had quite a little battle, though fortunately the donor and the architect were both very much on my side, and the donor was a wealthy man and an extremely generous patron of the church, so in the end we licked those stuffy middlebrows, whose whole idea of art was that it should console and be uplifting. My design threw down a challenge to them, suggested conflict and division, instead of easy phoney comfort, or sickly piety. But even when we'd got the thing accepted, the hassles still weren't over. I had a devil of a job trying to get the glass. I needed a lot of subtle neutral colours, which no one seemed to have in stock, so I was rattling around from one supplier to another, wasting time and petrol.' He hurtled round a corner, as if in demonstration, hands clenched on the wheel. 'And to cap it all, I wasn't that enamoured with Saint Jerome anyway. In fact, it beats me how he made it as a saint. He was fanatical, vindictive, spiteful and self-centred; hated Jews, hated competition, and was so obsessed with fasting and asceticism, he encouraged anorexia in all his female pupils. One of them actually starved herself to death, and there was said to be a scandal at her funeral. And it's always seemed suspicious that he had so many women flocking round him, when he spent his whole damn life denouncing sex – even sex in marriage.'

Jane looked up, shading her eyes from the bold stare of the sun. 'So how did he imagine the race would carry on?'

'I doubt he cared that much. The next life was the important one, which was why he opposed every form of pleasure – food, reading, women, wine – anything which ties us to this transient wicked world. The only thing he could say for sex was that it renewed the supply of virgins, and he apparently assumed that the very few women who ever made it into heaven would be immediately transmuted into men.'

'Gosh! What a pig. I loathe him.'

The artist laughed, relaxed his hands, let the car slow down, as if all his own annoyance had suddenly evaporated, and he'd remembered it was Saturday, and he was off-duty and at leisure; no longer struggling with misogynist saints, or hostile PCCs. 'Well, don't loathe *my* Saint Jerome. I have to admit I did become quite fond of him, once I'd got stuck in. It's often the way when you're working on a job. The subject takes you over, and you begin to see the human side underneath the faults or the façade. I made my Jerome really haunted, pulled between his own strong sensuality and all the fasts and deprivations he inflicted on his body. And the evidence bears me out, you know. The more I read about him, the more I found a man divided. He was apparently a gourmet, and used to visit strip-shows in his youth, yet he had an obvious dread of his own voracious appetites, tried to douse them with hard work. It's said he studied Hebrew to discipline his mind, stop it recreating images of those topless dancing-girls.'

Jane glanced up at the artist – the lean ascetic face and troubled eyes. Weren't there certain parallels between him and harrowed Jerome? He called himself a gourmet, like the saint, but was always missing meals, hadn't eaten since last night, and then left half his food. He, too, had females fluttering around him, was fanatical and self-centred, and though clearly very sensual, still rationed all his pleasures, always put work first.

'Actually, I'm keen for you to see him, Rose. I'd like your view on the window as a whole. I've never been too sure about the lion. Because I knew the story was apocryphal, and there probably hadn't been a lion at all, let alone a new-style softie Jerome pulling out a thorn from its paw, I tried to make the creature very minimal, more the general feeling of a lion, the sense of strength and claw, rather than every hair and whisker painted in. But perhaps I went too far, played it down a shade too much. It'll be interesting to see it now, after all these years.'

Jane started as a flock of geese suddenly honked across the sky, the nearest they had got yet to a jet plane. She was both pleased and apprehensive that he wanted her opinion on the window: flattered that he thought her views worth hearing; scared she'd disappoint him by saying something crass. She was always short of words, didn't have his skill in clothing basic thoughts in velvet or shot-silk. And suppose she *didn't* like it? Should she lie, pretend, force empty smiles and phrases; or simply tell him it was 'interesting' or 'haunted' – terms he'd used himself?

She glanced through the car window at the stretch of tangled woodland, the murky stagnant stream. Despite the wreckage from the storm, the wreckage of the season – crippled hedgerows, beaten bracken, dead or fallen trees – there were also signs of spring: swollen buds on beeches, a pewter sheen on willows, glossy heart-shaped ivy-leaves garlanding dead elms. All life and vegetation seemed turned low, like a barely flickering flame, but both heat and light were there still, ready to burst forth again, once winter was defeated.

'Look, there's the signpost – Belthorpe.' Christopher swung right, following its white arm. 'I'd like to tell you it's an idyllic country village, but it's actually quite ordinary, and spoilt by modern housing.'

Jane could see nothing modern as they drove into the village, just a street of old stone houses, a timbered pub shaded by two ancient oaks, and a group of old age pensioners gossiping by the village store, which had yellowed windows and a mangy cat dozing on the sill.

Christopher scorched up the street, all the grey heads turning to goggle at his car; an overweight labrador suddenly trotting right in front of it, so that he was forced to swerve and slow. 'The church is further up, Rose. It's rather nicely sited on its own, with trees all around it, so you feel you're in the wilds.'

'We are,' said Jane. 'I've never seen such space and sort of emptiness. I mean, driving here, we hardly passed a soul.'

'Well, Lincolnshire especially is rather secretive. I suppose it's not en route to anywhere, so it keeps itself to itself. And even parts of Notts are pretty lonely. Right, here we are.' He pulled up outside the churchyard, which stood higher than the village, with a screen of naked beeches standing guard around it, their labyrinthine roots exposed, like gnarled arthritic fingers. She could glimpse the grey stone church through the frieze of dappled branches; a dour but solid building, with a squarish tower one end. Christopher was already at the door, impatient as she hovered by the gravestones.

'Some of these are really old. I can hardly read the inscriptions.' She peered closer at a moss-furred block of granite.

'I'm not surprised. The church is thirteenth-century – parts of it, at least. It's suffered horribly, lost half its nave and chancel, and all its early glass.' He plunged across to join her, pacing swiftly round the tombstones, the anger in his voice spilling to his feet. 'When I think about the destruction of stained glass, I get so hopping mad I'd like to line up those crass Puritans and shoot them in cold blood, like they shot their lethal musket-balls through precious jewels of windows, or smashed them into fragments with iron bars. D'you realise, Rose, they called them works of the devil, those fantastic works of art, said they were invented by Satan, who was the patron of pomp and pride. You ought to read their records, their almost gloating relish when they battered down another hundred windows, or demolished priceless statues, and then recorded their barbarities as "godly reformations".'

Jane stepped back, as if he were threatening her personally. She almost envied him his anger; the way he cared so passionately. She knew he would have risked his life if he'd been around in Cromwell's time, and if that life could save the glass. She had read about the Puritan devastation, but it had all seemed two-dimensional – long ago and far away, just something in her history book, taught by chilblained Miss McKay, who cared more about the heating in the classroom than about the loss of England's heritage.

The artist was still fretting round the churchyard, appeared to have forgotten what they'd come for, his mind now in the south. 'Every time I go to Canterbury Cathedral, I feel a sense of outrage. There's that splendid nave with all its windows just plain-glazed, when they were probably once as rich as the famous ones in Chartres. I'd like to believe in hell, Rose, so that bloody butcher Cromwell could burn down there for ever. He used the nave as a barracks, would you believe, let his troops run wild and tear the place to pieces. And Henry VIII was every bit as bad – filched twenty-six cartloads of treasure from Canterbury alone, then wrecked every other Becket shrine throughout the length and breadth of England.'

He suddenly swooped down, ripped out a piece of groundsel sprouting on a grave, flung it to one side. 'And what makes it even worse was that both men were well aware of the relish for destruction, which lurks beneath the surface of so-called civilised society, and both deliberately harnessed it, whipped up public fury against the cathedrals and the monasteries. Whole communities joined in, every thick-skulled clod and ruffian working off his personal frustration on the fabric of the church.'

Jane glanced up at his face, troubled by his bitter voice, the rancour in his eyes. Even the first day she had met him, he'd been berating human nature, its appetite for violence; denouncing violence violently. Was he angry just with vandals who'd lived four hundred years ago, or with people in his own life, here and now?

He wiped his hands, which were muddy from the groundsel, then tramped back to the entrance of the church, beckoning her to join him. 'Come and see these windows, Rose – monstrosities, the lot of them, nineteenth-century trash, in place of thirteenth-century masterpieces.'

She stepped inside; the cold but bracing winter air giving place to a dark and gloomy clamminess as she closed the door behind her. The windows he was rubbishing looked okay to her – the sort of thing she'd seen in all the books – worthy saints standing under canopies, haloes round their heads, Gothic scrolls twining round their feet.

'Look at this abortion! Absolutely lifeless, and made by some philistine who thought rich colours meant crude ones. It was probably churned out by a soulless firm, working on the cheap and rehashing old designs.'

'But where's yours?' she asked, glancing round the nave from pious face to pious face; one saint pointing to a book, another with a pilgrim's staff, two with lavish lilies. No lion, as yet, no stern but sensual Jerome dissolving into space.

'It's right up near the altar, in a side-chapel. Thank God! It would have been impossible, stylistically, to put a modern window in this nave, especially my Saint Jerome. You can't just stick a new work in and ignore the scale and colour of all the other windows, or discount the shapes and rhythms of the architecture. You have to consider the building as a whole. My muted low-key colour scheme would be completely overwhelmed here. I chose sober colours deliberately, to suit a sober saint, and because I . . .' He broke off in mid-sentence, stopping to examine a brass plaque on the wall, which seemed to claim his whole attention.

She turned back to the pilgrim-saint, wondering who he was. Christopher had taught her a lot about the saints, how real they were in medieval times, and how absolutely crucial – patron saints and local saints, saints for every day and cause; helping you and guiding you, like family and friends. She hoped Saint Rose would do her bit when they returned to the hotel, make the sex so special that the artist would remember it for years and years to come, maybe all his life. Though, judging by what she'd learnt about her name-saint, it didn't seem too likely. Saint Rose had been a virgin, and also a recluse, who had retired to a crumbling garden-shed and practised highly masochistic forms of penance. She'd hardly approve of dirty weekends with someone else's husband, let alone of Sybarites knocking back champagne.

She glanced around for Christopher, saw him near the altar, standing in the side-chapel, with his neck and head craned up. Couldn't he have waited for her before going to see his window? He always got edgy if she lingered over something he considered second-rate, and would express his disapproval by striding on ahead. She hurried to catch up with him, praying that she'd like his famous saint.

She tipped her head back, rubbed her eyes. There *wasn't* any saint – no ascetic haunted Jerome in subtle muted colours; no lion, not even minimal, no man or beast at all. She was looking at a waste of plain uncoloured glass, slightly rippled in its texture, but basically so humdrum you wouldn't even notice it – the sort of glass they had in their Shrepton loo.

She held her breath, listened to the silence, which had stifled everything – nature, traffic, even their own heartbeats. No bird was singing, no car had dared to pass, and there was no sound or stir from Christopher, who was standing shocked beside her, like a statue in cold stone. Then, suddenly, she heard the din of smashed and shattering windows, the barbaric crack of musket shots, and battering of cruel iron bars lobbed through radiant glass; the mocking ring of horses' hooves as the Roundheads clattered off. Virile saints had been trampled into fragments, angels pulverised; bright birds no longer flying, but broken-backed and mute; lush Madonna lilies hacked down like common weeds.

'So they won,' the artist murmured, his voice so low she could barely make the words out.

He turned on his heel, walked swiftly to the door.

16

Jane could feel the pikes still, now stabbing through her body, Cromwell's vicious metal bar battering her and battering, his fury flooding into her. She fought back with all her strength, furious herself at the waste, the desecration; sweating, grinding under him, as she tried to heave him off. Somehow, she'd succeeded and she was lying now on top, gripping with her thighs, clawing with her nails; her breath too fast and heavy, a different harsher rhythm from the one which seemed dictated by her body and the battle. She was fighting everyone at once, not just the brutal Roundheads, but all her stupid family: her mother – both her mothers – the one who'd left her and the one who'd scooped her up; the father who had shammed the name, and the first and fleeting father who had grappled in a bed like this, shot his seed, then scarpered. She was raging at them all, raging at the mess they'd made through their carelessness, deceit; smashing things to pieces, destroying history and heredity, shooting lethal musket-balls through identity and safety.

They were angry, too – angry that she'd discovered all their secrets, bitter that she'd run away, shocked and scandalised that she was sleeping with a married man, an older man, a violent man – no, not sleeping, struggling – wrestling with him even now, as she slammed against his chest, thwacked and thrust on top of him, used every muscle, every shred of strength. His body seemed much larger than it had done just this morning, larger and more ruthless, yet she herself was part of that brute body, joined to it and bonded; her hair entangled round his neck, their arms and legs entwined, their two mouths clamped together, their sweat, saliva, mingling. They had lost their separateness, their boundaries, lost their sense of time, lost their human language; were making only noises – grunts and racking gasps of breath, sudden sobbing cries.

She shut her eyes, ducked her head, as she bent into the wind, let the storm gust and rampage through her, assault her with its own sounds – maddened howls and whinings, a steady soughing roar, which she could feel squalling through her body, like the night of the great hurricane. She could smell those smells again – the reek of crushed and bleeding leaves, the tang of splitting wood and sea-blitzed shingle; could feel the same abandonment as she had done in November, the same loss of all control; could do nothing but submit, fall as trees were falling, crack and smash to pieces.

She bit him as she came, bit him on the shoulder, hardly knew what she was doing until he yelped in pain, pushed her off, then slumped back on the bed, turned round the other way from her, his back against her spine. She pulled her hair free, tried to calm her breathing. How still it was, uncanny – total shaky silence after such an uproar. The wind had dropped, the storm died down, her separate self and tamer self now creeping slowly back, appalled at what she'd done. She had let him rip her skin off, her chrysalis, her shell; all those safe and careful layers she'd spent eighteen years assembling, destroyed in half an hour. The Jane she knew wasn't madly sexual, didn't show her anger, or express her feelings savagely, didn't lose control.

She glanced down at her body, which felt strange and incomplete, as if it had been wrenched apart, then put back the wrong way; parts of it still missing, or maybe swapped with Christopher's; other parts duplicated, like those cockeyed Cubist pictures in the art books. She touched her breasts, which were still smarting from his mouth; her whole body marked and branded with him – a love-bite purpling on her neck, faint red bracelets round each arm, where he'd gripped her by the wrists. She tried to swallow, but her throat felt husky-dry, her own mouth sore and out of shape, from her wild ferocious kisses. He'd shown her who she truly was; revealed the greed and violence spitting underneath; proved what she'd denied – the excitement in that violence, how close it was to ecstasy.

'C . . . Christopher?' she stammered, suddenly needing him to talk to her, reassure her, make things safe and small again. He didn't seem to hear, was lying like a fallen trunk, his body touching hers, yet no longer feeling part of it, seeming like a stranger's, a stranger who had frightened her. She had been scared all afternoon, from the moment that he'd marched out of the church and stormed round to the vicarage to discover what had happened to his window; found the vicar out, only a dumb child playing in the garden, whom he'd left confused and crying. He had charged on to the pub, burst into the public bar, started interrogating the barman, as if he was personally responsible. There'd been a sudden chilling hush, with everybody staring, eyes hostile at his hectoring tone, no one saying anything to the Intruder and the Enemy, then beer-mugs raised to mouths again, in a conspiracy of silence. He'd stampeded out, sprinted down the narrow street to the dozy village store, found it closed for lunch. He had dithered for a moment, then wheeled back to the vicarage, she following like his shadow, a silent cringing shadow, trying to compress herself to nothing. The large stone house was empty still – empty like the church, where he chafed for fifteen minutes more, examining his window from the inside and the outside, finally subsiding in a pew, exhausted and defeated.

She had known she ought to comfort him, but couldn't find the words. His reaction seemed excessive, as if he were grieving for a murdered child. But perhaps his windows were his children. He had no others, after all, no flesh and blood descendants to perpetuate his line. The glass would do it for him, keep his name and memory alive. She had already seen the mother-love he lavished on it, the time and patience he poured out, when he was not a patient man. He was less generous with real people, offhand and even curt; saved his true affection for his Resurrection Angels, his Saint Jeromes, his red birds. But now a favourite child had been destroyed.

They had driven back in silence to the Swan. She'd felt embarrassed by the sun, which continued shining tactlessly, lighting up the landscape and the sky, when his face and mood were so clearly overcast. As soon as they got in, he rang his wife. She felt totally negated, like some odd bod he'd forgotten. He didn't find a private phone, or explain what he was doing, but just sat down on the bed, and started telling Anne the story, then asked if she could dig out his address book and find the number of the architect he had worked with on the window, a Mr Howard Gray. Next, he rang the architect – or tried to. The man who answered claimed he'd never heard of Mr Gray, had lived there only eighteen months, and had bought the place from a doctor, not an architect.

She herself had crept into the bathroom, as if to hide from Anne. She always tried to blank her out, pretend Christopher was single; often lived in fear that Mrs Harville-Shaw might stroll into the studio and start asking awkward questions. Christopher had told his wife that he'd hired a young assistant, but had surely not revealed the extent of her new duties, nor admitted he was with her this weekend. When, at last, she'd ventured out, the artist was still sitting on the bed, an ashtray balanced on his knee, though his cigarette was spewing ash

224

on the bedclothes and the carpet. The sky had clouded over, the room gloomy now, and cold.

'I'm sorry,' he'd said suddenly. 'This is not much fun for you, Rose. And we never had our lunch. Shall we ring down now for some sandwiches and fruit?'

She shook her head, couldn't eat, felt too upset by Anne still – the wife at home, who knew where his address book was, could dig out numbers from the past, who'd shared that past, shared his bed each night.

He had kissed her very tenderly, assumed she was distressed about the window, shared his own outrage and dejection. She'd kissed him back with Anne's lips, astonished at herself – the way her teeth and tongue were joining in, the anger in her mouth, the open thrusting force of it, as if it had grown up overnight and could rival any wife's. She was a bitter wife, a fierce wife, attacking him with kisses, stripping off his sweater, removing both the cigarette and ashtray. He had fought her back immediately, tearing off her own clothes, straddling her and muzzling her, leaving bite-marks on her breasts.

It had been light still when they'd started, the murky grudging light of a winter's afternoon. Now a sombre dusk was falling, all the objects in the room blurring and dissolving. She could feel herself unravelling as well, hated the grey silence, the unfriendly feel of the artist's bony back. In the films she'd seen, the books she'd read, sex was more companionable. People chatted afterwards, lay face to face, or lolled against the pillows, still fondling one another, or sharing confidences. She longed for him to talk, to tell her it had been all right, that she hadn't broken rules, or gone too far; that he was fond of her, committed, still admired her breasts and body. She rolled over in the bed, let those breasts push gently at his spine; suddenly imagined him a baby, a tiny puny infant, born eight weeks prematurely, and battling for his life. Was that why he was small still, and still a stubborn fighter? She'd been touched when he admitted that he'd wanted to complete himself, instead of lying passive in the womb. It seemed crazy, yet courageous, to challenge the whole scheme of things, defy the force of nature, when you were a pathetic scrap who could barely suck or squall.

At last, he turned towards her, humped over half-reluctantly, brows drawn down, face frowning. 'You see, they never liked my window, Rose.'

She tensed, removed her hand. So his mind was in the church still. All that time in bed, he had been thinking of his window, not of her.

Her convulsive scorching body, her scourging grown-up mouth, had been just a muted background to Saint Jerome.

'So I suppose if something happened to it – if it was damaged in the storm, or attacked by vandals, they were relieved to have an excuse to do away with it, or were even getting their own back. I still can't understand, though, why they didn't get in touch with me. It would have been courteous, to say the least, to have informed me in a letter. Perhaps they assumed that I was dead, or so decrepit I was past taking any interest.' He eased stiffly out of bed, shambled to the wardrobe, as if in imitation of that old decrepit man; his voice querulous, disgruntled, as he continued complaining about the Chancellor of the Diocese, and how it was impossible to put anything in a church – or take it out, for that matter – without his formal diktat. 'But he might well have remembered all the wrangling in the past, Rose, or have re-read all the records, and if the committee were still hostile to any sort of modern art, they probably advised him to avoid any more controversy, and replace the bloody window with plain glass, which can't offend anyone. Except me,' he added, slouching to the bathroom with his clothes.

She heard the bolt ram home, felt excluded and shut out, not just by the bolted door, but from the whole contentious world of church committees, which she had never really understood, despite the many times he'd cursed their tedious rigmarole. She fumbled for the light-switch, snapped on the bedside lamp. Everything was sharper now, solid, redefined. She felt too tired to move. The sex had drained her, left her wrecked and spent. The roses, too, looked jaded; two or three keeled over, as if their stems were too inert to bear their weight. She reached out for a bloom, one still full and healthy, held it to her nose. It smelt of nothing, not like summer roses, whose scent was so intense it was the whole essence of the flower, literally as well as metaphorically. These were forced – a violent word – violence everywhere: the violence of the Roundheads, the violence of the storm, the relish for destruction lurking beneath the civilised exterior of every Tom, Dick, Harry, Jane. Christopher had told her that red roses were created by a sacrifice of blood – Aphrodite's blood – and that the flower was sacred to all the gods of love; its very name an anagram of Eros; love and suffering linked.

She lay back on the bed and shut her eyes. She'd return to yesterday, those first romantic moments they had spent in bed together, before she spoilt things with her fears; those marvellous lines he'd quoted from *The Romance of the Rose*.

'For she so worthy is of love
That well she may be called the Rose . . .'

It had seemed another christening, another sanction and endorsement of her name – a name not yet stained with blood.

The bathroom door clicked open, and Christopher emerged, now spruced and dressed, and with a completely different face on – a strong incisive face, ready to do battle with Roundheads, vicars, even age and death. He sat down by her feet, reached across and took the rose, touched it to her Venus mound in a flirtatious teasing gesture. 'Have you ever heard the phrase *sub rosa*?'

She shook her head, resentful of more questions and more no's. Couldn't they simply chat, for once, lounge and laugh like lovers, without him playing pedant all the time?

'It means secret, confidential – comes from the Latin "under the rose". You see, as well as all its other connotations, the rose is an emblem of silence, so they used to carve it on the ceilings of council chambers, or engrave it on confessionals, to remind all those involved that what was said beneath it was strictly private.' He lay back beside her for a moment, held the rose above them, as he stretched out on the bed. 'What I'm trying to say is that everything which happens this weekend is *sub rosa* and our secret, not to be repeated to Isobel or . . .'

She flounced up out of bed, furious that he felt he had to warn her, couldn't trust her own discretion. She wouldn't dream of telling Isobel – or anyone. He had destroyed all the romance, made things sordid and disreputable between them.

'It's the private view, remember, Rose, the day after tomorrow, and the whole crew will be there – Isobel, my wife, the vicar, Stanton Martin – so please be very careful what you say.'

She didn't answer, just focused on the words 'my wife'. It was Anne he was concerned about, quite clearly; Anne he was deceiving – both of them deceiving her, herself as well as him. How could she ever face that wife, a scant two days from now, look her in the eye, pretend she knew the artist as mere cool aloof employer, instead of panting lover? All the same, she was relieved that he'd invited her – at last. He had left it long enough, for heaven's sake, only asked her very casually once she'd told him she'd arranged to see Hadley and his play. It was another bribe, perhaps – first this weekend at the Swan, then the fancy do on Monday – both bait to tug her *his* way, entice her from Southampton.

'I only hope the bloody organisers know what the hell they're

227

doing. You can kill stained glass if you have the room too bright. The last stained-glass exhibition they held at the RIBA looked pretty much a mess. The lights were too intrusive, and they failed to get the press lined up, or . . .'

Jane reached across and grabbed her brush, tore it through her snarled and sweaty hair. How could she compete with private views or pressmen, or ever hold his interest for more than half an hour? She should have gone to Southampton, not Lincolnshire, resisted all his lures; spent the night safely with Hadley's female friend, in the chaste single bed laid on for her in a fellow student's flat. Hadley was unmarried, relaxed and easy-going, not obsessed with work; someone her own age whom she could relate to far more freely. She would have avoided all the lies and complications – the cheating on a wife, which made her feel uneasy and a traitor to her sex; the pretence to Isobel; the crisis of the window, which was still unresolved and shadowing the evening. The clock struck from the courtyard – five o'clock. Hadley and his friends would be letting down their hair – drinking, dancing, larking still, at Alexandra's flat. He'd arranged a second party in her honour, and she wasn't there to share the fun. Spanish plonk and red-hot curry he had promised her – or warned her. She shrugged, swapped brush for comb, still fighting with the tangles.

The artist seemed uneasy, as if he'd picked up on her mood, groping for his cigarettes, placing one between his lips, but leaving it unlit, then removing it, abandoning it, while still fiddling with his lighter. 'Well, Rose,' he said, at last. 'What d'you want to do now? I know it's early, but I suggest we take the car and go and find a meal, or maybe have a drink first. I've had nothing all damned day except half a cup of tea this morning. Is that all right with you?' he asked, almost as an afterthought.

'Fine,' she said, checking through the wardrobe to pick out something suitable for a casual student party. 'I'd like a pint of Spanish plonk, please, and a plate of red-hot curry.'

17

Jane faltered up the imposing marble staircase, trying to lose herself behind Isobel's billowing blue silk skirt – a rather girlish though expensive skirt, strangely contradicted by the butch and scruffy sweater she was wearing over it. Jane smoothed her own red dress – red to match the artist's bird – wished they weren't so late. She could hear a bray of conversation erupting from the hall, even strains of music. Christopher would be wondering where they were, though he must surely be familiar with the chaotic Mackenzie household, where no one ever left on time, or allowed an extra hour or so for fuming in thick traffic on the busy road to London, or finding non-existent parking-spaces in clogged and squeezed W1.

The journey had been gruelling, and not simply on account of Isobel's erratic style of driving. She herself had been sitting next to Hadley in the back – thrown against him, even, when his mother braked too sharply and took corners on two wheels – a Hadley she'd imagined was safely down in Southampton, finishing his term. He certainly hadn't been invited to the RIBA private view, though that hadn't stopped him coming, despite the fact he was only home because he claimed he wasn't well; had more or less collapsed the last night of his play from a mixture of exhaustion and too much cheap red wine. He had pumped her for a good half-hour about her own weekend – the Shrepton friend who'd moved down south and now had cancer of the breast – that fictitious invalid she'd been nursing for three days. The lies had escalated, especially as the vicar had been sitting in the front, a kindly and compassionate man, who kept offering his assistance: could he visit the poor girl, or put her on his prayer-list; did she know about the cancer-diet; was she too ill to come to church?

The Reverend A. F. Hargreaves was nothing like the Anthony

she had heard about from Christopher – not difficult, pedantic, but affable and wise; a short and rather chubby man, with benevolent blue eyes and very little hair. Jane glanced at his bald pate, bobbing just ahead of her, beside Isobel's wild curls; Hadley a head taller, and looking more dishevelled; the three of them now entering the majestic crowded hall. Isobel looked round for her, beckoned her to follow. She stopped, daunted, on the topmost stair, overawed by the massive marble columns, the bronze busts set on pedestals, the huge glass doors to the hall – everything so showy, ostentatious. Yet if she didn't cling to Isobel, she would be lost in all that crush, overwhelmed by cultivated people who knew the clever thing to say, weren't wearing borrowed shoes.

Suddenly, she herself was part of the whole mêlée, had somehow ventured through the doors, and been swallowed up in noise and smells and colours – women's perfumes fighting the faint whiff of hot prawn pastries; their gaudy dresses rivalling the brilliance of the glass-panels. The room-lights were subdued, so that the glass itself could blaze with more intensity, exploding in the quiet-toned hall with a dramatic jewel-like radiance. She shook her head as a waiter offered canapés, needed a few moments to take in the whole scene – the sheer impact of the panels, their electrifying colours and sunburst energy; the string quartet in evening dress, playing on a dais; the obsequious stewards pouring pink champagne; the swarm and shrill of guests – everyone from sober-suited businessmen to an arty-looking female whose flowing hennaed hair almost reached her thigh-length purple boots.

'Where's Christopher?' asked Isobel, scanning all the faces, then craning her plump neck to try to see past panels and exhibits. 'I doubt we'll ever find him in this scrum. Ah! There he is,' she cried, gesturing triumphantly, 'surrounded by his entourage.' She tried to rally Anthony, divert Hadley from the food-trays, and steer a shrinking Jane, while still clutching her champagne glass and an oozing lobster vol-au-vent as she swooped towards the far side of the room.

Jane dodged a man in a ponytail and pinstripes, and a diminutive old lady with a poodle tucked beneath her arm, as if it were her handbag; the dog's crisp white coat echoed by its owner's frizzy perm. She could feel her stomach lurching, a film of perspiration clammying her hands; wished she could borrow steely nerves as easily as shoes. She felt naked, undefended, as she prepared to meet the wife, rehearsed her next few lies; her scarlet dress too flimsy to keep the terror out. She could already see the artist, who seemed to tower above the crowd, despite his modest height, the only one with solid lines; the only one not blurring in the heat and raucous jostle. He looked dapper and distinguished in a dark grey suit and flamboyant crimson shirt. How strange that their colours matched. Her own shoes and bag were grey, the silky scarf she'd knotted at her neck. Would people notice, comment, see it as a bond between them, a private signal denoting their relationship? He caught her eye, and she tried to freeze her face, prevent it giving anything away, acknowledging his greeting with just a casual nod. Yet she was disturbingly aware that his eyes were saying one thing, his formal smile another.

She was grateful for Isobel's exuberance, the way the older woman fell on necks and names, hugged and kissed the ones she knew, pumped the others by the hand, repeated introductions, began jaunty little anecdotes, then broke off in the middle to clasp another friend, and made so much happy stir that Jane could simply stand there, sharing in the ebullience, yet not required to shine herself, or even speak, beyond a few 'hallos'. She tried to fit the faces to the names – Felice she remembered from Adrian's dinner party; Adrian himself was tête-à-tête with a thin young man called Aubrey; Stanton Martin was the VIP who looked more like a dropout, and Daniel Boyd, his colleague, another architect. Lorna in the mini-dress was from the *Sunday Times*, and Frederick ('Call me Freddie') a top tycoon from Pilkingtons, who were sponsoring the exhibition, along with a large insurance company, a contractor, and the Crafts Council. But where was Anne, the wife?

Isobel suddenly lunged forward, shook a new small hand – a hand with exotic rings on every finger, a hand which could be lethal, loaded down with so much dangerous metal, so many spiky stones. 'Veronica!' she bubbled. 'How very nice to see you! How's things? How are the girls? Do meet Rose. She's working as Christopher's assistant. Rose – Veronica Harville-Shaw.'

Veronica! The *ex*-wife. Another woman with his name. Jane took a step towards her, felt her fingers close on hot damp flesh; recoiled instinctively. She disliked the fastidious features masked with make-up, the expensive preening clothes, the cloying scent swamping her own cheap and weak cologne. The voice was Radio 3, self-confident and cultured, asking duty questions about where she lived, where she'd trained, what was her opinion of the show.

'I haven't really seen it yet,' she flurried. Her own voice sounded ordinary, inferior, something from a pop commercial station, rather than the BBC, and with that trace of northern accent she was always trying to conceal.

'Yes, where is Christopher's panel?' Isobel enquired. 'It seems rather naughty, doesn't it, to be guzzling their champagne when we've hardly looked at anything.'

Veronica stretched out a slim arm, her four rings glinting, threatening. 'In pride of place, over by the window. We were all paying homage to it, half an hour ago, but then Gerald dragged us over here, to see his model for the Clarendon Centre.'

Jane had been so nervous of the company, she had hardly spared a glance for the architectural models arranged on perspex stands – a shopping mall in Bristol, a country club in Japan, a Saudi Arabian airport, a synagogue in Arles – all made to scale, in miniature, like little wooden dolls' houses, and all resplendent with stained glass. She wished she had two separate pairs of eyes, one to view the exhibition, one to watch the wives. There was still no sign of Anne, but maybe she was guardian of her husband's scarlet bird, still standing by his panel, protecting it from any hostile comments.

'Come on, Rose. Let's see it,' Isobel enthused.

Jane was relieved to leave the artist, had been achingly aware of him throughout the endless introductions, though he'd barely said a word to her, had saved his voice and energies for the more important guests. They had also lost the others in their party – the vicar to the *Sunday Times* reporter, and Hadley to a waitress, or her wares. Isobel herself kept stopping on her ambling zigzag way towards the window, magnetised by striking glass or photographs, exclaiming at tall panels, zingy colours, or meeting some new crony who must be fêted and embraced. Jane found it hard to concentrate, didn't want to look at other, rival exhibits until she'd seen the artist's; wished to save her freshness for his bird, keep her mind open and uncluttered.

'Good gracious me! That's strong.' Isobel pretended to reel backwards when at last they'd reached the fifteen feet of glass – one of the tallest entries in the hall. Jane stood silent, her hand across her stomach. She could feel the bird's convulsive movements shocking through her own insides; hear the frantic beating of its wings, as it hurled its fragile body against the cruel and steely nothing of the window – a window which slammed back. The engorged and gory crimson of its plumage suggested fresh-spilt blood; the high blank walls surrounding it stirred memories of nightmare.

'Bird Inside', she spelt out slowly, cringing at the title, which itself seemed cruel and taunting. Birds belonged outside, soaring into space and freedom, untrammelled, unconfined. Was Christopher confined himself – in his marriage or his home, perhaps – and so venting his own feelings? Or enjoying some sadistic urge, as he trapped a helpless bird in glass, held it captive in his power? It hardly seemed to matter. The panel was so charged, she had no choice but submit to it, let it work on her emotions, disturb her mind and body. She suddenly realised you could love a man less for what he was than for what he could create; love him for skills, even while they harrowed you.

'Powerful,' murmured someone, a tall man with a Vandyke beard, who had pushed in front of them. 'Powerful, but contrived. Can't he be more subtle?'

'You should read what it says here,' the man's female friend sniggered, pointing to her catalogue and then reciting from it sardonically. '"The red bird is a symbol, a winged soul representing transcendence and the ascent to higher realms, but trapped in this material world, caught between two opposing realities. The colour red signifies the masculine – the active energetic colour of fire and sun and war, martyrdom and blood." Christ! It's so pretentious. A bird's a bird, for God's sake.'

'Birds aren't red, though, are they?'

'I've seen red ones in the zoo – well, pinkish, anyway.'

'They were probably flamingos – or maybe you'd had too much pink champagne.'

Titters now from both of them. Jane unclenched her fists. No point lashing into them in public. If they were such blind and stupid philistines, then better to ignore them. She turned away, started studying the screen behind her, which showed the artist's drawings, and also studies of his work in progress, and other big commissions, including several photographs of Adrian's leisure-centre, all preceded by a brief biography. 'Born in 1930,' she read, eyes halting on the figures, unable to move on. She had never quite believed that the artist could be sixty, yet he was actually sixty-one. It was there in bold black capitals, for all the world to see. She stabbed the '3' with her finger, as if trying to rub it out. It was too much of a shock. The thirties seemed so long ago, a faint and faded era in jerky black and white, with no TVs or computers, no microwaves or washing-machines, no Kentucky Fried. He'd been alive in the time of Churchill, Hitler, Stalin – even the swooned-over Clark Gable – a relic and museum-piece himself. She glanced back at his bird. It seemed so vigorous, so spunky, the work of someone full of verve and sap. He wasn't old at all, in the sense of withered, stagnant, but moody and tempestuous, a sexagenarian adolescent, still making waves, still champing at the bit.

She forced herself to jump two decades and start reading through the long list of his commissions, astonished by the things he had done, the works he'd never mentioned – a palace in Oman, twelve heraldic panels in a famous Cambridge college, a casino in Knightsbridge and a mosque in Abu Dhabi – his windows glowing right across the globe, from cathedrals in Ohio to banks in Tokyo. He had won awards and scholarships; had examples of his work included in museums in Sweden, France and Germany, even in the V & A – Harville-Shaw, the Artist, sanitised and laurel-crowned, the unqualified success. But what about the private man, the other, uncrowned Christopher, who had been rigorously excluded from this exemplary CV – his two wrecked marriages, his failure to have children, the violence locked inside him, the hostility he roused?

She looked around, hoping she might see him, check on the two versions, maybe fuse them both together. There was no sign of him at all, only a troupe of twittering yuppies, and a still fizzy Isobel, now babbling to a woman who was just a stretch of white silk back, a fall of straight brown hair.

'Ah, Rose,' pounced Isobel, as they caught each other's eye. 'Let me introduce you to Anne Harville-Shaw. Anne says she's never met you.'

The white silk back turned round, revealed a smiling face, a small and well-shaped mouth, tiny lines around the eyes, the coral lipstick smudged. The hair reached to her shoulders, so straight it looked like child's hair, though the breasts were full and womanly.

Jane stared. She was looking at her mother – the mother who had borne her – the final and definitive one who had ousted all the variations, taken over from the countess and the slut, the sculptress and the pop star, the druggie teenage dropout. She had gradually fixed the picture in her mind, adding a few details every night, building up her mother stroke by stroke, line by line, like the artist with his portraits. She wanted certain striking likenesses between them, so there could be no shred or scrap of doubt that they were biological mother and her child, so she had endowed her fantasy-mother with her own straight hair in the exact same shade of brown, and also the same eyes, dark-lashed eyes in a rather timid blue. But she also wanted differences – what she saw as faults in herself would be abolished in her mother: her too-wide mouth scaled down, her meagre breasts made generous. Anne's breasts were really bosoms, an old-fashioned comfy word, but she was not plump and slack like Isobel; smaller altogether, less arty and untidy. She had decided fairly recently that she didn't want an artist for a mother. Artists were too selfish and too moody. Yet she yearned for someone less tight and crimped than Amy – someone in between, who'd be free and easy-going, but still responsible; attractive yet still motherly, and about the age of forty, so she would have had her daughter young, not wasted all her twenties being bitter and infertile. Anne looked fortyish, much younger than the artist, but still old enough to have gained her first grey hairs – only two or three of them, but snaking rather sadly through the glossy autumn-brown.

Jane realised she was staring – rudely, unforgivably – and that she and Anne were now standing on their own; Isobel deep in conversation with the vicar, who must have come to find them. She tried to respond to Anne's well-meaning overtures, not play the cretin who had also lost her voice. Yet she was still astonished by this wife, who was nothing like the model she'd imagined – not the brash hard-headed businesswoman, or the cold and perfect beauty, not the sexy siren.

Anne suddenly bent down and slipped her shoe off, balancing on one leg, the other foot just stocking-clad and with a small hole in the toe. 'I broke my heel on that dratted marble staircase. I've been stuck in the loo trying my best to mend it, but it still feels rather wobbly.'

Jane answered with a sympathetic mumble. Anne looked lamed and flawed – vulnerable, endearing. The shoes were boring brown, too heavy for the white silk dress. How odd that it was white. The mother in her mind wore white – deliberately, defiantly – to counter all the shame and scandal, the murk and darkness of her birth. She had learnt enough from Christopher to know that colours mattered – white for innocence, redemption; also white for brides and marriage. Her eyes moved slowly up to Anne's left hand, the gold ring on her wedding finger, a wide one, carved with flowers. She longed to tug it off, hurt that slender finger as she did so. This was still her rival, the hated woman who shared the artist's life, the hated feckless mother who had given her away. Her gaze continued travelling up – to the breasts which Christopher must kiss, the pale throat he would fondle, the jewelled cross round her neck, perhaps a present from her husband, a sentimental keepsake to mark some anniversary – a tasteful and expensive gift, with the cross-shape edged in tiny pearls, and the finest of gold chains.

Anne seemed a little flustered by this long and fierce inspection, touched the cross, as if protecting it from damage, or her neck from further scrutiny. 'It's . . . pretty, isn't it?'

'Mm,' grudged Jane. 'Did you have it as a present?'

Anne shook her head. 'No, I found it in an antique shop, just two months ago, and bought it for myself. It's Georgian, the man said, though the chain's a good bit later. I've become really quite attached to it, never take it off now, except in bed.' She laughed. 'I was really looking for a plant-stand, but then I saw this in the back room and felt it was appropriate because I was going to be confirmed that very week.'

'Confirmed?'

'Yes, rather late in life, at the ripe old age of forty-two.' She laughed again, an easy friendly laugh. 'I think thirteen is more usual, but my parents were agnostics.'

Jane was lost for words. A newly Christian Anne seemed absolutely wrong, didn't fit the image of the worldly marketing manager, who jetted to New York. And how did Christopher relate to a wife who'd just found God, when he himself attacked that God, deplored what he called the violence and hypocrisy of the Christian faith?

'Ah, there you are, Anne. I've been looking for you everywhere.'

He was suddenly beside them, his red shirt like a warning, threatening danger. She responded to the danger, her body leaping into overdrive, pulse and heart both pounding double time. There seemed neither space nor air enough for the three of them to stand together, to keep on breathing normally, control their throttled voices. Was he as tense as she was; could Anne not pick up vibes between them? Now she'd met the wife, it seemed even worse to have cheated on her, when she was nothing like the heartless bitch she'd pictured. Her own arm was brushing Christopher's one side, his love-bite flaunting on her neck, though hidden by the scarf, yet Anne's warm trusting smile was embracing both of them – artist and assistant, not husband with his bed-mate. They were standing near the string quartet, who had reached a dazzling climax; the music trilling out with a sprightly teasing grace; capering, cavorting, chiding any jaundiced guest who dared resist its mood. The artist's voice sounded sombre and subdued beside that ecstatic chortling cello, those boisterous violins.

'So how do you like my bird?' he asked, turning now to her.

She tried to find an answer, keep her mind on art, rather than adultery, but the subject of that art was almost equally disturbing. She could see the bird again, feel its pain, its panic – maybe even its resentment. She was relieved when her first fumbling words were swamped in a loud chorus of congratulations, greetings. A new group of boozy friends had come to claim the artist, tangle him in flattery and faddle. She let their talk wash over her, still tuned in to her inner

236

thoughts, still fretting over Anne; only pricked her ears up when the subject turned to Christmas.

'Yes, we're going to Nice on the twenty-third,' she heard the artist say. 'Staying for two weeks. We've got friends out there who own this stunning villa. It'll be quite a little house-party – at least a dozen guests and even the chance of a new commission, if I'm lucky. You see, they've invited a French architect, who already knows my work and . . .'

Jane slunk away, unnoticed. He hadn't mentioned Christmas, not to her; hadn't said a single word about villas in the sun, house-parties, commissions. And she loathed that casual 'we' – him and bridal Anne, not him and wilting Rose. Rose had been rationed to one brief weekend in the winter wilds of Lincolnshire, while Anne was rewarded with a whole fortnight on the Côte d'Azur.

She glanced up at an oblong of strange geometric glass, mainly horizontal lines, and mainly dreary greys. She'd better concentrate on that, distract herself by looking round the exhibition, which was what she'd come for anyway. The artist was a German, judging by his name. Christopher had told her that the Germans were important in the modern revival of stained glass – not to mention pushy and aggressive – but she had never seen their work before, found this particular sample extremely hard to like. She moved on to another work: a large rectangular panel, with a repeated pattern of squiggles set in squares, which reminded her of wallpaper. She wished Christopher was with her, to help her sift the cream from the crap; to explain why some exhibits looked so different from his own – the glass unpainted, the leadlines sharp, insistent, the whole impression one of stark high-tech rigidity.

'There's a real sense of dialogue,' said a well-stacked blonde beside her, a sultry-looking girl in skin-tight leather trousers and a frilly low-necked blouse. 'I mean, it may be abstract in its form, but there's still a narrative in progress, an argument between active/passive, translucent and transparent.'

The girl was talking to her friend, both of them with drawly Sloane Street accents, both only in their twenties, yet clearly well-informed, able to discriminate, make deep, incisive comments, see things in the glass which were invisible to her. Anne had mentioned the ladies' room. Perhaps she'd hide in there, escape these sophisticated highbrows, all superior to her. This would never be her world, and she was stupid to have come at all, or craved an invitation. Had she imagined that the artist would be free to pay her court, show her off to people as his mistress? She turned to look at him.

He was posing by his panel for a photograph; a reporter with a notebook hovering just behind, waiting for her turn. He'd be busy all the evening, galvanising journalists, charming wealthy sponsors, wooing architects. She hadn't even seen his panel, beyond that first quick glance, had hoped to study it in detail, so she could discuss it with him later, learn from his own skills. She was still helping him cut the glass for the Resurrection window, had improved by leaps and bounds after two weeks' solid practice, but was still basically a novice. Yet how could she go back there to examine 'Bird Inside', when the press had joined his fans, and he was surrounded by a circle of gawpers, hangers-on?

She mooched on to the door, weaving through the crowds, caught a glimpse of Adrian, standing by a glass-screen whose lowering blues and purples made his mouse-grey suit look timid and washed-out. She dashed towards him, pleased. He seemed almost an old friend in this room of arty strangers. He returned her eager greeting, then gestured to the tall man at his side. 'You've met Aubrey, haven't you?'

'Yes,' she said, trying to make it gracious. She had hoped to have Adrian to herself. 'You're the international equities portfolio manager.'

'Brilliant!' Aubrey grinned. 'What a memory. I'm sorry I haven't had a chance to get to know you, but we're just off now to a very boring dinner.'

'Poor you,' she said with envy, then watched the two men disappear; Adrian's limp and sandy hair contrasting with his companion's tight black curls. Could the two be lovers, she wondered with a sudden sense of shock; Aubrey's 'we', like Christopher's, denoting union? Gays were on her mind. Christopher had told her that Jonathan was gay – the owner of the Swan – and the news had somehow troubled her. She mustn't be censorious like Amy, who damned all 'queers' as perverted and promiscuous, but it still wasn't all that easy to be as casual as the artist was, especially when the gay in question was Adrian, not Jon. It seemed to cut him off from her, make him someone alien.

The string quartet was tuning up, a scratchy strident sound, which matched the discord in her head. She was glad to see a steward approaching with a tray of drinks, must try to change her mood.

'Champagne for you, Madame?'

She helped herself, eyes lingering on the steward's face. He looked a little like her father – solemn and sad-eyed, with neat grey hair, cut short. She'd love to see her father there, so she could join him, take his arm, prove that she belonged to someone, wasn't just a gatecrasher.

'Rose! At last!' a male voice cried. 'You've been avoiding me all evening.'

Jane swung round, saw a dishevelled grinning Hadley, holding out a loaded tray of canapés. 'Here, help yourself. I'm doing waitress duty.'

'How did you get those?'

'I told the waitress I'd spent the last six gruelling months as a hostage in a prison in Beirut, eating only bread and water. The poor soul cried her heart out. She's gone to get reserves. Please do dig in. I'm feeling rather sick myself.' He rubbed his nose, transferred a blob of mayonnaise from his top lip to his sleeve.

Jane took a small prawn bouchée. She had eaten nothing yet. The food had seemed taboo, snobby itsy-bitsy food for wives and artists, architects and sponsors, not for mere plain Janes. She reached out for a delicate concoction of asparagus and salmon, gulped it swiftly down; realised she was starving, had eaten very little over the whole weekend with Christopher, and still felt famished, hollow. She crammed in a large vol-au-vent, and then two lobster tartlets, continued eating avidly, as if in compensation for the artist's constant dieting, and also his excluding her from Le Gourmandin. He was going on to dinner there with Anne and Stanton Martin, and a few important others in that cliquish inner circle – the most original new brasserie in London, or so the critics claimed. She wouldn't know, hadn't been invited. Her dinner would be cheese on toast at Isobel's, if they ever made it back, or a Marmite sandwich in the cold and empty studio. She stuffed in two more tartlets, washed them down with pink champagne.

'Ah! I recognise you now,' said Hadley. 'You were the hostage in the next-door cell, whose rations were even more prison-fare than mine – the odd dry crust and a slurp of dirty rainwater.'

She giggled, allowed a passing steward to refill her empty glass. She had forgotten how relaxed she felt with Hadley; liked the fact he'd sought her out.

'I hate these do's, don't you, Rose?'

'I haven't been to many.' *Any*, she corrected in her head.

'They're all very much alike. Well, this is more pretentious. You often get just cheapo wine and a few odd nuts and crisps, rather than champagne and lobster whatsits, but it's still the same old arty-farty crowd. And you know my views on splurging all this cash on prestige buildings, when a lot of people still haven't got a decent inside loo. I mean, think what this lot cost!' He gestured to the silver tray, speared half a dozen scampi morsels on one overloaded cocktail-stick and transferred all six to his mouth.

'I thought you said you were feeling sick.'

'Yes, sick with indignation.'

Jane's laugh froze. She had seen the artist's crest of hair, the scarlet of his shirt, bearing down towards them, making for their corner. She felt irrationally guilty to be caught alone with Hadley, especially a Hadley who had no right to be there, and was dressed most inappropriately in a casual sweatshirt with 'Brixton University' blazoned on the chest. He was still holding out the food-tray, still grinning to himself, his hair tousled and exuberant, his dirty trainers scuffed.

'Rose,' the artist frowned, ignoring Hadley totally. 'I know you said you'd like to meet Keith New. Well, he's here, at last, after a hold-up on the South Circular.'

'Fine,' she said. 'Give me just a jiff and I'll be with you. I'm a bit tied up at present.' She helped herself to another canapé, as if to indicate it was Hadley she was tied to, Hadley and his sustenance. She was even using Hadley's words. 'Just a jiff' was his phrase. She was astonished at her daring. Keith New was a well-known stained-glass artist, one she'd heard a lot about from Christopher, one she'd asked to meet. You didn't put a nineteen-year-old student at a provincial university before a man who'd made the windows for Coventry Cathedral, had helped put stained glass on the post-war map, reinstate it as no longer a lost art. And Christopher was doing her a favour in remembering her request, coming to get her specially when he was busy with his friends. 'I'll join you in a minute,' she said airily, draining her champagne.

'Don't,' begged Hadley, once the artist had stalked off. 'He's bound to be a wally, and anyway, I've hardly had a chance to say a word to you myself. I only came this evening because of you.'

She flushed. 'Really?'

'Yes, really. I should be back at college. I had two important lectures today and a paper to give in. I intended driving back on Sunday evening, but Mum told me you were expected the next day, so I thought, what the hell, I'll stick around – can't miss a chance like that. You surely don't imagine I'd flog up here just to see the glass, do you?' He put the tray down, grabbed her hand. 'Look, why don't we cut loose, Rose, go and have a drink together? There's this marvellous joint off Oxford Street, with really great music and . . .'

'But what about your mother?' Jane tried to release her hand, could feel the artist's gimlet eyes boring into it, though she realised he'd returned to the far corner of the room.

'Oh, she won't care. She'll probably go on somewhere herself – dinner with the Reverend, or a nightcap with some lame-duck artist she's scooped out of the crowd, who can only paint with his big toe, or has cut off both his ears, or . . .'

'But we'll lose her then. I mean, how will we get home?'

'We'll fly.'

'No, seriously.'

'You're always far too serious. What's wrong with British Rail?'

'But the trains don't run that late, do they?'

'It isn't late. It won't be. Look, if you're that concerned about getting home, let's escape for a mingy half an hour, and arrange to meet Mum somewhere – either right back here, or in Oxford Street, or . . . I'll go and have a word with her, while you fetch your coat and stuff.'

'But I haven't said goodbye.'

'You don't need to if we're coming back.'

'But I told Christopher I'd join him, meet this famous artist . . .'

'I'm sure they'll both recover from the fearful disappointment. And anyway, I'm a famous physicist, and you need a change from art. See you downstairs in the foyer. And don't go off with anyone else – I can't trust you for a minute.'

'What's the time?' Jane mumbled, opening her eyes and blinking against the light.

'Ten past two.'

'You mean two A.M.?' She shook off the old blanket, which felt heavy, claustrophobic.

'Yup.'

'It can't be.'

'Eleven and a quarter minutes past.' Hadley slammed his book shut, yawned and stretched dramatically. 'You've been fast asleep.'

'Asleep?' She rubbed her eyes, tried to knead away her headache. Her mouth felt dry and dirty.

'Yes. You crashed out on that sofa, while everyone else was dancing. You looked so sweet and peaceful, we didn't have the heart to move you. Though it beats me how you snoozed through all that racket.'

Jane struggled to sit up, glanced around the room, a rather squalid room, with a stained and fraying carpet and too much ugly furniture jostling for more space. Empty glasses were littering the floor, almost-empty bottles dribbling on their sides, cigarettes stubbed out in hardened pizza crusts. Only one small lamp was on, but an intrusive light with a garish orange shade. 'I'm sorry, Hadley, honestly. I just don't know what happened. I suppose I . . .'

'Why be sorry? It gave me a chance to re-read *Lady Chatterley*.' He gestured to his book. 'I read it first when I was nine, couldn't really see what all the fuss was about. It's better this time round.' She tugged her skirt down, feeling suddenly exposed, though relieved she was still decent, and someone hadn't tried to make her nap more comfortable by unzipping her red dress. Hadley had removed his shoes, but nothing else, thank God; seemed remarkably sane and sober, sitting upright in a chair with a pile of books beside him, rather than sprawled sozzled on the floor. 'Where are all the others?'

'Sue's retired to bed, and the rest pushed off about half an hour ago.'

'Why didn't you wake me?'

'Why should I? We'd missed the train anyway, and Sue said we could stay the night if we didn't mind the sofa. How was it? Comfortable?'

She didn't answer, needed all her concentration to backtrack to the time they'd left the show, so she could catch up on their movements, remember where and why she'd faded out. They had gone first to Smoky Joe's, where Hadley met a friend called Jazz, and they'd ordered Blue Lagoons, then on to Frederico's, which Jazz claimed was 'far out' and where they'd drunk some bitter whitish stuff which looked innocent enough; then reeled back to the private view to tell Isobel they'd be later than they'd said and would catch the last train back. After that, Jazz had rustled up more pals, and they had driven to his girlfriend's flat, and she'd forgotten all about last trains, or artists' wives, or how the hell she'd report for work at the studio next morning; had simply let her hair down, enjoyed herself for once.

She grinned as she recalled it. 'You're a fantastic dancer, Hadley.'

'Well, not quite the slow foxtrot.'

'I can't do that myself.'

'Shall we try it now?' He leapt up to his feet, started hunting through the records, already rasping his own raucous tune, more hip-hop than slow foxtrot.

'Ssh. We'll wake Sue. And I'm far too fagged to dance.' She collapsed back on the sofa, feet curled underneath her.

'Nothing will wake Sue. Judging by the amount she drank, she'll sleep till the last trump. Hey, d'you want another drink yourself? There's still an inch of vodka left.'

242

She grimaced. 'No thanks.'

'You're not much fun, Rose, are you? – no drink, no dance, no music. How about a kiss?' He lunged towards her, before she could escape, pressed his lips to hers. She hardly struggled, didn't have the energy for arguments, refusals. And, anyway, the kiss felt very innocent, a brother's kiss, light and brief and teasing. The artist's mouth was so much fiercer, Hadley's kiss hardly seemed to count, didn't involve her tongue or teeth, didn't shock through her whole body, or turn it inside out.

She edged up on the sofa, to make more room for him. He pressed closer, squeezed her hand. 'You're sweet, Rose.'

'I'm not.' She tugged her hand back. She was feeling anything but sweet, had glimpsed the artist in her head, kissing Anne – not her – his teeth grazing down those generous swelling breasts.

'You've creased your dress.' Hadley's hand now lingered on the fabric, seemed especially taken with the fastening at the back.

She shrugged. 'It's only cheap.'

'I like it.'

He was already heaving down the zip. She didn't try to stop him. If she could no longer sleep with Christopher, had lost him to his wife, then why not formalise the fact, deliberately renounce him in some cold-blooded casual act, prove she didn't care a toss, show him there were other men who wanted her – younger men, good dancers, men who liked their food? Hadley's lips were fumbling hers again. The kiss was chilli-flavoured. They had shared a plate at Frederico's and then pigged themselves on a gigantic banana split. He had paid for everything. Okay, she'd pay him back. He had somehow got her dress off. She hadn't helped, or hindered, just let him pull and scrabble; his eyes gulping down her body as if it were another ice-cream sundae. Now he was peeling off his sweatshirt and the grubby off-white vest-thing underneath it. She felt angry with his chest – its hairlessness, its paleness – angry with his stomach, which wasn't taut or flat enough, didn't have that grizzled pelt she expected on all men now. How could Hadley, at nineteen, have flab around his belly, and why did he wear vests?

The vest was on the floor, and he was stripped to his grey cords; seemed embarrassed and self-conscious as he groped in his back pocket. 'I suppose we'd better use one of these.'

She shut her eyes, didn't want to see, loathed the thought of condoms, which were connected in her mind with AIDS and silly jokes. Did Hadley always carry them, or had he bought them for this evening, planned the whole routine? That 'spontaneous' suggestion of a drink looked rather suspect now; that 'chance' meeting with a mate of his whose girlfriend owned a flat. Who cared, anyway? At least he was considerate, wouldn't land her with a baby.

She slipped her bra and pants off, lay back on the sofa, tried to make things easy for him. She liked him, didn't she? He was good-natured and amusing, even making wisecracks as he pulled the Durex on. He was much bigger than the artist, bigger everywhere, yet tamer altogether, not hurting her or fighting her, but easing gently in. The trick was not to think, to banish Christopher – and Anne – to wipe out the weekend. It was Friday again, and this was her first time, a normal happy time with a nice boy her own age, who was doing his level best to please her. Odd she felt so little. It must be just the drink, the nagging spoilsport headache. She ought to make an effort, do something in return – move her hips, grind and thrash a bit, toss her hair about.

'Christ, Rose, that's bloody marvellous! Don't stop. Oh, God! I'm coming!' His voice was hoarse; his whole body heaved and jerked. She clung on underneath him, praying that the condom wouldn't slip or break, trying not to think of babies. At last, he slumped on top of her, out of breath and panting, his sweaty hair tickling on her neck. There was silence for two minutes. She could hear a stealthy clock ticking, one she hadn't noticed before; the odd car droning past. She was sure the cars were driverless. There seemed to be no other living person in the world.

Slowly, he rolled off her, did something with the Durex. Again she shut her eyes. 'Did you come as well?' he asked, flopping back on the sofa with a sigh of deep contentment.

'Yes.'

'Fantastic! I've been rehearsing this for weeks, you know – ever since I met you at my mother's. When you said you couldn't make it to the play, I almost charged up to the studio and dragged you down to Southampton by force. I thought at first you were lying, inventing that sick-girlfriend stuff just to fob me off.'

'No, I . . .'

'In fact, I'm sure that's why I got ill. It wasn't just the wine and all the build-up of the play. I collapsed from deprivation!' He laughed. 'Let's kiss again.'

Kissing stopped him talking, so she moved her lips to his. Mouths should taste of nicotine, not chilli. Funny how you missed things – the explosion of a match, the lazy curl of smoke drifting to the ceiling.

He smoothed her hair, coiled it in his hands. 'It's quite the longest mane I've ever seen. Even Rowan's wasn't this length, and sisters don't count anyway.'

'I bought it in a sale – two yards for the price of one.' It wasn't difficult to please him. The odd joke, like his own; the odd remark, to prove that she was listening.

He squeezed a breast, too hard. 'Let's do it again in the morning.'

'It *is* morning.'

'No, it's not. It's time for kip!' He reached out to switch the lamp off, hauled the blanket back. 'Do you like the left side or the right?'

'I don't mind.'

'It's a good job this old sofa's such a whopper. There's almost room for two.'

Three, she thought, still watching the bright point of the Marlboro glimmer in the darkened room.

'Goodnight, Rose, super-Rose.'

' 'Night.'

'I promise I shan't snore.'

'Same here.' She lay as still as possible. Snoring was no problem, since she knew she'd never get to sleep at all, but it wasn't easy not to fidget on such a makeshift bed, and with Hadley's bulk beside her. She wished she knew exactly where they were – in London certainly, in Fulham probably, but she didn't have a street-name, or a surname for the enigmatic Sue. It might make her feel less disoriented to fill in a few details, and maybe less alone. She hated it when someone else was sleeping and she was wide awake, especially when her mind was so determined to be cruel, kept dwelling on the horrors: the probing from a tactless Isobel, the suspicion of the artist; the shameful fact that she'd spent two consecutive nights with two quite different men. Which meant she was a slut; had obviously inherited sluttish genes. If she ever met her birth-mother and asked her who her father was, she could imagine the reply: 'Let's think now. If I conceived you on the Sunday, then your Dad was old John Smith; if it was Monday, then young Harry, and if Tuesday, well . . .'

No. Her mother looked like Anne, faithful Christian Anne, who'd be entwined with Christopher in bed as she was hinged to Hadley. Trapped was more the word, trapped by his left arm, trapped by her involvement. She shut her eyes, could see the scarlet bird panicking and plunging in the now-empty exhibition hall. She wished she could go back there, check through Christopher's biography and scoop up all those scholarships, commissions; take them back and lay them out like treasures. She had slept with that CV, had felt all those works

245

and windows thrusting, scorching into her, his talent seeding hers. She was glad the artist didn't wear a condom, disliked the thought of any barrier between them.

'Rose?'

'Mm?'

'Are you awake?'

'Yes.'

Hadley guffawed, sat up with a jerk. 'What a waste! I've been lying like a corpse trying not to wake you, and we could have been talking all this time. I can't sleep for sheer excitement. I've just got to see you again – next week, I mean, or sooner – and I'm trying to work out how. Term ends this coming Friday, and then I push straight off to Paris.'

'Paris?'

'Yup. A student trip – dirt-cheap. We're spending Christmas there, and it should be quite a party. I was wondering if there was any chance that you could come as well? The organiser's a friend of mine, so I could probably wangle you a place. What d'you think? How are you fixed for Christmas?'

She didn't answer, was working out the mileage from Paris to the Côte d'Azur – Nice, to be exact. Three hundred miles? Four hundred? Both were France, at least.

'It would be great if you could make it. We'd have a ball, I know we would. Do you speak French, by the way?'

'A bit.'

'Terrific! Mine's only the "bonjour" kind. Listen, Rose, promise me you'll try to come. What's wrong? You've gone all quiet. Look, if you're worried about the cash side, I'll take care of that. It's not a problem, honestly. If you really want to know, Dad left us quite a stash, and I haven't liked to touch it yet. It seemed all wrong, just splurging it on nothing. But to have you there at Christmas – I mean, waking up beside you and saying "Happy Christmas, Rose."'

'Happy Christmas,' she thought dully. Yes, madly wildly happy.

18

'Happy Christmas, Rose!'

'Happy Christmas.'

'A little present for you, dear.'

'Oh, thank you, Mrs Brooking.' Jane unwrapped lemon hand-cream, Boots' own, in a gift-box. She already had bath-oil and cologne, soap and matching talc, two sets of lacy handkerchiefs, a woolly scarf, a silk scarf, and a box of Cadbury's Milk Tray – and those were just the small presents, the extras, as it were.

Mrs Brooking took the last free chair. Rowan and her boyfriend, Neville, were sprawling on the floor, with Rowan's married cousin, her boys, aged three and four, a highly nervous whippet, and two men from Neville's office, who appeared to have neither homes nor parents. Jane hadn't quite sorted out all the names and faces, and Isobel seemed blithely vague about how many friends and neighbours she had actually invited, though judging by the amount of food she was preparing in the kitchen, it must be half of Sussex. Some were bona fide relatives, others walking wounded. Mrs Brooking, for example, with her two sticks and her hearing-aid, and the other elderly widow who'd brought her heart-pills and her Pekinese, and had passed a dramatic Christmas morning describing the horror and indignity of her hip replacement operation, and how she was lucky to be here at all, when she'd almost died in theatre. Jane wondered what category she herself would fit – lame duck or genuine friend. Has Isobel taken pity on her because she had no other plans for Christmas, shouldn't spend it in a cold and empty studio?

'Sherry for you, Mrs Brooking? Or would you prefer a G and T?' A tall man in a green home-knitted cardigan, who seemed to answer to three names – Robert, Bob and Kipper – had been appointed duty barman and was presiding over an impressive range of bottles.

'No, sherry, Robert, please – a sweet one. Gin's so acid, isn't it?'

'Rose, do you want a refill?'

'No, thanks.' Jane put her glass down. Her own sherry had been sweet, and she'd already guzzled glacé fruits and dates; opened the Milk Tray, and picked out half the creams, accepted dampish Smarties from Billy's grubby hand, and even sampled Isobel's mince pies. She checked her watch. Still no sign of lunch. Her parents would have finished theirs by now, and would be halfway through the washing up; the table cleared, the coffee brewed, the turkey carcass neatly wrapped in Clingfilm. No, she mustn't think of home. Not only did it churn her up, but it was unfair to make comparisons. Easy for Amy to have dinner on the table at the dot of one o'clock, when she'd had only three to cook for all her life.

She glanced around the crowded room, which seemed to swarm and hum – not just the tribe of guests, all babbling, prattling, laughing, but the ceaseless shift and murmur of the fire, as it devoured itself, kept gobbling up more hissing sparking logs. The strange lop-sided Christmas tree was typical of Isobel. She had taken in a cripple, then tried to make it happy, hung its stunted branches with such a wild assortment of baubles, trinkets, tinsel, toys, it looked in imminent danger of collapse. Many of the Christmas cards were already on their faces, blown down by the draught as people darted in and out, or the two boys played at choo-choo trains and went steaming round the room. Nice to be a child again, to transform yourself to something else – an engine or a tree, so you couldn't think, or mope. She pushed Byron off her foot, reached out for a coffee cream, though chocolate didn't seem to fill the strange emptiness inside her. This was the happiest day of the year – or so people tried to kid you – yet she felt she was in mourning.

Perhaps she should have gone to France with Hadley, after all, instead of inventing all those reasons why she had to stay in England, piling up excuses, most of which were lies. The true reasons were so complicated, included things like vests and condoms, hairless chests, red birds. And there was one overwhelming reason that she was reluctant to admit, even to herself, let alone to Hadley: she was so obsessed with Christopher that any other relationship seemed meaningless and wrong. Yet the artist was away in Nice, padlocked to his wife, caught up with his friends, so busy and involved she'd be just a casual doodle in the margin of his mind.

She rammed the lid back on the chocolate box, wiped her sticky hands. She ought to make an effort, play her part as guest. It would be far more wretched sitting on her own with a Wall's pork pie for Christmas dinner, and no Christmas decorations except the odd cobweb in a corner of the studio.

She edged her chair a little closer to portly Uncle Rory's, though she hadn't really gathered yet exactly who he was – Tom's brother, or Isobel's, or merely an honorary uncle like 'Aunties' Meg and Martha. 'D'you live locally?' she asked him, wishing for the umpteenth time that she was a sparkling conversationalist with a bold and witty repertoire – a Felice, for example.

'Oh no, I'm a northerner.'

She changed the subject quickly – it was dangerous to get so near her parents – tried another tack. 'Did you have anything exciting for Christmas?'

'Just a Marks and Spencer dressing gown and a rather boring tie. I'm too old for excitement, Rose.'

She glanced at his red face – red from heat and Scotch. He couldn't be much older than the artist.

'And what did you get yourself, dear?'

'Oh, loads of things.' More than any Christmas in her life. Everything was lavish in the unstinting Mackenzie household, and Isobel had showered her with a cornucopia of gifts, then Rowan added more. Uncle Rory was waiting for the details, so she obliged with scarves and sweaters, then tried to describe her most important present – the framed drawing of a bird, which Christopher had given her. She'd been disappointed that it wasn't his own work, and he in turn had seemed a little piqued that she'd never heard of the artist who had drawn it, a household name apparently, whose work was in demand, snapped up by the dealers. She had clearly failed to realise the value of the drawing, its rarity, its vigour, the trouble it had taken him to hunt it down at all. Once he'd put her right, she had tried to thank him as profusely as she could, but secretly she'd wished the gift had been more personal – a present for a mistress, a heart-shaped locket on a chain, or a ring with her own birthstone in.

'Hey, Billy, don't! That hurts.' Billy's favourite Christmas game was pulling her long hair. He seemed fascinated by it, kept creeping back to tug it, when he thought she wasn't looking. His mother switched on the television, in the hope it would distract him – a commercial for Courvoisier, which reminded her of Christopher – again: sophisticated brandy-drinkers gathered at some house-party, the men all sleek and soigné, the women dripping jewels. She was glad when brandy changed to cat-food. She had spent too long already peering through the windows of that villa on the Côte d'Azur, seeing Anne and Christopher entwined, watching them trip up to bed, then hearing all the night-sounds – not just birds and pounding waves, but creaking bed-springs, wild impassioned cries.

Uncle Rory raised his voice to defeat the competition. She could hardly hear him anyway, since Billy's younger brother had broken his toy gun, and was letting out frustrated wails, which had upset the anguished whippet, now shivering and howling in its turn. Several aunties flurried with hankies, admonitions. Martha spilt her drink.

'I . . . I'll get a cloth,' Jane murmured, seizing the excuse to slip away, though every time she had sneaked out to the kitchen, to escape or lend a hand, Isobel had tried to coax her back.

'Are you sure you don't want any help?' she offered once again.

'No, absolutely not. I'm only sorry it's so late. The turkey's still half-raw inside. I suppose we could start with the goose, and have the turkey later. What d'you think?'

'Yes,' said Jane. 'Good idea.'

'Except Martha doesn't eat goose. And Edith's bound to say it's too fatty for her heart condition. There is the ham, as well, of course, but I never feel that ham quite counts, do you? I mean, it seems so sort of ordinary – what I'd call a Monday food, when you've had a host of weekend guests and can't rustle up the energy to cook another meal, so you dish out cold damp ham.'

'But your ham's hot.'

'Yes, 'course it is. And I did that nice brown sugar crust, and apple rings to go with it, but all the same . . .' She dabbed a grease-spot off her dress, pushed back a skein of hair. 'You should have seen the hams we had in Oban. You know, a Scottish Christmas is really something, Rose. In fact, when Tom and I were young, we used to spend the . . . Oh, drat, the pudding's boiling dry. Could you be an angel and top it up with water? Tibs, get down from there immediately! D'you know, I'm sure those greedy cats think I'm cooking just for them.'

'Isobel, I wish you'd let me help.'

'You are helping, darling. And if you really want another job, you can whip this cream up, then spread it on the trifle. Gosh! It's hot in here, isn't it?'

'Boiling.' Jane undid the top two buttons of her blouse. The sitting-room had been warm enough, with its huge log fire and the fug from all the guests, but the kitchen was a furnace; the Aga blasting heat, the windows all steamed up, Isobel's flushed face dripping perspiration as she checked the ovens, basted roast potatoes. Everything seemed galvanised by her own bubbling-over energy; the Christmas pudding shuddering in its pan, a squad of other saucepans singing on the hob, parsnips spluttering in the oven,

250

turkey spitting fat, the air itself panting in hot eddies as it swirled around the room.

Isobel dived across and took the egg-whisk from her. 'No, don't use that. Try this one.' The cream was stiff in minutes, as the older woman assaulted it with elbow-grease and metal. She was an enthusiastic cook, yet there was still a sense of chaos, nothing quite controlled; clutter spreading everywhere, presents piled on worktops, hats and coats dumped on kitchen chairs.

Jane thought back to eight o'clock – a very different Isobel kneeling like a statue in the hushed and chilly church, nothing moving this time save her lips. Had she been praying for her child, her abandoned baby Angela, who would now be middle-aged? 'You never forget the child you've given birth to,' Isobel had told her, 'and Christmas and birthdays are always rather sad times, when you wonder specially where and how she is.' The words kept nudging in Jane's head. Was her own birth-mother praying at this moment, speculating, missing her, trying to build a picture in her mind, or had she forgotten clean about her eighteen years ago?

'Isobel?' she said.

'Yes.'

'You know Saint Jerome.'

'Well,' she smiled, 'not personally.'

'Was he all mixed up – I mean, spiteful and vindictive and always having rows with people, and hating Jews and women and . . . ?'

'Good gracious, no! Whatever gave you that idea? He's one of the great Doctors of the Church – a tremendous scholar who gave us a new translation of the Bible. And for several years he was a hermit in the desert – I mean, frightfully holy and austere, a man who believed in loving God quite passionately, and renouncing anything and everything which could distract him from that aim, and . . .' Isobel paused for breath, retrieved a whoosh of cream which had flown across the table, then continued with the holy man's achievements.

Jane chewed a strand of hair. Why was nothing ever simple or clear-cut; no one truth or viewpoint which everyone could hold to? Hadley had remarked that faith was believing what you knew to be untrue. Was *he* right, or his mother?

'Why this sudden interest in Saint Jerome?'

'Just something I read.' Jane could feel herself blushing as she recalled her weekend with the artist, followed almost instantly by that reckless night with Isobel's own son. She'd made Hadley swear he wouldn't tell a soul, but, all the same, she still felt very threatened

251

by it, embarrassed with his mother. Thank God he was in Paris, though Isobel had mentioned him several times already, and each time had made her nervous, as if she expected the next question to be 'How's Hadley as a lover?' rather than 'D'you think he'll get a proper Christmas dinner in that dreadful student hostel?'

'By the way, how are you getting on with Trish?' Isobel enquired, licking gobs of cream from her fingers and the whisk.

'All right.'

'She's a nice girl, isn't she?'

'Mm.'

'In fact, I was wondering if you two would like to go out for a walk – enjoy this bit of sunshine before it gets all dark and gloomy.'

'What, now?'

'Why not? It's a lovely day, completely wrong for Christmas, but that's probably global warming, or whatever it is they threaten in all those fatalistic articles which insist the planet's heading for destruction. I expect they wrote much the same thing in the 1990s BC.'

Jane ignored BC, was more concerned with lunch. Dates and sweets were fine as just an appetiser, but her stomach was demanding a proper solid meal. 'But aren't we going to eat now? I mean, I thought you said we'd start with the goose and . . .'

'No, better not. You know what all the aunts are like. It isn't Christmas dinner without the blessed turkey. And anyway Byron needs a walk. He'll be impossible this afternoon if someone doesn't take him out. Trish came in her car, so you could drive down to the beach with her and have a really bracing jog along the sands.'

'Okay,' she said reluctantly. She hadn't warmed to Trish, who was petite and cutely pretty, and had clearly been invited not just because her mother was ill in hospital, but to demonstrate the point that adopted children could be happy, normal, grateful, well-adjusted. She had talked to her for half an hour, just to be polite, but kept to safe and stilted subjects – the mildness of the weather, the intelligence of cats compared with dogs. Trish's mother was an old schoolfriend of Isobel, and had adopted Trish as a child of three: a 'special' child, a 'wanted' child, as Isobel had pointed out in her worthy little spiel last night; one chosen by her adoptive parents, not a mere mistake. Jane had tried to close her ears to what seemed like special pleading. Isobel could never be objective. She'd had her own 'mistake' adopted, so she needed to believe that all adoptive parents acted from the best of motives; all adopted children could grow up fine and dandy. Oh, she'd probably meant it well, intended to be helpful, provide some reassurance, but Jane still resented the intrusion, the whole artificial set-up, the fact she was expected to communicate with a twenty-year-old stranger she didn't even like.

'I'll fetch the lead,' she muttered, stopping in the cloakroom first, to change her tampon. Her period was a heavy one, and had started late last night. She'd been exceptionally relieved, since it meant she wasn't pregnant. In the sixteen (endless) days since that business on the sofa, she had been recalling all the horror stories about condoms leaking, condoms with small holes in, condoms slipping off. Yet she'd also felt a twinge of disappointment. Getting pregnant by the artist was a different thing entirely, and she'd been indulging in wild unlikely fantasies about saving him from sterility, proving one up on the wives. She would have also proved herself, of course, allayed her secret fears. One part of her was terrified of landing up like Amy – barren, babyless.

'Byron!' she called, pulling on her jacket and jingling the red lead. The boxer erupted into the hall. almost knocked her over; the whippet cringing out as well, though shrinking from her hand. She traipsed back to the sitting-room to ask if she should take him too, prised Trish from her corner, where she was providing a mute audience for Edith's hip-replacement saga, instalments nine and ten. All the others called goodbye or started asking teasing questions – were they going carol-singing, or had they given up all hope of lunch and were headed for the chip shop; would they be back in time for Boxing Day; did they want the odd crumb saved?

It was a relief to shake them off. Strange how other people's families, however kind and jolly, could make you feel so desolate – the private jokes or references you didn't understand, the bonhomie you couldn't really share. Her parents were her own family, the only one she had, and she'd missed them more today than any other time in the preceding eleven weeks. She'd often complained that their Christmases were dull, just the boring three of them most years. Now she realised she'd always been the centre and the star. She'd had no competition. The presents and the tree, the turkey and the Christmas cake, had been laid on in her honour, the whole extended holiday woven round her pleasures and her needs.

She banged the front door shut, bewildered by her thoughts, the whole confusing mixture of resentment, guilt and gratitude; the sheer longing to be back with them, resuming her star role. She stood a moment longer on the step, though Trish was already waiting by the car, and Byron straining wildly at his leash, rebuking her as spoilsport. She needed to compose herself, struggle for control. It

253

would be terrible to cry on Christmas Day, blubber for her Mummy like a lost and frantic two-year-old. She breathed in the fresh air – that would help to calm her – stern no-nonsense air which slapped her burning cheeks, smelt of winter cold rather than turkey grease or overheated kitchens.

'Are you okay?' called Trish.

'No,' she mumbled to herself, letting Byron tow her to the car. Even Trish's name annoyed her, its brief and jaunty intimacy suggesting they were bosom pals already. She'd rather call her Patricia, the name that she'd been christened; keep her distance, keep things cool and formal. 'D'you know the way?' she asked her, once she'd settled Byron in the back. 'Turn right at the gate, then straight on for a mile or so.'

'It's lovely country,' Trish remarked, as they swung out of the drive.

'Yes,' said Jane. 'It is.' How in heaven's name would they talk for a whole hour, how move from 'lovely country' to the intimate details of their adopted lives? Trish seemed quite reserved, could well be fighting misery herself. Things were pretty bad for her, in fact. She'd lost her father fourteen months ago, and now her mother was recovering from a stroke. 'You must be worried about your mother,' Jane forced herself to say.

'Yes, I am a bit.'

'Is the hospital a good one?' She tried to sound less hostile. It was hardly Trish's fault that she'd been invited to meet a misery, who was so concerned with her own petty little grouches she couldn't spare a thought for anyone else.

'Well, it's ancient, but it's said to be quite good. I'll be visiting this evening. My sister's there right now, so Mum shouldn't feel too lonely. And the nurses always make a special effort over Christmas.'

'Oh, you've got a sister?'

'Yes. Susan. Four years older.'

Is she also adopted, Jane knew she ought to ask. Then they'd sail into The Subject, and she could report smugly back to Isobel that after a heart-to-heart with Trish, she no longer felt upset by the facts of her adoption, and had undone eighteen years' betrayal in one walk.

'Any brothers?' she asked instead.

'No, thank God,' Trish grinned, trying to push a slobbering Byron off her neck. She was driving fast, like Christopher, and Jane was reminded of the empty roads in Lincolnshire, the December sun thawing frosty fields. She felt torn between her lover and her home;

one scared and childish part of her yearning for her parents, while the adult half ached and throbbed for Christopher. And even Hadley wouldn't stay in Paris, but kept nipping back to plague her. Yet, despite her fears and guilts about her night with him in Fulham, there was still a small vindictive voice whispering to her secretly that she was not entirely sorry to have paid the artist out, evened up the score a little. If he had Anne each night, shared his bed and body, then was it really so horrendous for her to have had another man for a paltry fifteen minutes?

'Trish,' she said suddenly, 'I wondered if you'd mind if we took a little detour?'

'No, of course not. Where d'you want to go?'

'Just to see a . . . house.'

'What, one you want to buy?'

She laughed. 'I couldn't afford a garden shed at present. No, one I . . .' She paused to shape the lie. A friend of hers had gone away for Christmas and asked her to keep an eye on the place. That sounded pretty plausible and the first half was true, at least. She had always been curious to see the artist's home, had never had a chance before. Houses were important – extensions of their owners, statements of their values and their taste. Christopher kept his private life so private, she felt constantly intrigued by it; sometimes wildly curious, other times resentful, but always keen to gather up some clues, set him in his context, so to speak. 'Spy!' her conscience nagged, but she tried to drown it out, concentrated on giving Trish directions. Strange how well she knew the way, when she had only walked her fingers on a map.

'That's it,' she said, at last, after what had seemed a journey of several hundred miles, though it had lasted twelve brief minutes. She took a deep breath in. She was actually looking at the artist's house, sitting right outside it; disappointed somehow that it wasn't a palace or a castle, or some fantastic modern construction made wholly of stained glass, but just a large, though unimposing, red brick villa. Dreary laurels mobbed the wooden fence, and one unwieldy cedar was blocking half the light from all the right-hand windows. The house stood on its own, as if it had been transplanted from a village, and resited in a wilderness; its only neighbour a copse of trees and the wide sweep of a hill. It was like the barn in that respect – self-sufficient, solitary. Typical of Christopher to shrug off human contact, avoid a gossipy street or prying neighbours. Yet, in other ways, the house didn't seem to suit him; looked too staid and sober, as if had stiffened in its joints; the house of someone prosperous

255

but dull. A car was parked outside; a car which contradicted it: a low-slung sporty model in a zingy gleaming silver – Anne's car, she presumed.

'No wonder they're scared of burglars,' Trish observed, winding down the window. 'I mean, the place seems so cut off. D'you want to take a look around?'

Jane shook her head. The house was not a friendly one, seemed to be staring with its heavy red-rimmed eyes, warning her to keep away, telling her it didn't welcome strangers. And she *was* a stranger here, had no rights to the artist except on weekdays in the studio; banned from all his evenings, from his breakfasts, baths, and shavings, from his late-night drinks or early-morning wakenings. 'No, it looks all right to me,' she said, turning round to Trish with a falsely casual smile. 'No papers on the step, or milk bottles piling up. Let's push on to the beach.'

Her eyes sneaked back as Trish switched on the ignition, still watching the blank windows, the sombre slated roof. She wanted to remember them, store them in her head along with Christopher's CV, and all the shreds and scraps she'd gleaned about him from Rowan, Adrian, Isobel – her Christopher compendium.

'Hey, stop!' she cried suddenly ducking down to make herself invisible, and praying Byron wouldn't bark. Someone had moved into the window of the downstairs room, and was fiddling with the curtain, glancing out a moment. She knew the woman, recognised the ample breasts, the straight brown hair gleaming in the light. Anne – Anne Harville-Shaw. She stared a moment longer, to make absolutely certain, then leant across and tugged Trish's skirt. 'Quick!' she begged, crouching out of sight herself. 'Drive on!'

'What's wrong?'

'Nothing. Just get away from here.' She couldn't talk. Her voice felt choked and clogged, and a whole cannonade of questions was bombarding her bruised mind. Christopher and Anne were seven hundred miles away in a villa on the Côte d'Azur, so how could Anne be standing at the window of her own house? Had they come back suddenly? Had they gone at all? Could the artist have deceived her, invented the whole story of a holiday in Nice because he didn't want to see her over Christmas, craved a quiet two weeks at home with no company but his wife?

'Rose, are you all right?' Trish changed gear, slowed down to a crawl. 'And where d'you want to go now? I'm driving round in circles.'

'Anywhere. You choose.'

256

'But can't you tell me what . . .'

'It's nothing. I'm feeling a bit sick, that's all. I . . . ate too many chocolates.'

'Why don't we go back then? I expect Isobel can find some Alka Seltzer.'

'No, honestly. I'll be better for a walk. The fresh air will do me good. And, anyway, Byron needs some exercise. Let's drive on to the beach, if you don't mind.'

Thank God Trish was easy-going – obliging and amenable – all the things which had annoyed her earlier on. Now she was relieved to have a chauffeur, a reason to stay out. She couldn't return to all that jollity and babble until she'd sorted out the confusion in her mind. Christopher had phoned her from the Côte d'Azur, actually spelt out details of the villa, described the guests, the meals. He must be there, he must be. And she had even asked how Anne was; somehow couldn't stop herself, despite her jealousy. 'Fine,' he'd said, straight off.

She gazed out of the window, hardly taking in the scenery, except as it reminded her of the artist and his wife; the blighted trees like those in Christopher's landscapes; the bare brown furrows straight-combed like Anne's brown hair. Should they drive back to the house, she wondered, conceal the car, but hang around outside, try to see if Christopher was there as well as Anne? Maybe Trish could even knock, pretend she'd missed her turning and landed up in the wilds, and could they please direct her back to the main road. But if Christopher appeared, it would mean he was a liar, and the whole of Christmas would be punctured like a child's balloon. He was a liar anyway. Just last night he'd told her on the phone that he'd be away two days less than he'd planned originally, and would be returning on 4 January. How could he play false like that, mystify her, baffle her – except that all grown-ups did the same: lied to you, deceived you, made things seem quite different from the facts.

'Rose, don't cry.' Trish stopped the car, reached out an awkward hand. 'Won't you let me help? I've no idea what's going on, but . . .'

'They didn't tell me,' Jane blurted out, tears sliding down her face.

'Who didn't tell you what?'

'That I . . . I'm adopted.'

'*Are* you? So am I.'

'I know.'

'But I didn't know that you were.' Trish scrabbled for the Kleenex, passed the box across. 'That's really quite a coincidence.'

'No it isn't.' Jane grabbed a fistful of Kleenex, so fiercely that she tore them. 'Isobel arranged for us to meet. She couldn't tell you because I made her promise not to, but she was hoping that I'd confide in you myself.' She let out a sudden hoot, laughing now as well as crying, a crazy hurting laugh. 'Oh, Trish, it's so ridiculous. I'd vowed I'd never say a word, would keep off the whole subject, just to prove to Isobel that she shouldn't interfere, and now I've fallen right into her trap.'

Jane's feet were sore and aching, a blister on one heel. She and Trish could hardly see to walk. Dusk was falling, a clammy mist seeping all along the coast, curdling with the darkness, laying a damp pall on their skin, their hair, their clothes. Trish stopped a moment to extract a pebble from her shoe. 'It's terribly late,' she flustered, peering at her watch. 'They'll be sending out a search-party. I simply didn't realise what the time was.'

'We'd better phone,' said Jane, anxious now herself. It would seem rude and very casual to have disappeared so long.

'I hope they haven't finished lunch.'

'They probably haven't started yet.' Jane was still reluctant to return, to resume her public mask when she'd only just succeeded in removing it, had let Trish see her naked; even stripped the 'Rose' off and admitted her real name.

'I'm glad we've got the dog, Jane. It's a bit spooky out here, isn't it?'

Jane stared up at the sky, the swollen threatening clouds, the wedge of sullen moon, grudging in its light. She had been blind to her surroundings, oblivious of the encroaching sea until it frothed around their feet, and they'd had to move up higher to the shingle. Only now was she aware of the shrill sea-birds, of Byron's frantic barking as he challenged ghosts or gulls; of the smells of tar and salt. She had never meant to walk so far – nor talk so long and freely.

'Trish, I . . . I'm sorry if I've bored you.'

'Bored me? Don't be stupid.'

'I don't know how it all poured out – I mean Christopher and everything. I haven't shocked you, have I?'

'I've heard worse than that, I promise you.'

'Yes, but he's sixty – sixty-one. My mother would be scandalised, probably want him clapped in jail, with "Dirty Old Man" branded on his forehead.'

Trish laughed. 'Mothers never like their daughters' men-friends, however old or young they are. I envy you in one way, Jane, just to have a man at all. I haven't dared admit this to anyone before, but I'm nearly twenty-one, and I've never had . . . you know.'

Jane looked up in surprise. Trish's face was blurring in the darkness, but it was a pretty face – too pretty, she had thought at first – the sort of pink and white complexion you rarely saw outside TV commercials, contrasting with dark eyes and hair – curly, springy, bouncy hair, which seemed alive in its own right, bobbing as she walked, a frisky fringe untidy on her forehead. She'd have imagined such a girl would have had boyfriends flocking round her, be almost spoilt for choice, mobbed by men, invaded. But then the Trish she'd met four hours ago, dismissed as prim and priggish, was nothing like the real one. It had been a great relief to talk to her, to confide in someone totally objective, someone not much older, who understood about adoption, knew it from the inside out. And yet the confusion hadn't gone – was worse, if anything. All the things which Trish had told her had stirred her up still more, added new resentment, new guilts as well as insights.

Byron suddenly shook himself, the slow but wild vibration spreading from his head to his non-existent tail. Jane longed to do the same, shake off all the complexities, the endless circling thoughts. 'Let's run,' she said to Trish, envying the dog again as he streaked towards a breakwater, hurtled back full-steam.

'Run! You must be joking. I'm flagging as it is.'

'Well, jog-trot then. If we don't get a move on, they'll be ringing the police.'

They jogged the last half-mile, then made a call to Isobel from the phone-box on the promenade, reported they were safe.

'Thank God!' said Isobel, expressing her relief in a dramatic exhalation. 'We were getting really worried.'

'I hope you've started lunch.'

'I'm afraid it's still not ready.'

'Told you so,' said Jane, once she'd put down the receiver. She and Trish collapsed in helpless giggles.

'My mother says she's always been the same – late for everything. I love her, though, don't you?'

'Yes,' said Jane; bit back a wary 'sometimes'. 'Listen, Trish, for goodness sake don't call me Jane, not in front of Isobel or anyone.'

'Okay, Jane – Rose.'

They laughed again, conspirators; flopped back in the car, only realising how chilled they were once they'd switched the heater on and began to let their cold cramped limbs relax. Jane sat silent as they speeded back to Isobel's. She knew the road so well, knew every public phone-box on the route; the last one just three hundred yards from Windy Hollow House. She was watching for it now, praying it would work, not be out of order, vandalised.

'Could you let me off here? I want to make a phone-call. I'll walk the last bit back.'

'No, I'll wait. Don't worry.'

'Please don't. I know it's stupid, but it's a rather hairy call, and if anyone's around it'll make it even harder.'

'I'll stay here in the car, though, promise not to eavesdrop.'

'It's not that, Trish. I . . . I've got to be alone.'

'You mean you're going to ring your guy?'

Jane nodded. 'Tell the others I'll only be a minute.'

She waited till the car had disappeared, wished she'd taken Byron, not just to protect her from the bleak and lonely darkness, but to distract her from the turmoil in her head. She had no money on her, which would make the call still more tense and awkward. She'd have to reverse the charges, wait several frantic moments while the operator asked if they'd accept it.

No – she must outlaw words like 'frantic', keep the call dispassionate, remain as cool as possible, detached and unperturbed. It wouldn't be easy, but she couldn't chicken out now. It was her Christmas present to them, her recompense for not being there in person. Trish had made her see that her parents would be suffering just as much as she was – more, in fact, since they'd be racked with grief and worry, unable to enjoy their Christmas Day. She'd only realised half an hour ago that it was she, and only she, who made their Christmas for them, simply by her presence, her existence. Just as she had no one else, nor did they.

She checked her watch: half past four. They'd have come in from their walk – coats hung up, outdoor shoes away – and be putting on the kettle; her father fetching cups and plates, her mother cutting Christmas cake, everything shipshape and methodical. She had hardly needed to wear a watch when she'd been at home in Shrepton. Her parents had been living clocks, never running down, never fast or slow. She suddenly longed to join them in the quiet and tidy sitting-room, for a tranquil cup of tea, instead of braving lunch at Isobel's with all its rumpus and shemozzle. The efficiency she'd criticised was actually a virtue, had meant she wasn't late for things, or stuffing sweets instead of meals, not rushed or pushed or panicked; had provided an order and security she had never even valued. Couldn't she say thank you now, offer them an olive branch, take the first important step towards a reconciliation?

She picked up the receiver, eyes skimming the graffiti pencilled on the wall. Beneath the insults and obscenities were a few scribbled hearts and flowers: 'Sue loves Nicky', 'Pam loves hunky Joe'. If only love were as simple as those sentiments, and not always undercut by some opposite emotion; every surge of loyalty or fondness followed by a backwash of bitter indignation. And anyway, if she started making overtures, her parents would expect her to return. That was quite impossible. She couldn't leave the artist, despite the fact that her feelings for him were similarly confused, plunging like a switchback from passion to reproach. If she phoned him now, as she had let Trish think she'd meant to, she wouldn't even know whether to dial the code for Sussex or for France. She wiped her clammy palms across her coat. She'd been freezing just a minute ago; now she was perspiring – nervous from her dithering, from all the complications. If she didn't get a move on, Trish would come to find her, or Isobel come running in her grease-splashed dress and slippers, and with tinsel in her hair. She must do what she'd decided in the car – phone her parents, but keep the call as brief and bland as possible – no emotion, no disclosures; just 'Happy Christmas; she hoped that they were well; she was fine herself, and they really mustn't worry; she'd phone again next month – goodbye.'

Three long minutes passed before the operator answered, a rude man with a local Sussex accent, who was followed by a squall of whines and cracklings. She couldn't hear a word, but presumed he must be trying to connect her, arrange the transferred charge. 'Right, caller, go ahead,' he rapped at last.

'Hallo,' she said uncertainly, not even sure who was on the other end.

Her father's voice was wary, a frightened hopeless sort of voice she had never heard him use before.

'It's Jane,' she said, as coolly as she could.

'*Jane!*' She heard the voice break, stumble on the next few words, try desperately to right itself. 'Oh, darling, you're alive! Thank God. Don't put the phone down this time. Janey, please, for heaven's sake, tell us how you are.'

'I . . . I'm fine,' she stammered, trying to remember the formula she'd planned: were they well themselves, had they had a happy Christmas, she'd ring next month, goodbye.

'I'm missing you', she said instead. 'I'm missing you quite horribly. Oh, Dad,' she sobbed, 'don't cry, please don't. I love you and I'm coming home – right now.'

19

'Did you enjoy your Christmas?' Jane enquired nervously, mopping her sore nose.

'It wasn't bad.'

'No better than "not bad"?'

'Quite pleasant, then. Will that do?'

She crumpled up her sodden paper hanky. The artist seemed irritable already, and he had been back in the studio only a paltry seven minutes. True, he'd kissed her passionately, as soon as he'd walked in, told her that he'd missed her, brought her presents – French chocolates and French scent. He probably didn't like her questions – or her cold.

'Did Anne enjoy the trip?' she asked, reaching for more hankies, and trying to stop her voice from betraying any emotion beyond a mere idle curiosity.

He shrugged.

'Well, did she?'

'Yes, of course she did. Why shouldn't she?'

'Did you both stay there for New Year?' She slipped the 'both' in slyly, hoped it didn't sound intrusive.

'Till yesterday – I told you.'

Jane blew her nose more loudly than she needed. So he was lying to her – deliberately, cold-bloodedly, and for no reason she could see. He worshipped Truth in art, then kicked it in the gutter as far as personal relations were concerned.

'How about you? Did Isobel lay on the fatted calf?'

'A whole herd of fatted calves,' she said, forcing a fake smile. 'And roast sucking pig for New Year's Eve – well, pork chops, anyway, and about twenty other courses. By the way, you didn't phone again.'

'No.'

'You said you would.'

'I couldn't, could I, if you were staying at the Mackenzies'?'

'No, after that. I came back here on the third, remember, and we arranged you'd ring that evening.'

'I said I'd *try* to phone, Rose. It was very difficult, in fact.'

'With Anne around, you mean?'

The artist struck a match, almost burnt his fingers as he tried and failed to light his cigarette. 'There were fifteen people staying in the villa and one very ancient telephone.'

'Don't they have public phones in Nice?'

He didn't answer, removed his overcoat, then strode over to the hi-fi, selected a cassette. The music was some modern thing, which sounded very harrowing, screwed up the tension in the room another painful notch. She was annoyed he hadn't commented on her four days of hard work. She had returned from Isobel's earlier than she'd needed, attacked the barn with brushes, mops and elbow grease; spring-cleaning every room, clearing up the studio, putting all the glass away, emptying the cullet-box. They had finished all the cutting just before the Christmas break, and were about to start the painting, so this morning she had got up extra early, cleaned the surface of all the separate glass-pieces stuck up on the screens, to remove any trace of grease or dust. Then she'd prised off the first section – the Angel's head and halo – and placed it on the workbench, on top of the cartoon, exactly as he'd told her. She'd done everything he'd asked, and now wanted some acknowledgement, the briefest of brief thank-yous, not that wail of strident music.

He appeared to have picked up on her thoughts, since he turned the volume down a little, then joined her at the workbench. 'Okay, Rose, first I'm going to show you how to grind and mix the paint. It may sound like a chore, but it's actually a vital job. The ancient Japanese calligraphers used to spend an hour or more preparing their inks. They felt that the rhythm of the grinding focused their minds, built up a sense of peace and concentration.'

She watched him spoon dry pigment on to a square of roughened plate-glass, add a pungent-smelling cocktail of water and acetic acid, then grind it with a palette-knife, pressing, circling, mashing, establishing a rhythm. 'You want to get it smooth like custard – no lumps or powdery bits.'

She did her best to concentrate, envied those calligraphers their peaceful focused minds. She must take them as her model, leave the lies behind, stop fretting over Nice and why the artist had deceived her. She was his assistant, not his mistress, so it didn't matter anyway. She had vowed she wouldn't sleep with him again; should never have allowed that scorching kiss which was still throbbing in her mouth, confounding her decisions, unsettling and disturbing her.

'Next we mix in some gum arabic, and a little dab of sugar. That helps the pigment flow, makes it stick more firmly to the glass. Here, have a try yourself, Rose.'

She tried to copy him exactly, continually flipping back the mixture into the centre of the palette, cutting through it vertically, then scraping it all up again, and repeating the whole process. Strange how they had returned to work so swiftly. They'd been parted for sixteen and a quarter days, had a mass of news and feelings to exchange with one another, yet were talking gum and pigment. She stared at the dark sludge, which looked more like mud than custard. It still surprised her that you painted glass with such a limited range of colours, a few grey-greens and blackish-browns.

'Do you stain the glass yourself?' Trish had asked naïvely, when they'd been discussing their respective jobs last week. It was only when she'd explained to Trish the detail of her work, that she'd realised what a lot she'd learnt in a brief two months' apprenticeship.

'No,' she'd told her, 'the colour's in the glass already. You don't apply any other colour to it, apart from silver-stain . . .' She had broken off at that point. Silver-staining was quite a complex business in itself, and Trish was looking baffled, as it was. Her friend's job was less complicated. She was employed by a small firm of vegetarian caterers who cooked for private parties – everything from homely dinners to large-scale prestige gatherings; worked mostly from her home, liaising with three other girls, but using her own kitchen to prepare and cook the food, and sometimes waitressing as well, if she wanted extra money.

Jane had thought secretly that it sounded rather boring; much preferred her own work, especially now she was learning more about it. She'd been mugging up the books, aiming to keep a step ahead of Christopher, so as they started each new stage, she had grasped the basic principles, techniques. 'The craft's basically so simple,' the artist often said. 'You can pick up the essentials in a day or two.' She didn't contradict him, but to her it seemed extraordinarily involved, and there were always subtleties, refinements, she found difficult to grasp. Painting glass, for instance, was as much about controlling light coming through the window as depicting scenes and symbols. The paint also added richness, created form and texture, modified the brilliance of the colour. But, according to the books, removing paint

264

was as vital as applying it, and when the artist reached the second stage of painting, he would be using a whole armoury of different implements and brushes, to scrub and scratch and stipple it, sponge and stab and splatter.

But first he had to trace in all the details – fingers, features, halo, hair, feathers on the Angel's wings, petals on the roses. He was picking out a tracing-brush, selecting a long-handled one with very fine long hairs. 'I've just started using these Chinese brushes, and they're bloody good, you know – said to be the closest thing to what they used for painting medieval glass. This one's squirrel-hair, which the twelfth-century monk Theophilus specially recommended in his treatise on stained glass, though he also praised badger-hair, and even hair from the tail of a cat.'

'Perhaps Isobel should lend you Tibs, or chop off Orlando's tail.'

He ignored her little joke, stood keyed-up at his workbench, about to start the painting, peering intently at the lines on the cartoon which were showing through the glass. 'Paint ready yet?' he asked.

She nodded. If those calligraphers he'd praised had been mixing inks for *him*, he would never have allowed them their full and focused hour, but would have been hassling them to finish, so he could get on with his own job. She gave the mixture one last grind, praying that she'd got it right, that it wouldn't be too runny on the one hand, nor too stiff on the other. She watched him dip his brush in, trace the first line of the Angel's face – *her* face. They were bonded by this window, not just by their bodies. She longed for him to recognise the fact, rebuild their intimacy, say how much she meant to him, how sad and grey the days had seemed in Nice – if he'd gone, that is.

'Don't watch me, Rose. It puts me off my stroke. Can't you find a job or something?'

She backed away. 'There's nothing left to do, I've cleaned up all the glass-screens and . . .'

'Well, go and make some coffee.'

She trailed out to the kitchen, banged the cups around. Christopher never had coffee till eleven at the earliest; simply wanted her to scat, stay out of his hair. She filled the kettle, stood musing at the sink. He must have been to France. The chocolates were hand-made, had the name of the supplier on both the wrappings and the box – a Monsieur Jacques Lemercier, with a local Nice address. So why had Anne not accompanied him? Had he taken someone else, another woman she didn't even know about, some model from the Art School, or . . . ? She rammed the Maxwell House back, started grinding coffee beans. At least it would take longer, and it was essential she kept busy, pulverised her angry thoughts, as well as just the beans. Grinding coffee, grinding paint – that was all that she was good for.

She plugged in the percolator, started scouring down the worktops while she waited for it to brew, though they were clean and clear already; arranged biscuits on a gold-rimmed plate, home-made ones from Isobel's. The artist simply grunted when she carried in the tray, didn't seem to notice that she'd made a special effort. His total concentration was on his brush, the glass – the curved line of the eyebrow which he was feathering in with tiny delicate strokes. 'I like the way your eyebrows sit,' he had told her all those weeks ago, but now her brows had been translated to the Angel, and all his passion and commitment were directed at that Spirit, and not to her as mere superseded mortal.

She bit into a biscuit, to remove the taste of jealousy, bitter in her mouth. She was jealous of so many things – of the Angel, and the artist's wife, and his (female) friends in Nice; jealous of his talents, his absorption in his work. 'Christopher?' she said.

'Mm.'

'I need a job myself. I hardly did a thing at the Mackenzies' – Isobel wouldn't let me. I just stuffed myself and sat around, and now I'm feeling fat and sort of fidgety. Can't I help you with the painting? It doesn't look too difficult.'

'You'd be surprised. Drawing with a brush takes years of practice. It's a matter of control, you see, and you've no training or experience at all. You can't even draw with a pencil.'

'Well, I'll never learn, will I, if you don't let me have a bash.'

'Okay.' He straightened up, took a sip of coffee, seeming slightly puzzled at how it had arrived there. 'If you root around in that cupboard on the right, you'll find some old cartoons. Pick out a hand, or foot, or flower – something that you'd like to paint, and practise on some scrap glass. But go and do it on that table by the window. I need total peace and quiet. Working on a face is always rather tricky. It never seems to come right first time round.'

She went to fetch some scraps of glass, unrolled a few cartoons; found a long and slender foot belonging to a female saint, which looked suitable to paint. She tied an apron round her waist, stood eager at the table. She was a child of six again, helping Mummy make the pastry, not the steak and kidney pie they would eat for supper, later, but a meagre offcut, soon grubby from her hands. Amy had always humoured her, had bought her a small rolling pin, encouraged her attempts to make pastry leaves and flowers – and Alec had gone further – actually eaten up the greyish leaden lumps which eventually emerged from the oven along with the meat pie.

She tipped pigment on a glass-palette, began preparing her own paint, glad to have a simple task, while her mind was mired in the complexities of mothers, fathers, home. Trish had pointed out that a 'real' mother was the one who did the mothering: played the pastry-making games, read the bedtime stories, got up in the night if you were sick or scared or thirsty, fed and taught and nursed you. Amy had done all those things, and done them lovingly. Trish had also said that maybe her parents hadn't told her the truth about her adoption because they'd feared she'd be upset about her origins, and had tried to save her pain; or perhaps they'd dreaded losing her affection to the mother who had borne her, which, however wrong, still proved they cared, proved her great importance to them.

She jabbed the paint with her palette-knife, trying to break up any tiny lumps. If only it were as easy to remove the clots and polyps in her own life – the entanglement with Christopher, the seesaw-lurch of feelings her parents kept provoking: first love, then fear, then fury. The two relationships were linked, in fact. She had changed her mind about going home to Shrepton because she had to see the artist, knew she'd lose him totally if she went back north, became her parents' child again. And now she'd lost him anyway, lost him in deceit; had upset her parents terribly, caused more pain all round.

She placed a rectangle of glass above the tapering foot, tried to trace the outline of the toes. Despite the hand-rest she was using, her fingers felt unsteady, and all she managed to produce was a few gungy little blobs, not the precise and sinuous lines the artist had achieved. It was a completely different process from trying to paint on paper. Glass was not absorbent, so she kept using too much paint; dabbed it with her hanky, then forgot what she was doing, so that when she blew her nose she transferred brown streaks to her face. No wonder Christopher had banished her to the far end of the studio, like a stupid messy child. She glanced across to see what he was doing. He seemed tense, on edge, picking up his cigarette as often as the brush, inhaling deeply, coughing; then suddenly rubbing off the paint with a piece of dirty rag, as if he too had made a mess.

She wished he wouldn't smoke. She didn't usually mind, but her nose was blocked and stuffy from her cold, and smoky rooms made it difficult to breathe. And did he have to have that music on? It was so dissonant and screechy – a trumpet and two violins competing with each other to see which could sound the shrillest. It wasn't just the noise she found depressing, but the fact that she and Christopher were so utterly divided by it – what for him was pleasure and involvement, for her was pain and ignorance. She didn't know the composer, couldn't understand the work, couldn't even begin to grasp how anyone could like it.

Her eyes strayed to the pinboard, level with her head – sketches, letters, postcards, tacked up in profusion, including a stiff white invitation from the Worshipful Company of Glaziers, its coat of arms in colour at the top. She read their Latin motto: *'Lucem Tuam Da Nobis Deus'* – 'God, give us your light' – repeated the phrase softly, as if it were a prayer. If only she could find a God like Isobel's, a kindly God who would bring light to all the mystery – the mystery of her birth, the mystery over Nice.

'Right,' said Christopher. 'That's the face done – and about time too! It took me seven shots to bring it off.' He laid his brush down, stretched to ease his back. 'No wonder half my colleagues are into geometric abstracts. It saves them a heck of a lot of time – not only all this painting, but the firing too, and maybe a second bloody painting, and then a second firing and . . .'

'Don't you have to fire then, if you haven't painted the glass?'

' 'Course not.' He grimaced at her ignorance. 'The only reason for firing is to fix the paint, rather like a pottery-glaze, make it fuse permanently with the surface of the glass. That's elementary, Rose.'

She crammed a biscuit in her mouth, feeling rebuked and almost cretinous; sat in silence staring at the hash she'd made – not a graceful female foot, but a mess of blots and splodges. At least the silence was a bonus. The cassette had ended with a final anguished death-throe, and the artist hadn't resurrected it as yet. He was finishing his coffee, which was now scummy, with a skin on top. He picked out a small biscuit, started crumbling it to pieces, as if its only function was to give his restless hands a task while their owner took a minute's break, allowed himself to talk.

'Actually, painted glass is very much out of fashion – has been since the fifties. I regret that, in a way. You can add much more depth and detail if you paint it, and a whole range of different textures. But all the Young Turks nowadays are churning out acres of glorified leaded lights, and I suspect they're sometimes simply tempted by the fact that it's so much quicker, not to mention cheaper – obviously, since it cuts out two whole processes.' He removed a moustache of coffee from his lip, swallowed the last mouthful with a frown.

'What's even worse, in my view, is the way they just design their windows or whatever, then hand them over to be cartooned and cut and finished in some bloody great factory of a studio, instead of doing all the work themselves. There's this famous place in Germany – infamous, I'd say – which is always touting for new work. I chuck their letters straight into the bin. Why call yourself an artist and a craftsman, if you can't be bothered with the art and craft, but just delegate to a bunch of Krauts, who'll make a slavish copy of your sketch, but won't add those tiny changes which are the life-blood of the thing?' He gestured with his teaspoon to the workbench. 'Even now, I'm making alterations – modifying a colour, re-drawing a nostril or an eye – and when I come to do the matting, I'll be making individual decisions on almost every piece of glass – how much paint to keep or scrape away; how much texture to create; whether to stipple it, or scratch it, or leave it smooth or . . .'

'You mean, some artists leave all that to someone else?'

'Oh, yes, increasingly – if they bother to paint at all. I suppose it's a bit like the old Victorian trade-firms, when all the different processes were done by different people. It got so specialised in the largest of the studios that some chaps painted only feet, or only hands, or only flowers or borders. I'm naïve enough to think that any artist worth the name should carry out each stage himself. That way, the finished window ends up alive and personal.' He pushed his cup away, stubbed out his cigarette. 'I'm talking far too much. We've got work to do.'

You have, she thought enviously, wishing they could take a longer break, talk not about pernicious German studios, but about themselves – their Christmases, their future. If he hadn't taken Anne with him to France, perhaps that meant the marriage was a dud, so she'd no longer have to worry about betrayal and deceit, and could sleep with him again. His mind was so much on his work, but hers was on his body – the little she could see of it: the V of flesh closed off by his shirt-buttons, the coarse hairs on his wrists, his tanned and nervy hands. Those hands were so involved, with the paint again, the brush again, and she craved them for herself; longed to feel their warmth against her breasts, the cunning fingers tracing not an angel's neck, but the slow curve of her hip. He seemed to be almost flirting with the brush, coaxing it, seducing it, giving it his full attention, all his tenderness, devotion. She'd been pushed aside, back in her own corner, so she wouldn't interrupt that eager twosome. What would happen later, when he was forced to stop his work because the light had dwindled and dusk about to fall? Would she have his hands herself then, another kiss, perhaps, or would he shun her cold-germs and return to healthy Anne?

She was almost glad to hear the phone ring, pounced on it

immediately. It might distract her from her anxious circling thoughts. 'It's for you,' she said dejectedly, slouching back to Christopher.

'I'm busy.'

'I know. I told her that, but she . . .'

'"She"'! Who's "she"? I've told you several times before, ask for people's names.'

'I did.'

'*And?*'

'She didn't answer, said you'd . . .'

'Okay, hand it over.'

She listened to his voice change, the first brief and barked 'hello' mellowing to intimacy as he reclined back in his chair, kept nodding, smiling, emitting exclamations. He had told her he was busy, yet here he was, enthralled by some long saga, now on his feet and weaving round the room. Portable phones were made for men like Christopher, who could work off excess energy while chatting to their strings of fancy females. It also meant he could frustrate her curiosity by wandering out of the studio and continuing the conversation in the kitchen or the firing-room, where she couldn't listen in. He was almost through the door, though he didn't close it – strangely – so she could still hear his lively voice, his animated laugh. He'd been crotchety with her, hadn't even deigned to smile, let alone reward her with that delighted husky chuckle. Was this the woman he'd whisked away to France – some famous painter, sculptor, who was also wonderful in bed?

She skidded to the door, banged it shut herself. She mustn't be so paranoid, turn every casual caller into Mrs Harville-Shaw the Fourth. It could be a prospective client, someone he was flattering in the hope of an important new commission, or a client's wife who had to be kept sweet. She sat down at his workbench, admiring the blue face, which he had totally transformed. It was no longer blank and featureless, but had a deep expressive eye, a sensuous mouth, half-open, as if about to sing, or weep. She could recognise herself in it – Rose immortalised. She must concentrate on that, on the fact that he'd employed her as his model, engaged her as his helpmate, still needed her around.

She bent a little closer, to examine the detail of the brush-strokes, then shrank back anxiously. One of her long hairs had fallen right across the Angel's eye. She blew on it, to shift it, but it refused to budge at all, appeared to be caught in the fine grains of the paint. Impossible to leave it there. The artist would start cursing, make the atmosphere between them even more inflammable, yet if she tried to pick it up, she might smudge the painted face. She held her breath, used the very tips of her fingers to try to tweeze it up, managed to get hold of it, remove it from the glass. Relief gave place to horror as she realised she had left a tiny scratch – must have nicked the surface with her fingernail, disturbed the fragile paint.

She whipped up to her feet, and over to the glass-screens, pretended to be busy, deep in concentration. She had heard the artist breezing through the door.

'What are you doing, Rose?'

'J . . . just taking down some more glass for you to paint.'

'Good girl! That's what I call initiative. I'd like the chest bit next, please, and the top part of the wing.' He replaced the phone in its cradle, then went back to his workbench, examining his palette, remoistening the paint. He rinsed his brush, sat waiting, watching Jane impatiently as she dithered by the screens. 'Get a move on, Rose. I haven't got all night.'

'Coming,' she said frantically, trying to detach the fiddly glass-shapes with an oyster-knife, her hands so tense and clumsy she was terrified she'd break a piece, ruin something else.

'What's wrong with you today?' he asked, tapping out a descant with his brush. 'You're not yourself at all. Why don't you spend the day in bed? You've got a lousy cold, and a bit of rest would probably do you good. Go and put your head down, and I'll bring you up some hot soup later on.'

Don't be kind, she prayed. It'll only make it worse. 'No, I . . . I'd rather stay and help.'

'There's very little to do. To be perfectly honest, it's probably almost easier if I . . . Hell's teeth! What's happened here? How in God's name did that scratch appear? Rose, have you been messing about with this?'

'Well, no – yes – I only . . .'

'Christ All-bloody-mighty! Can't I leave you for a second without you bungling something? I had the devil of a job working on that face, and now you've mucked the whole thing up.'

'I'm sorry.'

'It's no good being sorry. That won't put it right. You can't retouch unfired paint – which means I'll have to wipe it off and do the bloody thing all over again. And we're pushed for time as it is.'

'You shouldn't have gone away, then.'

'*What* did you say?' He lunged towards her, caught her by the shoulder.

'Nothing.' Her shoulder twinged and scalded underneath his grip,

271

her whole body hot and feverish, as if her trifling cold had exploded into fever.

'Rose, it's none of your fucking business whether I go away or not.'

'It *is* my business. And I hate you swearing at me and . . . and telling all those lies. Okay, I've spoilt your precious Angel's face, and I'm sorry, really sorry – I can't apologise enough – but you've spoilt things as well, ruined them, in fact. I can't bear it when you lie to me, so I've no idea what's going on, and everything's a mystery. It's always been like that – people pulling the wool over my eyes, imagining I won't find out, until some stupid sozzled Uncle Peter starts letting out the secrets and . . .' She broke off in confusion, hardly aware what she was saying, then jerked out from his grasp and stumbled to the door. 'I'm leaving anyway. I'm no use here – you told me so yourself – so find another girl to help, that one you took to Nice, for instance. I'm sure she'd be less bungling.' She spat out his own word, ripped her paint-splashed apron off, then slammed the door behind her.

20

Jane paused a moment on her bike, to mop her nose and eyes. It was madness to be out in such bitter winter weather, with a stinking cold and no coat or scarf or gloves, but her only thought when she'd run out on the artist had been to escape as quickly as she could, put miles and miles between them. She blew on her numb fingers, tried to slap them back to life. She couldn't simply cycle on for ever, with no goal in sight, no idea where she was going. Her instinct was to hurtle straight to Isobel's, but Hadley would be there. He'd flown back last night from Paris, and had already phoned, suggesting that they meet. She had tried to sound more stuffed up than she was, added a cough and a sore throat to her other (genuine) symptoms. But no cold would last indefinitely, and eventually she'd need a new excuse, some reason why she couldn't – wouldn't – sleep with him.

She pedalled on wretchedly, eyes watering in the wind; too cut up about the artist to spend more time on Hadley. If only she were back in Shrepton, with all her friends around her – Helen, Sarah, Rita, Sue – girls of her own age and background, whom she could confide in, open up to. Was she crazy to have left them, made herself so solitary, a runaway, a stray? There were so many things she missed about her home, and it had been worse these last two weeks, when she'd felt a refugee, mooching round at Isobel's because there was nowhere else to go. Yet when her mother had come on the phone, not weeping like her father, but insisting that they drive straight down to fetch her, and could she let them know exactly where she was, some warning-bell had sounded in her head and she'd refused to tell them; said she couldn't leave her job quite yet, was still confused about coming home and needed far more time to think it out. She had really feared the clash of her two worlds, her parents' disapproval of the person she'd become.

She slowed again, glanced behind her, now hoping quite irrationally that Christopher's sleek car would come purring up to rescue her; that he'd drive her back to the studio, take her up to bed. She dithered at a signpost, realised if she turned right there, she would be on the road to Adrian's.

'*Lucem Tuam Da Nobis Deus*'. The words chimed in her head again. Adrian had a chapel and a God. He was single, unentangled, kindly, a true Christian – and still desperate for a cleaner. He'd told Isobel at the private view that his latest Irish 'treasure' had walked off with the fish-knives. She could offer him her services instead, keep quiet about the row, but simply say she hadn't much to do while Christopher was painting, so it would help them all if he could employ her for a week or two. Suddenly, the bike seemed lighter, the weather not so cruel. At least she had a refuge and a plan.

She was sweating by the time she reached his house. It was much further than she realised, with more puffing gruelling hills. The heat seemed overwhelming when she entered the front hall: three radiators sweltering, and a real coal fire panting in the majestic marble grate. Nick had let her in – the man who looked like Keats, whom she remembered from her first visit. He also remembered her, flashed her a Keatsian smile, which spread from his full mouth to his spirited dark eyes.

'Adrian's busy at the moment, with a client. Can you wait?'

'Yes, 'course.'

'Park yourself on that sofa there. Or if you fancy a quick dip, the pool's just down the corridor.' He gave a dramatic stagey shiver. 'I wouldn't recommend it. We're all so busy here, no one's used it for an age, or even turned the heating on, and it's probably got ice on top by now.'

'No thanks! I'd like to see the glass, though. D'you think Adrian would object if I took a quick look round?'

'I'm sure he'd be delighted.' Nick was juggling with the letters he was holding, then shuffling them, like cards. 'He'll be tied up for a good half-hour, so there's no rush – take your time. I'll come and fetch you when his client's left.'

She wandered down the passage, still furious with Christopher, yet tempted by his glass. She had never seen the panels finished and installed. He had planned to take her with him the first day of the fixing, maybe let her watch awhile on several subsequent days, as part of her training in the various stages of stained glass, but she'd never gone at all, in fact. It had been very close to Christmas, and the artist was het up, getting really jittery that the job would not be finished before he left for France. Then the chief glazier, Big Joe –

whom he trusted and respected – had phoned to say he'd gone down with pharyngitis and would have to send a substitute. Christopher had blown his top, turned on her as well when she tried to put a word in, told her not to waste her breath when she didn't understand the problems. A less experienced glazier might handle a panel carelessly, or even line them up wrong, and with the 'bloody fucking rain' on top of everything, he doubted they could start the job at all, let alone complete it in well under a week.

She had escaped to the Mackenzies', offended by his language. Isobel had hugged her, tried to calm her down. He was always in a state, she claimed, when any major work of his was due to be installed; always feared the worst – that he'd somehow got the scale wrong, or had measured incorrectly, so that the panels wouldn't fit. He was a perfectionist, said Isobel, who criticised himself even more harshly than the glaziers; picked on tiny footling faults which no one else would notice – a nose was overpainted, or a fleck of red too bright. She had let herself be comforted, but decided none the less to keep away; simply listened to the hassles, as Christopher reported them – the uncertainty of working with aluminium glazing-bars, the continuing heavy rain, the surliness of Big Joe's callow stand-in.

Christmas brought its own problems, submerged the whole kerfuffle, switched her thoughts from Adrian's house to that villa in the South of France. But now she was experiencing the artist's fears herself, as she stopped outside the leisure-centre, hand nervous on the doorknob. Supposing he was right, and the panels looked a mess? That might well explain why he'd been so brusque and stroppy. Perhaps he'd spent his Christmas not cavorting with wild females, but brooding over failure.

She pushed the heavy door, bewildered for a second by the total striking change in the whole impact of the room. The plain glass wall behind the pool had been replaced by whorls of colour; Adrian's bare and wintry garden no longer even visible, but overlaid by exotic scarlet birds – birds plunging, soaring, spiralling, wrestling with each other in a dance of love or war. She knew those birds so well, had shared the studio with them, studied them a hundred times on Christopher's design. Yet now they'd been translated from a small-scale paper sketch and from unfinished separate panels to a full-fledged panorama, and the effect was shattering. Leisure-centre was no longer the right word. The whole room was busy, agitated, goaded to a frenzy. It looked bigger, somehow, yet also felt confining, as if she were trapped with those oppressive birds, their jagged beaks and talons menacing her personally. The colours seemed alive –

aching purples, strutting reds, frisky crowing yellows, so delighted with themselves that they'd flung their bold reflections on the water, and she could admire them in the pool as well, upside-down and quivering.

She took a few steps forward, so she could look more closely at the leads, try to grasp the way he'd used them – to give an added sense of urgency and movement. Those around the birds were all swooping down diagonally, to suggest flight, or gusts of wind. You never saw that in medieval glass, which used the leads more strictly to outline shapes and figures, not expressively, as he did. She walked right up to the glass, touched a feathered head, ran her finger round an eye-socket, traced a gaping beak. She couldn't get away from him, despite the fact she'd just stalked out; all the things he told her vibrating in her head; his skills licking at her fury and thawing it, like ice.

'Rose!' Nick hollered, bounding through the door. 'I've been calling till I'm hoarse.'

She whirled round in confusion, had totally forgotten Nick, lost all sense of why she'd come to Adrian's. Even now, she couldn't leave the birds, kept gazing at the panels as she backed away reluctantly; asked Nick what he thought of them.

'Pretty wild!' he grinned, though he wasn't even looking. Probably no one in this house had paid true homage to them, or really under-stood how much skill and effort they had cost, or how Christopher's own energy had sparked that swirling movement in the glass. They were just another acquisition, more icing on the cake.

'Now, about this cleaning job,' said Nick. 'I've had a word with Adrian and he says he's thrilled that Santa's sent you. Apparently, he wrote a note to Santa Claus, asking for a cleaner, and got a Maserati instead, but he's glad to know that Santa's sorted out his priorities, at last.' Nick jingled his loose change, to accompany his laugh. 'Could you hoover the whole place, Rose, not just the offices, but the top two floors as well? Adrian says they've not been touched for weeks.'

She nodded, chewed her thumb. Did she even want the job now, or should she gallop back to Christopher, tell him how she loved the birds, how thrilled she was, how . . . ? No. He'd probably still be tetchy, refuse to listen, or fling her own words back at her – she was leaving, so he understood, and had advised him to employ another woman. Safer to wait till he'd left for home himself. Then she could creep back to the studio in peace, spend the evening deciding what to do. Meanwhile, a bit of hoovering would help – mop up her spare energies, stop her fretting over Nice – and other women.

'Have a word with Sally first. She'll show you all the cleaning gear. If you go along that passage, her office is the third door on the right. Okay? See you later.'

She returned Nick's jaunty wave, then crept along the passage, embarrassed by her cold. She shouldn't really spread her germs, especially in an office full of vital people who probably couldn't afford to be off sick. She had better ring her leper's bell, warn Sally and the others to keep a cautious distance. She paused outside the first door on the right, could hear Adrian talking on the phone, his voice far more decisive than it was in conversation. She peeked in as she passed, saw Aubrey sitting on the desk, swilling back a Coke, and dressed in the same canary-yellow waistcoat he'd been wearing at the private view. Did he work here now, she wondered, or simply follow Adrian like a fond and faithful dog? She shrugged, walked on. What was it to her that Adrian had a boyfriend? The grown-up world was like that – nothing what it seemed. She'd get used to it in time.

She knocked on Sally's door, explained her presence, explained about her cold.

'Don't worry. I've got a stinker too, Rob's gone down with flu, and Adrian's top client has landed up in hospital with a very nasty case of glandular fever. Your germs will hardly count, Rose.' Sally pushed back her fair hair, which was now an exotic shade of platinum, and looking even brighter against her sultry black crêpe top. 'How are you otherwise? Did you have a decent Christmas?'

'Pretty good,' she lied, 'How about you?'

'Terrific! I spent Christmas Day and Boxing Day just lazing, then I went to Lanzarote with my boyfriend, and he bought me this really fabulous ring. I've also got a new company car – a BMW convertible. It's out of this world. Here, come and take a look at it before you get stuck in to the hoovering. I'm showing it off to everyone.' She gestured to the window, pointed out a stylish silver car. 'Isn't it fantastic?'

Jane joined her at the window, too surprised to speak. The car she was admiring was the one she'd thought was Anne's. The registration was the same, as well as just the colour and the shape. She had remembered it distinctly because the last three letters were her father's initials, A.R.N. Anne and Sally must be friends, and if they'd both been home on Christmas Day, perhaps they'd got together for a drink or cup of tea. Christopher had told her that he and Anne had known Adrian for years, so Sally could have met Anne here, or at one of Adrian's parties. Anyway, in this cosy part of Sussex, everyone knew everyone else – Isobel, for instance, with bosom friends all round her, neighbours popping in, and a network of acquaintances stretching ten or twenty miles. She suddenly felt lonely, a strange creature like a wyvern – which she'd seen in a heraldic window – who didn't have a mate, didn't belong in any habitat, and would be labelled an enigma and an outcast.

'You haven't said a word, Rose. Aren't you into cars?'

She turned back from the window, tried to put some gusto in her voice. 'Well, I don't know much about them, but yours looks really great. And a bit faster than my 1950s bike.'

'You bet! Tell you what, when we break for lunch, why don't we take a run in it, go up to the pub, and put it through its paces on the bypass?'

'Great!' said Jane, meaning it this time. If Anne and Sally were friends, she could spend the lunch-hour not just trying out a swanky BMW, but solving a few mysteries. She must steer the conversation back to Christmas, listen very carefully to see if Nice was mentioned.

'I'd better get a move on, then. It's not that long till lunch, and I've got three whole floors to clean.'

Sally smoothed an eyebrow with her pen. 'We'll have our lunch latish, if you like, then you can do the offices while the others are all out. It makes it so much easier. Start with the first floor, Rose. It's mainly empty rooms up there, apart from Adrian's bedroom and the bathroom. Come with me and I'll show you the glory-hole where we keep the hoover and the mops and stuff.'

Jane lugged the hoover up the curving wooden staircase. She'd become quite an expert char in just the last few days, though there was more sense of satisfaction in sprucing up a Jacobean manor house than in de-cobwebbing a barn. She always felt that Adrian's stately mansion needed a devoted slave or nanny, somehow permanent, full-time, who cared passionately about it; would keep the parquet shining and the panelling well-polished, and have time to fuss with brass and flowers and silver.

The first floor seemed conspicuously bare, compared with the opulence downstairs; no paintings on the walls, or antique furniture; and Adrian's bedroom in particular looked spartan in its simplicity. She was touched by that in one way: the sturdy single bed and ancient wardrobe, the rough-hewn wooden crucifix hanging on the wall. This was Adrian the monk, compared with Adrian the financial speculator. Perhaps his house and treasures – and even his stained glass – were simply business assets, bought to impress his clients, provide an appropriate setting for bankers, brokers, millionaires, whereas the real and private Adrian preferred things plain and simple.

She plugged in the hoover, lined up Jif and Ajax on the windowsill. She had better clean as thoroughly as possible, prove she didn't 'bungle' every job she touched. She'd move the bed to start with, vacuum underneath it, as her mother always did. It was difficult to move – an old bed with no castors – and was sticking at the headboard end. She bent down to try to shift it, saw something glinting in the bedsprings; what looked like a gold chain, caught up in a coil of wire. She worked it free, stared in shock at the tiny antique cross with its border of seed pearls – Anne's cross – the one she'd bought the week she was confirmed. She heard Anne's gentle voice, saw her friendly guileless smile. 'I never take it off, except in bed.'

She sank down on the bed herself, the hoovering forgotten. Had Adrian taken Anne to bed; had they lain between these very sheets while the artist was in Nice? Impossible. Anne was older than Adrian, at least a decade older, and had just become a Christian – publicly, officially – wearing crosses round her neck to tell the world she shunned such sins as adultery, deceit. Jane glanced from the gold chain to the large cross on the wall. And Adrian was similarly devout, a self-proclaimed believer who prayed daily in his chapel and had dared criticise the artist for mocking that great Faith of his. The hypocrite! To sleep with Christopher's own wife, then invite him round to dinner and play the role of faithful friend. She lurched towards the wall, slammed her fist against the dying Christ.

'Fool!' she told herself, as she nursed her reddened knuckles. She was overreacting, jumping to conclusions, had no real proof of anything. Anne might have come up to his bedroom just to comb her hair – except the mirror and the dressing-table were nowhere near the bed, and even if her chain had come undone, it would have fallen on the carpet, not got tangled in the bedsprings. It was obvious, wasn't it, that they'd been to bed together, however much she loathed the thought?

She stuffed the chain in her pocket, dragged over to the window, staring out at the bare and shivering trees. It was the hypocrisy she hated, the total sham of people mouthing one thing, but actually behaving quite contrary to their principles, kicking out all sense of trust, all loyalty and openness. Yet wasn't she as bad, deceiving Anne, deceiving Isobel, deceiving even Adrian – posing to the lot of them as an innocent young virgin? And what about her one-night stand with Hadley, the lies she'd told to Christopher to explain her disappearance on that giddy Monday night; all the lies she'd told in general since she'd run away from home? Perhaps lying was simply part of growing up, an adult skill you had to learn, like cooking, driving, typing. She could develop the new skill, try to get an 'A' in it, then take a cynical line, relish her discovery of Anne's affair with Adrian, since it left her free to sleep with Christopher. She could hardly wreck a marriage which was already headed for the scrapheap.

She grabbed her cleaning rags, started attacking all the surfaces, whisking off every trace of dust, climbing on a chair to reach the upper walls, determined to purge and purify the room. She hurtled back downstairs to fetch different cleaners – stronger ones – disinfectants, scourers, heavy cloudy bottles promising to kill every dangerous germ. She moved on to the bathroom, sluiced the basin, scrubbed the floor. Anne had probably gone in there as well, washed herself, prepared herself. Or perhaps she and Adrian had wallowed in the bath together – afterwards, before. She tipped antiseptic into the bath, swabbed down every inch of it, then marched back to the hoover, vacuumed the passage, all the other rooms. She had to restore this house to its former pristine state – an impregnable and spotless house with a chapel at its core; its owner praying on his knees, not bonking in a rumpled sweaty bed.

'Good God, Rose! It smells like Sussex County Hospital up here. Are you trying to put me off my lunch?' Sally tottered on to the landing in high stiletto heels, brandishing her car-keys, buttoning up her coat. 'We'd better get off now. I know I said a late lunch, but Adrian wants me back by half past two. Just leave everything, and you can carry on this afternoon.'

'I can't go out like this. I look a fright.'

'Yes, you can. If you want to put your war-paint on, do it in the car.'

'But I haven't got . . .'

'Borrow mine. Stop fussing. We're only going for a drive, not taking part in Miss United Kingdom.' Sally coaxed the duster from Jane's reluctant hand, then towed her down the stairs. 'I only hope Adrian hasn't nicked the car ahead of us. He seems to have taken quite a fancy to it, despite the fact he's just swapped his Aston Martin for a Maserati coupé. Crazy, isn't it? He buys the thing for me, then hogs it himself. He used it over Christmas, wasn't going to tell me, but he scratched the paint quite badly, so he had to own up. I was livid, I can tell you, but I couldn't really say anything, when he'd been decent enough to get it in the first place.'

Jane stood stock-still on the stairs. Things were slotting into place, perfectly, revoltingly. It wasn't Sally who had called on Anne for a drink on Christmas Day, but Adrian in Sally's car. Anne hadn't gone to Nice because she preferred to stay at home and entertain her lover – in the marriage-bed, this time. Maybe Adrian was the one who had persuaded Anne to be confirmed, so they'd have a little more in common, could swap prayers and crosses, as well as beds and bodies.

'What's wrong, Rose? You look awful.'

'I . . . I'm feeling a bit weird.'

'Sit down for a moment. You've probably overdone it, with that rotten cold and everything.'

'No, I need the loo.' She dived along the passage and out through the front door, grabbed her bike, started pedalling furiously, before Sally could realise she wasn't in the lavatory. She didn't want a BMW speeding in pursuit of her; had to see the artist, had to pour things out to him – the whole tangled hopeless mess; all her fears, disgust and misery – had to share them with him, even if it ended in some disastrous explosion.

She burst in at the door, hair tangled round her shoulders, cheeks flaming from the wind, nose running like an urchin's, right into her mouth. She wiped it with her hand, slumped against the wall. Christopher was tracing still, the brush poised in his hand, the feathers on the Angel's wing exquisitely defined. All the time that she'd been agonising, struggling with the hills, the cold, the turmoil in her mind, he'd been quietly painting, worshipping the god of Art. He didn't seem the slightest bit upset that she'd flounced out in a fury, calling him a liar and threatening never to return, but was standing there serenely, continuing with his work.

Slowly, he looked up, raised one ironic eyebrow. 'Back already?'

The storm of words raging in her head dwindled to a feeble mocking breeze. The vital things she'd planned to say seemed futile now, hysterical. 'I . . . I need to talk to you,' she stammered out half-heartedly.

'I don't think now's the time, do you? You're unwell and over-wrought, and I need all my concentration for my work.'

'I'm not unwell. I've only got a cold. And it's never the right time. You've been away for ages, and now you're trying to shut me up.' She could hear her voice rising – the storm again, and perhaps a highly dangerous one – a squalling hurricane which could strike down Anne and Adrian, if she let rip with raging words. She gripped the workbench, hard, trying to ground herself, control herself, by hanging on to something strong and solid. 'Listen, I think we ought to . . .'

They both swung round as someone hammered on the window-pane behind them. Jane glimpsed an orange sweatshirt, a thatch of gingery hair, shrank back in confusion.

'Can you let me in?' yelled Hadley. 'I couldn't find the bell, and I've brought some food and drink and stuff.'

Christopher rinsed his brush in water, flicked it dry; angry droplets spattering the floor. 'Will you kindly tell your impetuous young friend that this is my private workplace and not a public restaurant.'

Jane dashed to the front door, suddenly aware that she must smell of disinfectant, had paint-stains on her jersey, and a crust of mud hemming her old jeans. 'Hadley, look, we're working. You can't . . .'

'But you told me you were ill – too bad to move at all, you said. Mum was really worried. She's out herself, visiting some poor old gent in hospital, but she sent me round with this lot.' He plonked his basket down, a large old-fashioned wicker one, which held two covered Pyrex dishes and a tartan Thermos flask. 'That's camomile and whatsit,' he said, pointing to the flask. 'She made it for you specially, says it's marvellous for sore throats.'

'But I haven't got a . . .' Jane bit the words back quickly, had told Hadley just last night that every time she swallowed, it felt like broken glass. 'That's . . . er . . . very kind. Thank you.'

Hadley grabbed her hand. 'You don't have to sound so formal. I was jolly glad to have the chance to see you. I've missed you fearfully, you know, thought about you every single day – and night. You did get all my postcards?'

'Yes.' She disengaged the hand, praying Christopher wouldn't join them at the door.

'I wish you'd written back.'

She glanced nervously behind her. 'I . . . I didn't think a letter would get to you in time. Aren't the posts a bit fouled-up in France?'

Hadley shook his head, reached across to touch her hair. 'Far better than they are in Merry England. After all, you got my six, didn't you?' He twined a lock of hair between his fingers. 'I think I'll cut this strand off and wear it in my helmet like a plume. Then, when I fight for you in the lists, I'll win every single tournament, and you'll reward me with your favours.' He tried to demonstrate the favours, drew her closer, both hands round her waist.

She stepped away so swiftly, she banged her elbow on the wall. 'Ssh! Christopher will hear us.'

'What's he doing?'

'Working. In fact, I really ought to . . .'

'Great! I'd love to watch. I've heard so much from Mum about this famous studio, I've got to see the place in action, so to speak.'

'He can't stand being watched, especially now. He's bang in the middle of some really tricky painting.'

'I won't disturb him, honestly. I'll only be a jiff. By the way, where d'you want this food put?' He seized the basket, the two dishes rattling wildly as he swung it. 'Mum said you had a kitchen here, so if you could point me in the direction of the fridge . . .' He was already streaking past her, right into the studio, halted by the workbench where Christopher was painting, peered across his shoulder. 'Gosh! That's fascinating. I've never seen stained glass close up. It looks completely different, as if it's been dismembered. Poor Dad! He can't seem to get away from things in bits. What's that brownish stuff? Oh, I see, it's paint. How odd. I always thought the details were somehow engraved on the glass, not painted. And what a funny brush!'

Christopher laid his 'funny' brush down, looked through Hadley as if he wasn't there. 'Rose,' he said, his voice ominously controlled. 'I wonder if you and your friend could find another venue for your party? It's impossible to work with these distractions, and we appear to have had more than our fair share today already.'

Jane shook back her hair, tried to keep her own voice calm and pleasant. 'It's all right, Hadley's going. He . . . he only came to bring this food from Isobel.'

'The fridge is full of food. I brought back cheese from France, and several different pâtés.'

'No, it's special food for me.'

'What d'you mean, special food? Does Isobel imagine that I starve you, as well as overwork you, so you need your own supplies, extra rations delivered personally at lunch-time?'

Hadley laughed, perched on the workbench, swinging his long legs. 'Actually, that's quite a good idea. Perhaps I could set up a delivery service, earn some money in the vac – a Cordon Bleu rival to lousy Meals on Wheels. Mind you, this lot's pretty vile,' he said, gesturing to the basket. 'Mum made very mushy things on purpose, 'cause Rose can't swallow at the moment.'

'Can't swallow?' Christopher removed himself from both Hadley and his basket, stood by the window, lighting up another cigarette.

'No,' said Hadley, following. 'She's got this rotten flu and a terrible sore throat. We thought she'd be in bed.'

'Couldn't Isobel have phoned me first, to check?'

'She didn't know you were here, told me you were expected back tomorrow. She'll be popping in herself this afternoon.'

Christopher closed in on Rose, exhaled a spurt of smoke. 'I'm not sure what's been happening here during the last fortnight, but I think you know already, Rose, that I discourage casual visitors. I'm not keen on interruptions when I'm working.'

'Hold on a minute, Christopher,' Hadley interjected. 'That's totally unfair. Mum's hardly a casual visitor. Perhaps you've overlooked the fact that she put up all the cash for this damned window. And anyway, I think it's pretty decent of her to bother as she does. Rose said she had a temperature last night, so Mum felt she ought to help, maybe call a doctor.'

Christopher snapped his lighter on, extinguished it again. 'As far as I'm aware, there's nothing wrong with Rose, apart from a slight cold. She appeared to have no trouble swallowing half a dozen biscuits, and she's just been out for a long and bracing bike-ride.' He was still fiddling with his lighter, the tiny flame twitching on and off with an impatient hissing sound. 'In fact, why don't the pair of you get out of my hair, go for another joyride, or eat your mushy picnic somewhere else, and leave me to get on with my "damned window", as you call it.'

He strode back to his workbench, seized the wicker basket and thrust it into Rose's arms. 'I suggest you take your coat this time. I'll see you in the morning – nine o'clock sharp – if you're not too near death's door, that is.'

21

'And so I slept with him, you see – a second time, I mean.'

'And you didn't really want to?' Trish was sprinkling the cut aubergines with salt, then leaving them to sweat in three large colanders.

'No.' Jane flexed her aching hand. She had peeled seven pounds of carrots without a break. 'I know it sounds awful, as if I'm just a slut or something, but I was so mixed up and miserable, and we were in the house alone, and he kept . . . well – sort of groping me, even during lunch, undoing my top buttons and . . . I felt so ill by then, Trish, I think I really did have flu, and I couldn't seem to rustle up the energy to keep saying no, and arguing. And he was so mad-keen and everything, one part of me was rather touched. Or maybe I was just getting back at Christopher. He'd been so cold and distant, you see, and really quite sarcastic, whereas Hadley was all over me.'

'Literally, it seems.'

Jane laughed, half-ashamed. 'I've shocked you, Trish, I bet.'

'Of course you haven't. I suppose I'm simply jealous, in a way. You've got two men, I've got none.'

'Well, I wish you'd take him off me.'

'No fear! I've known Hadley Mackenzie since he was a strapping lad of three. We even shared a bath, once. It removes all the romance if you've sat cross-legged on the carpet watching *Play School* together, and fighting over the peanut-butter sandwiches.'

'I wish *we*'d stuck to that.' Jane coiled a carrot-peeling round and round her finger.

'I wish I could get past it,' Trish rejoined. 'The last guy I went out with sat me down in the living-room, switched on the TV, then went to make the sandwiches, and we had a lovely cosy evening watching

The Big Sleep. The only difference was the sandwiches were ham, not peanut butter.'

'Well, at least he wasn't vegetarian.'

'No – thank heavens. D'you know, the longer I've been working for Green Cuisine, the more I crave good red wicked meat.'

'They're vegans, aren't they, this time?'

Trish nodded. 'Ninety-seven vegan rebirthers, if you can imagine such a thing – all meeting for some weirdo celebration. In fact, we'd better get a move on. Maeve's coming to collect the food at five o'clock sharp, and we've hardly done a thing yet.'

Jane checked her watch, continued with the peeling. 'Vegetarian cooking's quite a con. I used to think it was just rabbit-food and stuff, not all these spinach soufflés and aubergine terrines, which take twice as long as something quick and simple like lamb chops and two veg.'

'Well, at least we're not waitressing tonight.'

'I wish we were. I made fifty pounds on Saturday, including all the tips.'

'Yes, but we weren't in bed till three.'

'I still think it's worth it.'

'So do I.' Trish trickled olive oil into the frying pan, about to fry the aubergines. 'I've saved enough for my holiday already, even upgraded it to Greece, instead of Spain. Why don't you come with us? Easter in Corfu. I can hardly wait!'

Jane shook her head. 'The window's being dedicated on Easter Sunday.'

'You mean, you're still expected to go? Won't it be embarrassing now you've walked out on Christopher?'

'Yes,' she said. 'It will.'

'Don't bother then. Join us in Acharavi. Maeve won't mind. The more the merrier. Her boyfriend's probably coming anyway.'

'I'll see,' Jane mumbled vaguely. Trish could never really fathom how much the window meant to her, how fiercely she missed working on it. Chopping up the vegetables for leek and carrot soup was not quite in the same league as helping to create a deathless Angel. Food was so ephemeral, vanished in an evening, didn't have that heady power to transport you to a different realm, one where Spirits bridged the gulf between earth and boggling heaven, but which sounded total gobbledygook if you tried to put it into words, or explain it to someone down-to-earth like Trish. She couldn't understand now how she had ever scrawled that letter to the artist – an impulsive tetchy letter, saying she thought it would be better if she found some different work, since she didn't have the expertise he required in an assistant. Perhaps she'd simply burned to show she didn't need his job – nor Adrian's, for that matter – was employable elsewhere, not dependent on their charity, or whims.

She was also worried about money, especially when she realised that if she wanted to run off again, escape from Christopher this time, instead of from her parents – run east or west, or even go abroad – she simply wouldn't have the fare. Her life with the artist was so uncertain, insecure. Even the way he paid her made her feel a child – just money in her hand – no slips or cheques or vouchers, no lists of hours spent working or official duties done. She had welcomed it at first, since it saved her paying tax, but now it seemed haphazard, as casual as the job itself. She had hardly saved a penny, had no place of her own, no prospects and no future. She jabbed the peeler in her palm. Was there any more future in preparing vegetables? She hadn't even graduated to making pies or pâtés. Trish did all the fancy cooking, while she scrubbed and peeled and sliced. All the same, she was earning more at Trish's, slaving long hours in the kitchen, or dressing up in her frilly cap and apron, then topping up her piggy-bank each night.

She stared out of the window at the dreary treeless street, then back to the small kitchen with its ugly yellow paint, its turquoise-squiggled lino. The bleak and poky bungalow seemed to hem her in, constrain her, after the high roof of the barn, and she missed the blaze and brilliance of the glass-screens; fretted at the thought that the Resurrection Window was taking shape without her; Christopher alone with it, maybe as hurt and peeved as she was. She had been away ten days now, which meant he would have matted it, be involved in all that business with the badger brush, the stippling brush, the scrubs and sticks and needles. She had read about it in the books, but not seen it in reality, and she jibbed at the exclusion, despite the fact she had brought it on herself.

She hacked a carrot into discs, taking out her anger on the knife. She mustn't keep returning to the studio, had made a wise decision in deciding to come here. It gave her steady work, and was company for Trish, who was living in the house alone while her mother was in hospital, and had jumped at the idea. She couldn't stay at Isobel's with Hadley on vacation, Hadley on the prowl, and it had seemed a merciful escape to live with someone single, quiet and punctual, who was completely unencumbered by relations, sons, lame ducks. Now she was less sure. Trish had been extremely kind, yet she didn't feel at home, disliked the frumpy furnishings in the cramped and dowdy sitting-room; the roar of passing trains which shook her chilly bedroom; found herself thinking back to Isobel's, the artistic vibrant house and peaceful jungly garden, even missing all the chaos and the clutter.

She tipped her carrot-slices into the largest of the bowls, joined Trish at the hob. 'Shall we invite Isobel for supper here one evening? I'd like to pay her back for all her hospitality. I'll do the cooking and you can put your feet up.'

'But won't she bring Hadley? I thought you were trying to avoid him.'

'No,' she said, then 'Yes. He buzzed off back to college at least three days ago.'

Trish was silent for a moment, stirred her sizzling aubergines. 'I wish you'd told me earlier – about your sleeping with him.'

Jane flushed. 'I'm sorry, Trish.'

'I mean, is that the real reason why you came here, just to find a bolt-hole and put thirty miles between you?'

'Of course not.' Jane's flush deepened. 'I was really keen to live with you, get to know you better. I mean, we seemed to hit it off so well, right from our first walk.'

'So why couldn't you have trusted me?'

'I did – I do.'

'Except about Hadley, it appears. When I asked you on Christmas Day if the artist was the only man you'd slept with, you said yes, emphatically.'

Jane trailed back to the table, swept her pile of peelings in the bin. 'I suppose I was ashamed – and . . . and . . .'

'And what?'

'Well, the fact you've known Isobel so long. I mean, I haven't breathed a word to her.'

'And you were scared I'd blurt it out, you mean?'

'No.' Jane paused a moment, wiped her hands. 'If you really want to know, it did cross my mind that you might have had a . . . thing with Hadley yourself.'

'No such luck.'

'But I thought you said . . .' She stared at Trish, who looked away, sagged down at the table.

'Okay. You've caught me out. I suppose I can't complain that you don't trust me, if I keep things back from you.' She pulled roughly at a hangnail on her thumb, her voice tight and slightly bitter. 'I've been mad about Hadley since the age of twelve or so, and he's never shown the slightest sign of interest in me, treated me like his sister, or the girl next door or something.'

'Isobel married the boy next door, remember.' Jane forced a laugh, tried to keep things light.

'Lucky Isobel.'

'Oh, Trish, I'm sorry, honestly. I don't know what to say.'

'Don't say anything. It only makes it worse. I've never admitted this before, but I think the reason why I never warm to other men is just that they're not Hadley – haven't got his hair or eyes or laugh or . . .' She broke off, sat staring at her hands.

Jane pretended to be busy swabbing down the worktops. She had taken Hadley's hair and eyes for granted, been annoyed by his wild laugh the last time they'd been together. She could see him in her mind again, naked in his bedroom; that shock of hair which Trish admired tickling on her neck, those greenish eyes sparking with excitement as he peeled her pants down, stroked her own dark thatch. He *was* good-looking, generous, relaxed, amusing, fun, and now she knew the strength of Trish's feelings for him, she somehow felt uneasy, as if she herself had misjudged him and short-changed him. Wouldn't it actually be better to have a boyfriend her own age, someone unattached, whom she could be seen with in a restaurant without other people smirking or tut-tutting? And, if she were honest with herself, one sneaky shameful part of her had secretly enjoyed the sex, relishing the fact that Hadley seemed so avid for her. It had been so different from the first time, when she'd slumped on Sue's old sofa, feeling, doing nothing; just an automaton, a robot. This time, she'd colluded, returned his frantic kisses, responded to his body, despite the turmoil and confusion in her mind. She'd even found herself whooping silently to Christopher while Hadley slammed on top of her: 'He's forty-two years younger than you, and nearly six foot tall. Any normal girl would regard you as antique, not to mention bloody difficult. It may surprise you, Christopher, but Hadley thinks I'm wonderful.'

She blushed as she recalled the words she had used to Trish just now: 'groping', 'pawing', 'slobber', 'snog'; the way she'd made it obvious that she didn't really care for him; denied the other side, as if she didn't dare admit, even to herself, that she had actually come with Hadley – yes, right at the same moment as his own blazing breathless climax, and just as she was yelling at the artist. She had landed up in bed with him mainly because of Christopher – a crazy way of getting her revenge, and also paying out Adrian and Anne – trying desperately to prove she didn't care a fig about their own affair, and that she herself could be every bit as casual. How unfair to Hadley that seemed now, as cold-blooded as her crass attempt to tell him she didn't want to see him any more – or at least not until she'd sorted out her future: what to do and where to live. Hadley had immediately offered help: had she considered vocational guidance, or going on to college; would she like to see prospectuses, or talk to this old chap he knew who'd been a careers adviser half his life?

'No,' she'd said to all of them, 'I'd like to go to bed – alone.' And she'd padded across the landing to the spare room, locked the door, then crept beneath the covers, pulled the bedspread right across her head. She had cried, in fact, not slept, but it had still been cruel to Hadley.

Trish was sitting tense and hunched, still pulling at her hangnail, her feet hooked round the chair-leg, her face expressionless. Jane cursed herself for prattling. She'd upset her friend, quite clearly – upset everyone. Relationships were like that – embittering, confusing. Perhaps Anne had only gone to bed with Adrian because she, too, was resentful; had found out about her husband and his mistress, and was determined to get even. Which meant that she herself had driven them together. 'Oh, Trish,' she groaned aloud.

'What's wrong?'

'Nothing. Everything. Tell you what, let's finish all this veggie muck, then buy ourselves a huge great steak for supper and a bottle of retsina, and pretend it's Easter in Corfu instead of January in Railway Road.'

'To Easter,' Trish enthused, clinking her glass to Jane's.

'To Easter,' Jane repeated, her thoughts leaping to the window – the Resurrection Angel defying death and winter. She had drawn the thin beige curtains, but was still aware of the soft-footed stealthy snow drifting down outside; the sense of bareness, barrenness, things hibernating, shrinking, in a sleepy sapless limbo. She grimaced at the taste of her Greek wine, tried to counter it with a mouthful of tournedos. 'Fantastic steak!' she said.

'Fantastic wine!' Trish echoed, splashing more into both glasses. 'Let's pig ourselves for once. We'll probably be eating invalid food once Mum returns from hospital – steamed cod and Lucozade.'

Jane put down her fork. 'When's she coming out?'

'Pretty soon. The doctor said next week.'

'Won't she mind my being here?'

' 'Course not. She'll enjoy it. I've told her all about you.'

Jane said nothing, could hardly admit that she wasn't looking

290

forward to the return of Mrs Carter, who was still partially paralysed. Would she be expected to play nursemaid as well as vegetable cook? And would there be room enough for three in the dumpy little bungalow? She gulped her wine, determined not to spoil the evening. They'd worked hard enough for heaven's sake, deserved a celebration. She sneaked a glance in the mirror over the sideboard, wished Christopher could see her in her low-necked black silk blouse, and with her hair in a French pleat. She and Trish had both dressed up, done each other's hair, messed about with blusher, eye-gloss, lipstick; and now outclassed their drab surroundings – too soignée and sophisticated for the all-beige room with its fussy little ornaments marching down the mantelpiece, its fake-coal fire glowing garish-red. She was surprised that Trish hadn't modernised the place, or at least added artistic touches of her own. It seemed very much the home of someone middle-aged and boring, who bought her curtains and her furniture from some cheap mail-order catalogue.

She forked in more tournedos, looked across at Trish's plate, empty now save for a parsley sprig and a smear of Madeira sauce. 'Gosh! You walloped that lot down!'

'I'm sorry. I was ravenous. And I suppose I've got so used to bolting meals, I've forgotten how to eat at a normal leisurely pace. Who's talking, though? You've almost finished yourself.'

Jane laughed, mopping up her own sauce with a piece of crusty bread. 'It's because we had no vegetables.'

'I couldn't face them, could you?'

'No, especially not aubergines. D'you realise, Trish, we've cooked aubergines, in some form or another, every single day since I've been here. They ought to call it Purple Cuisine, not Green.'

'We've got a green pudding, by the way.'

'What, lettuce mousse?'

'No, avocado ice-cream. I made several gallons a month ago, for a rather swanky dinner party; kept back a jarful for myself, and stored it in the freezer.'

'It sounds revolting.' Jane screwed up her face. 'And I don't want pudding anyway. I'd like to sprawl out on that rug with a nice big cup of coffee and a bar of fruit and nut.'

'Will wholenut do? I bought a bar this morning.'

'Trish, you're great! A mind-reader.' She switched on the television, while Trish went to make the coffee, watched the tail-end of the News – a general strike in Bulgaria, a shooting in Armagh. She turned the sound to nothing; was more concerned with Christopher: had he heard any more about his Manchester commission? Was he missing her, annoyed with her? Why couldn't he have written back, cajoled her address from Isobel and told her how he was?

'Coffee up!' Trish announced, returning with a tray. 'Chocolate for you, ice-cream for me, and some Turkish Delight for both of us – left over from Christmas. I also brought you this,' she said, passing Jane a loose-leafed folder with a stiff-backed orange cover.

'What is it?'

'My Life-Story Book. I thought you might be interested. A lot of adopted children make them with their parents. I kept mine up for years. Here, look at me at seven! Wasn't I a podge?'

Jane stretched out on the rug, staring at the photo of a smaller, fatter Trish – the same dark curly hair, the same engaging smile. She leafed back to the beginning of the book – more photographs, and drawings, childish scribbles, letters – Trish as wobbly toddler, Trish as babe-in-arms. 'This is me with my first Mum', was written underneath in a smudgy purple crayon. 'She used to cuddle me.' Jane met the wary eyes of the mother in the picture, a schoolgirl of sixteen or so, with a sullen mouth, a cascade of wavy hair. She wasn't cuddling Trish, rather clutching her uncomfortably, as if frightened she might fall, or fall apart.

'I grew in my Mum's tummy', Trish had printed boldly beside a picture of a baby in the womb – well, more a sort of froglet in a hollow Easter-egg. 'When I was born, I weighed 8lbs 6oz, which is nearly as heavy as three big bags of flour'. The bags were crayoned in underneath, each neatly labelled 'McDougall's flour, self-raising'.

'At two months old, I went to live with Pam and Eric Stokes. Pam got ill, so I moved to Elm Street Children's Home, and stayed there for six months, then moved into The Lees.'

Jane glanced across at Trish, who looked totally absorbed in her ice-cream, scooping it up with a wafer, rather than a spoon. 'I didn't know you'd been in children's homes.'

'Yes, four in eighteen months, then two more sets of foster parents – and all before I was three. It was quite a record, apparently.'

Jane peered down at the book again, studying the photo of the ugly red-brick building which Trish had labelled 'The Lees'; one bare tree standing guard outside it like a thin and shivering sentry. Had she herself been parked in institutions, or passed back and forth like a parcel to feckless foster parents? No. There wouldn't have been time. She remembered her own photo on the mantelpiece at home – a tiny baby in Amy's arms, just a few weeks old. Amy and Alec had saved her from the homes, from constant moves, upheavals.

'What happened to your mother?' she asked, trying to calm the surge of feeling which both photographs had roused.

'Nothing much. I suppose she was too young to land up with a baby. Then she met an older man who wasn't keen on threesomes, so . . .' Trish shrugged. 'It was either him or me. That's partly why we made the book, to keep track of all the changes.' Trish put her dish and wafer down, pointed out a photocopied map of Sussex, Surrey, Hampshire, with two coloured lines meandering across it. 'The social worker suggested that, so I'd understand all the different moves. The red line is my mother's life. She moved eleven times herself, before she was sixteen, so I suppose I can't complain. The blue line's me. You can see I got around a bit.' Trish abandoned her ice-cream, tore the wrappings from the box of Turkish Delight. 'Don't forget your coffee, Jane. It's getting cold.'

Jane ignored the coffee, waved away the sweets. She was magnetised by Trish's book, fighting a strange tangle of jealousy and pity. Trish had facts, however harsh – a family tree, a life-graph, a calendar, a map – all blazoned on these pages, with arrows, captions, pictures, dates. She even had a copy of her birth certificate pasted in the front, with her father's name, her mother's name, her own original surname. However insecure her early life, at least she had a sense of continuity. Trish had never known her father, but there were still solid facts about him, facts she'd written out herself, this time in leaky pen: 'My Dad was tall and slim. His eyes were grey. His hair was dark, like mine. He liked dogs and cats and chocolate'. Jane slammed the book shut suddenly, bit into her own bar, crunching through a hazelnut, as if she was chewing up all mothers, fathers, foster-parents – reducing them to pulp.

'You could make your own book,' Trish was saying. 'Oh, I don't mean literally. It's too late to be drawing pictures of your pet rabbit or your nursery-school. But you could try to get the facts, Jane, or even trace your mother.'

'How can I?' Jane retorted. 'I don't know anything about her. She might be dead for all I know, or in the outback of Australia.' She remembered Angela – Isobel's first child – completely lost, swallowed up in bureaucracy and mystery: no clues, no links at all. 'Once your child's adopted,' Isobel had told her, 'you, as the real mother, are legally erased, might as well be dead and buried.'

'It's not impossible,' Trish observed, picking out a chunk of Turkish Delight. 'There are agencies which help, and something called a National Contact Register. It's much easier now than it used to be. You could see it as a challenge, a sort of New Year resolution.

By next New Year, you might have tracked her down, or have just spent Christmas with her. And even if it takes much longer, I still think it's worthwhile. I mean, it's yourself you're searching for – your whole origins and background. And it's not as if you're tied, Jane, by a houseful of young children, or some job which chains you down. You're free to go wherever you want – well, maybe not to the outback of Australia, but I doubt your mother's there.'

Jane licked chocolate off her fingers, edged away a little from the fierce heat of the fire. She *was* tied in a way, tied to Christopher; should be back there, working on his window. She had watched it grow from initial sketch through cartooning, cutting, painting, and had now severed the relationship before it was completed. She envied Trish her sense of continuity, yet had chucked away her chance of something similar. Of course, a life was much more complex than a window, and she had only known the artist less than three brief months, but, all the same, if she hadn't left the studio, she would have had the opportunity to work on other windows, see them through, right from their conception to their final dedication.

'I had quite a bit of aggro myself,' Trish admitted, brushing off the icing sugar which snowed her emerald skirt. 'I hadn't seen my "born-to mother", as the social workers call them, since I was an infant of eight weeks. She was single when she had me, but then she married twice, and divorced twice, and moved all over the place. It took me six months of detective work, before I met up with her last year.'

'And did she welcome you with open arms?'

'No.' Trish paused a moment, to let a train roar past. 'I turned up at this dingy pub in Basingstoke at ten to one instead of one o'clock, and she told me I was early. Early, after twenty years! Actually, I think I caught her out. She was smooching with some man, who slunk away immediately, as if he'd no right to be there. It was quite a shock to see her. I knew she was only thirty-six, and I'd always had that photo of her, so I imagined her as young and pretty, but she looked quite old and ill, in fact. Her hair had gone all stringy, and had started to turn grey already, and she chain-smoked the whole lunch-hour, which somehow seemed all wrong. Mum and Dad had never smoked, and had never gone to pubs, so I felt sort of torn between them, and terribly embarrassed, especially when I realised she had a slightly Cockney accent, so my own voice sounded rather posh and snobby, as if I was trying to show her up.'

Trish wiped her sticky hands, took a sip of coffee. 'And then she made it pretty clear she didn't want to keep in touch. She'd just married number three – a man ten years younger this time – and I suppose it would have ruined things entirely for a daughter to turn up like a rabbit from a hat, only six years younger than her husband.' Trish hunched her knees up, nursed them with her arms. 'I wasn't sure whether the man I'd seen was her husband or some boyfriend. But she told me if the guy came back, she'd introduce me as a new employee who'd just started at her office. That was almost the worst part. It really hurt, you know.'

Jane crumpled up her chocolate wrapper, flung it in the bin. 'And you're trying to encourage me to go through all that aggro. No thanks! I'd rather live with my fantasies.' Anne's face was suddenly smiling in her head, as if she'd pasted it in her own Life-Story Book and labelled it 'My first Mum'. She tried to shift the picture, blank it out, negate it.

'It might not be as bad for you. And anyway, I'm still glad I went, in spite of everything.'

'How can you be? It sounds quite vile. And it's more or less asking for rejection. I mean, if they didn't want us when we were born, why should they want us now?'

'Lots of reasons. I've known people have these really great reunions, or find whole new families when they were thirty-five or forty – brothers, sisters, grandmas, aunts. It's changed their life, transformed it.'

'Well, it didn't transform yours.'

'No.' Trish spread her hands, as if giving up her mother, her whole extended family, letting them go free. 'But it still helped, you know, laid a lot of fears to rest. And it made my mother real, which is vitally important. After all, she . . .'

Jane thrust the book into Trish's arms, cutting off the sentence. Trish was so damned cheerful, so positive, accepting. All those treacly smiles beaming from the photographs, denying all the traumas of her babyhood. It was inhuman in a way to be so placid and unfeeling. She was still babbling on about that pathetic hopeless mother, who had kicked her out twice over.

'You see, she told me about her own life, Jane, so I could sympathise much more. She'd had such a ghastly time herself, I couldn't really blame her.'

'Well, I would. I'd chop her into pieces.'

'Don't say that. It's horrid.'

'I'll say what I like.'

'Look, I still feel something for her. I don't want you attacking her.'

295

'She needs attacking. Stupid bitch! Fancy a mother disowning her own daughter.'

'She's not a bitch. I . . . love her, if you really want to know.'

'Then you must be soft in the head. If she was *my* mother, I'd kill her.'

Trish shot up from the rug, lashing out at Jane, pummelling her and kicking, clawing with her nails. Jane fought back, butting with her head until she had brought Trish to the floor, falling spreadeagled on top of her. She could smell the dirty carpet – a smell of cat and sweaty feet; feel its scratchy pile grazing her hot cheeks as Trish forced her over and sat astride her back. She bucked like a wild horse until she'd thrown Trish off, then clutched out at her skirt to prevent her from escaping. She heard the fabric tear, clung on doggedly, but Trish hit out again, then grabbed a fistful of her hair and almost pulled it from the roots.

'Get off,' yelled Jane. 'You brute!'

Trish suddenly let go, rocked back on her heels with her arms around her body, as if protecting it from any new attack. A bruise was already swelling on her leg, the skin puffing up around it, angry and inflamed. She was breathing very heavily, her voice shaky and accusing as she spewed out fractured words. 'I've never shown my book to anyone before. I . . . I only let you see it because I thought it might help, but now you've ruined everything.' She touched the hole in her green skirt, her fingers moving through it to the stockinged leg beneath. 'Don't think you're the only one who . . . who's . . . I mean, just because I don't go round wailing all the time . . . Oh, forget it. What's the use? You'll never understand.' She seized her book, stumbled to the door, tripping on the carpet, staggering like a drunk. Jane followed, tried to stop her, but Trish shook her roughly off, bolted down the passage to her room.

Jane listened to the door slam, the key turn in the lock, then limped back to the sitting-room, hid herself in the largest of the chairs, curling up to nothing like a foetus. The television was still playing to itself, a smiling man and woman sitting down to dinner in a restaurant. You couldn't trust a smile. It might be fixed with Sellotape, to hide a running wound, or switched on for the grown-ups, to kid them all was fine. The Trish she'd called unfeeling and inhuman must have stockpiled smiles like gas-masks in a war.

She should have done the same herself, worn a smiling mask, and never let it slip, whatever the provocation. She had taunted Trish and lost her as a friend, turned her into a dangerous snarling animal. There was hardly a relationship she hadn't overturned. She'd walked out on her parents, walked out on the artist, messed up things with Hadley, and now picked a fight with someone who could have been a sister – and all because she couldn't keep her mouth shut. She clutched the chair-arm, relieved to feel it firm beneath her hand. Nothing else was solid. There seemed to be a deep black hole in the centre of her body, as if all her organs and intestines had shrivelled up and atrophied, leaving only pain.

She switched the lights off, locked the house up, then trailed along the passage to her room, pausing for a moment outside Trish's door. Should she knock, try to have a word with her, tell her she was sorry, and did truly understand? No. The words might come out wrong, and she dared not face another brawl when she was still shaking from the first one. She slipped in to her own room, scrubbed her make-up off, exchanged her slinky skirt and blouse for a pair of old pyjamas; tugged the hairpins from her hair and brushed it straight and free. Safer to be a child, the sort of placid easy child mothers loved and wanted – the kind she'd never been.

She paced the tiny room, up and down, up and down, from door to wall, and back again. Was Trish asleep, she wondered, or equally upset? How would they ever face each other, heal the broken night, sit down to cheerful morning with tea and Sugar Puffs? Maybe Trish would not appear, just leave a frigid note, telling her to leave. She couldn't leave, had nowhere else to go. It was only early February – the whole bleak year stretching on indefinitely. She fumbled in the bedside drawer for the stiff-backed diary she'd been given as a Christmas present. She had written almost nothing in it yet, apart from 'Christopher comes back' on January 4, and 'Start work studio', on January 6. She had lost heart after that, couldn't be bothered to record the dates and details of Green Cuisine conferences or vegetarian dinner parties. But without those there'd be nothing, just an infinity of empty days, all lacking point and purpose.

She climbed between the chilly sheets, slumped against the pillow. She'd never sleep, but her body ached and throbbed, and she couldn't spend the whole night on her feet. She leafed on through the diary, every page a blank. Better to go back – back not just months, but decades. She turned to the front page, crossed out the year printed in the centre, and substituted '1974'; then flicked on to mid-April and wrote laboriously in what she'd used to call her joined-up writing: 'I grew in my Mum's tummy'. She drew the froglet in the Easter-egg, though it came out like a tadpole in a pond, then kept riffling through the pages until she came to 5 October. 'When I was born', she wrote a little smaller, underneath that date, 'I weighed 6lbs 2oz, which is slightly more than two big bags of flour'. She pencilled in the flour-bags, added two neat labels: 'Spiller's Homepride, Plain'. Amy had given her the figure of 6lbs – the only solid fact she had, though it could have been invention, she'd realised since her eighteenth birthday party. She turned the page, picked up a different pen and wrote along the bottom: 'This is my first Mum. She used to cuddle me'.

She sat staring at the blank white sheet of paper, empty save for days and dates; 'Columbus Day (US)', 'Full moon'. She tried to fill the face in – the hair, the eyes, the smile – but nothing seemed to come. Anne's face would no longer do. Her first mother could be young and sad, ill or old with stringy hair, even a chain-smoker who loafed around in pubs all day, but she mustn't be involved in lies.

A train rattled past the window, seemed to roar right through her body and out the other side; leave her deafened, hollow. Then silence swathed the room again, stealing over everything like sly concealing snow.

She glanced back at her diary, with its cosy lulling words – 'She used to cuddle me' – ripped the page out violently, screwed it into nothing.

22

'Thank you, darlings,' Isobel enthused, hugging Jane and Trish together, then reaching for her coat. 'That was a really marvellous lunch – and tea. Rose, you've become quite a master-chef in the time you've been with Trish.'

'Well, I'm certainly a whiz at scrubbing spuds.'

'But you made the pudding, didn't you? And meringues are really tricky.'

Jane nodded, passed Isobel her gloves – red wool mittens which shouted at the purple bouclé coat. 'I'll be taking over from Trish soon. She can retire and draw her pension.'

'Can't wait!' grinned Trish, moving down the passage to the door.

'Hold on a minute, girls. Rowan's coming over for Sunday lunch tomorrow, with Neville and a pal or three. Why don't you come too?'

'I'm afraid I can't leave Mum,' Trish said, lowering her voice, so that her mother wouldn't hear. 'You saw how bad she was today. You go, Jane.'

Jane winced at the wrong name. Trish had kept up 'Rose' all day, until this final lapse. 'I can't get there on my own,' she said. 'It's a bit too far to cycle.'

Isobel rummaged for her car-keys. 'Well, you could come with me now, and stay the night. I'd love that. And Neville can drive you back on Sunday evening. He lives in this direction.'

'Would you mind, Trish?'

''Course not. Run and get your night things.'

Jane sprinted to her bedroom, collected up pyjamas, toothbrush, handbag, sweater, coat; felt a sense of real excitement and release. Mrs Carter's presence had somehow acted like a straitjacket, and also roused opposing feelings of compassion and revulsion. Illness was so harrowing, especially at close quarters. Trish's mother and Isobel were exactly the same age, had been in the same class together, yet the latter seemed a good two decades younger. Jane watched her zip along the path, auburn hair bouncing on her shoulder, eager words spewing out in spurts of frosty breath; tried to quash the image of a cruelly contrasting Margarita Carter – shuffling, stumbling, stuttering, from bed to chair to bed.

She climbed into the passenger-seat, lolled back against the scruffy brown suedette, enjoying the sensation of hurtling through the darkness in their own snug and warm cocoon. It was only five o'clock, yet felt much later – timeless – as they sped between blurred fields and ghostly sky.

'Are you enjoying it at Trish's?' Isobel enquired, slowing down a little as she forked right at a junction.

'Mm. In a way. We get on pretty well . . .' The sentence faded out, as Jane reeled back from Trish's flailing fists. She could feel the blows bludgeoning her body, the sense of shock and outrage as they wrestled on the carpet. The image of that savage fight wouldn't leave her mind. She and Trish had made it up next morning, apologised, blamed the wine, done their desperate best to laugh it off, but even after all these weeks, there was still a certain wariness between them. They laughed and joked and chattered on the surface, but underneath was suspicion and distrust.

She cleared her throat, knew Isobel was waiting for more details. She tried to fill the silence, switch to less distressing problems. 'The job's not all that marvellous. I mean, I'm glad I've learnt to cook, and I'm earning a fair bit, but it's not the sort of work I really want to do. I can't get wildly passionate about it, or feel I'm being stretched or . . .'

'Like you did about Christopher's work, you mean?'

'I wasn't any good at that,' she snapped. 'He told me so himself.'

'Really? So what happened? I never understood why you left in such a rush.'

Jane mumbled some excuse, as she had done before with Isobel – every time the older woman had tried to probe or question her. She hadn't meant to sound so sharp, but the whole business made her irritable, including the questioning itself, the kind but snooping phone-calls. She changed the subject quickly, started a long anecdote about their latest Green Cuisine event – a three-day conference for Glaswegian New Age meditators who had complained because the organic wholemeal stoneground bread had been made with dried

300

yeast instead of live. While she talked, she was aware that she was counting miles – only six or seven now until they passed the track which led to Christopher's barn. She waited five more minutes, then casually remarked: 'By the way, I left some things in the studio, and I've never had a chance to go and get them. Would you mind if we stopped off?'

'Not at all, but how will you get in? It's Saturday, remember, so Christopher won't be there.'

'I've still got my front-door key.' It was in her handbag, along with one of the red roses from the Swan, one she'd dried and pressed, kept as a memento of what she called their honeymoon, the first time they'd been to bed together. She was counting days now, instead of miles: fifty-seven since they'd last made love; forty since she'd seen him. Time had never passed so slowly, as if she'd had to start again at the beginning of her life and relive her eighteen years at tortoise pace, crawling from infancy to childhood, through endless wretched teens. Yet she'd been determined not to weaken, unless Christopher himself gave some sign that he wanted to communicate. And she wouldn't weaken now. She was going to see the Angel, not the artist; had to check the window, see how far he'd got, catch up on the stages that she'd missed.

She tried to keep on chatting, but her mouth felt stiff and dry. She couldn't understand it, when all she planned was a brief glance at some glass-screens in an empty studio. Why that desperate churning in her stomach; that sense of almost danger as the car swung right along the track, bumped and jolted down the stony lane?

'Look, he *is* there!' Isobel exclaimed. 'The lights are on. How nice. We can go and have a drink with him.'

'No!' Jane almost shouted. 'He . . . he hates people dropping in. He must be really busy if he's working late at the weekend. Quick! Turn back.'

'But what about your things?'

'I'll . . . er . . . phone him sometime. They're not important anyway.'

'Listen, Rose, I think I ought to have a word with you – about Christopher, I mean. I've been intending to for ages, and now we're . . .'

'*Please* drive on. I don't want him to see us.'

'How can he? It's pitch-dark out here, and I've turned the headlights off. Keep your hair on, darling. You're sounding quite worked up.' Isobel reversed the car, stalling twice on the narrow rutted track. 'You're missing Christopher, aren't you?'

301

'Not especially, no.'

'That's the trouble – one of them. You just won't open up. You can trust me, Rose, you know that.'

Jane said nothing, skewed round in her seat and peered back at the bright lights of the barn. Was the artist really working, and was he on his own? Could Anne be there, or Stanton Martin, come to see his sketches, or was he busy with some voluptuous new assistant?

'Hey, stop!' she said suddenly. 'I've just remembered, I'll have to fetch my best red dress. I need it for a do we're . . .' The sentence petered out, didn't sound convincing. She had already collected her belongings from the studio, a month or more ago, one Sunday morning, when Christopher was out. Trish had taken her, and they'd called at Windy Hollow House for a cup of coffee afterwards.

Isobel turned round again with a grind and snort of gears. 'Want me to come in with you?'

'Oh, no. In fact . . .' Jane hesitated, reluctant to sound rude. 'I wondered if you'd mind driving back without me? I'll come on later. I won't be very long.'

'But you've got no transport.'

'No,' she said, pondering. Perhaps Christopher would drive her – if she found him on his own. If only she could stay with him, return to her own bed, high up in the gallery, with his paintings looking down on her, and the Angel bright below.

Isobel switched her headlamps on to full, to give more light in the murky tree-lined lane. 'Look, give me a ring when you're ready, and I'll come and pick you up.'

'Oh, Isobel, you angel! Are you sure it's not a nuisance?'

'No. I'm on my own this evening, and I won't even need to cook, after that slap-up lunch you and Trish laid on.' She stopped the car outside the barn, reached across and squeezed Jane's hand. 'Be careful.'

'What d'you mean, "be careful"?' She had made it sound quite menacing, as if the artist were a murderer or rapist.

'I don't want you to be hurt, Rose.'

'I'm only going to fetch a dress, for heaven's sake.'

'Well, in that case, let me wait for you. I won't come in, I promise. I'll just park here outside.'

'No, please.'

She watched the car drive off, almost yelled it back again. If her substitute were there, would she really want to stay and watch them operate together? She had never known Christopher work at six o'clock on Saturday, though if Anne had gone abroad again, he might have grabbed the opportunity to show his new assistant round, become more intimately acquainted with her.

She fumbled for her key, had no wish to disturb them by ringing the bell. The artist would be furious if she slunk in unannounced, but she couldn't lose this chance of checking up on him. She tiptoed through the door and on into the studio – no one there at all, although the lights had been left on. They must be up in bed – *her* bed. She fought an urge to scream at them, command them to come down; instead crept up the stairs herself, barely breathing, pausing on each step. If she found him there with someone else, she'd murder both of them. She stopped a moment, afraid of her own anger, hearing in her mind the wild noises of the Swan – heavy panting breathing, sudden whimpering cries. The door was open just a crack. She pushed it with her hand, shut her eyes, as if she couldn't bear to see their bodies, naked and entwined. She counted up to five, then forced her lids to open.

The gallery was empty, the bed neatly made, just as she had left it, all those days and days and days ago. Her relief was so enormous, she let out a shuddering sigh; patted the smooth duvet, as if rewarding a good dog. She rattled down the stairs again, realising only now that the glass-screens were no longer in position – no Resurrection Angel exulting to the sky. She glanced around in panic. Had something happened to it, some vandals smashed it up, as had occurred with Saint Jerome? She stood silent by the table, recalling Christopher's anguished face when he'd finally ferreted out the story of what had happened to his Belthorpe window. A gang of louts, on the boozy rampage after a pop festival near Lincoln, had attacked it with both catapults and shotguns, then fled to the next village and turned their freaked-out rage on something else. He'd been wretched when he heard; all the more demoralised because no one had informed him at the time, nor suggested he replace it, and all he could conclude was that the vicar and the PCC were actually relieved to be rid of what they saw as an embarrassment. If he lost a second window, one not even finished, he might begin to feel a victim.

She walked slowly to the far end of the studio. Everything was so vulnerable, so fragile – babies and their parents, works of art, relationships. Peaceful easy-going Trish had lashed out with tooth and claw, and she herself had instantly retaliated, two good friends fighting like wild cats. Supposing Trish bore grudges, was still chafing at the slight to her first mother, or still jealous over Hadley? And Hadley was another problem; would be home again on his spring vacation in just a month or so, expecting a decision, and one made in his favour.

She squeezed past the workbench, her mind circling on itself; suddenly saw two screens propped against the wall, the glass on them intact and safe. They had been taken down, that's all, left in a corner where she'd almost overlooked them. She subsided on a chair, so she could relish her relief, switch from problems to achievements; remember her success in cutting that blue foot, those strips of emerald field. So much of her was in that stained-glass window – not just her hair and features; but her exhaustion and her tension, her care and concentration, her name, her love, her labour.

She loped back to the workbench, unrolled the cutline, spread it flat. That now-grubby length of paper contained the history of the cutting of the glass – crossings-out, reworkings, where Christopher had changed a shape or added a new leadline; scribbled memos to himself, instructions jotted down for her, initials representing colours: R, DG, LB. It was also a record of their relationship – their two bloods mingled in several darkish stains, a grease-spot from a cake they'd shared, a heart he'd doodled in her honour, after a rare impulsive mid-work kiss. She placed her finger on the heart, as if she could almost feel it beating; admired Christopher's bold scrawlings, the energetic writing as assertive as himself. This cutline would be taken to the glazing-shop, used as the master-plan for leading up the window, and she'd no longer be a part of it, would miss that whole last stage; never watch the glaziers positioning the glass-shapes – a giant jigsaw on their bench – tugging lengths of limp lead taut, cutting them to size round each individual piece of glass, then soldering the joints, the hissing silver solder setting fast like sealing-wax.

She rolled the cutline up again, stowed it in a drawer, couldn't bear to be reminded of what she'd lost, renounced. As she stooped to close the drawer, she noticed a trail of fine white powder on the floor, which she recognised immediately as plaster of Paris. The artist used that powder in the firing-trays, as a smooth base for the glass. He must be firing in the kiln-room, have the rest of the window there, painted but dismantled, waiting its turn in the kiln.

She nipped out of the side door, and a few steps down the passage, knocked before she entered, stepping into stifling heat from the draughty chill outside. Christopher wheeled round, naked save for a pair of ancient corduroys, sweat shining on his body, trickling down his chest. His hair was tousled, sticking to his forehead, his whole face flushed and damp. She had only seen him look like that when they'd just finished making love. Instinctively, she checked the room, but could see no panting woman – only glass and tools, empty wooden boxes, dusty metal trays, a workbench with a rack above it, holding saws and hammers.

'Rose!' he said, and took a step towards her, his voice slightly husky, as if he'd been suffering from a cold. She could smell his heat and sweat, felt almost scared of this wild and unkempt Christopher – white dust on his battered shoes, a smear of dirt blazoning one cheek. She began to pour out words, as a barrier and shield against him; to prevent him coming any closer – empty babbling words about her job with Trish, her lunch with Isobel; how she had come to fetch her dress, then seen the lights on, stopped . . . He made no response at all, simply kept his eyes on her; steel eyes drilling through her eye-sockets and on into her skull. She could feel herself faltering, the phrases petering out, shrivelling up to nothing like scraps of flimsy paper in a fire.

He suddenly let out a curse, whipped back to the kiln. 'Christ!' he said, 'the glass.' He grabbed a pair of asbestos gloves and a long iron handle-thing, transferred a tray of red-hot glass to a lower part of the kiln. She flinched back from the firing-chamber, glowing hectic-red; nervous of the heavy trays he was shifting up and down. It seemed almost a barbaric process, roasting fragile glass-paint in a furnace. The cool blue Angel must be suffocating, broiling; its wings ablaze, its long hair charred and singed. She could feel the heat in her own body, melting her to liquid, blistering her tongue. She threw off her coat, her cardigan, longed to strip as naked as the artist.

She hardly recognised him. He had turned into a navvy, heaving loaded trays about; the muscles in his naked back rippling from the effort; an oblong of bare sweaty skin gleaming through a tear in his old cords. Even his fine hands had become rough and hulking paws in their clumsy firing-gloves. He clanged the metal doors shut, then removed one final tray from the bottom of the kiln. 'Goddammit!' he exclaimed.

'What's wrong?' she asked, unnerved, but unable to see anything, since he was standing in the way.

'The face has flown, for Christ's sake.'

'What d'you mean?' 'Flown' suggested wings, a small blue face winging through the air, another minor angel.

'Broken right across – ruined, in effect.'

'Oh, no!' She stared down at the tray – the Angel's head and hair laid out in its separate pieces on a bed of fine white powder; the blue face cracked in three, which made it look distorted – weeping or grimacing, instead of gazing wide-eyed up to God. She felt angry with him suddenly, as if he, too, were a vandal, destroying his own glass. How could he be so careless, risking something precious, which meant so much to both of them? Yet she had spoilt it first time round, by scratching it with her fingernail. Was it jinxed, this face, or could it be her fault again, for barging in so suddenly?

'That's the last bloody straw, Rose! I've been firing since ten o'clock this morning – which is why it's so damned hot in here – and everything's gone wrong. Firstly, I forgot my keys, and had to go back and fetch them, next we had a power-cut for an hour, then I had some breakages on the top part of the wing, and now the face, of all things. It means cutting it again, painting it again, going right back to square one.' He set the tray down on the bench, sank down himself, exhausted. 'I could have done with an assistant this last fortnight. Why the hell did you walk out on me like that?'

She tensed. 'You made it pretty clear I wasn't any use.'

'Nonsense, Rose. I never said a word about your skills or lack of them. As far as I remember, you kept hassling and distracting me, asking stupid questions . . .'

'Which you answered with lies.'

'For God's sake, Rose, not that again. We've been through it all already.'

'No we haven't. You just clammed up, didn't care how much it meant to me. Don't you see, it's terribly important? If you lie to me on one thing, then I can't trust you on the rest.' She fretted to the window, stared out at the darkness. 'I know Anne didn't go with you to Nice, so why pretend she did?'

Christopher pounced up to his feet, made a punching motion through the air. 'Okay, she bloody didn't. Does that make you feel better?'

She shook her head, recoiling from the rancour in his voice.

'All right, let's spell it out, if it's going to make you happy. Never mind how miserable *I*'ve been.' He suddenly lurched off at a tangent, as if he'd forgotten Anne entirely. 'I'd no idea where you were, or why you'd bloody gone. You waltz off with that oaf Hadley for the evening, then stay away six weeks. All I get is one brief note, telling me damn all. You didn't even leave me your address.'

'You could have got it if you'd tried.'

'I don't pester people, Rose, if I assume they no longer want my company.'

'Look, you *told* me to get out – well, not exactly in those words, but you said I was a bungler and . . .'

'You accused me first.'

Jane gripped the windowsill. They were sounding like a pair of squabbling brats, each out for the last word. If she wasn't careful, there'd be another brawl. She tried to calm her voice, behave more like an adult, but without capitulating. 'Okay, I did – I do. You lied to me, Christopher, and I need you to explain.'

He fidgeted away from her, picked up a rag to mop his sweaty face. Several minutes passed before he spoke again, his tone chilly and restrained now. 'Anne and I don't see eye to eye as far as Christmas is concerned. She likes to stay at home, and take things very quietly. She's away a lot on business and has a high-powered pressured job, whereas I work mainly on my own, so naturally I prefer a bit of company, a trip abroad, something much more lively. We've been away for Christmas five years running, so I admit she's got a point. The problem was she changed her mind – first she said she would come, then she said she wouldn't, which made it very awkward for me, since I'd fixed up all the flights, arranged things with my friends. We had quite a dust-up over it, but finally we compromised: this year we'd go abroad, to Nice, so we wouldn't let our friends down; next year we'd stay at home.'

He broke off for a moment to remove a tray of glass from the firing-chamber, transfer it to a lower shelf, to cool, first pulling on his asbestos gloves, then manoeuvring it with the handle. 'Right, I'll turn the kiln down now, and we'll take a break before I fire the last batch.' He lit a cigarette, striking several matches before he could get one to ignite, as if he'd infected them with his own unease in explaining the débâcle over Christmas. 'Where was I?' he asked tersely.

'Just setting off for Nice.'

'Ah, yes. We'd even packed, cancelled milk and papers. But the day before we were due to leave, Anne went down with a filthy cold and refused point-blank to go; said the cold was on her chest, so it would be dangerous for her to fly.'

'But why couldn't you have told me that?' Jane demanded, feeling both baffled and relieved. 'I mean, there's no mystery about a chest-cold. I'd have understood, wouldn't I, even felt quite sorry for you both?'

'Would you, Rose, or d'you think you might have blamed me for not staying behind with my wife; called me selfish for leaving her alone and jetting off myself?'

Jane paused before she answered. That was exactly the thought just passing through her mind. 'So you lied to me because you didn't want me to think of you as heartless?'

He nodded. 'Something on those lines.'

'I'm not sure I believe you. You don't care what I think – except about your work.'

'It was work which was the problem. My friends in Nice had invited this French architect who particularly wanted to see me. I couldn't let him down at such short notice. In fact, I've got a new commission – two windows for a church in Lyons – which is pretty damned miraculous, since the French always tend to keep things for themselves, don't hand out work to foreigners.'

'Congratulations.'

'You're too young to be sarcastic, Rose. It doesn't suit you.'

'I'm not sarcastic, just upset.'

Christopher inhaled so deeply he appeared to be sucking down the cigarette itself. 'You're making such a meal of it. It's a trifle, Rose, which you're blowing up sky-high. Okay, I'm selfish, I like to do things my way, overrule my wife, and I suppose I'd prefer you not to know.' He put down his cigarette, reached out for a duster, started cleaning up the pieces of glass, removing them from the firing-trays and transferring them to shallow wooden boxes. 'We all try to hide our baser side, even from ourselves, make out we're virtuous, and never get involved in sordid little quarrels. I mean, it's humiliating, isn't it, wives and husbands fighting tooth and nail over something so damned trivial?'

She was touched, despite herself. So he valued her opinion, wanted to seem blameless in her eyes, someone reasonable, fair-minded, who didn't insist on his own way. But what about Anne's affair with Adrian? That was not a trifle. He clearly couldn't know about it, and she'd no intention of upsetting him by blurting out the facts. Perhaps Anne had exaggerated her cold, inflating a slight sniffle to a bronchial infection, so she could cry off at the last moment, well aware that Christopher would have to go himself, and she'd be free to meet her lover. She ought to feel sorry for the artist, married to a woman who lied to him, betrayed him; should treat him with compassion, not keep hectoring and riling him. It was obvious that he'd missed her – though he was far too proud to say so – and felt hurt because she hadn't left him her address. She leaned across, eased the duster gently from his hand. 'Look, I'm sorry, Christopher. It's all been such a muddle. I thought you didn't want me here.'

He was still holding a small piece of glass, peering at it closely. 'Six weeks have never seemed so long,' he said, almost in a whisper. 'I caught your cold, you know, and it hung around for ages, as if I couldn't get you out of my damned system.'

'Well, maybe I caught Anne's cold,' she replied. 'Remember, you and I slept together just before you left for Nice, and you could have been carrying her germs.'

'But you'd have got it sooner then, been snuffling over Christmas.'

She didn't answer. Whoever had caught what from whom, there was an obvious intimacy of germs; she and Anne and Christopher passing on their moods, their lies, their colds. She kissed his neck and throat, as if trying to soothe the hoarseness in his voice, which had deepened it an octave. Selfishly, she was glad he'd caught her cold. It seemed a bond between them, something of herself affecting his whole body, taking hold, lingering for weeks.

He returned the kiss impatiently, his open mouth moving to her lips. 'So why don't you come back?' he murmured. 'Take off those fancy clothes and help me with the firing.'

Her hands crept down his naked sweaty back. 'Do you have to do it now?'

'I'm afraid I do.' He edged away reluctantly, pulled between her body and the glass. 'I'm going up to Manchester tomorrow, and will be there for most of the week. I've had some pretty hellish problems on my new commission, which is why I'm so behind on *this* job.' He gestured to the firing-trays, began continuing his work of dusting off the glass-pieces, packing them in boxes. 'There's all the leading still to be done, which will take a good two weeks, and the glaziers are always up to their eyes when it's getting close to Easter. It's such an early Easter – that's the trouble. And I'd like to have the window in at least a fortnight before the actual dedication, in case there are any problems with the fixing.' He blew powder off a piece of glass, whisked the duster over it, then glanced down at his watch. 'I should be home already, but it seems stupid not to finish off these last half dozen trays, now the kiln's at the right temperature, and my assistant's here to help.'

Jane smiled and rolled her sleeves up, found another duster, and starting easing into the rhythm of the task. 'I mustn't be too long though. Isobel's expecting me. She told me to ring and she'd come and pick me up.'

'Well, I hope she doesn't stay and chat.'

'I'll make sure she doesn't. I'll meet her just outside.'

He met her eyes, exchanged a grin – two conspirators.

She dusted off a wing-piece, laid it gently in the box. 'What happens to the glass now?' she enquired, trying to catch up on the stages she had missed. 'Is it ready to be leaded yet?'

'Not quite. First it has to go back on the screens. After firing, I always check the whole thing up against the light. Some sections need rematting, or the tracing might have fired away, so I have to do a second painting, which means a second firing, and only after that it is sent off to the glazing-shop, packed in these same boxes, by the way.'

Jane shook out her duster. The more she saw of Christopher's work, the more she realised what patience it required – so many different stages, so much that could go wrong. 'I think I'd scream,' she grimaced, 'if I had to keep redoing things. It was bad enough when I burnt the meringues and had to beat another dozen egg-whites.'

The artist leant towards her, touched her hand. 'How soon can I lure you back from burnt meringues? Could you start work here on Monday week? I'll be back myself from Manchester by then.'

She nodded. A week should be enough to wind up her job with Green Cuisine, and settle things with Trish, who could well be secretly relieved that she was returning to the studio. Their friendship might recover once they no longer lived and worked together; the memory of that shameful fight slowly fade and dwindle. It had been too much of a strain, cooped up in the kitchen every day, then taking turns to mother-sit, whilst the other one waitressed half the night.

The artist was smoothing out the plaster of Paris on the now empty firing-trays, breaking up any tiny lumps, raking over the surface with a piece of plywood cut to the width of the tray. 'Actually, there's not much more for you to do on the Resurrection window, but I'd like you to stay on, Rose, and help me with my new commissions. I'm going to be quite pushed. They want the Lyons windows by next Christmas. I've already got some good ideas buzzing about in my head. The architect, Jean-François, is keen to have a maze theme. Last April, his son, Pierre, went on a student pilgrimage to Chartres, with several thousand others – all the kids trudging thirty miles or more, and praying as they footslogged. They arrived in the cathedral on Sunday afternoon, for a dramatic solemn Mass, where everyone was given lighted candles, and processed through the Royal Portal with the organ playing and the congregation singing and a real feeling of *communauté*. Pierre stayed overnight, returned to the cathedral soon after it opened in the morning, and found this group of English pilgrims walking the labyrinth, which is marked out on the floor of the nave and uncovered only once or twice a year, when they remove the chairs to make room for all the crowds. He joined them and got talking, walked the maze along with them, and witnessed what he called a miracle – some young girl from Ireland suddenly healed in the very centre of the labyrinth.'

'Healed of what?' asked Jane.

'I'm not too sure. Jean-François talks faster and at greater length than any man I've met, and though my French is pretty good, I did miss the odd subordinate clause. I think he said she'd been reborn, though that does sound quite incredible – I mean, reborn without her handicap. She apparently experienced this sense of being in the womb, and travelling out and down from it through the pathway of the maze. That may be Irish blarney, or a case of simple hysteria, but he assured me that his son was a solid down-to-earth type, not given to exaggeration, and he was definitely aware of this tremendous sense of energy, centred on the labyrinth. In fact, he was so *bouleversé* by the whole experience, he returned home supercharged, spouting mystical geometry and cosmology and gematria, and God alone knows what else. Jean-François was impressed, began reading up on labyrinths himself, and was soon equally agog – I mean, all that heady symbolism about man's journey through the path of life, with its vicissitudes, meanderings, until he finally reaches the hereafter – so when he heard I'd also walked the Chartres maze as a student of eighteen, he was absolutely fascinated.'

'You never told me, Christopher.'

The artist stubbed his fag-end out, using a paint-tin as an ashtray. 'I suppose it was so lost in the mists of time, I'd forgotten all about it. It was my very first visit to the cathedral and I was exactly your own age, and extremely interested in all things mystical. The maze is quite remarkable, one of the very few still left in Europe, and among the biggest Christian mazes ever made. No – I mustn't call it a maze – it's strictly speaking a labyrinth.'

'I thought they were the same.'

'No. Though a lot of books use the two words interchangeably, and even the Oxford English Dictionary fails to make the distinction, but simply reflects most people's ignorance. A maze has false turnings and dead ends, and is something which "amazes", whereas a labyrinth has just one single pathway – the longest possible route confined to the smallest possible area. The most famous one was the Knossos labyrinth, though some modern scholars insist it was a maze.' He picked up his piece of wood again, continued smoothing out the plaster, removing one last nodule with his fingers. 'You see, Theseus was warned that he'd never find his own way out, without the help of Ariadne's thread, which suggests it must have been more complex than a labyrinth – or does if you insist on sticking to the factual truth, rather than considering poetic truth, which has more muscle in mythology. It's one of those huge subjects of controversy, with all the pundits citing different arguments, or submitting learned papers to the journals.'

Jane wished she could contribute to the scholarship herself, but she was floundering, as usual. They seemed to have moved from modern France to ancient Greece before she'd even grasped the basic concepts. Didn't mazes have hedges, like the yew-hedge maze she'd walked once in a stately home near Durham, when she was still living with her parents? You could hardly plant a yew-hedge in the middle of a cathedral.

Christopher was working fast, to match his flow of words, now reloading his empty tray, pressing down each glass-piece into the soft white plaster bed, paint-side upwards, ready to be fired. 'The Chartres labyrinth is actually based on the Knossos one, but the medieval masons extended the arms of the Cross, and so Christianised its symbolism. The basic idea was still the same – a laborious journey, requiring perseverance – a search for one's true self through the tortuous path of life. But in the Christian case, the end is not just death, but death as the means of entry into heaven, and Ariadne's thread is interpreted as grace, which helps man fight the "Minotaur" of evil. Poetic truth again, you see, and pretty powerful stuff.'

He nestled two more pieces into the corner of the tray, fingers deft and cosseting, like a father with his children. Jane watched him half-resentfully. He appeared to have forgotten both their quarrel and their kiss, but that was typical. Once he started on a subject which absorbed him, mere personal relationships shifted into second place. She envied him his knowledge and his travels; longed to go to Chartres herself – not to mention Nice and Knossos – browse through learned journals, take sides in deep controversies with highbrow culture-vultures. Up till just this moment, a maze for her had been nothing more than a trivial diversion, an amusing puzzle to while away an hour or so, not an academic subject, awash with heady symbols.

The artist swapped three glass-shapes round, to make room for one last piece, ensured that none was touching. 'There's definitely a sense of power arising from that labyrinth. According to the dowsers, it's sited on the junction of half a dozen power-lines, which give it quite some charge. And its whole design is "charged" in a more complex sense, with deep mystical significance. Its basic form and structure ties in with the dimensions of the cathedral itself, and is a key to its geometry, but don't ask me to explain. It's so damned complicated, it would take me half a lifetime.' He paused a moment, brow creased in concentration as he tracked back forty years. 'I walked it in a state of near elation, Rose. Even at that age, I knew it was significant – a winding track through eleven concentric circles which inevitably lead "home" – bring you to fulfilment, to your goal. I was already doing a painting course at St Martin's, though I hadn't yet decided I wanted to work with glass. But the impact of the Chartres windows seemed to make my mind up for me, as if I were being "led" by the labyrinth itself, brought to a decision by some outside force or power.'

He shivered suddenly, despite the stifling heat. 'Perhaps I was imagining things. The atmosphere was very other-worldly. They'd had some special celebration earlier that day, and moved out all the chairs to make more room in the nave. The crowds had mostly gone, but there were still a lot of people lighting candles at the shrines, or just kneeling on the hard stone floor, and a Bach toccata was rumbling on the organ, and the whole cathedral seemed to flicker and vibrate, and there was this amazing sense of prayer and . . .' He left the sentence hanging, reached down to brush white powder off her skirt. 'Why not fetch an apron, Rose? You're ruining your clothes. And can't you get a move on? You've hardly done a thing yet.'

She stared at him, bewildered. His mood had changed completely, the earlier irritation returned in his brusque voice. Perhaps he'd regretted what he'd told her, decided to clam up before he gave himself away, or permitted her a glimpse into his soul. If she'd 'hardly done a thing' it was because she'd been engrossed in what he'd said, trying to take it in. It was too late to help, in any case. If she stayed there any longer, Isobel would worry – or worse – begin suspecting things.

'Look, I'm sorry, Christopher, but I'll really have to go now. Isobel's already very curious about why I left the studio, and if I don't get back, she'll only start cross-questioning me.' She shook herself, like Byron, to remove any more loose powder, then went to fetch her coat. 'May I use the phone?'

'Help yourself. And forgive me if I snapped. I've been working too damned hard, that's all.' He took both her hands in his, kissed her on the forehead. 'Listen, Rose, let's go away again. We need a break – both of us. Christmas didn't count. As soon as this window's safely at the glazier's, we'll book a weekend somewhere – and I promise not to talk about cathedrals or labyrinths, or say one single word about my work.' He laughed. 'You don't believe me, do you?' He kissed each hand in turn, still clasping them in his. 'D'you mind if I don't come and see you off? I must get these last trays in.'

313

'No, that's fine. Isobel should only be ten minutes, and by the time I've tidied up a bit . . .'

He seemed reluctant to release her, scooping up her hair, and holding it in two long reins, as if he were controlling a small pony. She tossed her coat behind her, pressed herself against his naked chest; was aware of him responding. Perhaps he'd changed his mind, at last, and decided work could wait. She could almost feel the conflict in his body; his hands and shoulders tense still, while, lower down, his excitement was quite obvious. Then, decisively, abruptly, he thrust his tongue between her lips, bit her own tongue, hard. She flinched in pain, but he simply forced her tongue aside, started exploring her whole mouth like some dark and secret cave, his teeth grating against hers, grazing along the outside of her lips.

'You're hurting,' she choked out.

He fumbled with his corduroys, pushed her back against the wall, tugged off her pants and tights, and suddenly she felt him hard inside her. She could barely move in that position, but she shut her eyes, used all her effort to grind and churn against him, tensing up her muscles, trying to hold him in a vice. Her skirt was creased around her middle, her flower-sprigged blouse soaking up his sweat. She had to bridge the gulf between them, muss and soil her prissy clothes till she was as hot and brute as he was.

'Stand on my feet,' he ordered.

She placed her bare and powdery feet on his clumping white-snowed shoes, feeling some strange sense that she was growing out of him, two bodies with one root.

'Now climb me.' He cupped his hands beneath her buttocks, helped her clamber up. She latched her legs around his waist, gripping with her thighs, clutching at his shoulders, her fall of hair cascading back behind her. He was bearing her full weight now, his legs trembling from the strain, his mouth still scalding hers. He hadn't courted her or wooed her, or asked her if she wanted him – simply given orders – but she could almost hear his body howling out its own needs: how it craved her and desired her, yet also sought to punish her, pay her out for leaving.

He was moving faster, faster, driven by some wild relentless rhythm, and she tried to steel herself against the sense of being overwhelmed, annihilated; fought an instinct to shrink back, escape into the safety of her mind.

'No!' he rasped, his voice gravelly and ragged, unable to compete with the violence of his breathing, the convulsive jerking movements of his body. 'I love you, Rose, don't you understand?'

His nails were digging into her flesh, and she could feel her helpless spine scraping up and down against rough and rutted stone. She hardly registered the pain, focused only on the words he'd said – red-hot words, molten from the kiln, exploding now in his headstrong hurting climax.

23

'I love you, Rose,' she murmured, faking Christopher's gruff voice. 'I love you, Rose. I love you.' However many times she said it, the words still stupefied. She fumbled for the light-switch, sat up in bed again. It was impossible to sleep. Not only did Rowan's room seem wildly large and colourful after the cramped beige of the bungalow, but the artist had sneaked into it, left his home and wife, and come running – eager, ardent – to Windy Hollow House. She sat him in the wicker chair with its pink and orange cushions, had him explain about the labyrinth again, and this time she responded with deep and searching questions, trenchant observations about the symbolism of mazes. Then they discussed the Manchester commission, and she made him repeat his comforting remarks about how busy he could keep her, how useful she would be; how he could offer her employment for eighteen months at least, and also up her wages.

She had returned from the studio skittish, effervescent, but had tried to keep the bubbles down, stop herself from fizzing. Isobel had probed, of course, but she had answered very casually, given nothing much away, except the fact that she'd be returning there to work. Isobel had seemed subdued, not quite her jolly self, complained she had a headache, and finally retired to bed at ten. She herself had stayed up till after midnight, wandering through the downstairs rooms, relishing the sense of space, admiring all the works of art, comparing them with Trish's china horses and the picture of a flower-girl with a puppy and a parasol, which graced the Carters' sitting-room.

She threw the covers back, reaching for her handbag, fished her diary out of it and started checking on weekends, keen to write in every one: 'Away, with Christopher'. She wondered where they'd go – perhaps abroad this time – knew from Trish's brochures all the exotic destinations: Amsterdam, Vienna, Rome, Sofia, Leningrad.

316

Imagine Russia in a weekend! It sounded quite incredible, when her grandmother had told her once that it used to take them two whole days to drive from Kent to Cornwall. Though even Russia paled beside Vienna, the romantic city she'd always longed to see. There'd been a picture in the brochure of a Viennese palace with at least a thousand windows and a lake so blue it blazed, and the statue in the fountain had looked distinctly like Christopher – small, lean, muscly and intense – with water spouting from his loins and a dolphin as his sofa. Palaces were two a penny, according to the write-up, and so many famous composers had lived in old Vienna it must disgorge music like other towns belched smoke. Christopher would warm to that, and she could also surprise him with her German. She had dropped it after GCSE, but Miss Monteith had always said that her accent was remarkably good; even gone so far as to ask if she'd lived some time in Germany, or had a German relative. 'Ringstrasse,' she practised, remembering the caption to another sun-drenched picture in the brochure: an attractive tree-lined boulevard with elegant shops and coffee-houses enticing people in.

She stuffed the diary back again, her fingers grating on the rough side of a matchbox, an empty one she had picked up from the studio. She pushed it open, unwrapped the two pink Kleenex folded tight inside, drew out the cross and chain.

'I didn't steal it,' she told the stern policeman in her head. 'I simply shoved it in my pocket when I discovered it at Adrian's, and I've been wondering ever since how on earth I could return it.' She had never dared to try it on; somehow feared the tiny trinket, which seemed more potent than a wedding ring, more lethal than a gun.

She moved over to the dressing-table, pulled off her pyjama top, dithered for a moment before shaking back her hair, then fastened the fiddly clasp around her neck. She edged nearer to the mirror, so she could admire the pearls gleaming on her skin. The cross felt strangely heavy, despite its trifling size; weighed her down with new responsibilities. By wearing Anne's jewellery, she had somehow also taken on her character, and so become the artist's wedded wife. Which meant that she could sleep with him, stay with him all night, wake with him in the morning, make love not standing up, but lying in the marriage-bed, a good eight miles from glass-screens, hungry kilns.

She slipped off her pyjama bottoms, so that she was now completely naked, then luxuriated back in bed, rolling to one side, to make more room for Christopher. She shut her eyes, could hear the clop of horse-drawn cabs spanking down the Ringstrasse; Strauss waltzes thumping out above the pealing bells of Karlskirche; the Vienna Boys' Choir joining in, and above all the happy hubbub, the artist's voice, pounding, thrusting into her: '*Ich liebe dich, Rose.*'

Jane was still in Austria, eating *Sachertorte*, Hadley sitting opposite, gnawing not the chocolate cake, but soft lumps of her flesh, which he dug out with a long red-handled spoon. She had only half her stomach left, which was oozing bloody cream. Hadley's spoon had struck a bone, and was rapping it and rapping, so that the noise went through her head.

'Come in,' she mumbled peevishly, suddenly awake.

'Tea up!' boomed Isobel.

'But it's the middle of the night.' Jane shrank away from the intrusive voice, from the flood of light frisking through the window, as Isobel drew the curtains with a rattle and a swoosh.

'It's twenty past eleven – in the morning. I've just come back from church. I thought I'd better wake you, as Rowan and the rest will be here in half an hour.'

Jane sat up in bed, relieved she had her pyjamas on. She had dragged them back in the dark of six A.M., woken by the cold; must have returned to sleep again, slept ten hours in all. 'Gosh! I'm sorry, Isobel. I meant to help you with the lunch.'

'No – my turn today. And it's mostly done, in any case. Getting up for church is the only thing which seems to make me organised. I always feel that God's a bit like Tom was – prefers the potatoes to be peeled and the roast beef browning nicely in the oven, before we sing the hymns.' Isobel plumped down on the bed, stretched out her stripey legs. She was wearing woolly winter socks in stripes of green and gold, beneath a pale blue summer skirt, with a jerkin in autumnal brown linking the two seasons. 'Don't let your tea get cold.'

Jane reached out for her mug, sipped appreciatively. 'What luxury! The first time I've had tea in bed for weeks.' She screwed up her eyes against the light – not the reluctant bleary light of recent mornings, but a flamboyant glare and shimmer more suited to midsummer than to February. Christopher had made her so much more aware of light – shown her its mysterious power of changing everything it touched; blurring lines, or sharpening them; continually working on the quilt of fields which spread beyond the studio, dousing them with mist or dusk, then rekindling them at sunrise, like stained glass brought to life again after dying in the night hours.

She shifted in the bed, so that a shaft of sun fell directly on her face. She, too, had died, in one sense, lost her glow and sparkle, let

318

all her colours darken. Today was a new start, and she was glad that she was spending it at Isobel's, in a lively house with a sunburst on the door; roast beef on the table and good friends to share it with. 'How was church?' she asked, cupping both hands round her mug.

'Well, it's the first Sunday of Lent today, so the service was a bit subdued – no flowers or organ or Gloria. But although Anthony may disapprove, I always find Lent rather exciting. I mean, Easter's round the corner, and I like that sense of stripping off the old self and preparing for the new, as if we're leaves or bulbs or something, shooting up in spring. And we're given forty days to do it, which seems to me just perfect. Oh, I know it's penitential – forty days in the desert, forty years in the wilderness – all that sort of thing, but it's psychologically right, you know. A month would be too short for all that spiritual spring-cleaning, and two months far too long, so that we'd lose all heart, or begin to get quite corpse-like from the fasting. Happy Lent, Rose, anyway.' She stretched a hand out, endangering the tea. 'I saw Veronica in church, which was a nice surprise, as well.'

'Veronica?'

'You know, Christopher's ex-wife.'

'I didn't realise she still lived in the area.'

'She doesn't. She moved up to St Albans after the divorce. But she's staying with the Mortimers, a mile or two from here. She said she tried to ring me yesterday, to let me know she was in my neck of the woods – three times in all, she phoned – but of course I was out all day with you and Trish, and *she* was out all evening. I'll pop and see her later on, leave you to hold the fort.' Isobel kicked off a navy patent shoe, wiggled her green toes. 'I've missed her in the last few years. We got very close when she was breaking up with Christopher, used to meet each Sunday for tea and a long walk. Which reminds me, Rose, I ought to have a word with you about our dear friend Christopher.'

'What about him?' Jane put her mug down, pulled the bedclothes tight around her chest.

'Well, I'm very glad you're going back to work with him. That's marvellous news, but . . .'

'But what?'

Isobel clasped her hands, as if in prayer, the fingers tense and tight. 'I don't know quite how to put this, but . . . well – try not to get involved.'

'Involved?'

'I hate to gossip, Rose. I think it's very dangerous and definitely unkind, but poor Veronica got badly hurt, so I feel it's only fair to warn you.'

'What d'you mean, "hurt"?' Jane could suddenly see Veronica cringing on the floor in pain, white dust on her stylish clothes, bloody spittle in her mouth; the artist's lips too wild for her, his nail-marks on her bruised and naked back.

'I'm not too keen to go into the details, and after all, I've only heard her side, so it's not really fair to Christopher, but I'm aware that you're quite fond of him . . .'

'I'm not!' Jane slammed out of bed and over to the window. 'Look, if you're trying to insinuate that I'm having an affair with him or something, you must be out of your mind. He's old enough to be my grandfather.'

'Yes, of course he is – I realise that, but . . .'

'And, anyway, I . . . I've got another boyfriend.'

'Really, darling? Who?'

Jane kept her back turned, fiddling with the curtain. 'Someone Trish knows. She thinks he's great, and I know you will, as well.' That was true, at least. Isobel adored her only son.

'Oh, Rose, I'm so relieved! I'd really love to meet him. You'd better introduce me, invite him here for lunch one day, or supper or high tea, or . . .'

Jane slouched back from the sill. 'He's not around at the moment. He's away at university.'

'Oh, I see. Well, wait till Easter, then.' Isobel jumped up to let the ginger tom in. He was scratching at the door, flounced in with his tail held high, sniffing round her legs. 'I must admit I have been rather worried. You see, Hadley brought the subject up, and . . .'

'Hadley?'

'Yes. He drove up here one Saturday, from college, said he was depressed about his course and wanted to have a chat with me about it. I was rather touched, you know, the way he thought his totally unscientific mother could grasp the ins and outs of modern physics. Anyway, we stayed up very late, drinking this quite frightful wine he'd had left over from a party, and he suddenly asked me if I thought you were in love with Christopher.'

Jane picked up her hairbrush, tore it through her hair. 'That's total utter rubbish. How on earth could I . . . ?'

'Don't be angry, Rose. I'm sure he meant it well. He was probably just a bit concerned about you working there.'

'Concerned?' Jane kept on brushing, her head tipped down, so all the blood was rushing to her face. 'Why should he be?'

'Let's forget it, shall we? I think I've said enough.' Isobel collapsed into the wicker chair, nursing a pink cushion.

'You haven't said a thing – just hints and innuendoes. I don't know what you're getting at, and it's not your business, anyway.'

'I'm sorry, Rose, I don't want to interfere, but I suppose I feel responsible. I mean, your own parents aren't around to help, so someone ought to talk to you . . .'

'But you're *not* talking. You keep going round in circles, saying how concerned you are, and how Veronica got hurt, and how it's only fair to warn me, and all the rest of it, and I'm still completely in the dark. If you've got something to tell me, why not just come out with it?'

'It's not an issue now – if you're tied up with someone else. I didn't know that, did I, so I imagined you and Christopher might . . .'

'Look, I'm working with Christopher, going back to live there for eighteen months or more. Of course I'm involved with him, in one sense, and if you think I shouldn't be, then I ought to know the reason.'

Isobel winced as the cat sprang on her lap, its sharp claws digging into her thighs. 'Working there's no problem. I was just a little worried about . . . a more personal involvement. You see, Christopher believes in . . .' She paused, released Orlando's claws from the thin fabric of her skirt. 'What's the word when you have affairs quite openly, despite the fact you're married – sort of write them into the contract? Perhaps there isn't any word, but Christopher does it anyway.' She shook her head, as if to express her deep regret. 'I'm not breaking any confidences – he makes no secret of the fact. There was even an article about it at the time of his divorce, when he said quite openly to a good half-million readers – including my two children, by the way – that fidelity was outmoded, and marriage had to change, and that loving someone meant allowing them complete fulfilment, which included sex with other partners.' Isobel started tugging at her wedding ring, trying to force it past her knuckle, twist it round and round. 'The trouble is, the more partners you have, the more risk there is of AIDS and things, so you can see why I was anxious, Rose. And, anyway, the whole concept seems so wrong – a contradiction in terms. The marriage vows say "forsaking all other".'

Jane clamped her hands together, to try to stop them shaking. Strange how small the room seemed now, all its former space and colour contracting to a claustrophobic grey; Isobel too loud for it, her voice destroying everything. She unlocked her trembling fingers, groped for the small bump beneath the fabric of her pyjama top

– Anne's cross and chain, binding her in wedlock. 'Did . . . did Christopher get married in a church?'

'Yes, when he married Veronica, but not the other times. It was especially hard for her because when they first met up, his views were very different, but he expected her to change along with him; tried to talk her into taking lovers, so he could justify his own affairs.' Isobel's hand moved from ring to cat, ruffling the soft fur, then smoothing it down flat again. 'I felt torn between the two of them at first. I've always been extremely fond of Christopher, but Veronica was suffering such a lot, and it was affecting her three children.'

'And . . . and what about Anne? Did she agree to the arrangement?'

'I'm not too sure. We've never been that close. She was one of Christopher's "entanglements" while he was still married to Veronica, so it was really rather awkward for me to accept her with open arms once she became the official wife. I've nothing against her personally, but it was a question of basic loyalties, you see.'

'So Anne broke up the marriage?'

'No. I wouldn't go as far as that. Christopher had other girls besides her, and he's never found it easy to stick at a relationship, or lose himself in someone else, or build a sense of loyalty and trust.' Isobel ran slow and lulling fingers from head to furry tail, then flicked back to the ginger ears, tweaking them and fondling. 'It's not totally his fault, you know. He was starved of all affection in his childhood, and that always makes it difficult to love. Veronica claimed he couldn't love, he simply wasn't capable; said the only love he understood was free love, and that every time he used the word, he actually meant lust. But, you see, you have to *learn* to love, and Christopher never had the chance, Rose, nor anyone's example; no doting mother, or devoted father, not even a religious faith, with a loving God, to compensate.'

'Isobel, I . . . I need the loo.'

'Just a minute, darling. Let me finish. I feel worried that I've said too much, given you the wrong . . .'

'I'm sorry, but I'm bursting.' Jane cannoned from the room, locked the bathroom door, turned the shower to fierce, stripped off her pyjamas, and stood beneath the jet of scalding water. She had to wash the lies off – the lies of an ex-wife who was jealous and vindictive, out for her revenge; the lies of that crass journalist who'd reported Christopher's remarks, distorted them to make his paper sell, raked up dirt to libel him; dirt which everyone had read, including Hadley, who must have been a schoolboy then, young, idealistic and probably deeply scandalised. You couldn't trust the gutter press – everyone knew that – and you couldn't trust ex-wives. She had disliked Veronica the moment she'd set eyes on her at the RIBA affair – all those dangerous spiky rings and that condescending voice. Of course Christopher could love. He'd just told her that he loved her, with a vehemence which proved it wasn't fake. She heard the words again beneath the thunder of the shower, felt her back grazed against the rough stone wall as he ejaculated into her. 'Every time he used the word, he actually meant lust.'

It had been lust, hadn't it – his body craving hers – hurting hers, in fact; slamming wildly into her to relieve his own frustration. Perhaps Anne had been abroad again, and his other various 'entanglements' all busy or away, so he'd been desperate for some sex. She snatched the soap, lathered it all over her, trying to sluice the germs off – not just cold germs, Anne's germs, but all those casual women he'd slept with in his trendy open marriages; all those wives he'd wheedled with his spiel about fidelity being boring and outmoded; all those different partners he needed for fulfilment. Anne had never had a cold – that was obvious now. Their Christmas was simply part of an old pattern: Anne would stay behind and sleep with Adrian; he would go to Nice and sleep with . . . who? The other guests' obliging wives and girlfriends, Jean-François' svelte blonde mistress, the girls in the *confiserie* where he'd bought her fancy chocolates, the giggly plump French maids who cleaned the villa. Those germs were really dangerous – Isobel was right. Except Isobel had probably lied as well, and was certainly a hypocrite, trotting off to church to say her prayers, then slandering a man behind his back, a friend she'd known for over thirty years, and one she claimed to . . .

'Rose! Quick! There's someone on the phone for you.'

Jane turned the shower down, grimacing at the banging on the door. Isobel again. Couldn't she be left in peace even for five minutes? 'I can't come down. I'm in the shower.'

'Well, take it in my bedroom.'

'But I'm all wet and soapy.'

'Never mind, just pop out with a towel.'

'Who is it, though?' Her voice was hoarse from shouting through the door. 'Can't I ring them back?'

'No – and hurry. It's long-distance.'

Long-distance. That meant Christopher. He'd said he'd phone from Manchester if he could find a minute free. Well, she'd refuse to speak to him – not just now, but ever in her life again. She was nothing to him, nothing – some odd bod he picked up when no one else was free. Maybe he and Anne discussed her, compared her with the other girls he'd had last year, last week, and then began on Adrian – was he worse or better than Anne's previous one-off lover? She stepped back into the shower again, grabbed the scratchy loofah and rasped it right between her thighs, trying to scour him off. She dropped the slippery soap, banged her elbow on the bath as she groped to pick it up. Her hair was streaming wet, heavy on her shoulders, clammy down her back, her cheeks smarting from the pressure of the shower. She fumbled for the knob, turned the water to a trickle. Would it really hurt to talk to him? Supposing he was phoning to tell her that he loved her? She ought to hear the words again, and hear them when he wasn't making love to her; give him one last chance, prove they could mean more than simply lust. She flurried out of the bath, clutched a towel around her, ran into the bedroom, picked up the extension.

'Guess who?' whooped a male voice.

'Who?' she faltered. There was a buzzing on the line, so it was hard to make its owner out.

'What a stroke of luck, Rose! I only rang to have a word with Mum, never imagined you'd be there. She says you're staying the whole day. Hell! I wish I'd known. I'd have come charging up like Sir Lancelot on his steed. Except my damn steed's broken down – the big end's gone on my Capri.' He laughed delightedly, as if thrilled to have his car a wreck. 'I was going to write to you anyway, to ask if you'd . . . worked things out, decided what to do, and also find out if you'd any plans for Easter. I don't mean Easter Sunday – that's sacrosanct, of course. Mum would never forgive me if I wasn't there for the dedication of her precious stained-glass window, but I'm home the week before that, and I wondered if you'd like to . . . ? Hey, Rose, are you still there?'

'Yes,' she said. 'I am.'

'You okay? You sound a bit faint and far away.'

'No, I'm . . . fine.'

'Great! So am I. You know, it's amazing the effect you have. I was feeling rather down this morning, but now I'm on the rooftops. And talking of rooftops, how d'you fancy Paris in the spring? It was wonderful at Christmas-time – well, I told you that already – but what I didn't say was that I sussed out a few hotels, just in case I went again, or could persuade you to come with me. There's one on the Left Bank, which is frightfully cheap, but rather quaint and definitely romantic. And right next door is this really brilliant restaurant – three courses for a hundred francs, and wine thrown in as well. How are you placed for Easter, Rose, or rather the last week in March? Are you free?'

'Yes,' she said. 'I think so.'

'Well, how d'you feel? Would you like to come?'

She paused a moment, hearing not Hadley's voice, but Isobel's again. *Veronica got badly hurt, so I feel it's only fair to warn you.* 'Okay,' she shrugged. 'Why not?'

'You don't sound very keen.'

'I . . . I've just got out of the bath and I'm dripping on the carpet.'

'Gosh, I'm sorry. How exciting, though! I'm driving up – this minute. If my car won't work, I'll nick one, or grab myself a pair of wings. I've got to see you naked.'

'Ssh.'

'Why "ssh"? My mother isn't listening, is she? She told me you were taking this upstairs.'

'I am, but . . .'

'Oh, Rose, I've missed you terribly. You just don't understand. I've even . . .'

'Hadley?'

'Yes.'

'How far is Paris from Chartres?'

'Chartres? Let me think. It can't be far because two of our party went there on a train and got back the same day – in fact, they were back about teatime, and only left at twelve. Why? D'you want to go there?'

'I wouldn't mind.'

'You mean, instead of Paris?'

'I really meant as well. But instead of might be better still. Someone told me you could spend a whole week in the cathedral and still not have time to soak it up.'

'I'd rather spend my week soaking up your body.' He blew her noisy kisses down the phone. 'But we'll stay wherever you like. You can choose everything, fantastic darling Rose. D'you want to fly, or go by . . . ?'

'Rose!' called Rowan. 'Where are you hiding?' There was a sudden frantic barking from outside on the landing, the sound of eager footsteps thudding up the stairs. 'Mark insists on coming up to see you.'

Jane pounced on Isobel's dressing gown, scrambled swiftly into it, then swathed the towel around her dripping hair. 'I'm in your mother's bedroom, but . . .'

'What's going on, for heaven's sake?' Hadley bellowed down the phone.

Jane tied the belt firmly round her middle, then returned the receiver to her ear. 'Your sister's just arrived, and about half a hundred others, judging by the noise outside.'

'Great! I'll have a word with her. Goodbye, darling Rose. And you won't forget your promise?'

'No,' she said, and shook her head, kept shaking it and shaking it, as she tried to change her face for Rowan and her retinue; restore happy sunny normal jolly Sunday.

24

Jane stared up at the two towers of the cathedral, one taller than the other and a different style completely; the shorter one almost lost in scaffolding; the stone stained and dingy-grey. So this was Chartres, the most visited cathedral in the world, the most miraculously preserved example of Gothic architecture, a sacred place of healing for eleven centuries – and some said since the Druids. She tried to stifle a twinge of disappointment. It was not quite what she'd expected, not as overwhelming, not as special. Perhaps she'd read too many books – complicated books she'd found difficult to follow, which explained how nothing in the building was irrelevant or accidental, but all the proportions and the measurements had deep significance, and were steeped in mystic symbolism.

She scanned the towers again. So why didn't they match, if the proportions were so perfect? And why did this so-called Royal Portal look so dirty and neglected – the stone pitted, streaked with lichen, even worn away in parts? She dropped a woolly glove, stooped to retrieve it, angry with herself. She was niggling like her mother, criticising something before she'd given it a chance. She could hardly judge, in any case, standing at a distance, and with both eyes watering in the wind. She clutched her coat around her, struggled on, head down, towards the doors, wishing she'd packed fur-lined boots and thermal underwear. Chartres' bitter February made England's seem benign.

She still felt frazzled from the journey – two hours seesawing the Channel, then another half-millennium trying to quiet her stomach on a queasy throbbing coach. She'd been car-sick as a child, assumed she had outgrown it. It had been a relief to take the train at Paris, chunter down to Chartres on a tame suburban line. She had arrived at almost midnight, booked into the first hotel she found – a shabby run-down *pension* off the station, with cardboard walls, and neighbours who played poker half the night. The breakfast coffee hadn't been quite strong enough to undo the effects of only three hours' sleep.

She picked her way round two old tramps, sprawled sozzled on the ground, one coughing half his lungs up, the other dead to the world; pushed the heavy inner door, which seemed to fight her entry, so that she was forced to slam her way into the church. She could hardly see at first, stood blinking at the darkness, as if she had passed from day to night, then took a few uncertain steps, until she was standing in the main body of the nave. She stopped in shock, staggered by its almost threatening scale. She was a twentieth-century pilgrim, used to skyscrapers and tower-blocks, yet those seemed paltry Lego-land compared with this immensity, this teeming swooping space. She craned her neck to peer up at the vaulting, kept looking up and up, aware that she was soaring like the building, leaving cold and doubt behind; dazzled and electrified by the whoop and shout of glass. She had never seen such glass. It was nothing like the pictures in the books, which, however faithful or exact the reproduction, still looked dead and flat compared with the reality – the mysterious dusky glow of blues and purples, the gash of red, like wounds, the glitter of bright haloes or gold crowns. Different windows kindled as she watched them – flaming into scarlet or blazing sapphire-blue; the greens quieter but insistent, the yellows trilling out.

She walked slowly up the nave, trying to take in everything at once – the sense of movement and yet stillness: the columns leaping up beyond her to the dark and shadowy roof; the glass alive, vibrating, bursting through the gloom; the tongues of lighted candles licking the cold stone; the solemn weighty silence, which seemed made of stone itself. She didn't have the words for what she felt. All the terms that Christopher had used – numinousness, transcendence, *élévation spirituelle* – were just strings of letters, too cramped for this great height. He'd been closer when he'd mentioned eating glass. She could eat these windows, gorge on them, like the richest sort of food, nibble their small details, roll them round her mouth. She was already picking out the plums – a sumptuous-looking king, settling down to sleep, still wearing all his gear in bed, including his gold crown; a supercilious camel in an unlikely shade of mauve; a small but sturdy cow with twisty horns. But she was doing things all wrong. The guidebook had instructed her to 'read' the windows as if they were a book, take out her binoculars and study them page by page, in the right and proper order, not goggle indiscriminately, ignoring plot and story.

She fumbled in her shoulder-bag, then zipped it up again. Stuff the guidebook! Medieval peasants would not have had binoculars, and anyway she was far too restless and excited to stand still in one place; felt more like hurtling round the aisles, shouting greetings to all that brilliant company of angels, prophets, martyrs, virgins, saints. Apart from them, the church was almost empty – hers to relish on her own. She had expected far more tourists, but perhaps they didn't arrive till spring, or only at weekends, and it was still early in the morning and a bleak and wintry weekday. There were no guides or flashing cameras, no strident voices, intrusive tramp of feet. She was glad she was alone, didn't want Christopher confounding her with facts, or Hadley trying to flirt with her, asking when they could sneak back to the bedroom. She shared the huge cathedral with just a few old crones, huddled in the pews like sacks, or praying on their knees.

It must be built of prayer, this church – solid prayer plastering the walls, or concreting the floor; left behind like fossils after all those God-based centuries. She still hadn't got the facts quite straight, except there'd been at least half a dozen earlier churches on the same sacred hilltop site, a Roman temple before that, and perhaps a Druid settlement and a pre-Christian virgin-mother cult. She paused to touch a column, as if she were touching Faith itself, the Faith of ghostly worshippers who were now only bones or dust, yet seemed present in a way, shuffling there beside her, whispering and pointing; their prayers spiralling up like incense to the stone ribs of the roof.

She glanced back the way she'd come, trying to absorb the whole plan of the cathedral. If she wanted to make sense of it, study it in detail, she had better stay six months, not the few brief days she'd planned. Apart from all the carvings and the sculpture, there were a hundred and seventy-six separate stained-glass windows – twenty-seven thousand square feet of coloured glass. Perhaps she'd camp out in the nave, spread a rug and pillow in some dark nook or corner, and live there like a spider, hiding in the night-time, coming out by day. She liked the thought of hiding, took pleasure in the fact that no one in the world save Trish even knew where she had gone. After Hadley's phone-call, she had suddenly decided to go to Chartres immediately, not wait until the end of March and travel as his bed-mate, but go alone, as pilgrim.

She had reached the crossing now, stopped instinctively, overawed by the sense of height and mystery, which seemed even greater here, a breathless leap from human-scale to heaven. This was the exact centre of the church – she knew that from the books – the point of harmony, with man's world to the west, and God's realm to the east, and the two reconciled and balanced, so that the building was a slice of stone eternity. She liked that strange word 'slice'; imagined the cathedral as an elaborate sculpted loaf, stuffed with numbers, symbols, meanings, bursting like fat currants from its dough. The numbers hadn't meant much when she'd tried to work them out – all that stress on cold geometry, on theology, philosophy, astrological forces – pretentious words and theories swamping and perplexing her, making her a dunce who'd failed her GCSE when it came to Chartres Cathedral.

Now she knew she'd passed. It was a matter not of brain, but of instinct and gut-feeling. Whichever way she looked, she was aware of new complexities and depths – an infinity of shapes and details: arches and pilasters, capitals and columns, vaulting, carving, tracery – layer on layer on layer, waiting patiently and silently for her to soak them up, absorb them through her pores.

She was still astonished by the emptiness, by the fact no other person had come barging through the door, destroyed her precious peace. She'd been imagining the cathedral as it was when it was new – wide-eyed pilgrims swarming in like bargain-hunters on the first day of the sales, jostling for more elbow-room; carpenters and craftsmen touting for a job of work; merchants selling takeaways from a pie-stall in the nave (until they were kicked out to the cloister and told to learn respect); shrivelled crocks and cripples lying in the crypt like sacks, and praying for a cure. They'd have all recognised the glass – its colours stabbing-sharp from the recent twentieth-century cleaning, which had restored it to its thirteenth-century brilliance. Only the clerestory windows were still uncleaned as yet; their muted reds and blues looking murky and encrusted, as if they were trying to block the light out, rather than let it filter through.

As she gazed, the stone walls seemed to fall away, and leave the glass suspended in black space, detached from its surroundings, shimmering and floating in a void. She longed to pray, to know the words and rituals which made important things official, or could take her fret of feelings and hurl them up to God, like a rocket or a fax-machine. She knew this day was special, another sort of birthday, to replace the grim October one. She had some-how come of age, here in Chartres – alone – with no guests, no fussing parents, no witness save the figures in the windows; and part of growing up was accepting the whole balls-up of her party, the mess and tangle of other people's lives – even her own parents' lives.

She walked slowly round each transept, marking out the cross-shape with her feet, first north, then south; moving from bright pools of light to sombre smudgy shadow; aware of the huge crypt beneath her, the oldest and most secret part of Chartres, supporting the whole building on its broad submerged stone shoulders.

She drifted to the ambulatory, and on to the east end, which seemed a separate sacred region, closed off by double rows of massive columns, and lit chiefly by the radiance of the glass. She peered up at the window showing Charlemagne, remembered him from school – a big shot who could probably read, but had a lot of trouble writing; used to get up in the night to practise secretly. She had done the same herself – not with writing, but with cutting glass; had tried to impress Christopher by putting in a night-shift, stealing down to the light-box at two or three A.M., hoping to improve her skills by the time he arrived at nine. But Charlemagne was celebrated here because of the famous relic presented by his grandson – the tunic Mary wore when giving birth to Christ – a relic so miraculous it had made Chartres the star attraction for the next eleven hundred years, a sort of medieval Disneyland. According to the guidebook, the relic was depicted in the glass, but she'd have to use binoculars to make out that small detail from the mass of crowded scenes.

She took them out reluctantly, still feeling it was wrong to bring modern aids to medieval glass. She looped them round her neck, fiddled with the knob, then tilted back her head, almost losing her balance as faces leapt towards her, opening out like flowers; colours fizzed and stung. She was zooming in on heads – a skittish scarlet halo, a helmet in pea-green, a bay horse with a neat curled fringe which would have done credit to the best-trained girl at Snippers. She moved the glasses higher, found herself in the middle of a battle-scene; tried to tell the goodies from the baddies, identify the characters, distinguish shields and lances, helmets, spurs and crowns. The most impressive shield was one right at the bottom – heart-shaped and blood-red – which seemed to pulse as she examined it, and contrasted with its owner's slim white leg.

She rested her eyes a moment – the binoculars were heavy, and it hurt to keep her head tipped back. She was also stiff with cold; the dank chill of old stone numbing her whole body, even through her coat and two thick sweaters. Perhaps she'd take a break, go and get a coffee, to warm her from inside; buy a croissant or a sandwich so she wouldn't need to stop again for lunch, then return with her binoculars and feast herself on windows.

She tracked back to the transept and out through the south door, astonished at the fierceness of the light. The weather had been cloudy when she had first set off this morning, the day still dull and leaden, with a heavy curdled sky, yet emerging from the twilit church was like exchanging a dark tranquil womb for the glare of the delivery-room. The noise was startling, too. She had been lapped in timeless peace, the only sound the faint breath of a candle, or the slither of a rosary slipping through a gnarled old hand. Now two angry drivers were indulging in a hooting-match; a man outside a restaurant bellowing instructions to a van; a stroppy toddler wailing from its pushchair.

She crossed the square, lost herself in the maze of streets around it, searching for a café which looked quiet and inexpensive. She stopped at a *boulangerie*, drooling at the smell of new-baked bread. The town was packed not with arty tourists, but with bustling local matrons stocking up their larders. A customer squeezed past her, loaded down with five *baguettes*, already nibbling at the end of one, as if she couldn't wait for breakfast. Another woman was arguing with the fishmonger, poking the oysters with the tip of her umbrella. Jane stood marvelling at the range of unfamiliar fish, grotesque and spiny creatures with beards and claws and pincers, some still alive and waving the odd feeler. '*Torteaux vivants*,' she spelled out, watching the faint shift and sigh in a pile of dozy crab-shells. Their flame of life seemed turned to low, a last desperate weary flicker before they expired in someone's stewpan.

It was too cold to linger long, a ruthless wind ripping the last tattered leaves from a row of puny maples. She could sense snow in the air, snow held back like unshed tears, creating a strange tension, as if the nervous and unhappy sky was struggling to control itself. She ventured into a homely-looking café, muttered her '*Bonjour*', found a secluded table at the back. Two men were playing draughts, a woman with a baby feeding it a brioche dunked in coffee. Jane ordered a hot chocolate and a croissant, relieved the waitress understood her French. The only time she'd been abroad before was on a school trip to Bayeux, when they'd been packed into a dormitory with Mademoiselle Roux as chaperone, and no real chance to wander on their own. It was much more of a challenge to travel independently, almost a luxury not to have to talk to people, or feign a cheerful mood to hide the misery inside. The last few days had been something of a strain. She had decided not to tell Trish what Isobel had said to her about the artist's views on marriage; still felt some sense of loyalty to Christopher, didn't want him damned as promiscuous, deceitful. She knew what Trish would say – forget him, write him off – and neither had seemed possible. Yet here in Chartres, the whole tangled sordid story had faded in importance, no longer hurt so bitterly. Perhaps this truly was a place of healing, where miracles still happened, relics still had power.

She scooped froth off her chocolate, ate it with a spoon. She actually felt cheerful, for the first time since Sunday morning. Okay, she'd probably never know the truth about Christopher's affairs – whether he'd lied to her (again) about Anne's bad cold at Christmas; whether he genuinely loved her, or simply wanted a quick screw. But then she'd probably never know the truth about God, or Faith, or even Chartres itself – whether the Druids had been here before the Romans, whether the famous relic was just a trumped-up fake to extort money from the gullible; or if all the mysterious forces people claimed to experience in every part of the building, from the sanctuary to the crypt, were mere wishful thinking, or the result of too much *vin du pays*. Yet somehow she could live with the uncertainties, accept them as another sort of truth; was more concerned with simple things: the warm fug of the café, the taste of good French bread.

She removed her hood and scarf, cooed at the plump baby regurgitating brioche down its front. She'd relax here for a while, soaking up the heat, spinning out her brunch, revelling in the fact that she had no one to consider save herself; no Mademoiselle Roux to chivvy her, no Hadley to keep sweet, no tetchy artist with half his mind on work. She dipped into her jam – strawberry jam, which brought her father rushing to the café. She could see his hand beside her own, reaching out to pile some on his bread – a solid squarish hand, with dark hairs on the back, which always looked untidy. She'd been surprised as a young kid that Amy hadn't hoovered up those hairs, or scoured them off with Brillo pads, as she did with all the other things which upset her sense of order. Jane bit into her croissant, smiling at the thought. At least her tidy parents had stayed faithful to each other, kept their own lives neat, hadn't carved up her whole childhood by flaunting their adulteries, or suing for divorce. She suddenly felt lighter, as if she'd shed some crippling burden; could see herself pulsating on the fish-stall, labelled '*Jane vivante*' – not just waving one frail and feeble claw, but bursting clean out of her shell.

When she left the café, the first weak sun was breaking through, dappling the wan sky with pearl; the twin towers of the cathedral glinting in its light. Whichever way you walked, those towers

333

seemed always visible, rearing up beyond the shops and houses like a reassuring presence; a compass and a magnet summoning you back. She let them lead her on through the narrow crowded streets, only stopping at a flower-stall to admire the early tulips, sniff the scent of fat pink clotted hyacinths. She'd return here later on, buy flowers for her room – not six dozen hothouse roses, but a small bunch of spring narcissi.

She jogged the last few yards to the south porch of the cathedral, horrified to think that when she'd first entered through the west doors, she'd been so chilled and mopish she'd ignored the amazing carvings, lumbered blindly past them with her head down. These doors were just as famous, and still more packed with sculpted figures – apostles, martyrs, popes, confessors, flanking a Last Judgement in the centre. She did her best to identify the cast, picked out James the Greater by his scallop-shells, James the Lesser by his club. She had learnt a lot from Christopher – how to recognise a bishop by his mitre, a martyr by his palm and crown, Gabriel by his lily, Saint Peter by his keys. He had brought so much alive for her. All the symbols, stories, parables, which medieval people understood instinctively, she was beginning to grasp herself, through working on the glass or studying other windows. Four months ago, angels hadn't figured in her life. Now she saw them everywhere, and just above her head the entire celestial court had assembled for the Judgement: Seraphim and Cherubim, Thrones and Dominations, Virtues, Powers and Princedoms, Archangels and Angels. She wondered if her father would know a Virtue from a Throne, or her mother fret about the problem of dusting Seraphim, who had half a dozen wings apiece, to symbolise the swiftness of their thought.

The Cherubim were holding flames – another symbol, representing light, this time, though the stone looked dull and grey. All the same, she wished they'd turn their flames towards her, provide some instant heat. She'd better go inside again, and find the Passion window, compare the artist's Resurrection Angel with the smaller one at Chartres. She had seen it on a postcard in the studio, but the scale had been so tiny, it had been just a jumbled blur. She entered through the wooden doors, prepared now for the gloom, but not for the striking difference in the glass. The sun outside had lightened it in tone, made the blues more dominant, so that they slapped down even racy reds, while the diamond-patterned borders seemed to glitter and ignite, like illuminated Persian carpets woven with gold thread. She strode down to the west end, determined to blank out all distractions on the way; start at the beginning with the earliest of the windows – the Passion window and the two famous ones beside it.

She was annoyed to find a group of people already standing with their necks craned up and their camera lenses pointing. She'd laid claim to Chartres Cathedral as her own individual property, had no wish to share it with cocky brash-voiced Yanks, so loaded down with hardware they looked as if they'd ransacked the largest branch of Dixons. They were gawping at the central window, so she edged more to the left, used her binoculars to locate the green crucifix which the guidebook had described – the Tree of Life defying Death, in resurrection-green.

'Gee!' exclaimed the fat blonde on her right. 'How d'you figure they ever got ladders up high enough to paint that stuff? Some of those darn windows are like as big as the state of Florida.'

'They don't paint it, honeybun. They buy these ready-coloured pieces and stick 'em all together. Like in a jigsaw puzzle.'

'No, they don't,' a younger girl objected, a Twiggy with no breasts. 'That's mosaic, not stained glass. I guess what they do is melt it till it's hot, and pour it into moulds. In fact, that's probably how they dye it in the first place – tip it into separate containers and add a different colour to each one, like when you frost a birthday cake – you know, strawberry-pink in one lot, chocolate in another.'

'Well, if you want my honest opinion, they've used too many colours. It's a mishmash, isn't it? You can't make out what's goin' on at all.'

'They should've left more plain glass,' a swarthy man chipped in. 'It's so dark in here, you can't hardly see. I guess I'm gonna have to use my tripod, and probably the flash, too.'

Jane wheeled round in fury. 'Listen,' she protested, no longer able to contain herself. 'The men who made these windows were bloody geniuses. Of course they painted the glass, but first they had to cut it – every single tiny piece is cut by hand, you realise, not just ready-made. And none of your fancy modern glass-cutters. All they had was a sort of red-hot poker-thing, which cracked the glass apart. Imagine cutting really fiddly shapes with a clumsy piece of iron! And they couldn't waste a fragment. Coloured glass was worth a bomb. Medieval people treasured it, like we treasure precious jewels. And there wasn't any paper then, so they didn't have our cutlines or . . .' She broke off in confusion, hadn't meant to speak at all, let alone come over like a battleaxe. And anyway, how could she expect a bunch of casual tourists to know what cutlines were? It had taken her long enough to grasp the fundamentals, and she'd been actually working on the glass. But wasn't that the point? She had started blind and ignorant, and Christopher had made her see. She must play his role herself, but do it with less virulence, turn down her fishwife voice.

'Look,' she said, in Trish's tones: warm milk and clover honey. 'It's not exactly easy to make a stained-glass window, and it was even harder then. I mean, when they came to paint the glass, they had it lying flat on whitewashed benches, never saw it up against the light, like artists do today. They just had to imagine the effect they were creating, and also judge how it would impress a congregation from a distance, like we're looking at it now. That takes bags of confidence, and a sense of almost daring. Of course, they handed down traditions, which must have helped a lot. There was this twelfth-century monk, you see – a German called Theophilus, who wrote a whole long treatise on the . . . ' Her words faltered to a stop. She was going far too fast, muddling theory up with craft, probably boring the plaid pants off them. She moved her eyes despondently from the window to their faces, astonished to see six pairs of eyes fixed on her with the sort of doggy rapture Byron beamed at Isobel when she went to fetch his lead. Then all six voices started chiming out at once, plying her with questions – where, what, why, how, when?

'Are you the tour-guide here, Ma'am?' the wobbly blonde enquired, gazing at the glass with new respect.

'Er, no, I . . . '

'You just gotta be an expert, spoutin' all that stuff.'

Jane shook back her hair, wondering how she'd ever dared to give her one-man lecture, uninvited. 'I . . . I work for a stained-glass artist, in his studio.'

The group now gathered round her, encircling her and pressing close, as if she were some rare and precious creature unknown in modern times; a unicorn or griffin who had popped up from the Middle Ages and must be caught before it vanished. They invited her to coffee, or to lunch at their hotel – the best in town, they claimed.

'I'm sorry, but I've had lunch.'

'Well, listen, how's about dinner? We've found this real neat restaurant, about ten miles out of town. It puts on like medieval banquets – you know, roast wild boar and sucking pig, and this old-fashioned beer called mead.'

'The waitresses are all dressed up like Elizabethan serving-maids. It's just so cute, you gotta see it.'

Jane shifted from foot to foot. 'I'm afraid I'm really pushed for time. I'm only here for . . .'

'Don't hassle the kid, Dee-Dee.' The dark man checked his watch. 'Hey, you guys, the tour of the crypt starts in seven minutes, and we don't even have our tickets yet.'

The other five gathered up their clutter, then all shook her by the hand, left their names – and cards – told her if she was ever in Wisconsin, or Denver, Colorado, she must be sure to look them up.

She watched them shamble out with a mixture of relief and secret pride. She was now the guide, the expert, the professional stained-glass artist too busy for a banquet. She grinned to herself as she thought of her own supper – a *croque monsieur* in one of the cheapest of the cafés, or a bread-and-pâté picnic in her dingy hotel room, with herself the only serving-wench.

She refocused her binoculars, until she'd located the green crucifix, then moved from death and suffering in the centre of the window to resurrection at the top. At last, she found the angel, which was far less overwhelming than the artist's – just an inconspicuous figure in one of the small roundels. Yet she liked its strange red face and feet, its Persil-gleaming robe; the way it was sitting with its legs apart, looking casual and relaxed, as if about to go off-duty and pour itself a pint. She moved her glasses a fraction to the right, admired the skilful details of the painting: the three white lamps hanging in the tomb, the empty shroud below them. She could appreciate the subtleties now she'd worked with glass herself; the expressive use of colour which could reverberate and jolt, sizzle through your body as if you'd swallowed a live firework.

She abandoned the binoculars, took a few steps back, so she could scan the three tall windows as a triptych, let them seep into her mind, stain it with their reds and aching blues. Maybe all the tourists brought back a splash of colour with them, with their other souvenirs, so these windows were reseeded in every country of the world. Perhaps they'd come as far to see Christopher's new window, flocking into Sussex from Denver and Wisconsin, Tokyo and Delhi – and still be coming seven centuries on. She'd be dust and maggots then, like the Druids and the Romans were; a heap of bones like Charlemagne. Yet part of her would still live on – in the Resurrection Angel's face and features, its long straight streaming hair; and also in the glass she'd cut: the Angel's bony feet, the landscape they were planted on, a good half of the wings, the streaky startled sky above the halo.

She wandered down the central aisle, suddenly missing Christopher, his solidity, his seriousness, the way he knew his way about a church, as if he'd grown up in one from childhood, with God a moody, distant (often absent) Father. She stumbled on a rough patch in the pavement, glanced down at the markings underneath her feet – loops and coilings in lighter stone and darker, cut into the floor, until they were swallowed up by rows and rows of chairs. She took a closer look, realised that the pattern was not haphazard, as it first appeared, but enclosed a flower-shape in its centre, with six petals and a stem; recognised it instantly from the pictures in the books. The labyrinth! She'd totally forgotten it, hadn't even noticed it the first time she'd come in. But then the light was very dim, and the neat concentric circles she'd studied in the photographs were simply not apparent here, but cut off by the chairs, their symmetrical pattern lost.

She stooped down to examine the winding coils still showing; felt them rough and gritty underneath her hand, chilly to the touch. Could that uneven stretch of patterned stone really be a model of the universe, contain such complex symbolism, such marvels of geometry, that several well-known scholars had lavished a whole lifetime on its measurements and meaning? A maze to her still meant bulky hedges – yew or beech or holly, standing solid and 3-D – not a flat expanse of worn and dirty pavement.

She remained squatting on her heels, trying to remember what the various books had said. Most of it she hadn't understood; had soon got lost and storm-tossed by alchemy and ideograms, solar cycles, Gnostics, but at least she'd grasped the basic concept that it symbolised the path through life, the journey of the soul to heaven or the afterlife.

'I walked that labyrinth in a state of near elation, Rose.'

She could hear the artist's rasping voice, husky from his cold; see him standing on this precise spot in the nave, at exactly her own age. His crest of hair was tawny-brown, not grey, but he seemed little different otherwise from how he was today, still moody and impassioned, as he paced around the labyrinth, the flames of eager candles reflected in his eyes. She closed her own eyes, groped up to her feet. She could smell the incense from the service, hear the organ rumbling through the echo-chamber walls, his footsteps growing louder as he circled round and round. Thirteenth-century peasants had danced the maze, he'd told her; their prancing feet beating out the rhythm of the universe. The two images were fusing in her mind – the artist with the peasants, no longer tramping staidly, but whirling through the paths and right on into the centre, while the spinning cosmos orbited in time with them.

She opened her eyes, dizzy from her fantasy, but itching to walk the maze herself, repeat the artist's ritual. He'd been lucky – or well-organised – to find himself in Chartres on the one day of the year when the chairs were cleared away. She could hardly shift two hundred single-handed, would only bring some verger rushing out in fury from his spy-hole in the vestry. But at least the entrance to the maze was clear, and also its flower-centre, both marked out on the central aisle between the flanks of chairs. Perhaps she could climb over them, or push her way between. They were only light rush-seated things, not great hulking pews.

She retraced her steps until she was standing on the narrow path which led into the labyrinth. She had left her bag behind, had no wish to be encumbered, weighed down with trivialities – make-up, mirror, chocolate – or even maps and guidebooks, which were for another sort of journey. She glanced behind her, nervous, relieved the church was so deserted; even the old women gone, just one grubby bundle, doubled on itself, slumped down in the last row at the back. Light was filtering through the West Rose window, which showed Christ as Judge on Judgement Day, and Saint Michael and a black-horned devil, representing good and evil, weighing souls on a pair of scales. She couldn't make the scenes out, but she knew them from the guidebook; was suddenly reminded of their meaning in her own life – good decisions, bad ones; openness, or lies. The maze might help her choose. Christopher had made her see that it was a path not just to heaven, but to peace, or home, or certainty, or the true centre of one's self.

Her neck was aching from the strain of looking up, but she kept gazing at the Rose – a window with her name – aware that, like the maze, it also contained twelve circles – three sets of twelve, in fact – and that if it were hinged down to the floor of the nave, its centre would correspond precisely with the centre of the labyrinth, both circles the same size. When she'd read that in the book, it had seemed a curiosity, a quaint statistic she could usefully forget. Yet now she was actually experiencing the symmetry, could feel it in her body, as if she were being pulled between the forces which linked stolid stone with iridescent glass.

She turned back to face the altar, took her first few steps along the maze, stopped, frustrated, as the path branched to the left, then disappeared beneath a mass of blockish chairs. She slipped between the first two, but the four in front were joined together by a wooden bar nailed below their seats, and impossible to move. She clambered swiftly over them, feeling guilty, disrespectful, then squeezed between the next two, then the next, the next, the next.

339

If this was symbolic of the Path of Life, then it was a halting and restrictive path, with no sense of achievement. It was hard to keep on course at all, because the light was even dimmer once she'd moved out from the central aisle, and the grey-blue shadows of the chairs blurred the blue-grey outlines of the maze. She envied Christopher the scope he'd had to walk the path unhindered; even envied those medieval peasants who'd walked it on their knees, seen it as the equivalent of a pilgrimage to Jerusalem. It was a pilgrimage for her, as well, yet she was scrambling over chair-seats, rather than circling round a powerful path charged with mystery and meaning.

She could always take the easy course, simply cut across the windings of the circles, instead of following them laboriously, back and forth, back and forth. But then she'd reach the centre in just a few brief paces, instead of a meandering two hundred yards; would attain her goal in seconds, rather than a convoluted lifetime.

She stood dithering, uncertain, peering down at the faint and fading tracks. She could hardly see at all now. The cathedral was darkening, the windows guttering like burnt-down candles, then finally snuffing out. The weather must have changed, the sky outside be completely overcast – not snow, as she had feared, but torrential winter rain. She strained her ears, but could hear no drenching downpour, hear no sound at all, only the silence of the centuries silted up like sand. The great West Rose looked dead, Christ Himself blanked out, Saint Michael overthrown. The demons in that window, shown hurling the lost souls into the gaping jaws of hell, seemed to have climbed down from the glass and be closing in around her, their breath clammy on her face, their scaly touch erasing her, like another of the damned. She turned from west to east. Those windows, too, were blank, all the exuberance of the glass-makers doused with a black pall.

She crouched down on all fours, the stone rough beneath her knees, the darkness like the night of the great storm. She could hear the wind again, baiting the frail walls of her cottage on the beach; the sea pounding on the shingle, then sucking, swirling back. She had slept outside a church that night, woken to black cold, then crept inside for sanctuary, groping in the shadows until she was startled by a torch.

The torch was weak this time, wavering, uncertain, barely showing up the dim outline of the paths. She took two blind steps ahead, towards the centre of the labyrinth, aware that she was cheating, jumping gaps instead of tracing circles, but too panicky to care. She couldn't see to walk, but a hand was reaching out to her, a steel hand like a magnet, guiding her, restoring her, seeing she got home.

The torch was brighter now, illuminating six stone petals opening out around her. She was standing in the centre of the maze's central flower; could feel peace seeping up like heat, as if some hidden vent had been let into the floor, thawing the bleak darkness, quickening the dead windows. The blues were singing out again, a choir of peacock altos resounding through the nave, outshrilling the more timid greens and browns. The gold of crowns and thuribles looked newly shined and polished; the white robes freshly washed. She could see another figure in another shining robe – a figure in her mind – Ariadne with her guiding saving thread, leading Theseus from the labyrinth. She suddenly realised she'd been guided in her turn, led to a decision, as Christopher himself had been, in exactly the same spot. She had to work with glass – she knew that now, instinctively – had to stay with Christopher, despite the complications, and continue learning her new craft; not fritter time and skills away pushing papers in an office, or stuffing poncy aubergines. She would even have a faith – a faith in her own work, like the faith of all these stone-masons and glass-makers who had made themselves eternal with their church.

She could hear her stomach rumbling, realised she was ravenous – and not just for a sandwich. She needed a whole sucking pig, a whacking ten-course banquet, to give her instant energy to start on Christopher's windows. If she replanned her stay, she could report to work on Monday, as he'd asked. Today was Friday morning. She would get up at dawn tomorrow and see everything in Chartres – all the other churches, the old medieval town – then travel back on Sunday. But first she'd celebrate – buy up the whole cake-shop, fill her room with tulips, strip the flower-stall bare. She had discovered her true role in life, cut through all the turmoil, so why shouldn't she splash out?

She took a last look at the Rose as she sailed towards the doors; the angels in the circles blowing their bright trumpets, the shroud–clad dead struggling from their tombs. She couldn't see the details, but one scene in particular was blazing in her head: a triumphant green-winged angel pointing out the way, leading the elect towards Paradise Regained.

25

Jane stood clinging to the rail on the top deck of the ferry, the wind snatching up the long strands of her hair, then letting them whip back against her face. The decks were shining-wet from the hiss and swoosh of spray which was smoking from the breakers, softening their dark green. The horizon stretched ahead of her, lost in hazy mist, blue smudging into grey. A gull dived low towards the deck, then spiralled up again, blown away like a flimsy paper-bag. She envied it its wings, wished she could soar back to France, start her trip again – or travel further, see the world. She hadn't once been lonely in the past three days in Chartres, was thrilled that she could be alone, no longer had to cling to friends or parents. Even now, she was on her own, all the other passengers cowering down below, sheltering from the cold; a few brave souls huddled on the lower decks. This top one was deserted, hers to share with the hugeness of the sky, with the swooping pilgrim gulls.

Another ferry was passing, almost identical with theirs. She spelt out its name – St Anselm – knew the saint from one of Christopher's windows, a tall lancet in a Catholic church in Canterbury, which he had made ten years ago. She even knew his emblem: a gold ship with silver sails, and flying three white pennants with red crosses. She had learnt so much already, and if she continued working in the studio for eighteen months or more, she'd be as familiar with the saints as any thirteenth-century abbess. She must live as nun herself, though, and refuse to sleep with Christopher, serve him as assistant, not as mistress. She had been struggling with the problem since she'd decided to stay on with him; torn between the memories of their last explosive love-making, and her distaste at being just another casual conquest, a way of spicing up his marriage, providing some variety. She had finally decided to put her interests

342

first, develop her own talents, not join the list of his discarded other women.

She glanced down at the sea again, the green like reamy glass – the same flowing rippled movements through its colour, the same glints and restless shimmer. Strange they seemed so far from land, breakers swirling on all sides, their lace-topped crests repeated in the spumy clouds above her. An hour had passed already, so they should be close to Dover, yet she could see nothing but unbroken sea and sky. Perhaps she'd go inside, grab a snack before they docked, now that her stomach had recovered from the coach trip.

She passed from one world to another as she stepped inside the fuggy crowded restaurant, breathing in fried onions instead of clean salt air. The lights were glaring, garish; frowsty whey-faced passengers guzzling buns and sausages, a howling child drowning out the muzak. She joined the long queue at the counter, trying not to look at breadcrumbed haddock oozing yellow fat, or mounds of greasy chips; picked out a plain bread roll instead, and two red shiny apples. She paid with English money, loath to use her last French francs, which she'd keep for luck, or as a spur to visit France again, perhaps return to Chartres in spring.

Every seat was taken, so she squeezed out to the passage, where groups of people were squatting on the floor, some swilling cans of beer, one or two sprawled out on their backs, drunk, or maybe seasick. She wove her way between them, lurching with the ship. The sea seemed rougher now, and though she tried to eat her roll, it was difficult to swallow, stuck in her gullet, as if refusing to risk the indignity of being vomited up again. She threw it in the bin, jolted on to the duty-free shop, determined to distract herself from food. She'd buy some scent for Trish, an arty scarf for Isobel. She manoeuvred round a shrill of schoolgirls giggling by the fruit machines, dodged an old man in a duffel coat who tried to paw her hair. The shop felt claustrophobic – low-ceilinged, overheated, and full of jostling bodies. A sleek red-taloned salesgirl was promoting a new perfume, squirting it on wrists, each generous squirt accompanied by a dazzling Colgate smile. The scent was cloying, sickly, curdled in Jane's head with the smell of chips and onions. She moved over to the scarves, asked the girl behind the counter if she had any more exciting ones. Her voice was interrupted by an announcement on the tannoy – the captain speaking, reporting a delay – what he called 'an industrial dispute' at Dover, which would prevent them berthing for an hour, or maybe more.

An instant brouhaha broke out, people groaning and complaining

343

about wildcat strikes and bloody commie layabouts; two teenage boys even booing at full volume. The captain was still talking, giving information about boat-trains and connections, but his voice was all but swamped. Jane leant against the counter. The 'hour or maybe more' might extend itself indefinitely, depended on the whim of a bunch of bolshie dockers. She'd miss the last coach back to London, when it was vitally important that she turned up in the studio first thing Monday morning. She could almost hear the artist's querulous voice, asking where the hell she'd been. And if she told the truth, then more trouble. He'd be annoyed and even hurt that she'd gone haring off to Chartres without so much as mentioning the fact; hadn't shared the trip with him, at least in planning and anticipation.

She drifted from the shop into the video lounge, trying to find somewhere with less intrusive lights, so she could rest her eyes and mind. Two men with loaded guns were bawling at each other on the screen, one already scarred, the skin taut and puckered down his cheek, as if the wound had been cobbled up too tight by some bungling novice-surgeon. She flopped down in a seat, felt she'd travelled a million miles from Chartres. There, man soared up to God; here, he stuffed and tippled, made love to one-armed bandits, socked his fellows in the face, tried to blow their brains out.

The boat was juddering and rocking, its motion out of time with the car chase on the screen, but both churning through her stomach. The police car took the corner on two wheels. She longed to turn the film off, commandeer this dim-lit lounge as a place of quiet and meditation. There was so little you could switch off – not storms, or strikes, or people's moods, not colds or sex or wives.

Scarface had been nabbed, at last, though not by the police. A new gloating baddie dived down from a balcony and punched him in the kidneys. She caught the blow in the middle of her own gut, clapped her hand across her mouth, made a sudden desperate dash towards the exit.

She emerged from the lavatory, her coat stained with flecks of vomit. She had sicked up a thin mucus, yellowish and slimy, watched it slither down the plug-hole, while she retched and spat, retched and spat, hating the indignity, the offensive shaming stench. She took a few uncertain steps, testing out her legs, appeared to have lost her balance as well as half her stomach. She had also lost the daylight, a black void through the windows now, a sense of time running down, weak from its exertions. The boat seemed still more packed; bodies cluttering the corridors like overflowing dustbin-bags disgorging

344

empty cans. A low descant of complaint rumbled from the tired and crumpled passengers, which matched the fractious throbbing of the ferry. The lingering reek of frying-oil cut across the smells of beer, stale feet.

She ploughed her way upstairs and out on to the deck, needed some fresh air, though she was unprepared for the lake-sized pools of water sloshing round her feet, and the vicious wind slamming into her face. She found it hard to walk straight, with the boat rolling underneath her; was forced to weave and zigzag, experienced the same sensation as she had done in the hurricane – blown off course and buffeted by some sadistic force of nature which saw her as fair game. Had she grown no deeper roots since then? She'd felt so strong in Chartres – a tall majestic tree which could never be uprooted – but now her leaves and branches were being stripped and wrenched away. She couldn't bear to see herself go crashing down again, lose that new elation. Her mother would dismiss her state as mere adolescent moodiness, blame it on her age. 'Jane's up one minute, down the next,' she was always telling friends, but that was far too pat – the sort of thing all mothers said when their daughters couldn't settle down and accept the boring blandness on offer as 'maturity'. Okay, so she had moods, but then so did Christopher, and anyway, the confidence she'd felt in Chartres was much more than a fleeting high – more to do with healing and real insight. Perhaps its magic only worked when you were close to the cathedral, spellbound by its glass; or perhaps she needed longer to ground herself, and grow.

She clutched a metal seat-back, peered out at the sea. It looked black beyond redemption, vastly dark and treacherous, as if it had engulfed the moon and stars, drowned all other craft. She battled on to the stern, leaned against the rail, gazing at the foaming wake, which seemed to be pointing back to France. She longed to be washed up there, like a log or bottle bobbing into Calais, so she could escape the problems of returning home – not just the endless journey, but Christopher and Hadley. Easy enough to decide to give up sex, live life on her own terms, allow herself a breathing space until she'd found a man who was right for her, but another thing entirely to make Christopher accept it. He'd override her, force her to submit. And, in one way, she desired that; kept remembering his mouth, its wildness, its sheer skills. They had parted from each other in a blaze and stab of passion, and planning a weekend away – a whole weekend in bed. He'd never fathom why she'd changed her mind, and she could hardly mention what Isobel had told her about his messy married life, his women on the side.

345

She pushed back her tangled hair, tried to anchor it inside her coat, stop it streaming like a pennant in the wind. She might even lose her job if she refused to sleep with him. He could engineer it easily, tell her he was so hard-pressed with two big new commissions, that he was forced to employ a fully-trained assistant – a female one, of course. She glanced behind her, could hear boozy shouts and catcalls, a group of boys staggering towards her, their cigarettes glowing red. She tried to slink away, but the tallest of them pounced, grasped her round the middle, and pretended to throw her overboard. The others yelped with laughter, clustering around her, tugging at her hair, wolf-whistling and crowing.

'Get off!' she yelled, lashing out, wrestling with the ringleader until she had worked her body free, surprised by her own fury and her strength.

'Can't you take a joke?' he jeered.

'No!' she shouted back.

'Cunt!' he muttered, stomping off, then turning round to spit at her. The whole group slouched away, at last, taunting one another now, lobbing empty beer-cans across the deck. She remained huddled at the rail, not daring to make any move, in case they returned to the attack. She was still shaken by the incident, by that gob of dirty spittle aimed right at her face, by the crudeness of the swear-word. And the fight itself had brought back shaming memories of her savage brawl with Trish. There was so much violence running wild, not just in these drunken yobs, but in friends and lovers, even in herself.

She stared down at the breakers, their constant kick and thresh bullying the ship, retching up white spume. She could climb up on the rail and simply fall – let herself be blown into the sea like the fag-end that tall lout had dropped, her tiny fire extinguished in its depths. Wouldn't it be easier than fighting on so many fronts, torn between two mothers, not knowing who she was? She unzipped her coat, feeling suddenly too heavy, weighed down by her thoughts, by her bulky winter clothes. If she slipped them off, she would fall like a white streak, unencumbered, naked . . .

'Ladies and gentlemen, this is Captain Langley speaking. I am pleased to inform you that we have just received clearance to enter the port of Dover, and will be berthing in approximately twenty minutes.'

She swung back from the rail, plunged across the deck, tripping on the spray-drenched wood, but hauling herself up again, struggling to the front of the ship. She must try to beat the crowds, get off as soon as possible, grab any coach still waiting. She was surprised to see the harbour lights far closer than she'd thought; the famous white cliffs looming from the darkness like pale but solid shoulders. A revolving beacon was flashing on and off, as if in reassurance, lighting the ship home. This *was* her home, the country she belonged to, and she longed to disembark, plant her feet on solid land, lay claim to it as hers. She'd been born here, spoke the language, knew the customs and traditions; felt a sudden sweet relief that she was back, and safe – alive.

Other passengers began venturing from the lounges, crowding all the decks, some pressing, pushing close to her, jabbing with their bags; all trying to see the harbour. Everyone seemed miraculously revived, impatience and exhaustion discarded like old clothes. A few boys began to cheer and stamp, linking arms and singing, no longer raucous lager-louts but a halleluiah choir. A bearded man with a knapsack on his back unwound his long home-knitted scarf, absurd in green and yellow stripes, and waved it like a flag. Jane gripped the rail, refused to give her place up at the front, despite the burly man behind her who was trying to muscle in. She stood watching the bright strings of lights hung along the shore; longed to simply jump from deck to dock, instead of waiting for the dogged ship to edge in slowly, cautiously.

Everything seemed quieter and becalmed. The wind had dropped, the waves nudged gently at the hull, rather than pummelling it, and thwacking. She checked her watch, surprised to see it wasn't late at all, still only early evening. Of course she'd catch the last coach, would be back in the studio by eleven at the latest, and up for work next morning on the dot of eight o'clock. She was a professional now, committed, and if any fully trained replacement tried to wrest her job away from her, she would fight them all the way. She was involved in both the artist's new commissions; had already served as model for the Muses, and now she'd seen the labyrinth, soaked up all its mystery, she could help him with the Lyons windows, right from the design stage. He would be starting on the sketch soon, since the Resurrection window was almost off his hands, probably in the glazing-shop, being leaded-up, cemented. She'd insist the artist took her there, so she could watch the final stages; had to see the Angel in all its finished glory.

Flocks of gulls were flying up, flushed out by the ship's approach, wheeling to the right with a mournful keening cry. If she stayed and worked with Christopher, she could fly high on his wings, make sure he pulled her up with him. The harbour was so close now, she could see blurred and shadowy figures standing on the pier, one man waving boisterously, as if he'd been stationed there to welcome them. Suddenly more lights snapped on, floodlighting the boat. 'May Christ, by His light, dispel from heart and mind the sombre night.' The words flashed through her head – the inscription of a window which Christopher had made – another Easter window with a theme of light restored. She had seen the sketch in the studio, must have banked the words unconsciously, like treasure in her mind. She kept her eyes on the winking circling beacon; a gigantic paschal candle beckoning them in. It was only thirty days till Easter – light returning, spring returning, the Resurrection window triumphantly in place. She would be kneeling in the Sussex church where she'd first encountered Christopher, and where he'd saved her from the darkness, celebrating not just Resurrection, but her own deliverance, rebirth.

26

'The Day of Resurrection!
Earth, tell it out abroad;
The Passover of gladness,
The Passover of God!
From death to life eternal,
From earth unto the sky,
Our God hath brought us over
With hymns of victory.'

Jane tried to make her voice heard above Isobel's rich contralto.
She was eager to sing out, to swell the burst of happy sound surging
through the nave. The throb of hymn and organ seemed to make the
stone walls hum, as if the church itself was an instrument twanging
and resounding. She was right up in the front, a spear of sunlight
falling on her dress – blue to match the Angel; blue flowers in her
hat. She had never worn a hat before, not even at a wedding, but it
made her feel both festive and exotic. She had been nudging brims
with Isobel, when both of them knelt down. Isobel's dramatic straw
was banded with red ribbons, which kept fluttering and tossing as
she swung round to smile at some new guest, or check on her young
nephew who was sitting just behind her.

The church was packed, an overflow of people even standing at the back. The normal congregation was always large on
Easter Sunday morning, but Isobel's friends and relatives had
more than doubled it. Tom's colleagues, fellow surgeons, were
dapper in dark suits, and contrasted with her arty friends in their
cloaks and coloured boots. Rowan had brought her own contin-
gent, who were in the pew behind, a fidget of small children on
their laps.

'Our hearts be pure from evil,
That we may see aright
The Lord in rays eternal
Of Resurrection-light . . .'

Jane couldn't see Christopher, but she could hear his steady
tenor bulking out the weedier voices further down the row. He
was wearing a velvet jacket the colour of black grapes, and an
expensive purply tie. She had arrived in church before him, watched
him striding in impatiently with Anne latched to his arm, an Anne
who looked a mess – no hat, no special hair-do, and half an inch of
petticoat showing beneath her skirt. He had reached the front and
smiled at her, the smile freezing on his face when he saw Hadley
parked beside her – a Hadley in blue jeans. Isobel had saved her,
jumped up to her feet and given him such an enthusiastic (and highly
public) kiss, he'd been far too disconcerted to do anything but detach
himself and retire to his own seat.

Jane watched the sun glinting on the bishop's ring, brightening
the brass candlesticks, competing with the flickering flame of the
flower-wreathed paschal candle. It had been showery early on;
fast-moving bloated rain-clouds churning across a restless moody
sky. She had sat in her pyjamas, gazing through the window at
the battle going on – a contest between sun and shower, blue
and grey, hope and gloom. Sun and hope had won. It was now
a perfect Easter Day, as if Isobel's benevolent God had laid it on
deliberately – puffed up the white clouds, strewn the dappled fields
with primroses and dog-violets. The church was bright with more
luxurious flowers – freesias, stiff-necked iris, stately Easter lilies,
whose embroidered white and gold matched the bishop's vestments.
Anthony, the vicar, was also robed in white, but his short, plump,
balding figure provided an almost comic contrast to the tall and
raw-boned bishop, with his lion's mane of grey hair.

Both were now processing to the Resurrection window, preceded
by three servers carrying candles and a cross; the organ pumping out
a triumphant Handel voluntary, to underline the importance of the
moment. Isobel clasped her hand, and she and the Mackenzie tribe
trickled from their pews and followed the procession, Christopher
and Anne bringing up the rear. Jane was thrilled to be included.
She wasn't standing in that special group as Isobel's protégée, but
as Christopher's assistant, his almost fellow-artist. She hadn't seen
the window yet – not finished, not in place – save for the briefest
of brief glances when she'd first walked into the church. She had

350

hoped to watch it being fixed, was still very disappointed that she'd missed the installation of Adrian's red birds, but the artist had said no; wanted her to see it at its unencumbered best, without the obstruction of the scaffolding, the glaziers' fuss and clutter. He had returned from the fixing moody and depressed, slating himself for a whole list of faults and failings. 'The bloody useless window' didn't have the vigour he'd intended, looked smaller, less dynamic, less impressive altogether. The borders were too fussy, when he'd been aiming for simplicity, and both the eagle and the dove were slightly overpainted. She remembered Isobel had told her, way back in December, how he always overreacted, agonising endlessly over trifles or minutiae which no one else would notice, but all the same she'd still felt sick with dread. Supposing he was right this time, and the whole thing was somehow ruined. It could be her own fault. She had flounced out of the studio at the crucial painting stage, maybe put him off his stroke.

Even now, she felt a strange reluctance to share his disappointment; had to force herself to raise her head, look up at the window. She immediately stepped back, startled by its impact. It was totally transformed since the last time she had seen it. The painting, firing, glazing, had kindled it into life, a richer and more detailed life; the dark lattice of the leads defining each small piece of glass, yet also tying everything together, emphasising the sense of rushing upward movement. The Angel was a power-source, a charismatic Spirit exploding up to heaven, and demanding faith in God by its own vehement intensity. The angels in the other windows looked insipid in comparison, earthbound and quiescent, whereas Christopher's had broken free of all material ties. Its thrusting figure cut across both lights, and appeared to soar still further, beyond the mullions and the glass, beyond the solid stocky church to the infinity of sky. And the spectator soared along with it, had no other option, however gross and crass he was; was carried up beyond himself, beyond the froth and faddle to a new and higher realm.

Jane glanced back a moment at Hadley's shock of hair, which he was growing for a part in a new play; knew that he was wrong about the window. The thousands that it cost shouldn't be given to the homeless, or turned into hot soup. This was a different sort of rescue work, but every bit as vital – to pluck man from the pig-trough and fling him into heaven.

She was aware that eyes were on her face, not Hadley's but the artist's; allowed herself to meet his gaze, tried to put a hundred heady adjectives into one brief smile and nod. All the strenuous effort which had gone into the job, all the hours at bench and easel, the standing, stooping, stretching, the decisions and anxieties, had been somehow cancelled out. The window looked spontaneous, as if it had been created out of nothing, or out of light itself; a magnetic presence, inevitable and changeless.

The bishop's voice cut through her reflections. She was so caught up in the window, she'd hardly realised he was speaking, but she did her best to concentrate, to become part of the whole ceremony. He was thanking God for Tom's great gift of healing, for his compassion and his skills, the importance of his life. Isobel was smiling, while mascara-smudged grey tears ran slowly down her face. She didn't use a handkerchief, let them fall unchecked, as if she owed the tears to Tom, as another sort of tribute. Her son and daughter were standing either side, Rowan linking arms with her, a selfconscious-looking Hadley squeezing her gloved hand. The entire congregation had turned to face the window, and were listening to the bishop's rumbling baritone.

'We also thank Thee, Lord, for the gift of this new window, which speaks to us of hope, and reminds us there is life beyond the grave, everlasting life and light. We give Thee praise for all who have widened our vision, or helped to lead us to the truth: the prophets, thinkers and artists of this and every age. Thou art glorified, great God, by things of beauty, and so we earnestly beseech Thee to bless this window in memory of Thomas Hugh Mackenzie, that all who see it may be enriched, inspired, and brought to life eternal.'

Jane longed to shout 'Amen'. Okay, so she didn't know the great God he was addressing, but he was also praising truth and beauty – Keats's truth and beauty – making them important, exalting Christopher. Even the small children, who had been yammering and squirming, or wailing to go home, seemed impressed by his tall figure, his intense and solemn voice, the majestic shield-shaped mitre and jewel-encrusted cope. There was total pin-drop silence as he lifted both his arms to give the formal blessing, the gold crozier in his left hand, his right tracing out a dramatic sign of the Cross. Each word was slow and reverent, as if he were forging it anew, chipping it like silver from a mine.

'Holy Spirit of the living God, Who proceedeth from the Father and the Son, we dedicate this window to Thine honour and glory, and we pray that those who look on it may find in it a way to Thy great Truth. May the ignorant find wisdom, the weary find peace, and those in darkness and confusion find the light.'

Jane did now say 'Amen'. The last few words seemed directed at her personally, and she was touched by them, inspired. The organ thundered out again, as the servers with their lighted candles led the procession back to the chancel, Isobel now arm in arm with Christopher, Hadley grinning sheepishly, and the fervent congregation hurling a new hymn up to the roofbeams.

'Angel voices ever singing
Round thy throne of light,
Angel harps for ever ringing,
Rest not day or night . . .'

Jane turned back to steal a last look at her own Angel. It, too, would never rest, since the Bishop had entrusted it with a pretty weighty mission for the next few hundred years: to bring all those who looked on it to Truth and light and life.

'It's all a con,' said Hadley. 'I mean, in Chaucer's time people only put up cash for windows so they could save their souls, or escape the frightful fate of being pitchforked into hell. It was just a form of insurance, and jolly egotistical, not spiritual at all. My flat-mate, Duncan, told me. He's doing English Lit., and said these fourteenth-century Holy Joes sold bits of tatty pillowcase and passed them off as Our Lady's veil. Roll up! Roll up! Buy your way to heaven with a pig's bone – the genuine right femur of the Blessed Osbert Pugwash.'

'So you think your mother's simply trying to save her soul?' enquired a tow-haired surgeon, gesturing with his fork, then turning his attention to his loaded plate of food.

'*Dad's* soul, more likely,' Hadley muttered sulkily.

'I'm sure, if there's a heaven, your father's already there, old chap.'

Hadley shrugged. 'We haven't dealt with heaven yet, in our first-year physics course.'

Jane tensed. The surgeon looked offended by Hadley's jeering tone, shifted round to talk to someone else. Hadley still had a small audience, mostly doctors and their wives, his father's former colleagues. He swigged down more champagne, reached behind him for the bottle, so he could refill his dwindling glass before he returned to the attack.

'And the portraits of the donors in the windows got gradually larger and larger, until they were bigger than the saints themselves. It was a form of self-advertisement. "Look at me, look at me, kneeling right next to the Blessed Virgin Whatsit in my best doublet and hose. Aren't I rich and powerful? Aren't I a big wheel?"'

Jane jabbed her fork into a piece of salmon quiche, bit into it angrily. Hadley was quoting not just Duncan, but distorting her own words, rehashing what she'd told him and serving it up with a completely different gloss.

'What are you trying to say, young man?' asked another, older doctor, who appeared to be having difficulty cutting into a chicken breast with what looked like a cake-fork. 'That your mother had this window made out of a sense of self-importance, to perpetuate her name, and Tom's?'

'Well, both their names are plastered there, for all the world to see. You can hardly miss that socking great plaque right underneath the window, which gives them both a plug. I'm not too sure whether it's intended for God's eyes, so He'll save them two front stalls in heaven, or to impress the villagers.'

Jane stalked into the hall, fuming silently. She had never known Hadley so boorish and sarcastic. He was clearly drunk, but that was no excuse. It was a betrayal of his parents, a betrayal of the artist. Okay, so he felt bitter about his paragon of a father, who had never actually had the time to play the father's role, but couldn't he be loyal to him on this one important day, for his mother's sake, at least? She looked around for Isobel, saw her in the dining-room, garrulous and flushed, her large hat knocked askew, spilling coleslaw from her plate as she reached forward for a spoonful of crab mousse. Jane stood uncertain in the doorway, recoiling from the crush of guests, the loud guffaws, the roar of conversation. Why did parties seem so frightening – people larger, wilder, noisier, than they were in normal life? She could hear the music from her own eighteenth birthday party mocking in her head; the yearning strains of a romantic lovesick foxtrot mixed up with Uncle Peter's sozzled voice. 'Who's my mother, Mummy? Who's my . . . ?'

She lurched on to Tom's old study, the only room not invaded by the guests, shut the door behind her, slumped down at the desk. It was her fault really, wasn't it, that Hadley was so truculent? He'd discovered that she'd gone to Chartres alone, and been desperately upset; said she'd promised that they'd go together, and he'd already spent a fortune phoning French hotels, to find a really decent one; and had done badly in his course-work because he could think of nothing else but the excitement of the trip. She had made things worse by refusing to discuss it with him, refusing to go out with him. She hadn't intended to be cruel, had needed all her wits to deal with

Christopher; couldn't get involved in bitter arguments with both men at the same time.

She checked her watch – two o'clock. She should be helping with the lunch, clearing up the plates, passing puddings round, joining Rowan and her crew of giggly waitresses. She had drunk too much herself, felt tired and slightly dizzy, but she forced herself to walk down to the kitchen.

'Rose! How nice to see you. I've been trying to catch up with you since I first came through the door, but somehow we keep missing one another. How are things, my dear?'

'Fine,' she said mechanically, stopping in the passage to shake the vicar's hand. Anthony had changed from his elaborate white silk chasuble into a comfy tweedy suit, which made him look like an old-fashioned country vet.

'It's a marvellous day, isn't it?'

'Yes,' she said, uncertain if he was referring to the weather, or to the occasion generally.

'And there's dear Meg – and Alice. Shall we go and say hello?'

More smiles and bland 'how-are-yous'. Jane kept repeating 'Fine', kept bumping into people she'd met on Christmas Day – Uncle Rory, Aunties Meg and Martha. There were also swarms of strangers, daunting-looking men in formal suits with top-drawer accents and braying laughs which shook the room like shell-bursts. Even the untidy cluttered kitchen was bursting at the seams – an overflow of guests sitting on the table, or perched up on the worktops. Three small children were squashed into the dog-basket, playing dogs themselves, and a baby in a carrycot had been left beside the Aga and was chuntering to itself.

She suddenly spotted Christopher standing in the corner, talking to a woman – not Anne, a younger girl – a pretty one with tousled hair and a tarty scarlet dress. He was leaning forward, feeding her a celery-stick, slipping it between her lips, but still holding it in his fingers right against her mouth, while she laughed and nibbled, then offered him her own half-bitten pizza-slice. Jane turned on her heel, squeezed her stop-start way into the garden, returning jolly greetings, refusing plates of vol-au-vents, top-ups of champagne.

She strode across the lawn, lost herself in the thick shrubs at the back. Despite the sun, it was still cold and very windy, so no one else had strayed outside. She leant against a tree-trunk, trying to block out the girl's provocative mouth, the way her breasts drew attention to themselves by pushing at the low neck of her dress, as if impatient to burst out and be admired. You couldn't win with

Christopher. She had let him overrule her, accepted all his arguments about the importance of their bond, and why it must be sexual as well as artistic and professional, since one enhanced the other, and high creativity was linked to high libido; and how she could shrivel his ideas and skills if she rejected him in bed. Yet there he was, ogling other women, almost under her nose.

She closed her eyes, saw him in the studio their first day back at work together, heard his gruff and waspish voice demolishing her own ideas, her need for space and separateness; annoyed with her for voicing them at all. And then his voice had changed, become passionate and pleading, and they were suddenly making violent love, still dressed, and on the floor. She had responded like an animal – physically, instinctively – but resentment had wormed in, resentment on both sides, which had undermined their bodies, as well as just their minds. He couldn't come, and blamed her. She hadn't said a word, but she'd been thinking secretly: 'It's not my fault. It's because you're old and past it.' Her own anger had alarmed her, but he did seem old, seemed different altogether, less powerful, less distinguished.

'Rose!' called Isobel. 'Rose, are you all right?'

Jane slunk out of the bushes, still confused, still pulled between desire and indignation, longing and distaste. 'I . . . I just needed some fresh air.'

'I was getting rather worried. Rowan said she hadn't seen you for an hour, and then I caught a glimpse of you heading for the cabbage-patch! Gosh! It's chilly out here, isn't it?' Isobel hunched her shoulders, rubbed the gooseflesh on her arms. 'You'll catch your death in that flimsy frock of yours.'

'No. I'm boiling.' Still hot from Christopher – all the other times he'd rammed into her, laid claim to her – almost daily since she'd returned from Chartres, as if trying to repair his injured pride, or prove who gave the orders in the bedroom.

'The shrubbery's still looking rather battered,' Isobel remarked, breaking off a laurel leaf and crushing it between her fingers. 'It never really recovered from the storm. And then we lost our cedar.' She drifted on a yard or two, bent down to stroke its butchered stump. 'That's all that's left of a wonderful old warrior, sixty-five foot high, which battled with the elements for a hundred years or more, and sheltered half the birds in Sussex.' She straightened up, still shredding the now mangled leaf. 'And yet I was talking to old Abner, and he was claiming cheerfully that the storm wasn't a disaster, despite the fact ten million trees went down. He said destruction is just part of the natural cycle, and always followed by regrowth.' She tossed her leaf away, started fiddling with her hair instead, one long skein escaping from its pins. 'He told me that in thirty years we won't even know it happened, and that in certain ways the woodlands will actually be improved. More sunlight can flood in, you see, through all the gaps and clearings, which means more plants and shrubs will grow, and those encourage birds and insects . . .' Isobel broke off, secured two errant hairpins back in place. 'I felt almost glad there'd been a storm by the time I'd finished chatting to him!'

Jane subsided on to the tree-stump, drawing up her knees. 'Oh, Isobel, you're such a maddening optimist.'

'Of course I am. I must be. In fact, I can never understand why every Christian in the land isn't hanging out the flags today, or blowing golden trumpets from the rooftops. When you think what Resurrection means – *really* means . . .'

Jane shrugged, picked up a stray hairpin from the ground. 'We're not all Christians, are we? I only wish Christopher was happier. He seems so disappointed in the window.'

'Oh, that's just Christopher. I told you before, when he was so worked up about Adrian's leisure-centre, how he never does a job without feeling it's a failure. His standards are too high. He wants to be God, creating perfectly.'

Jane bent the hairpin's legs up, balanced it on her palm. 'I sometimes think God made an awful mess of things.'

'Of course He didn't, darling. Creation's quite amazing – a miracle, in my view. And talking of God, I ought to go and say goodbye to John.'

'John?'

'The bishop. He's leaving at two-thirty, has to attend some other function back at Lewes. We were jolly lucky to get him, on Easter Day of all days. Isn't he a darling?'

'I haven't really spoken to him.'

'Oh dear. I'm sorry. I did mean to introduce you, but I've been feeling rather . . .' Her voice appeared to slide downhill, lose its footing, fall. 'I suppose all those friends of Tom's brought back awful memories – of the funeral and . . . Now, steady on, Isobel, no more tears, you silly girl.' She slapped her own wrist, hard, like a strict no-nonsense nanny rebuking her young charge. 'I've disgraced myself already, crying in church like that.'

'No, you didn't,' Jane said vehemently. 'I liked the tears. They were right, and very special. They seemed almost part of the service – the dedication bit, I mean – as if you sort of . . .

357

owed them to the window. I can't explain. I'm probably sounding stupid.'

Isobel hugged her for reply. Jane could feel her generous breasts, voluptuous yet motherly; smell her flowery perfume, her lemony shampoo. If only she could be a child, push away all the complications of adult life and love, and cling to one really special person – someone she could trust. Isobel's arms were almost hurting, the hug was so intense. Jane shut her eyes, allowed herself to sink and merge, lose her boundaries. She was turning into Angela, Isobel's first child. 'You never forget the child you've given birth to.' Angela must have been present in the church this morning, unknown to Tom, to all the congregation; a child named for an Angel, then given up, and lost. Where was her own birth-mother on this important Easter Day – sitting down to Sunday lunch with a brood of rival daughters, or rotting in her coffin? Would she ever know the answer, ever feel her arms around her, holding her and holding her?

Isobel stepped back, at last, smoothed her crumpled blouse. Neither of them spoke, just walked shakily inside.

They found the bishop finishing off his trifle. His mystique had disappeared with his mitre and his cope. There was a dribble of spilt custard on his formal purple front, and his fruity churchman's voice was further mellowed by champagne.

'Must rush, Isobel my dear. I'm fearfully late already. Quite fantastic party, though. Congratulations! And who made the sherry trifle? One of the best I've ever tasted, and that's not flattery. In fact, there's so much sherry in it, I'm probably over the limit. It's a good thing David's driving. David! Get your coat – we're off.'

Jane shook the bishop's proffered hand. His huge jewelled ring looked as lethal as a knuckleduster, maybe holy ammunition in fighting the good fight, though he appeared to need a sling to support the weight of his right arm. Was he a man like Adrian, who regarded God as Chairman of the Board, who would promote him and reward him for good service?

She remained nervous in the hall, while Isobel took David's arm and saw him to the car, the bishop just behind them, scattering goodbyes like party favours. Jane edged on down the passage, then slipped into the sitting-room, still glancing round her anxiously. There were so many people she was trying to avoid – Christopher and Hadley, Adrian and Anne, not to mention the lame ducks: Edith and her yappy Pekinese, Mrs Brooking and her hearing-aid. There was no sign of the artist. Perhaps he'd found a bed upstairs, and was trying to convince his latest conquest that if they didn't take advantage of it, she might blight his inspiration, destroy his next commission. Hadley had collapsed, and been propped against the window-seat to prevent him being trodden on. He was still awake, but appeared to have left the party for a region of his own, a darker sadder region. Several other people looked slightly the worse for wear, not drunk, just dishevelled; hats abandoned, hair awry. The house had also suffered – wine-stains on the carpet, cushions on the floor, a china bowl in pieces, its pot-pourri scattered underfoot.

'Hello, Rose,' said a quiet unruffled voice. 'I've been looking for you everywhere.'

Jane swung round, came face to face with Anne's benevolent smile. She forced a smile herself, switched on her party talk – waffle and inanities, but underneath, her brain was working overtime. Did Anne not mind that her husband had absconded? Had she even noticed? Or was she far too busy awaiting Adrian's arrival? He'd had to miss the service, been involved with a new client, despite the fact it was Sunday and a holiday, and now it looked as if he'd miss the party too.

'Have you tried this chocolate mousse, Rose? It's delicious.'

Jane shook her head; hadn't had her first course yet, beyond one half-hearted mouthful of cold quiche. She couldn't concentrate on food, was transfixed at that moment by Anne's bare throat – bare of any chain. The tiny antique cross was in her own new handbag, now slung across her shoulder and clasped safe beneath one arm. She always took the cross with her, everywhere she went, for fear it might be stolen if she left it in the studio, even hidden in a drawer. She fought a sudden crazy urge to get it out, dangle it in front of Anne, and ask her casually, 'Hey! Guess where I discovered this.'

'You're not wearing your cross and chain,' she said instead, deadpan.

'No,' Anne concurred, in the same unflustered even tone she'd been using all along.

Jane watched her face intently, waiting for a flush of guilt, a flurry of confusion. Wouldn't she say more, give some explanation: she'd lost her cross, or sold it, felt it didn't suit her dress.

'You know, it beats me really how Isobel finds time to cook at all, with all the other things she does. Or did Rowan make the puddings?'

'I made some of them myself,' said Jane, squirming at Anne's praises. She didn't want compliments for her raspberry pavlova, but a straight answer to the question she didn't dare to ask: Are you having it off with Adrian?

359

'I'd no idea you could make meringues as well as stained-glass windows!' Anne put her empty bowl down, as if to make it clear that she'd finished with the subject of both puddings and gold chains, and had switched to more important things. 'You must be delighted with your window, Rose.'

'It's hardly mine, but yes, I'm thrilled.' Jane removed her fingers from the clasp of her small bag. Why make trouble on such a special day? The elation she had felt in church was slowly seeping back. It *was* her window, in a way, and just because she disliked big noisy parties, or was suspicious of the artist's wife, it was stupid to upset herself – or Anne. The window was still there, would be there for the next hundred years, acting like a force-field, drawing people to it. Even now, she felt its power, beckoning her back, insisting she admire it – on her own this time, without the distraction of a fizzy congregation.

She excused herself, pretended she needed the loo, but went to fetch her coat instead, then dived through the front door, hoping nobody was watching. She froze as she saw Anne again, coatless in the drive. Adrian had just roared up, and she was leaning down to greet him through the window of his car. They didn't touch or kiss, yet the pair seemed bonded, intimate. Why should Anne go out to meet him, if he were just a casual friend; why even notice he'd arrived? If only she could shrug them off, instead of getting so worked up about their every move. But she had never quite accepted the stubborn and unwelcome fact that the artist had a wife, and everything about that wife both tormented and enthralled her. That's why she had kept the cross – to possess a precious object which was Mrs Harville-Shaw's by right, and so give herself the name. Yet why the hell did she want the name when *Mr* Harville-Shaw had forgotten her existence, and was groping a third female in the attic or the glory-hole? She buttoned up her coat, fished in both the pockets for her gloves. She'd steal off to the church, as she'd decided, give herself a respite, away from crowds and crises.

She concealed herself in the bushes until Adrian and Anne had drifted back indoors, then grabbed her bike and pedalled furiously, wheeling left at the crossroads; hardly drawing breath till she dismounted at the church. She stood a moment, panting, revelling in the peace; the only sound the shrill song of a blackbird determined to upstage a rival thrush. The sky was busy, wisps of damasked cloud swelling and expanding, then dissolving into shreds again. Clumps of yellow daffodils trumpeted from graves, reproaching the bare trees which overhung them. Yellow everywhere – in primroses and

360

catkins, the first brash and glossy dandelions. She walked slowly up the path, relieved to find the door unlocked; breathed in the scents of candlewax and freesias as she stepped into the church. She went straight to the new window, which was marked out from the others because the sun was right behind it now, lasering through its blues, making them ethereal, while the lush greens of the landscape seemed to shimmer as she watched.

'May all who see it be enriched,' the bishop had implored. She had already been enriched. Whatever his deficiencies as far as women were concerned, Christopher had initiated her into the world of the artist, changed the way she looked at things. The whole universe was richer now, and she no longer went around half-philistine, half-blind. He had also taught her the importance of ambition – not Adrian's kind, which stockpiled swimming pools and sports cars he was too busy to enjoy – but the higher sort which centred on a vision.

She moved a little closer, so that the colours of the window spilled across her dress – blue for spirituality, green for new life. Easter had never meant so much before, had been just a day for chocolate eggs and simnel cake, outings to the wildlife park, cream teas in stately homes. She leaned against the wall, feeling faint and hollow suddenly, as scones and pastries trembled in her head. She had eaten nothing since supper yesterday; been too on edge to face a bite of breakfast; too uptight at the party to do anything but drink. She regretted the champagne now, which was making the church spin; the patterns of the windows rotating on the floor. She closed her eyes, tried to fight the darkness which was threatening to engulf her. She could feel the chill of Chartres again, when the sky outside had blackened and she had fallen on her knees at the entrance to the labyrinth. She groped out with her hands, touched the cold uneven stone, saw the spirals of the maze spread out all around her, no longer disappearing beneath rows and rows of chairs. Last time, she had cheated, simply jumped the gaps, failed to walk the blockaded outer circles, reached the centre far too soon.

She took her first uncertain step, her feet leaden, heavy, as if she were walking in a dream. The path was straight, to start with, but then branched left, began its first switchback loop, on and back, on and back; skirting right close to the centre, only to double slyly back again. She stumbled on, trying to drown her fear, remind herself of the reassuring structure of the labyrinth. There were no dead ends, no cul-de-sacs, only one way she could go, however long and serpentine. She would reach her goal if she persevered, concentrated only on the snakings of the path, the rhythm of her feet. She could hear another rhythm, a slow and steady beating she seemed to recognise, which was part of her and joined to her, though faint and far away.

She trudged another loop, then on again and round again, weary from the constant twists and turnings. Yet there was no way she could stop. Some force was driving her, a force she couldn't comprehend, yet could also neither question nor defy. Every time she flagged, she could feel it urging, goading, insisting she went on – a series of determined thrusts pulsing her along, each followed by a lull. The walls of the labyrinth were closing in around her. She was being squeezed and pummelled now, the pressure gradually increasing in brief but violent bursts, then tailing off again. Each time, she kicked and struggled, but her feeble limbs were powerless; her body taken over by some impetus outside her, with a relentless will of iron. She had completely lost her bearings, her sense of any path; seemed to have skewed round at an angle, her head pressing against some soft but stubborn barrier.

The squeezing stopped abruptly, and she hung paralysed, suspended, in a blank and timeless void. She focused on the rhythmic beat, which was growing more insistent, desperate to tune in to it, so that she could cut out all the other sounds – the vague but threatening booms and thuds resounding in the distance from some wild world far beyond her. But a sudden savage thrust propelled her through the barrier and into a dark passage. She could see the long black tunnel stretching out in front of her, its walls so tight, constricting, that her still-soft bones were corseted and crushed. She tried to force her way along it, struggling to grope forward, inch by painful inch, but continually slipping back. She was now so starved of oxygen, her spark of life was guttering like a candle, flickering and failing, about to be snuffed out. Yet someone else's breathing was shocking the whole tunnel, great laboured panting sobbing heaves, interspersed with cries of fear, cries so crazed and jagged they seemed to rip right through her skin. She couldn't cry herself. Neither her eyes nor mouth were working, and she needed her last gleam of strength to keep groping, butting down.

She stalled a moment, jammed against the tunnel-walls, her head too huge to clear them. She was close to suffocation, tempted to give up, stifled by the airlessness, deafened by the screams. Then a different voice cut through them, a voice urgent, but compelling. 'Push!' it shouted. 'Push, yes push. Push harder!'

Nothing happened – nothing – only blind and gagging panic. 'Push!' the voice insisted, a voice so loud and resolute, it seemed to create a new and stronger force from weakness and despair, a force which was releasing her. Sudden shuddering spasms began to shock through her whole body, sweeping her along. She had no choice but to submit, despite the pain and terror, the loss of all control, the juddering and jarring as she was banged against the tunnel walls. She heard a rush of water, was plunged into the cataract, shooting, jolting, over it, plummeting from darkness into life.

'It's a girl!' cried a triumphant voice, and she lost all sense of up or down, as she was slapped and jounced and swung, and a new booming, glaring, hurting world assaulted all her senses. A cruel steel blade sliced against her stomach; ruthless lights bombarded her weak eyes; gigantic rubber hands clamped her, top and bottom. Her mouth was gagged with tubing, a second tube stuck right up her nose; her flailing hands padlocked at the wrists. Then suddenly, miraculously, her fetters were removed, and someone swooped her down to a white expanse of bed. She felt her naked skin touch naked skin, closed her eyes in bliss. She was lying on a body whose taste and shape she trusted, and two strong arms enfolded her, protecting her from danger, cutting out the glare, and she could smell milk and warmth and safety, and knew that she'd reached home.

27

Jane was lying on the cold floor of the church, her arms curled round her head, her legs bent up and cramped. Her eyes blinked slowly open, troubled by the light. The sun was flickering through the inscription in the window, highlighting the letters – flowing gilded letters, now blazoned and aflame: 'Awake Thou That Sleepest'.

She struggled to her feet. She had been asleep too long – five months, in all – running in the wrong direction, making wrong decisions. She stood, still weak and shaky, leaning against a pew. The new-born were always weak. She must treat herself with care, take the journey slowly, dismount and wheel her bike up the steepest of the hills; buy some food when she reached the station buffet, allow herself to rest once she'd caught the train and was safely on her way.

The Resurrection symbols were shining from the window – the phoenix and the pomegranate, the ivy and the rose. She had helped to cut those symbols, done it well enough. She had a certain knack for cutting – a dexterity, a speed – but she would never be an artist. That was a delusion, one she'd wanted to believe. She was only an assistant, who had been hired for the wrong reasons – for her gender, not her skills. She stepped slowly forward, reached up on her toes, trying to touch the tiny thorns on the lowest of the roses. She must leave the name behind – it wasn't hers to use. She had let herself be trapped like the bird in 'Bird Inside', another dumb and passive creature subject to the artist's whim, ordered into cages or cajoled into bed. But she was more than just a panicked bird slamming into walls of glass. He had made her into an Angel, given her great powerful wings, so she could fly high, fly away.

She checked her purse, made sure she had the money for her fare – single, not return – rummaged for the matchbox which held Anne's cross and chain. She unwrapped it from its tissue, hung it from one finger, her naked wedding-finger. She could never be his wife – that, too, was a sham. She must return the cross to Anne, wrap a note around it, saying she had found it in the church. She had no proof of anything, would never know the truth about Adrian and Anne, so let it be her farewell gift, to make them innocent.

She tore a leaf out of her diary, scribbled a few words, sat frowning at her pen. She could write a hundred pages – to Christopher and Hadley, Isobel and Anne – trying to explain. Except that they wouldn't understand. And if she stopped to say goodbye, or called in to fetch her things, she would be lured back and distracted, lose her sense of purpose, her sudden total certainty of what she had to do.

She glanced up at the window next to Christopher's, a Saint Joseph window which had recently been restored – deceitfully, the artist claimed. New pieces of glass had been inserted, then deliberately pitted, painted, and begrimed, to make them blend and harmonise, look genuine fifteenth-century. A necessary deception, Christopher had called it. She was tired of all deception, necessary or no; must struggle for her own truth, however frail and ragged.

Saint Joseph was holding the Christchild, a plump and sallow infant, clutching at his robe – Mary's child, not his. He'd never fathered a child – too old, perhaps, or barren like the artist. She had to have her own child, prove that power Christopher had praised: the power of creating life itself, which made even an artist's talents look puny in comparison. Once she'd given birth, she would have a blood-relation, the only one she'd ever known – unless she found her mother, which she was determined now to do, at least try her dogged best. The two were bound together. If she had a baby, then she'd be passing on that mother: her nose, or mouth, or temperament, her ancestry and genes.

She crossed over to the north side, the shadow-side, the side of cold and darkness. The journey might be long and even gruelling, though she was travelling very light. She had no luggage and no certainties, no identity, no name. Her parents might refuse to help, even though she'd beg them, suggest they search together as a way of healing the rift. They might stall, or storm, or argue, warn her of the dangers – the rejection, disappointment, which Trish herself had suffered. But she still had to make the effort, had to take the risk; had to find that woman she'd known nine months already. She had listened to her heartbeat, shared her food-supply, been held by her, acknowledged, knew her voice and smell. She had received the gift of life from her, and must at least say thank you, even if they never met again.

She buttoned her thick coat across her flimsy dress. Strange to return in party clothes and frivolous blue shoes, when she had left in an old tracksuit and a grubby pair of trainers. She took a last, long, hungry look at the Resurrection window. The light was calm, subdued; no more frisking sunshine, but a serene and steady glow. The greens were already muted, even the blood-red of the roses beginning to recede. Only the blues were still insistent, smouldering and thrumming, and they too would fade at dusk; Christopher's bright window extinguished and obscured. 'May those in darkness and confusion find the light.'

She let the heavy door bang shut behind her, flinching as the bitter wind met her head-on in the porch. She unlocked her bike, wheeled it down the path, then along the steep and narrow road which meandered to the station. The trees were mostly bare – those that hadn't fallen in the storm. She paused a moment, to watch the setting sun – a sunset so extreme it looked as if Christopher had painted it in the most tempestuous of his moods, flung it on his canvas in a squall of orange-reds. The rags of cloud were all on fire, and showering their bright embers on the fields. Every tree was burning, whorls of gold and scarlet devouring their dark limbs. The anvil of West Woodbury Hill seemed blistered by the blaze, the smoking sky snagging on its surface. She took in the whole scene, swallowed it and relished it, like her first taste of solid food after forty days of fasting in the wilderness. Whatever else she chose to do, whatever job she found, she would never lose her artist's eyes. They were Christopher's own gift to her – more important than the trinkets she had craved.

The light was dwindling, a flock of noisy rooks suddenly flapping overhead, their scruffy tattered bodies littering the sky. She jumped on to her bike, as if spurred by their example, free-wheeled down the hill, panted up the other side. They were winging north, and so was she; had no time to waste if she wanted to reach Shrepton before her parents damped the fire down, retired upstairs to bed. It was Sunday – Easter Sunday – so there might well be fewer trains, and she had to get to London first; maybe wait an hour or more on the dingy local station. She could see Amy in her night-clothes, switching all the lights off, bolting the front door.

'No!' she shouted urgently, trying to make her parents hear; stop them drawing the thick curtains which would shut her out, muffle her small voice.

The birds were only specks now, buffeted by the wind, their

hoarse cries blown away with hers, like wisps of fading smoke, but following their instincts, flying to their roost.

'Wait!' she called more frantically, feet spinning on the pedals, hair streaming out behind her like the Angel's in the wind. 'Wait, I'm coming home.'